This Still Hearth

The story of Katherine Rose Beale

Charlotte Chidell

Busybird Publishing
2/118 Para Road
Montmorency, Victoria
Australia 3094
www.busybird.com.au

About the Author

The author has a Bachelor of Arts in literature and writing. She has published in professional nursing journals, poetry collections, in an anthology by the Diamond Creek based *Literary Optimists* and letters to the *Age*. Post working life, she is an oboist in several community orchestras in Melbourne and is an active volunteer.

This Still Hearth was intended to be a work of creative non-fiction, about an early pioneer of St Helena, Victoria. The limited information about Katherine Beale led to a decision to employ the genre of a biographical novel.

During a recent visit to England, the author discovered her nephew's local pub is the Prospect of Whitby. A noose and gallows hanging off the balcony mark the historical site of Execution Dock where Katherine observes the two hanged men. The adjoining stone steps to the River Thames are the same that Katherine descends to buy fish in December 1812.

Disclaimer

This work is a biographical novel about a real person: Katherine Rose Beale.

The journals in which Katherine records her thoughts, her interactions with others, her travels around London, Guildford, Portsmouth, St Helena, and Blackheath and Lee, the letters she writes to Elizabeth, and the various points in the book where she reflects on her life, are fictional, although the places are real. The style of writing aims to mirror similar surviving letters and journals of the era. The writing is informed by historical facts and real people, as well as by the author's professional background as a nurse and midwife, and her lifelong passion for church music.

A comprehensive, meticulously researched 'Descendant Report' that was generously shared with the author by Deborah Green, a great, great granddaughter of Katherine and Anthony Beale, included census data, genealogy reports, and other historical records that have been adhered to as closely as possible when writing about Katherine's family.

Primary sources used in the book include extracts from diaries, contemporaneous writers, newspaper reports, and quotations from real people. End notes link to a comprehensive bibliography for any person wishing to explore particular subjects in further detail. The references were re-checked and accessible at the time of the book going to press.

Acknowledgements

Iacknowledge the Wurundjeri Woiwurrung people as traditional custodians of the land on which part of this story takes place. I pay respect to all Elders, past and present who have resided in the area of St Helena, Victoria, and been an integral part of the region's history.

The writing of this book would not have been possible without the generous support of the following individuals and groups that have contributed to its genesis in varied ways, including: fostering and critiquing early ideas; provision of art work; lending a listening ear; reading and editing early drafts; giving me time to write, or just being a friend in need.

I would like to thank:

Elizabeth Bennett; Johno Bennett; Steph Boloutis; Daniel Car; Avril Chidell; Graham Chidell; Ray Chidell; Sue Chidell; Jim Gaudion; Anne Maree Grimaldi; Roy Gwyther Jones; Isla Heddle; Douglas McKenzie; Deborah Pearson; Lily Pearson; Oscar Pearson; Robin Pearson; Aquinas Purcell; Lou Purcell; Matthew Purcell; Resi Schlesinger; Rob Shackleton; and Bev Ward, for their support and assistance in bringing this book to fruition, as well as members of the following groups/organisations:

Christmas Hills Orchestral Players (CHOPs); Clarinet and Saxophone Society of Victoria (Clasax); Eltham Orchestras; Leith Park Life Group; Literary Optimists, Diamond Creek; Parishioners and staff St Katherine's St Helena and St John's Diamond Creek; University of Third Age Orchestra, Hawthorn.

Further assistance in answering specific questions was very much appreciated and given by:

Archivists on St Helena – I hope to visit in person in January 2025! Noel Croll, Profile Manager WikiTree; Tim Gatehouse, Local Historian; Deborah Green, Profile Manager WikiTree; Kev Howlett and Les Zigomanis, Busybird Publishing; Librarians in the Heritage Room, State Library of Victoria; Lesley Jones, nee Heddle, family permission to write about Katherine Rose Beale; Tourist office, George Town, Tasmania; and Noel Withers, Greensborough Historical Society Foundation President.

Charlotte Chidell, St Helena, Victoria, Australia October, 2024

Foreword

Katherine Rose Beale lived a remarkable life. Growing up in a poorer part of London, then beginning her adult life on the Island of St Helena, and later on in Australia, she was one of many women who left Georgian Britain in search of a husband. Indeed, the Honourable East India Company, which controlled St Helena at the time, facilitated young women travelling to India during its cooler months to find husbands from amongst its young male employees. These annual pilgrimages were disparagingly known as 'the fishing fleet'. Women who were unsuccessful in this quest and sailed back to England were equally disparagingly termed 'returned empties.'

Jane Austen's novel *Pride and Prejudice* was first published in 1813, the year it is believed Katherine sailed to St Helena. We might speculate, did she hope to meet and marry her Mr Darcy? Or would she have to be satisfied with her Mr Wickham or, perish the thought, her Mr Collins? Happily, she did meet her Mr Darcy in the person of Anthony Beale, and theirs was a long and happy marriage.

When they settled in the relatively young colony which later became Victoria, they named their property after their previous island home of St Helena. In time, the name transferred to the district. We can't be sure about the exact boundaries of their holding, as it predated the Torrens System of Title Deeds, and the 'Old Law' Title has been lost in the mists of time. Dianne H. Edwards (*The Diamond Valley Story*, 1979) locates the Beale holding to 160 acres, Lot 4 of Section 15, Parish of Nillumbik. It was purchased by Land Order issued by the Colonial Land and Emigration Commission, London, in the name of John Lindsay.

Katherine died in 1856, and Anthony constructed Rose Chapel to her memory. After Anthony's death in 1865, the building was remodelled and consecrated as a place of public worship. On the death of Lindsay Beale in 1917, Title to the land passed to the Melbourne Anglican Trust Corporation in accordance with Anthony's wishes. And so, St Katherine's Church, in the Melbourne suburb of St Helena, perpetuates the memory of this remarkable woman, and the birthplace of her husband.

Rob Shackleton

In loving memory of Isabel 'Isla' Heddle, nee Beale, 1929–2024

Great granddaughter of Katherine and Anthony Beale

'A faithful servant'

Table of contents

This Still Hearth[1]

Katherine Rose Beale, nee Young immediate family and timeline

- » **Father:** James Young 1746–1801, master mariner

- » **Mother:** Catherine Raitt 1758–1800

- » **Birth:** Katherine Rose Young 27 May, 1794 (1795 on gravestone)

- » **Older siblings:** Elizabeth 1779–1851; spouse James Halliburton, master mariner

- » James 1781–1840, master mariner; spouse Elizabeth Edsell Biggs

- » Isabella 1783–1870; spouse Adam Baildon, surgeon

- » Charles Cobb 1785–1838, master mariner; spouse Elizabeth Hay

- » Margaret 1789–1833; spouse John Lindsay, merchant

- » **Baptism:** 19 June, 1794, St George-in-the-East, Stepney, Parish of Shoreditch

- » **St Helena:** Travelled in 1813 (assumed)

- » **Marriage:** 15 June, 1814, St Helena, to Anthony Beale 1790–1865

- » **Children:** Onesiphorus James Beale 1815–1839

- » Edward Charles Beale 1816–1877, soldier; spouse Katherine Parr

- » Anthony Beale 1817–1880, surgeon

- » Robert Beale 1819–1819

- » Robert Beale 1820–1820

- » Katherine Ann Sibella Beale 1821–1907; spouse John Burt, late East India Company

- » Isabella Margaret Beale (Issy) 1822–1888; spouse (1) Francis Nodin, businessman (2) Charles Maplestone, architect

- » Elizabeth Maria Beale (Bessy) 1823–1899; spouse George James, wine merchant

- » Adam Beale 1825–1828

- » Rose Ellinor Beale 1826–1856, died in childbirth; spouse Herbert Foley

- » Margaret Lindsay Beale 1827–1914

- » Adam Beale 1829–1909

- » John Lindsay Beale 1830–1911; spouse Emma Bennett

- » James Young Beale 1831–1905; spouse Elizabeth Smith Grandfather of Isla Heddle nee Beale

- » Halliburton Beale 1833–1899; spouse Martha Ann Lewis

- » Charles Cobb Beale 1834–1834

- » Alexander Beale 1841–1897 (the only child born in Australia)

- » **1815:** Deaths of Adam Baildon (February) and James Halliburton (April), Katherine's brothers-in-law

- » Napoleon arrives St Helena (October). Governance of St Helena returns to British

- » **1816:** Sir Hudson Lowe appointed Governor. Wilks family returns to the Isle of Man

- » **1821:** Death of Napoleon. Governance reverts to the Honourable East India Company

» **1833:** St Helena Act: the Honourable East India Company sells St Helena to the British

» **1836:** Beales presumed to have left St Helena during this time and lived in England with relatives

» **1839:** 29 July, arrives Van Diemen's Land with husband, Anthony, and ten children on *Cecelia*

» 14 August, eldest son Onesiphorus (24 yrs) disappears

» 1 September, Anthony Beale and Adam (10 yrs) leave to purchase land in Melbourne

» 13 September, Onesiphorus's body found

» 14 September, Inquest in Launceston

» 4 November, travels to Port Phillip aboard the *Perseverance*

» 13 November, arrives Newtown (Fitzroy), where the house is erected on heavily timbered land

» **1841:** Moves to St Helena Park, River Plenty. Gives birth to final child, Alexander

» **1842:** November, Anthony Beale declared insolvent. John Lindsay and George James take on financial responsibility for his property

» **1856:** 5 April, daughter Rose dies in childbirth

» 5 August, Katherine dies

» **1858:** Rose Chapel completed, in memory of Katherine

» **1865:** 4 September, Anthony Beale dies

» **1867:** 25 February, creation of Deed of Family Arrangement, establishing a trust

» **1869:** 24 April, Builder John Dyer submits quote for 115 pounds to remodel the chapel

» **1876:** 16 May, St Katherine's Church consecrated following Anthony Beale's wish to leave it to the Church of England

» **1917:** 30 March, an indenture conveys the property to the Church of England Trusts Corporation. St Katherine's Church is now legally owned by the Church of England following the death of Lindsay Beale

» **1957:** Bushfire almost destroys the church, which is rebuilt following public donations

» **1958:** Sunday 13 July, the centenary of the church is celebrated

» **1999:** Land sale to Banyule Council, with church and cemetery only remaining

» **2008:** 150th anniversary of St Katherine's Church

» **2021:** 25 May, closure of St Katherine's Church for regular Sunday services

Character profiles

Honourable East India Company aka The Company

The Company owned St Helena, courtesy of a charter in 1657.[2] It was a vitally important strategic island whose safety was ensured through ~ 700 men employed in a garrison of three companies of artillery (the St Helena Artillery) or in the St Helena Regiment of four companies; its geographic location, its physical structure (very few landing places), and its impressive range of weapons. It is one of the most isolated places in the world. During Napoleon's captivity, governance of St Helena was vested in the British Government before returning to the Company following Napoleon's death in 1821.

The St Helena Act of 1833 was regarded as a great betrayal of employees of the Company, including most of the elite families on St Helena and the commanders and other senior crew on the East Indiamen ships. The Company sold back all their entitlements to the British Government for £100,000.00. In effect, its employees lost their homes, lifetime employment, and pension rights. Many moved to South Africa. The Beales chose to go to England initially, but it is likely their choice of Australia was prompted by Anthony Beale's inadequate pension and lack of transferable skills.

Today, St Helena, along with Ascension Island and Tristan da Cunha, are collectively a British overseas territory with equal status since 2009, due to their constitutional and historical links.

Napoleon

Napoleon's exile to St Helena in 1815 almost doubled the population, putting huge pressure on accommodation and food sources. He and his large entourage appeared in the harbour on *HMS Northumberland* with very little official warning. The flow-on effects of his captivity marked a time of deterioration in conditions for most of the Islanders, that continued following his death. His body was eventually repatriated to France.

Slavery

St Helena was to play a pivotal role in the eventual emancipation of slaves. When excavations were made for the first airport in 2017, the graves of thousands of slaves were discovered. Various projects are underway employing DNA testing to better understand their origin. The modern day 'Saints' are descendants of slaves, the Chinese indentured labourers, and the European settlers. Many slave names (originally from their owners) are held by local families on St Helena today.[3] Reparatory justice for the transatlantic slave trade is still being sought today.[4]

Principal families

Baildon family

Dr Adam Baildon was employed as a shore-based surgeon on St Helena by the Company from ~ 1807. He married Katherine's sister Isabella, and they had four daughters. He died prematurely in 1815 and is buried in St Helena. Their eldest daughter, Catherine, died aged 20 at Lee in January, 1823.

Balcombe family

William Balcombe was possibly an illegitimate son of the Prince Regent (George IV). He was a merchant who fell afoul of Sir Hudson Lowe and eventually moved to Sydney. They owned the Briars and the Briars Pavilion – the latter was where Napoleon lived when he first arrived on St Helena. Balcombe's younger daughter Betsy (Elizabeth Abell) was a great friend of Napoleon in his exile. Her younger brother Alexander had a property, The Briars, on the Mornington Peninsula in Melbourne.

Beale family (see also timeline of Katherine's life)

Katherine Rose Young married Captain Anthony Beale, an employee in the St Helena Pay Master's office, in June, 1814. Civilian employees of the Company were given a military equivalent rank. Many employees underwent training at the East India Company training establishment in Hertford England, that later became Haileybury School. The Beales had lived on the Island for generations, since it was captured from the Portuguese in the 1650s. Their properties included Terrace Knoll and Sunnyside. An ancestor, also Anthony Beale, was briefly the governor when St Helena was first settled. Katherine met her future husband (most likely in 1813) at a ball that was hosted at Plantation House, the official country residence of the Governor (personal communication with Mr Tim Gatehouse).

Katherine and Anthony eventually had seventeen children. Sixteen were born on St Helena. Three babies and a young boy died prematurely. Two of Katherine's adult children pre-deceased her in tragic circumstances. Onesiphorus drowned soon after their arrival in Launceston, and Rose died in childbirth. Ironically her sons Edward and Anthony, exposed to great dangers in their course of employment, survived.

Whilst Anthony is referred to as Major Beale in some literature, his equivalent rank was Lieutenant Colonel.

Halliburton family

James Halliburton was married to Katherine's sister Elizabeth. He was a commander of *Glatton,* an East Indiaman ship. He died at sea in 1815 and was interred with his brother-in-law Adam Baildon at St Helena. His son Charles, whom he never met, eventually lived with Katherine and Anthony Beale in Australia. There are many monumental inscriptions to the family at St Luke's Church near Woolwich.[5]

Lindsay family

John Lindsay was a wealthy merchant married to Katherine's sister Margaret. He assisted the Beales financially, especially when Anthony became insolvent. He initially lived in Laurence Poultney Lane before purchasing property just south of Greenwich in Blackheath and Lee where several of Katherine's siblings were to live. He and Margaret are also interred at St Luke's Church.

Wilks family

Colonel Mark Wilks,[6] a polyglot, served with distinction in India, and wrote a definitive history of his time as the Resident of Mysore. He returned to the Isle of Man after his brief incumbency on St Helena as Governor (1813-1816), where he became Speaker of the Manx parliament – the House of Keys – succeeding his father-in-law Major John Taubman. Wilks, a widower, married his second wife, Dorothy Taubman (born 1783), also from an established Manx family, in early 1813. His daughter Laura, from his first wife, Harriet MacLeane, was renowned as a great beauty. In her later life, she and her husband Sir John Buchan, endowed educational establishments on the Isle of Man, where the Buchan School continues to thrive in 2024. Wilks was highly regarded by Napoleon, unlike his successor Sir Hudson Lowe.

Yon family

Several members of the family were employed by the Beales. Chinese labourers were sourced from China in the early 19th century due to the gradual emancipation of slaves. Significant numbers were eventually repatriated. Their many descendants still live on St Helena.[7]

Young family

See also the timeline of Katherine's life and individual entries.

Charles Cobb Young

Katherine's second brother was also a master mariner. He died following a voyage on *Justina*.

James Young

Katherine's elder brother. He sponsored Katherine's second and third sons, Edward and Anthony, at the commencement of their careers in the military and medicine respectively. He lived in Lee, just south of Greenwich, and was a master mariner. He owned *Justina* that was captained by his brother, Charles.

Peter Young

Katherine's uncle was a ropemaker and sail maker in Wapping and named in the codicil of his presumed brother, James Young Senior's will (evidence from the Descendant Report). His wife, Margaret, was a sister of Katherine's mother. It is quite likely that they adopted Katherine and her older siblings when they were orphaned.

James Young (Senior)

Katherine's father added a codicil to his will of 14 May 1783, on 4 November 1799, naming three executors: his wife, Catherine nee Raitt, (who predeceased him); his presumed brother, Peter; and James Murray, merchant of Leadenhall Street (where the headquarters of the Honourable East India Company was located), providing for the support of his wife and children until they became self-supporting. It is quite possible that James Murray was the captain of the East Indiaman *Devonshire*.[8]

Minor characters

Governor Alexander Beatson

The previous Governor to Colonel Mark Wilks whose life was potentially saved by Dr Adam Baildon, Katherine's brother-in-law, during the 1811 riots on St Helena.

Reverend Richard Boys

One of two chaplains (the other was Reverend Jones) employed by the Honourable East India Company who were renowned for their uncompromising stance on morality.

John Burt

An employee of the Company and fellow traveller on *Cecelia*. He supported Katherine Ann Sibella Beale, giving evidence at her brother Onesiphorus's inquest. John and Katherine married the following January (1840) in Launceston, and eventually returned to England to live in Ramsgate, Kent. He was a Commissioner to the Court of Salvage.[9]

Captain Henry Christopher

Captain Christopher commanded *Sir William Pulteney* on five extended voyages between 1805 and 1814.

Doveton family

The Doveton family were related to the Beales. They were one of several significant families who had lived on the Island for generations, many of whom intermarried.

George James

A wine merchant who married Katherine's daughter Elizabeth (Bessie). They moved to Southampton, but supported Anthony financially following his insolvency.

Governor La Trobe

The family were neighbours to the Beales when they first settled in Newtown (present day Fitzroy).

Sir Hudson Lowe

Appointed by the British Government to supervise Napoleon from 1816 until the latter's death in 1821.

Charles Maplestone

Maplestone was a notable church architect and designer of lighthouses. He was a widower and artist, born in England. He married the widowed Isabella Nodin, nee Beale. She laid the foundation stone for St John's Church, Diamond Creek, Victoria, Australia. St John's marked the 157th anniversary on 11 November, 2024

Mason family

An eccentric landowner on St Helena, Miss Polly Mason, was known to ride an ox in preference to a horse. She apparently set up some sort of signalling system with Napoleon when he was exiled to St Helena in 1815.

Catherine Monk

A fellow traveller on *Cecelia*, she was called as a witness at Onesiphorus's inquest.

Francis Nodin

Isabella Beale's first husband, who died a few weeks before Katherine Beale. He had a colourful life.

Saul Solomon

His influence is still felt today, but originally, he had a large store that would have been one of the primary shops in Jamestown, and was involved in many other interests on the Island.

Lieutenant Colonel and Mrs Skelton

They travelled with the Wilks family on *Sir William Pulteney* and ultimately vacated their house at Longwood in order to accommodate Napoleon and his entourage. Mrs Skelton spoke French fluently and they made several visits to Napoleon before departing St Helena in 1816.

This Still Hearth

The story of Katherine Rose Beale

Prologue

June, 2016
St Katherine's Church, Anthony Beale Reserve,
St Helena, Victoria – a flight of imagination

The little church prompts memories of English churches, the sort one might find in small, rural villages, separate from other buildings, approached via a lychgate and surrounded by ancient graves and tufted grass.[10] It brings to mind St Mary's at Tyneham in Dorset. The village was confiscated by the government during the Second World War, with the villagers being given a week to pack up their lives, never to return. Nowadays, when the army tanks cease firing on the nearby ranges, visits are permitted to the partially ruined buildings. There is a lingering sadness that permeates Tyneham more than seventy years later, and inexplicably I am feeling a similar sense of poignancy here.

Set in remnant bush, shaded by magnificent trees, with a large grey bell hanging from a metal frame, the church and its graveyard exude an aura of calm. This is despite traffic passing on a nearby busy road and the high-pitched sounds of young voices. There is a sports ground on top of the small grassy hill in the lee of which the church sits. Colourful galahs, matching the trunks of the lemon-scented gums in their colours of pink and grey, are chattering to each other whilst sitting on a branch. The day is unusually warm for the start of winter, and the sky is deep blue with a few strands of cirrus cloud.

The churchyard is full of graves, unusual for Australia, where cemeteries tend to stand alone. Approximately half of the graves appear to belong to the Beale family and their descendants. A large, decorated, granite stone stands solidly near the entrance to the church, commemorating its one hundred and fiftieth anniversary some ten years previously. I try the door handle. Locked. I peer through the porch windows, but another door blocks the view of the inside. At my feet, a little memorial garden hosting striking winter roses or hellebores sits beneath a greyish-white rendered wall. The wall is contiguous with the church. Rectangular name plaques with spaces next to them, presumably for the remaining spouse, are affixed to the wall. Distinctive metal gates, dedicated to the pioneers, open onto the path leading to the church from a car park that is pitted with holes. Water sits in puddles even though it has not rained for a while.

I sit on a bench under the lemon scented gums. Enjoying the sounds and smells of nature, I start to drift off to sleep, imagining how the area might have looked before the Europeans arrived and changed it for ever …

Seedpods explode from the heat of a bushfire, started as part of planned land management by the people of the Wurundjeri indigenous culture. The Witchety Grub People are named for the manna gum – wurun – common along the Yarra River and its tributaries, and djeri – the grub found in or near the tree. Some seedpods land close to these local creeks and rivers. A few seeds settle in poor quality soil near the top of a hill. Small green shoots appear in late spring. The saplings are sheltered by larger trees that provide a forest canopy. Despite the odds, the small trees survive and thrive. Their roots thrust downwards searching for available moisture. Using a unique and complex chemical system, they communicate with and support each other to grow. Within ten years they reach half their mature height. The place where they are growing is rich with local flora and fauna, some of which are unique to this locale. Close by, the Sweet Bursaria shrub supports a population of striking yellow and copper-coloured butterflies. To the south, the Yarra River and Diamond Creek are full of fish and platypus. To the north, large mobs of kangaroos roam the extensive grasslands. They drink from the Plenty River that rises in the forested slopes of the southern Great Dividing Range, flowing south to join the Yarra.

Smaller animals regularly pass by the trees, foraging for food, particularly at night. Brush-tailed phascogale with pretty, triangular faces; blue tongue lizards, dwarfed by lace monitors that grow up to two metres; bandicoots; and sugar gliders. All live close by. The powerful owl frequently rests on the trees' higher branches. Honeyeaters and parrots provide colour, and feast on nectar and seeds from indigenous plants. Sulphur-crested cockatoos can be heard squawking as they fly over the valley. Flocks of long-billed corellas, with scarlet collars and blue smudged eyes, feed on the grasses. King parrots and kookaburras are frequent visitors. In the wooded areas, rare orchids thrive, their delicate hues of pink and yellow adding to the mix of colours. The two now-mature lemon-scented gum trees, with their magnificent, mottled pink and grey trunks, are fifty metres tall. Their long, slender, green leaves have a strong lemon fragrance when crushed. Essential oils distilled from their leaves can be used in perfumes, as well as in insect repellants. Their deciduous bark curls and flakes off in the spring. When their delicate white flowers appear in summer and autumn, they attract native stingless bees.[11] Small flocks of pink and grey galahs match the colours of the tree trunks. Together with colourful, noisy rainbow lorikeets, they make their homes here. The magnificent eucalypts tower above all the other trees and take in the sun's rays as it rises over distant mountains to the east. As the sun sets in the valleys to the west, the moonlight causes their branches to shimmer in silver light. They live in harmony with the flora, fauna and ancient peoples of the land.

Like silent sentinels the trees continue their annual cycle of life. People flock to mine gold in the local area. Gold is found near Mount Disappointment, with the tailings flowing in the local creeks and rivers. Townships are built. Diamond Creek is named for the crystalline stones on the creek bed, or possibly after a bull called Diamond that fell into the creek and drowned.[12] A reef of gold runs through its hills. Farms and orchards come and go. A train line is built to transport people and goods, mainly fruit such as apples and pears. Subdivisions and new homes are supported by bigger and faster roads until only remnants of bush remain.

A loud noise wakes me. What a strange dream! Despite the sun shining, there is a chill in the air. I start walking back towards home, hoping I won't lose the way as I only recently moved to the area. Three months later I become a regular attendee at the church and start to learn some of its history, kept alive by the efforts of the late Isla Heddle, a direct descendant of Anthony and Katherine Beale, and Bev Ward, the church warden. Cleaning and preparing the building for the twice-monthly Sunday services gives me plenty of time to explore the interior.

The inside of the church is striking. A two-light stained-glass window in the chancel of St Katherine's was erected to the memory of Anthony and Katherine Beale. A single-light window in the south wall, slightly damaged, is a memorial to Luther Maplestone, the stepson of Katherine Beale's daughter Isabella. It is next to the pew where I usually sit, so I often wonder what happened to Luther. He died so young – aged 23 – in a remote part of Queensland. Another stained-glass window depicts St Michael and was erected to as a tribute to the Beale descendants who lost their lives in the First World War. The young men's names are listed on a separate board.

These windows are detailed replicas of original windows that were lost to the 1957 bushfire. Yet another stained-glass window includes a picture of a possum, and was created to acknowledge the people who contributed to the rebuilding of the church through public donations. A large, grey plaque at the front of the church commemorates Katherine and Anthony Beale's oldest son, Onesiphorus. A photographic board near the entrance is used to illustrate the church history for visiting school and community groups. The wooden pews and the carved altar rails and lectern retain a scent of wood polish. The various brass candlesticks, other ornaments and fittings, and small plaques attached to the pews indicating historical donors, are shiny. A wooden font at the front of the church recalls baptisms, its brass cover mottled with dark spots. A nearby silver tray is a gift from the people of St Helena in the South Atlantic.

Many milestones have been observed since its humble beginnings as the Rose Chapel in 1861. The list of contributions dated 12 January, 1861, shows the cost was £505.16.8 with £450 from the late Anthony Beale. The building was originally a small, square room with a fireplace, built of handmade bricks by Major Beale. Building started in 1856 and was completed in 1858, with Divine Services first held in 1859, mostly for the Beale family. Money was donated by many relatives of the Beales. A copy of the list of contributors shows the amounts donated. They include Anthony and Katherine's daughters Elizabeth James and Katherine Burt;

her niece Katherine Halliburton; her son Anthony; CS Wingrove, her granddaughter Katherine Nodin's husband; and Charles Maplestone. For fifteen years this beautiful little place of worship remained the private chapel for Anthony Beale and his family in remembrance of his wife. Alterations to the original building were carried out around 1869. A letter from John Dyer, dated 24 April, 1869, states the total cost will be £115 and the works completed by 5 June, 1869. The fireplace was removed, and the square, domestic style gave place to a simple, pointed-arch style, with a door at the South end and three lancet windows on each side, a roomy porch with seats being added at the other end. Most of this refurbishing was closely supervised by Mr. Charles Maplestone, Architect of Heidelberg, a son-in-law of Major Beale. In these early days there was no belfry, so a bell placed in the forked branch of a gum tree called people to worship.

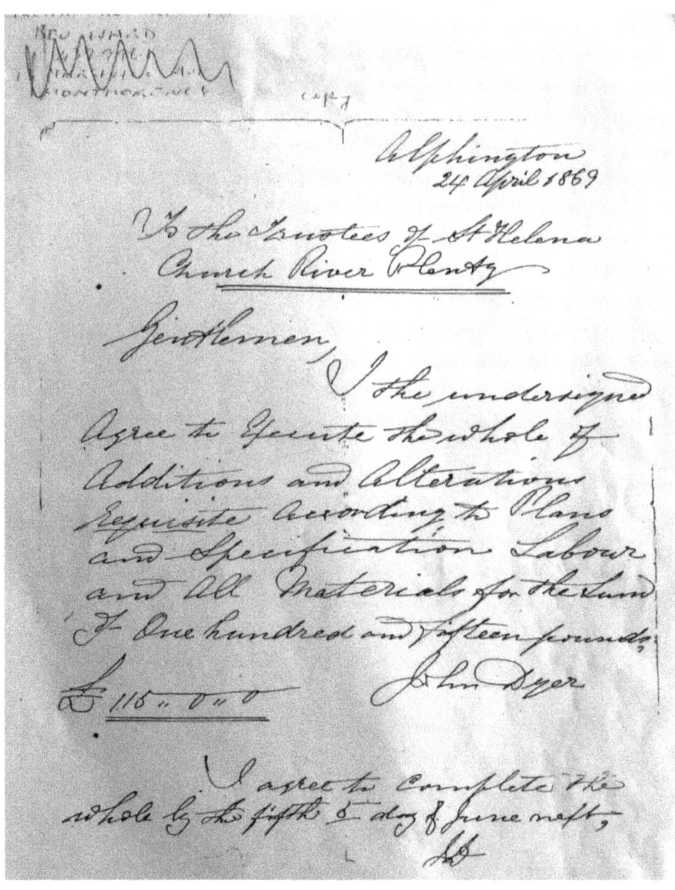

Quotation for improvement works from John Dyer 24 April 1869

8177 St Katherine's Chur
St Helena

List of Contributions in the erection of a *Church at S. Helena* ———————— in connection with the Church of England, under the 13th section of the Regulations of the 12th January, 1861, respecting the Grant in Aid of Public Worship.

NAMES	AMOUNT
The late Anthony Beale Sen. who originally built the church	450 . 0 . 0
Elizabeth James	3 . 0 . 0
Katharine A. Burt	2 . 0 . 0
Katharine Halliburton	5 . 0 . 0
Anthony Beale E.C.S.	20 . 0 . 0
— Ainkins	1 . 0 . 0
C. S. Wingrove	10 . 10 . 0
Charles Maplestone	11 . 11 . 0
Other Contributions to Dec. 26th 1870	2 . 15 . 8
TOTAL £	505 . 16 . 8

We certify that we have received the sums shown in the above Schedule, amounting in the whole to £ 505.11. for the erection of a *Church* ———————— and that that amount has been purely expended in the erection of the said building and for no other purpose.

Signature of Trustees { CM.
CSW.
JLB.

List of contributions in the erection of a Church at St Helena

The Church of England Messenger, **Thursday 12 August, 1869, records:**

'The little church at St Helena Park, near Eltham, built by the late Mr Beale in memory of his wife, and which together with three acres of land, including a cemetery, has recently been presented by the family to the Bishop, was re-opened on Sunday, 4th ultimo. A new chancel and vestry have been built and other improvements effected, and two beautiful stained-glass memorial windows, by Messrs Ferguson and Urie, have also been added.'[13] The Petition to consecrate the Rose Chapel that was to become St Katherine's Church was submitted to Charles Perry, the first Anglican Bishop of Melbourne on 1 March, 1876 by Arthur Pickering, Charles Maplestone, John L Beale, and C Wingrove, Trustees:

'Your petitioners therefore pray that your Lordship will be pleased, by virtue of your Pastoral and Episcopal authority, to separate the said building or Edifice from all profane uses, and to dedicate and consecrate the same to the Honour and Worship of Almighty God, and assign it to be perpetually the Church of St Katherine at St Helena.'

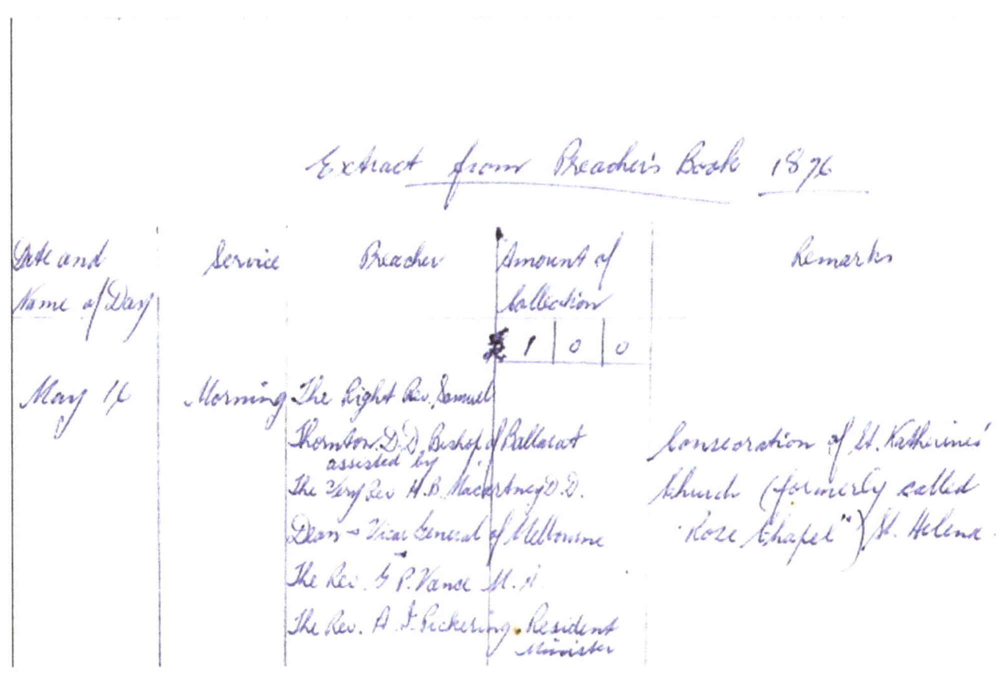

Extract from Preacher's Book 1876: Consecration of St Katherine's Church, St. Helena

Over the years, the church hosts many visitors. The stained-glass windows feature in articles about historical churches. People visit from all over the world. The grounds immediately surrounding the building are kept in good condition with grass regularly mowed, paths swept, and gravestones maintained. Tree branches that might be unstable are lopped and the remaining mulch is used to nurture local gardens. There is something about the interactions with this little church that invite many responses …

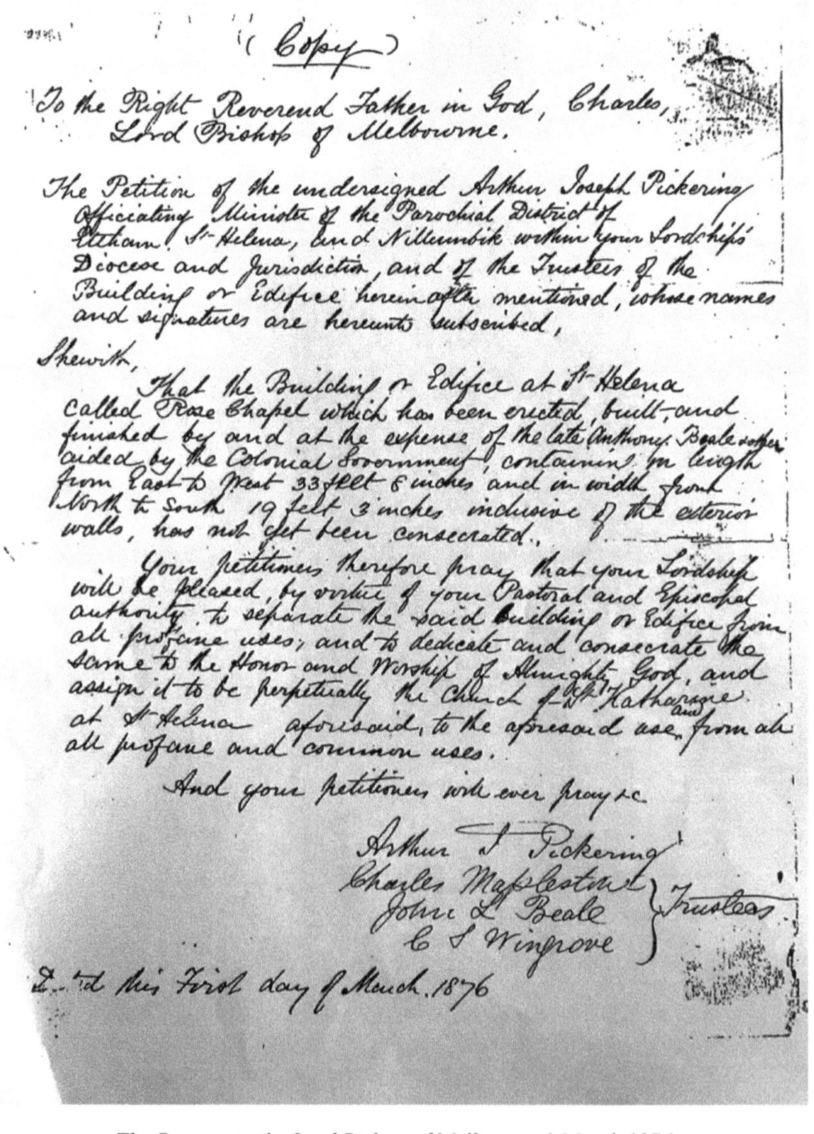

The Petition to the Lord Bishop of Melbourne 1 March 1876

In 1928 Robert Croll embarks on a series of one day walks around Melbourne 'The Open Road':[14]

'Greensborough is a revelation. You suddenly find that you are looking down into a valley of orchards and gardens, with the Plenty River making long loops and curves at their feet. [Take the right-hand track, St Helena 2 M]. You at once begin to climb Boyle's Hill. A cutting at the top has eased the grade, but on a warm day this will be found a pleasant pore opener.

'You have been walking on a whitish ground which looks alluvial: at a line on the St Helena estate, it alters abruptly to the rich black soil of a lava flow. It was not only the rich belt of soil and the neighbourhood of the river than made the early settler build his home here; it was also an appreciation of beauty. Go across the small reserve, open a second gate, and you will find yourself in a graveyard surrounding a church.

'Major Anthony Beale arrived from the island of St Helena in 1839. The Port Phillip Settlement was then four years old, and Melbourne had escaped the indignity of being named Bearbrass.'

The church is described as 'a substantial building with Gothic windows, some of them in stained glass to commemorate departed relatives. In the public portion [of the cemetery] lies the body of Walter Withers, an artist, who loved this picturesque countryside, but no stone bears his name.'

The Australian Women's Mirror of 28 October, 1930 responds to a letter about the granddaughter of Colonel Beale having goblets that were rejected by Napoleon in St Helena.[15] The writer 'Montrose' has just visited St Helena near Eltham:

'where in a picturesque setting among the quiet hills, is the little church of St Katherine (formerly Rose Chapel) built for Anthony Beale "in commemoration of the happy life and peaceful death of Katherine Rose Beale." Three great-grandsons gave their lives in the Great War. On the day of my visit there was inside the church a swallow's nest, high on a beam near the altar, calling to mind the words: "… and the swallow hath found a nest for itself … even thine altars" (Ps lxxxiv,3).'

In 1934, 'C.K.H.' writing in the Women's World, recalls the Historic Little Church at St Helena and the woman whom it commemorates:

'Hidden away in the heart of the bush, a mile or so from a main motor road, is a little spot of peculiar interest to those searching back to Victoria's early days. Where the road dips suddenly down to a bridge spanning a stream, an old road branches off the busy highway to wander leisurely away through the quiet bush. Mounting a hill, the old road reveals a tiny church, surrounded by a churchyard, guarded by high cypress trees, and looking like a scrap of old England set down in the midst of gum trees. [The] quaint church bell, placed high in the fork of an old gum tree, calls the country folk to worship.'

People have been inspired to write poetry and draw pictures of the church. The following poem is hung on the wall in a picture frame:

THE CHURCH OF ST KATHERINE, ST HELENA

†

It stands amid the fields afar,
A lowly church with door ajar,
The House of God, and there within
You'll find the peace and Grace of Him.

No stately pile confronts the view,
With tap'ring spires that pierce the blue,
A humble building old and grey
Fit place to worship and to pray.

He who in days of old bethought
To build this chapel quietly wrought
With careful hands to keep it free
From tinsel show and ribaldry.

There's something simple, holy, true,
Embodied here that brings to you
A quiet assurance all is well,
And Truth itself herein doth dwell.

Hard by beneath the trees that spread
Their shelt'ring branches overhead,
An older generation sleep,
And quietly their vigil keep.

Whatever their country, class or creed,
It matters not; if thou'rt in need
Of consolation for thy fear,
Kneel thou to God, for He is here.

JBC: 15/5/37

In 1946, in *Walkabout,* A.A. Burns writes 'In Memory of the Pioneers.'[16]

'A place of interest visited by many people is the quaint miniature church that stands on the estate known as St Helena, a few miles to the west of Greensborough, an outer suburb of Melbourne. In the story of the building of this church and its builder are associations not only with the years of early settlement in Victoria, but with the times of the great French conqueror, who criss-crossed Europe with his triumphant armies during the early 19th century, but who, in striking contrast to the height of power which he attained, ended his days lowly in exile on lonely St Helena Island.

'It is safe to say that few people who know the origins of St Katherine's and the story of its patriarchal founder will deny experiencing, when within the environs of this chapel, some perception of the historic atmosphere and the feeling of peaceful detachment which seems to be peculiar to the church and its surroundings.'

Twenty years later, disaster! *The Australian Women's Weekly* 6 November, 1957 article by Barbara Wallis headlines, 'Old lamp still lights church rebuilt from bushfire ruin'.[17]

'A thesis a young Melbourne man wrote for a degree in architecture has helped to rebuild to its original beauty a famous little century-old church destroyed by a bushfire. St Katherine's was visited by 4000 tourists a year until last February, when it was burnt to a smouldering ruin. Church Secretary Colonel F W MacLean told his wife and other parishioners gathered at the ruin: "This church will be rebuilt exactly as it has stood for 100 years."'

The plans taken by architect Kenneth Crosier were so detailed that the only difference in the new church was to be improved ventilation. However:

'there will be no electric light. The church was never used for evening service, and will still be lit by an old lamp brought from St Helena by Major Beale.'

The bell, still hanging in the old gum tree, survived the fire.

Despite the church at the time of the fire only having eight families of parishioners, it continued to flourish, and many weddings, christenings, and funerals were held over the years. Major celebrations were held to mark the 150th and 160th anniversaries. Further details of the local history of St John's Diamond Creek and the wider parish of which St Katherines is a part can be found in Roy Gwyther-Jones's book *Light on the Hill* (2017).[18] The Anthony Beale Reserve remains an important habitat, particularly its understorey, in conserving local flora and fauna.[19]

Chapter 1

1 August, 1856 – St Helena Park, Plenty, Victoria, Australia

There is a crispness in the air this morning, and a white frost makes the grass spiky. The house, like me, is feeling old, with familiar creaks and groans as it faces a new day. Possums live happily in the roof which rarely leaks nowadays. We eventually managed to rainproof it, but not before spending some nights under umbrellas when we first moved to Melbourne. What a strange time that was, settling into a new country.

I am obliged to spend the better part of most days in my bed due to my deteriorating health. I have always been an active person, so this enforced rest is a particularly bitter cross to bear. I try to compensate for this burden by reliving past times and remembering the many people I have met over a remarkable life, lived across three continents. I sometimes feel as though I am drowning, so I am propped up on pillows to try and ease my breathing.

The grief from Onesiphorus's disappearance within days of arriving in Van Diemen's Land and subsequent drowning, was different from the loss of my babies and young Adam in St Helena. At that time, I accepted that some babies and young children are destined to die. I had the other children to care for. But to lose my oldest son when we had made such a difficult decision to come to the other end of the world, tested me in a profoundly different way.

My initial reaction was to feel a deep anger towards Anthony that took a considerable while to abate. I was unable to pray or read my bible. I felt a despair that was compounded by a sense of disbelief when his body was found. My girls were so kind to me, taking over necessary chores and looking after the little boys when I was unable to. John Burt and Kas physically supported me at the inquest and spoke when I could not. At one point I felt I was losing my mind. I would smell the clothes that Onesiphorus had worn on the long journey and even wore some of them on occasion. In the end I was persuaded to give his clothes away as they did not fit anyone in the family, but I kept his pocket handkerchief which I would take out in private moments to try and recapture his scent, before it was finally gone forever. I still like to remember my firstborn son, and recently wrote this poem in his memory:

A Mother's Wish[20]

'What shall I wish for thee, darling?'
A fond young mother said
As she knelt to press a tender kiss
On her baby's golden head.

'Shall I pray that the unknown future
May be crowned with honour and fame,
That the palm of victory may be thine
And a soldier's glorious name?

Or shall the poet's tender dreams
Enshrine and grace thine heart?
Or sweet musician wilt thou be
And rapturous strains impart?

Tell me, my darling, which of these
My boy shall grow to be?'
The baby smiled with blue eyes mild
But ne'er a word spake he.

The long, long years have passed away
The mother is grey and old,
But in her bosom till this day
Lies hid a curl of gold.

But her sighs are hush'd when she kneels to pray,
And her murmuring heart is still'd,
For she knows in the Land of far away
Are her brightest hopes fulfilled.

And echoes come o'er the distant years
Where baby feet once trod –
Echoes of a little child at play
In the golden streets of God!

I am interrupted in my thoughts by a bang on the windowpane. A bird must have flown into it. The window looks east with a view of the rising sun that is beginning to appear over the distant mountains. The sky turns purple, orange, scarlet beneath black rolling clouds. The birds are singing as they do every morning; I can hear kookaburras laughing and see magpies carolling, their breath visible in the cold air.

There is a knock on the door. Margaret enters, carrying a tray that she places over my legs, making sure I am comfortable.

'Here is your breakfast, Mama. I will plump up your pillows. Do you need any assistance?'

'No thank you, Margaret. Perhaps you could bring a cup of tea once the men have finished eating?'

'Of course, Mama. You only need to ring your bell, and I will come at once.'

Margaret closes the door quietly.

My scrambled eggs are made from the eggs collected earlier today from our fowls and are always delicious. Margaret has removed the crusts from the toast and cut it into small squares, as I like it.

From my bed I can just see the heavy, grey bell Anthony placed in the fork of the lemon-scented gum nearest to the homestead. It is held securely by a metal plate, built to withstand storms.

Church bells have always been important to me. They link my past to my present, and the different churches I have been privileged to attend. *This* bell has no pendulum, so is struck with a stick or rod. *It is only missing a church*, I think with a wry smile. For Anthony, the bell is a tangible link to his beloved home where generations of his family had lived since an ancestor, also Anthony Beale, was briefly governor of St Helena, in the mid-17th century. In a lovely twist of fate, this first Anthony's wife also came from Stepney, not far from where I grew up.

It was not until the bell was put in its final resting place that I sensed a lightness about Anthony that had been sadly missing. The 1833 St Helena Act forced unwelcome change upon its loyal citizens, many of whom relocated to South Africa. We were so fortunate to be invited to live with my family in Blackheath and Lee. Each of my siblings were able to take a few of our children, who enjoyed getting to know their similar age cousins. Between my sister Elizabeth, my brother James, and my brother-in-law John Lindsay, and with occasional visits to my brother Charles in London, our large family was hosted in comparative luxury, for what turned out to be a three-year sabbatical.

Despite our many challenging journeys by sea, from St Helena to London, from London to Van Diemen's Land and perhaps the roughest trip of all, the final stretch across the Bass Strait that made us fearful for our lives, the bell survived unscathed, protected by its wrapping of goat hair and wedged firmly in the various holds of ships. Its provenance is possibly known by Anthony, but he has never shared this information with me. I believe it was once used in the Country Church, close by to Plantation House, the Governor's country house, where I lived with the Wilks family following our arrival on St Helena in June 1813. Sadly, I lost touch with Laura Wilks, the last letter received from her informing me of the death of her only son. By an extraordinary coincidence, her father, Mark, died of apoplexy on the same day that my young niece lost her life, the announcements of their deaths appearing side by side in the *Asiatic Journal*.

Almost the entire population of St Helena turned out to farewell the Wilks family in 1816, less than three years since Colonel Mark Wilks was appointed governor, such was the high regard in which they were held. Even Napoleon ensured he had a private audience with Mark and Laura prior to their departure. The exiled Emperor greatly respected Uncle Mark and was enchanted by Laura's striking beauty and intelligence.

Church bells instantly bring to mind all the important people and times in my life. I can just remember that Uncle Peter led the bell ringers at St George-in-the-East for Mama's funeral, the muffled sounds quite unlike what we were accustomed to hearing following Sunday services. Five years later, glorious peals sounded from churches all over London, celebrating Nelson's victory at Trafalgar. The reverberating sounds and patterns were unique to a particular church and always prompted a recitation of Oranges and Lemons, a favourite nursery rhyme, around the family table. There were alternative versions to the nursery rhyme that we used to sing when playing outside St George-in-the-East, often whilst skipping rope.

The leaves from the lemon-scented gum, where our bell is placed, have medicinal and other benefits. I crush them to release the oil that masks other more unpleasant odours, but they also seem to relieve my pain when I breathe in the scent. The local aboriginal women have many more uses for eucalyptus leaves, using them as an insect repellent and making teas that relieve colds and coughs.

Anthony and I no longer share a room as I frequently wake in the night. He cannot cope with broken sleep. Recently, he appears to have lost his ability to see humour in adversity and struggles in his faith. My legs are so swollen with fluid that I can barely walk. They are constantly wet as the skin has split in several places. There are raised bumps that feel rough to touch. It seems I may be destined to mark my first and last days in this country in a wet bed. We will never forget our first night in Newtown where all our bedding was thoroughly soaked following a heavy downpour of rain. The prefabricated house that had accompanied us from England was unable to withstand the onslaught of the late-spring deluge. Fortunately, we were eventually able to see the absurdity in it and I found one of Anthony's night shirts to replace my sodden gown. The thick quilt made from goose feathers took days to dry out and was never quite the same.

The days are long now, and I spend much of my time reading the bible and reflecting on my life, praying to God and thanking him for the good fortunes he has bestowed upon us. I like to look at the picture of our family sketched by John Burt when we were travelling on *Cecelia* and think about our dear children, as well as our sons Edward and Anthony who remained in England. In the sketch, the five boys are lined up beside Anthony in order of age, with the youngest to his immediate right: Hali, James, John, Adam, and Onesiphorus. On my left are our daughters: Margaret, Rose, Bessy, Isabella, and Katherine. I also dream about the children that are no longer with us – I am longing to see them all once more, and trust that we will be reunited before too long. In my prayers I ask for blessings on all my children and grandchildren, but I am saddened that I will never again set foot in a church. The visiting priest makes regular trips from Greensborough on his ageing horse to conduct Holy Communion services in our front parlour, using the Book of Common Prayer. I attend if I am well enough. Alternatively, families gather to read the church service at their own residences, to such as are disposed to attend. Nevertheless, I miss the churches of my youth. Anthony has promised to build a chapel he will name after me and our beloved daughter Rose. He intends to enlist the help of Charles Maplestone, a local church architect, who immigrated from England in 1852, barely twelve months after terrifying fires had swept through the Plenty River on 6 February. As a result of Black Thursday, the wife and five children of the M'Lelland family that lived between Plenty River and Diamond Creek were suffocated from the smoke of the fire. Other friends' farms were totally destroyed. These disasters made a significant impact on us all as we had settled in the area around about the same time.

Through our daughter Isabella (Issy), we have got to know Charles well. Issy and her recently-deceased husband, Francis, lived in an adjacent property in Richmond to Charles and his adored wife, Sarah, who died soon after their arrival at Port Phillip. Issy is a surrogate mother to his children, who are of similar ages to her own large family. Charles is currently working on preliminary designs for a church to be built in Diamond Creek and another in Kangaroo Ground, so is a frequent overnight guest. At these times, he likes to relax on our verandah when it is warm enough and make sketches of houses he would like to build – some of these drawings he has hung on the wall of our bedroom, as I like to look at them.

Charles managed his grief from losing his childhood sweetheart by engaging in several projects around Victoria, including designing lighthouses at Gabo Island and Cape Schank.[21] An agreeable and mutually satisfying arrangement was in place where his young children were cared for by Issy and her colourful husband, Francis, at their large home in Richmond. Charles paid for the necessary domestic help and additional monies to cover all expenses and incidentals, as Francis's income was precarious. Unfortunately, Francis's recent death has meant a reassessment of how best to manage the domestic arrangements, so I have not seen Issy since the funeral. Nor have I spent time with my husband who, it seems, is not unlike Charles. Both men become preoccupied with projects to avoid having to face some unpleasant situations. I fear that my prolonged illness has proved difficult for Anthony, as I have always tried to be the strong person in our marriage and this is no longer possible. It has been a considerable time since we engaged in any intimacy, and I sometimes fear that he is avoiding me.

For weeks, Anthony has been making brown bricks, packing the clay he gets from the Plenty River or its tributaries into wooden moulds. He and our daughter Margaret drive her pair of bullocks that are harnessed to a big wooden truck built by Anthony and our nephew Charles Halliburton, to carry the clay. Charles now lives with us following his arrival from England in March last year. Anthony stamps the bricks with a crude bell shape before ejecting them from the mould with his thumbs, leaving them to dry in the sun. He estimates that he has several hundred bricks and has been sketching possible designs for a chapel, aided by Margaret who carefully checks the dimensions. He intends to build the chapel adjacent to the family cemetery where Rose and her stillborn son were interred so recently. Soon afterwards there was another funeral: Francis died unexpectedly, barely four weeks later, leaving Isabella with seven children under fourteen.

I never truly warmed to Francis, although I did not share this with Issy. I regarded him as a bit of a rogue with an interesting but somewhat dubious past. I strained to understand him. His pronounced Scottish accent sounded almost like a foreign language, and the gestures he used to emphasise what he was saying were distracting. However, we were blessed with two grandsons and six granddaughters from their marriage, although sadly young Frank, a mirror image of his father, died in January, 1854, shortly after his first birthday.

I miss Kas, my namesake, and wish I could see her one final time, as I have always been close to my oldest daughter. I have enjoyed re-reading her most recent letter delivered to us by young Anthony who has taken two years' leave from his job to come out to Australia. Kas writes that they have moved to a house called Prospect Lodge in Ramsgate, Kent. John is soon to retire from his role as Commissioner to the Court of Salvage. Kas's letters to us are always full of information and reflect her usually sunny nature, although they were not blessed with a family. Katherine Anne Sibella Beale married John Burt from the Honourable East India Company service in January, 1840. He had been a fellow passenger on *Cecelia*. The day after our arrival in Van Diemen's Land, John formally asked Anthony's permission to marry his oldest daughter. They returned to England soon after their wedding. They visit Bessy when they can, as their husbands have become good friends. The Burts have been formally appointed as guardians of their nieces and nephews if any misfortune was to occur to their parents. Elizabeth – Bessy – also married well. She and her husband, George James, left for England with their seven young children in 1853. George was Anthony's wine merchant, the two meeting soon after we arrived in Melbourne Town. Our concerns about the ten-year age gap, as Bessy was not yet seventeen, were groundless. George, like John Lindsay, has been very generous to us. Anthony and I miss the grandchildren dreadfully, as does Margaret, who was close to her nieces and nephews. Bessy and George were keen to have the children educated in England and we supported their choice despite our sadness.

According to Bessy, they have a house full of servants, including a butler named Henry Bloomfield. She is expecting another baby, and is kept busy by two-year-old Elizabeth as well as the other children. Their house in Southampton is close to the partially ruined Southgate that forms part of the town walls. They are soon to move into newly built Ridgeway House with five bedrooms and extensive grounds, built on the site of a demolished castle. Young Anthony visited them in Southampton before making the long trip out to Australia, so we have enjoyed hearing about our grandchildren once more. I continued to exchange letters with my sister Elizabeth until she died in 1851. Her son Charles briefly lived in New York before joining us in Australia last year.

George James kindly treated Margaret to a team of bullocks two years ago that Anthony usually drives, but both are getting skilled at managing the pair due to the frequent trips to the Plenty River. The arrangement with our nephew Charles, who has also become a good driver, enables Margaret to explore the countryside around our property, parts of which are very steep, as well as making use of them around the St Helena homestead. She and Charles are thirteen years apart in age but enjoy each other's company. I have been fascinated by bullocks since first observing them on St Helena and seeing Miss Polly Mason riding her ox. On an early horse ride around the island, the blacksmith showed how harnesses and yokes were made for the bullocks on St Helena. Margaret's beasts are joined by a similar yoke that is roughly rectangular, but shaped to form curved depressions that allows it to rest across their necks. The two metal collars were made by the local blacksmith. The harness is made from scrap metal and bush timber, as are so many essential items in our new homeland, where very few items are wasted, and even broken objects can usually be reemployed in some way. The bullocks have a patient nature and are easy to control, despite their considerable strength. They make easy work of ploughing through the bush when harnessed in pairs. We have many implements which were made for us over the years by our local blacksmith, including the tools we use for stoking the fire in the kitchen and in our bedroom. I am grateful for the additional warmth as I need to have frequent changes of linen.[22]

This time last year Anthony took me to St James' Cathedral in Melbourne on the corner of Williams and Little Collins Street, probably the last time I was well enough to travel any distance. The cathedral foundation stone had been laid by our friend and neighbour Governor La Trobe, just five days before we had arrived on the Australian mainland on the ninth of November, 1839. We have felt an affinity with the church ever since, and regularly worshipped there – until my health deteriorated. Issy was married there in December, 1840, not long after it had been relocated from its original site further east on William Street, when it was not much more than a wooden shell and freezing cold on all but the warmest days. We all attended the first cathedral service on the second of October, 1842, just before Alexander's first birthday, although the building was not finally completed until 1847. I was looking forward to hearing its bells at the conclusion of the service, but was bitterly disappointed. A decade elapsed before the loud and sonorous ship's bell was replaced with Melbourne's first custom made peal of bells – six of them – that were hung in 1852.[23] Anthony reports there is some talk that the cathedral is already too small as so many people are arriving in Melbourne, attracted by the prospect of finding gold.

I am a passionate reader and very familiar with the Bible but as a young woman I had a particular fondness for the books of Jane Austen originally known as 'A Lady,' an ironic title as most books are written by men. I took *Sense and Sensibility* and the recently published *Pride and Prejudice* on *Sir William Pulteney* on my first great journey to St Helena. The travel to a distant land had been a blind leap of faith, but I was overwhelmed by a longing to escape overcrowded and polluted London. I naively identified with Lizzie Bennet, believing we shared characteristics such as intelligence and independence. In retrospect, I most likely shared Elizabeth Bennet's less charitable characteristic of making hasty or less than flattering judgements about people. I have prayed for this burden to be relieved, but fear it has become an ingrained habit. I wondered who might become my Mr Darcy, my favourite male character in *Pride and Prejudice* or possibly Colonel Brandon, the latter my hero from *Sense and Sensibility*. Both men, whilst quite different in character, have a certain depth that appealed to me. I remember seeing the heart-shaped waterfall soon after going ashore on St Helena and wondered if that was a good omen. My sense, when first introduced to Anthony at the Plantation House Ball not long after we arrived, was that he might become my perfect soulmate. The ball was attended by a veritable Who's Who of St Helena. Jane Austen would have felt at home if she too had been a guest at the ball, but it is likely her observations would have been informed by irony.

My life has taken so many unexpected turns since then. I feel as though I have been on an extended pilgrimage. My longing to find something that was hard to define gave me the courage to take the first big step into the unknown, leaving most of my beloved family in England. That restlessness and craving to search for something better was certainly not shared by my sisters when we engaged in more intimate conversations. The unexpected opposition to my travelling to St Helena initially caused me to question my motives. I used my journal to record my conflicting feelings alongside biblical quotations. I also spent time in prayer and reflection before I was convinced that it was a necessary journey on which to embark.

I have always drawn comfort from religious tracts, copying the ones I find most meaningful into Anthony's leatherbound journals, always mindful of paper shortages in the new colony. I have never been able to employ crosshatching as I feel it may be disrespectful in some way. The brown hide covers are imprinted with the seal of the Honourable East India Company, but the blue ink is fading. A hint of damp dispels any lingering odour of leather. Apart from the embossed seal, the covers are worn smooth to touch, any imperfections in the leather obliterated from frequent handling. It is when I am engaged in my writing, reflecting on the meaning of the words, or exploring the bush around our home, marvelling at the strange flora and fauna, that I feel most at peace.

I like to look back at old diaries of our early days in Newtown and the gay social life enjoyed by Issy, Bessy, and Rose. How we laughed when the little boys helped Anthony catch a pig. How nervous we were during our initial encounters with the local native population, but later we developed strong friendships with some of the women and children. It is almost hard to remember how frightened we were about the bushrangers that were coming so close to our properties in 1842. Anthony even purchased a pistol to protect us and, in a state of anger and nervousness, pointed it at one of our would-be saviours, Peter Snodgrass![24] These lawless men would hide in the forests of Montmorency. My friends and I, collectively the 'Resident Ladies of Plenty' sent a petition to Governor La Trobe on the fifth of May. We were fearful for our lives, living without protection so far from Melbourne Town. I believed our friendship with the La Trobe family, neighbours in Newtown with similarly aged children, may have encouraged action, as the bushrangers were caught before they were able to inflict further damage.[25]

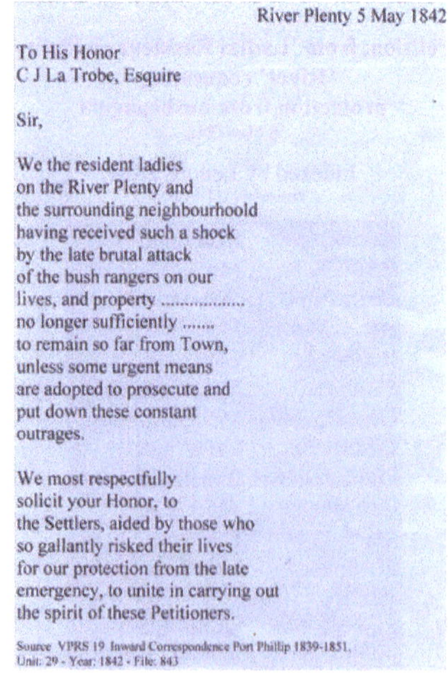

River Plenty 5 May 1842

To His Honor
C J La Trobe, Esquire

Sir,

We the resident ladies
on the River Plenty and
the surrounding neighbourhoold
having received such a shock
by the late brutal attack
of the bush rangers on our
lives, and property ....
no longer sufficiently ....
to remain so far from Town,
unless some urgent means
are adopted to prosecute and
put down these constant
outrages.

We most respectfully
solicit your Honor, to
the Settlers, aided by those who
so gallantly risked their lives
for our protection from the late
emergency, to unite in carrying out
the spirit of these Petitioners.

Source VPRS 19 Inward Correspondence Port Phillip 1839-1851.
Unit: 29 - Year: 1842 - File: 843

The 1842 Petition from the Ladies of Plenty (extract)

Anthony's crude sketches of the house he erected at Newtown when we first arrived on mainland Australia still make me smile. His original pens were old fashioned quills taken from our flock of chickens, with the nib shaped by a sharp knife and dipped into ink. I remember the scratchy sound of the quills on the linen pages and the occasional mild oath from Anthony if the ink flowed too fast. We brought our prefabricated house from England on the barque *Cecelia,* along with all our worldly possessions.

The first night, it rained heavily and leaked badly, leaving us cold, damp, and miserable the next morning. The absence of Onesiphorus felt as a heavy stone replacing my heart.

Anthony's sketch of our house[26]

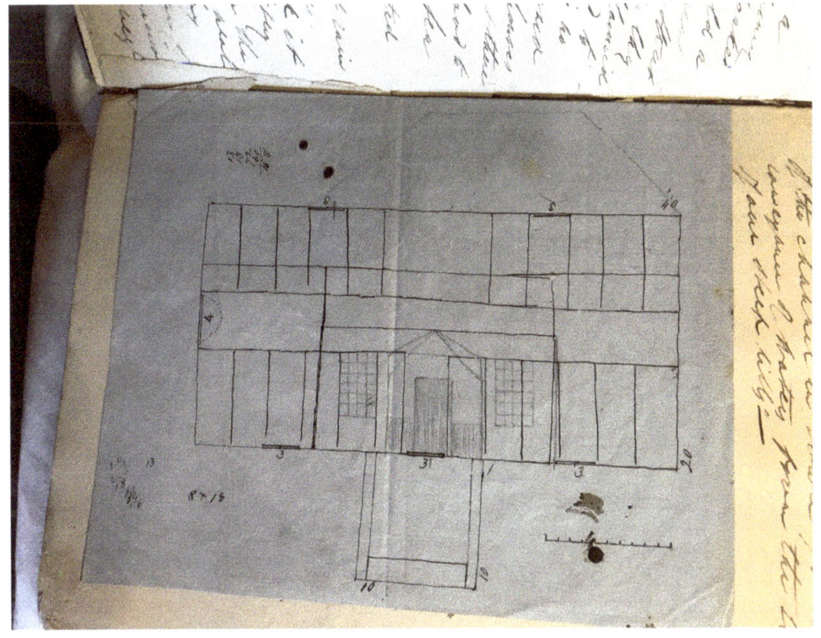

How the rooms may be divided

I miss my dear Rose, so recently departed with her stillborn son. Less than five years married. Anthony and I adored Rose, for her physical beauty was matched by an inner grace and we find it unbearable that we will never hold her or hear her laughter again. I have not felt well since Rose's sad passing. The grief from her unexpected death and that of her stillborn baby barely four months ago is still raw. We had enjoyed Easter together excited about the baby, with Rose looking radiant. Less than two weeks later, mother and child were both taken:

'my tears are flowing for a beloved child of 30 … I shall never hear that name again, that ever with such love wished me many happy returns, a painful thought. It is like a sad dream, but as it is indeed thus, since the 20th of last month we have been heavily visited: first the dear Infant, then the dear Mother.'[27]

It seems my time in this country has been marked by grief.

'My Rose.'[28]

They brought me a sweet young rose,

And laid it down at my feet,

And my heart and brain alike o'er flowed

With the breath of its perfume sweet.

And day after day it grew,

And gently one by one

Each petal opened its snowy folds

And turned its face to the sun

And I wept o'er its glowing heart

Tender and happy tears,

For it seemed to me that my eyes could see

Down a vista of golden years.

O! Rose so pure – so sweet

Sent me from Heaven above,

The Angels laid thee down at my feet

And whispered thy name was Love.

The swelling started in my legs, a heaviness that has spread upwards to my abdomen where the skin dimples when pressed, the hollow remaining long after the pressure is relieved. My legs are blistered and leak water, requiring frequent changes of the bed linen. Unfortunately, they are often odorous. Most days I am in pain. On occasions I get a frightening sensation where I struggle to breathe. I have noticed in the mirror that my lips turn dark blue with the effort. It is a cold winter this year with many frosts that often give way to sunny days. The men of the family keep the woodpile well stocked, so it ensures our home is kept warm.

I am pleased that our son Anthony has managed to take extended time away from his medical duties in India and can be a support to his father for as long as needed. He has also administered drugs to me that have made the pain more bearable and eased my breathing, although the medicine has a bitter taste. He is a skilled watercolour artist and has showed me some of his early drawings of places he has lived in India. I am fast running out of wall space, but it gives me pleasure to look at all the different types of art my family and others have created, as the individual works prompt memories of happier times. Young Anthony has nailed two of his works to the wall, next to a number of prints of St Helena published by George Bellasis in 1815 that Anthony gifted to me following the birth of several of my babies. The picture of Terrace Knoll painted by William Burchell[29] is hung on the opposite wall alongside a preliminary sketch of Sunnyside – named for Anthony's brother's home on St Helena – that Charles Maplestone has drawn of his neighbouring property. He sketched from our back veranda, whilst drinking Lapsang Souchong tea with its rich, smoky essence – also a favourite of mine – from a fine porcelain cup. Margaret has put a couple of her pictures on display in our bedroom. She continues to live with us and has some talent for drawing, but hers are cruder sketches of domestic scenes.

I shift around in the bed, finding it very difficult to get comfortable. A shaft of light from the rising sun is shining on the tree where Anthony has placed the bell. During its passage from St Helena and onwards to Australia it was carefully wrapped in layers of sackcloth made from the hair of goats collected at the time they threatened to overrun the Island. I remember our departure from St Helena was just prior to the naturalist Charles Darwin's visit for five days in July, 1836. Darwin was less than flattering about the damage goats had done to young trees causing much of the Island to be overtaken by indigenous wire grass. I am told that he found the strong winds challenging, whereas I had always appreciated their help in drying the never-ending stream of laundry generated by our large family. I miss the exotic and native trees that we had in our garden at Terrace Knoll where I used to hang out the clothes, particularly the Cedar of Lebanon with its deep woody scent and hints of citrus. Anthony and I spent many hours sitting under its benevolent shade. Its provenance was unknown, as similar trees were rare on St Helena and it grew at a lower elevation than in its native Lebanon.

Although from a different time and place, the lemon-scented gum tree evokes similar feelings of warmth and comfort. I love the heady lemony smell of the oil from the leaves. When the bark peels off, it forms little curls that are useful as fire starters. The striking pink and grey mottled trunks closely match the galahs with their grey feathers and deep-pink breasts. It amuses me when these birds walk, pigeon toed, over the surrounding grasslands, beaks down, grubbing for insects. They remind me of our firstborn, Onesiphorus. When he started crawling, his hands would turn inwards like a pigeon's toes and his hips would wriggle from side to side as he started to go faster. I am longing to see him and Adam and Rose and the babies lost to us on St Helena once again. At the same time, I cannot bear to think of all the things that I will leave behind when I no longer live on our bountiful Earth.

I will never tire of the beautiful birds and unusual animals that live in harmony around the homestead. Spring is my favourite season in Australia, but I am unsure if I will live to see it this year. Last year, the bluetongue lizard that starts to appear around October had a couple of babies. They would follow their mother as she was foraging for insects, miniature copies of their parent. At a similar time, a pair of scarlet-breasted king parrots made their home in a tree close by, nibbling at the new, green growth.

A shy brown and grey butcher bird with a hook on the end of its beak, reminding me in its size and shape of a drab kingfisher, regularly helped itself to leftover meat scraps which it hung on small twigs in another tree. The Australian wildlife is so different from anything I encountered in St Helena or England, but unlike some of my friends I was keen to find out more about native species and bush foods and to use them to enrich our diet.

I slowly learned the names of local animals and plants from two Indigenous women who befriended me during the early days of living at St Helena Park. I used the native plants and herbs to add colour, texture, and flavour to my cooking. I have written out the details and Margaret has collected them into a book to use as she prepares our meals that I can no longer do. As children, the boys enjoyed fishing in the local creeks and rivers and were very excited to be shown fish traps where the Diamond Creek merges with the Yarra River that the natives call *Birrarung*. Our boys were keen to learn from the local Indigenous men, who generously showed them some simple tools that could be made from river stones, and trees where the bark had been removed to make little boats. I am unclear how the lemon scented gums took root as I have been told they are not native to the area. The seeds were perhaps blown by the wind, or carried by the waters of the creeks and rivers. It is a strange country we live in now. I have never quite felt at home, always aware that the local peoples feel displaced from their lands. I feel an affinity for the aboriginal families that live near our property, and over the years I have learned some of the main words and phrases in their language. I am reminded of the slaves that populated St Helena, also displaced from their lands forever.[30] I have never been comfortable distinguishing between different races of people, sincerely believing that we are all made in God's image. I have tried wherever possible to learn from the natives and, in turn, shared some of my experiences with them.

Anthony and I elected not to have slaves in St Helena, unlike many of our neighbours. Instead, we were served faithfully for many years by a Chinese family. Peggy and Sarah Yon supported me in my domestic duties, whilst Henry, James, and John were responsible for manual labour. Peggy and Sarah assisted in the birth of my babies who were born after the Wilks family returned to the Isle of Man. For four weeks after the arrival of each baby, I was spoiled by them: they produced delicious food with extra treats for me, whilst looking after the younger children. One dish I enjoyed was pig's trotters cooked in ginger and vinegar which they assured me was an old Chinese method of food preparation that would restore my strength! At the time, I believed that these special foods did indeed help me to recover quickly from the births of so many children, but sadly there is no cure for my current condition. I can hear slight banging noises from the kitchen. Margaret has been fussing around me since very early this morning but was tactful enough to absent herself when her brother Anthony was here to give me some of his bitter medicine. He has suggested I take two teaspoons four times a day to help my breathing and pain.

Margaret was not old enough to join in the gaieties of our early days in Melbourne that were so enjoyed by Issy, Bessy, and Rose and enabled them to find suitable spouses. She has never shown any interest in finding a husband. She is the shadow to the brightness that her sisters bring to a room. Their love of company contrasts to Margaret's preference to be alone with her sketch book. At times, we struggle to know what to say to each other. Margaret was named after my sister and resembles her in her character. My sister was very reserved when we were growing up and rarely disclosed her feelings. In retrospect, she probably suffered most from the successive losses of our parents as she was such a vulnerable age. She also lived with our aunt and uncle, Peter and Margaret, until she married John Lindsay. I will forever be grateful for John's generosity during the time we were in England and, later, with Bessie's husband, George James, on the occasion in Australia when we were facing financial ruin. Soon after Alexander was born, Anthony had to attend court. We came close to losing our home before John Lindsay once again came to our rescue and agreed to purchase our land.

I sigh. It is so difficult to get comfortable. Remembering our lives is a good distraction from the pain and other unpleasantness that I find so difficult to bear at times.

Anthony is such a dreamer. He never really got over what he perceived as a betrayal by the Company and having to leave his beloved St Helena.

Most of his family moved to South Africa, but I begged him to return to England. My siblings and their spouses were extremely generous, offering accommodation and support for our large family. If I had been able to see into the future, I probably would have refused the move to Australia. I confess that I had regular feelings of resentment during the early days when Anthony and the older girls seemed to have all the fun. I was left with the daily drudge of trying to keep our household together with makeshift tools for cooking and domestic work. We had been spoiled with servants in St Helena, and in England I was rarely called upon to undertake domestic duties. Perhaps the biggest challenge of all, partly because it was so unexpected, was finding myself with child at the time we had moved to St Helena Park. There was so much physical work involved in creating our new home from virgin bush. I had not yet got to know our new neighbours, and it took time to find a woman who could assist me at the baby's birth.

I had constant nausea and a nagging backache. Alexander was born in October, 1841, only a few years short of my fiftieth birthday. Soon afterwards, I developed painful hands and wrists. It made holding a quill or pen to write, very difficult. At times it felt as though the tendons in my wrists would snap. Each movement was felt as a sharp thorn scraping inside my blood vessels. On the rare days that I was not in pain, I would copy some of my favourite poems and hymns into the family journal and reflect on the meaning of the words.

The days of my regular journal entries are now long past, and I am content to leave documenting our daily activities to Anthony. Essential dates about our family are recorded in the family bible I gave Anthony for a wedding present. Luckily it is large enough to include all the births, marriages, and deaths, as long as writing is kept small. Since the death of Rose and her baby I have been unable to look at the bible.

I love Anthony dearly, although I worry how he will manage when I am no longer here. His dark moods that were first apparent early in our marriage mask a vulnerability that is best managed by time alone. He relies on my strength, as his disposition can only be refreshed when he does not have to interact with others. I have tried to be a good wife and mother, but admit to myself I was closer to some of our children than others.

My first born, Onesiphorus, was most like me. His loss has been felt as a heavy weight in the centre of my chest for as long as I can remember. Anything I was required to do took greater effort. It was harder to get up in the mornings. Unwanted thoughts would repeatedly come into my head, suggesting ways in which I may have prevented him from going out that night. I wished I had better understood the strength of his bond with the Captain of *Cecelia*. In the early days, I felt an estrangement from Anthony, unfairly blaming him for insisting we come to this place, but never found the courage to speak these ruminations aloud. Not a day goes by when I do not yearn for my beloved son. He was a great comfort to me on *Cecelia* when all the small children were so seasick. He entertained them without complaint during the months we spent at sea. I am sorry he never got to meet Alexander, as they share a similar demeanour. Alexander seems to entertain himself, although I am never quite sure what he gets up to once he has finished his schoolwork. Margaret and Adam were the closest of all the siblings growing up, but since Adam moved away from home, Margaret has become more of a loner. John and James, come and go, but lately have been spending more time in the goldfields, with mixed results.

Adam does not keep in touch with us so we hear his news from his brothers. I fear that the burden we put on him when we first moved to Victoria, at only ten years old but now the oldest son, was too much for him. He and Anthony left for Melbourne with heavy hearts, to find a suitable piece of land for the house, before Onesiphorus's fate was discovered. Anthony took a wooden cart with him which he planned to use to deliver water locally. Edwards, a man we befriended in Van Diemen's land, travelled with them and was agreeable to working for Anthony whilst we established ourselves. The house was a tight fit, but we had been used to challenging living conditions on *Cecilia*. Edwards had a little nook near the chimney for his sleeping quarters. Katherine remained in Van Diemen's Land with her new beau, John Burt, whom Anthony knew from the East India Company. She gave evidence at the inquest into Onesiphorus when his body was located in the River Tamar.

John Lindsay is a fine young man of twenty-six years, and plans to marry Emma Bennett later this year. He recently bought a bullock cart and operates a team transport between Melbourne and Swan Hill. Like many others, he is caught up with gold fever, and for the last four years has been working diggings in various parts of Victoria although he has been staying with us for the last couple of months. James at twenty-four years is rather restless and still undecided on his path in life. He and Adam are close, with less than three years of difference in their age. They are living about sixteen miles away at the head of the Plenty River, but Adam plans to move to Rutherglen where he believes there is gold to be found. Hali is visiting his brothers, but is more of a homebody with no desire to travel. He still lives with us and helps Anthony on our extensive property, especially looking after the livestock and crops. We try to be as self-sufficient as possible. Recently we have had some success growing native plants, assisted by our aboriginal friends, whose ancestors owned the land all around us before the English settlement. We enjoy eating these bush foods and have used some with great success to treat various ailments. Alexander is fourteen but he is starting to grow tall and strong. He enjoys going for long walks and exploring the local area, which is very hilly. He is fascinated by Australian wildlife, particularly the mobs of kangaroos around the Plenty River. He enjoys fishing and frequently brings us our supper, fresh from the river or local creeks.

I shiver from a draught from under the door and another colder one through the window that does not quite fit its frame. It might be time to take some more of my medicine. Young Anthony explained to me that it may take several days to find the optimal dosage. He has taken a break from his career as a surgeon and is a great support to Anthony at this time. We have used the opportunity to catch up with family news from England and his life in India. He told us:

'I have been formally promoted from my role of surgeon with the Bengal Army in the Indian Medical Service, to Captain-Surgeon to the Royal Residency in Calcutta. I am close friends with Lord Canning, who was appointed Governor-General of India from February this year. I am afraid that during the course of my career I have seen some dreadful sights, especially during the Sikh wars which resulted in annexing of the Punjab.

'I recently caught up with Edward. As you know, he rents at Plumstead in Charlton, not far from Blackheath and Lee, when he is back in England. He has barely changed despite his distinguished career with the East India Colonial service, where he is currently ranked as Captain. Sadly, our careers to date have precluded meeting young ladies, but I am always delighted to meet all my nephews and nieces both in England and in Melbourne. Edward and I are eternally grateful for the practical and financial support given to us by Uncle James Young at the start of our careers.'

We are pleased that Edward continues to enjoy his military life in Bombay, but it saddens me that neither boy married. They seem to have inherited the desire to live and work in foreign lands from my late brothers and brothers-in-law. Our nation produces men who are prepared to leave their families and the relative comforts of home, risking their lives to travel to all ends of the earth, yet many English people reside for their entire lives within a few miles of where they were born,

I fear Anthony will not cope well with my death. I have written a short poem for him:

Not long[31]

It may not be for long my own beloved,

That we must part,

The same blest Voice that calls me from above

Will cheer your heart.

Not long! Ere in some tender twilit hour

As this might be,

That Voice may softly call thee up to where

I wait for thee.

And in that Unknown Land where angels bend

And Saints adore

Our love renewed again shall know no end,

For evermore.

Our marriage has been strong and forged by an unusual life, engaging with different cultures. From my first view of St Helena's rather forbidding façade, to meeting him at a ball, to our eventual marriage where we have been blessed with so many children, to our life as pioneers in Australia, and the grief of losing our two dear adult children, our faith has sustained us. My only regret is that our nearest church at Heidelberg is such a great distance away, that the services we were able to attend were rare. I have been fortunate that along with my bible I have enjoyed the works of English women writers. Through their strong characters I have experienced vicarious pleasure and delight. I started reading the works of Jane Austen and then the Bronte sisters, who had tragic lives back in England. Who knows how my life may have turned out if I had ignored the invitation to travel to St Helena? I recall the profound words of Julian of Norwich, the final prayer in the book gifted to me by the parishioners of St George-in-the-East, that has served me so well, her prayer confirming that all things will be well:

'[Jesus said to me] most reassuringly:

I am able to make everything well, and

I know how to make everything well, and

I wish to make everything well, and

I shall make everything well; and

You shall see for yourself that all manner of things shall be well.'

Julian of Norwich, Revelations of Divine Love[32]

Recently I have been dreaming about my early life in London before I left for St Helena, and in my dreams, I get to meet the family of my youth, particularly my mama, who for years I could barely remember. Sometimes the scent of rosewater that she loved will also bring back these memories.

I ring the little bell to summon Margaret to assist me to rearrange my pillows.

'I am coming, Mama,' she calls out.

Chapter 2

22 December, 1812 – East London, England

Katherine has to hurry. She had promised her uncle Peter to bring back some fresh fish for dinner. He is no longer working since hurting his back more than a month ago. The local doctor diagnosed a muscular problem that should improve over time. Her aunt Margaret is feeling unwell and has become increasingly frail, yearning to escape the dirty streets of London for her beloved Scotland. Katherine does her best to step over the puddles, thick with oily scum, partially fed by streams of water escaping from a nearby tannery. Many houses, built back-to-back, are still without access to cess pits. Urine gets tossed out onto the street after it has been used to wash clothes. The horses drop dung indiscriminately, before it is partially cleared overnight and sold on to fertilise crops in the country. Human dung, mixed with rotting vegetables, adds to the obnoxious mix. In summer, the smell is unbearable. As far as she can see there is filth. Thankfully, her strong leather boots, tightly laced, cover her ankles.

As her pace quickens, she lifts her dress a little higher, her arms crossed in front of her to keep her cape close to her body. Her bonnet is fastened around her chin covering most of her hair, but one of her eyes is tearing and she dabs at it in little pecking movements, reluctant to release the grip on the skirts of her dress. Her face is stinging, but whether from the cold, or the noxious air, or a bit of both, it is hard to determine. She breathes in the scent of her nosegay that she wears around her neck.[33] Like her handkerchief, it is made from silk from one of the leftover bolts woven by her late Mama. She has filled it with strongly scented dried flowers and small pieces of orange peel with the pith removed. She enjoys making clothes and other small gifts for family and friends, such as sachets de senteurs filled with fresh rosemary, or using dried thyme, lavender, rose petals, and bay leaves to protect against insects. Katherine and her sisters have made use of both bolts and oddments: the latter as an occasional double clout for flowers,[34] for small handkerchiefs, and for general cleaning purposes. Reflecting on her life after a busy day teaching, she avoids looking at people, and tries to block out the street sounds as she picks up her pace.

The street is noisy with the cries of ragged children, barefoot and covered in Thames mud up to their thighs. The tide is out so they most likely were mudlarking. The town crier in his resplendent red coat is ringing his bell and shouting out the latest news.

'Oyez, Oyez. Read all about it. Boney has been defeated in Russia. 500,000 lives are lost!

'Oyez, Oyez. New book of fairy tales published by the Grimm brothers. Come and see them!

'Oyez, Oyez. Would you like a paper, Ma'am?'

'No, thank you.'

At least he is not advising a hanging today.

'Hey, watch out!'

Katherine steps back from the kerb, not really focused on where she is going. Horses and carriages are clogging up the cobbled road. Earlier that day at the church school, one of the mothers was pleading on behalf of her children:

'Their father has been badly burned in an accident. He can no longer work. I am begging you to let my two children continue at the school. I will find the necessary money, but it may take a while.'

It was fortunate that Mary, her mentor and friend, had not yet left for the day. She was able to reassure the mother that St George-in-the-East has a certain amount of discretionary funding and that the children would be permitted to continue as pupils.

'I am truly thankful,' the mother said, her eyes tearing.

Katherine will always be grateful for her own schooling under the auspices of St George-in-the-East,[35] whose charter mandated the provision of education for local children. The church and school are like a second home. Her baptism in June, 1794, is recorded in the church records, along with the marriages of her three sisters and the burial of two siblings who predeceased her. Her Mama's funeral was held there, but Katherine was only six and had not really understood that she would never see her Mama again. Sadly, she was orphaned the following year. Papa never returned home. The mysterious disappearance of the ship he was captaining was never solved. It was presumed all the crew were lost at sea. Uncle Peter rings the bells at St George-in-the-East most Sundays, pulling on the beautifully plaited bell tails he made from leftover rope to replace the previously fraying cords.

The air is smoky with a faint odour of something long dead. Blackened building facades are thick with impregnated soot. It catches in her nose and throat and is making both her eyes water. She can almost taste it. A London fog is threatening. It mixes with the sea fogs rising from the Thames, visibility reduced to a couple of feet. It is dangerous to be out on the streets alone after dark. There are frequent muggings and pickpocketing, although Katherine suspects the assailants are not well rewarded for their audacity, often necessitated by poverty. There has been a spate of recent judicial hangings in London, men as well as women, announced by the local town crier dressed in an opulent red and gold coat, white breeches, black boots, and, balanced on his head, a tricorne hat. He grasps his looped leather handbell, ringing it vigorously and attracting huge crowds. Since the opening of the cotton mills in the midlands and north, work is scarce and poorly paid. Katherine knows of local families forced to share one bed in a damp, cold room. With the father injured, no longer able to work, the mother has to prostitute herself. Their children are frequently observed to beg in the street, their clothing reduced to rags, often shoeless, even in winter. Poverty, ironically, encourages truancy. Prayers and alms only go so far … too many of their family friends have succumbed to disease, unable to afford a doctor.

It is barely a year since the dreadful murders of the Marr family and their apprentice at their warehouse where Katherine used to purchase cheap silk and lace.[36] The baby had only been baptised at their church three months prior. Now all four victims are buried at St George-in-the-

East beneath a monument. Further murders occurred at the Kings Arms in New Gravel Lane barely a week later. The suspect, John Williams, was identified based on eyewitness accounts, but he had already hung himself. He was buried upside down with a stake hammered through his heart. The papers were full of the dreadful crimes. Katherine tries to avert her eyes from the spectacle of two men dangling from short ropes in a cage at Execution Dock, where a public hanging occurred the day before.[37] The cries from the crowd carried to their street. The barbarity of the punishment sickens her, although she has never attended a public execution. Death is prolonged for men convicted of piracy, as the hanging ropes are deliberately shortened. As a consequence, the hapless felon slowly suffocates, whilst all four limbs spasm and engage in a macabre set of movements nicknamed by spectators as the Marshals' Dance.[38]

The miscreants are frequently young.[39] At times, Katherine finds it very difficult to reconcile the sincere teaching they receive at church with the daily suffering she observes. As she nears the Thames, she hears shouts from some sailors who appear to have had too much to drink. A couple lurch towards her, holding on to each other, clutching bottles in their hands. They can barely stand, so she has no trouble avoiding them on this occasion. Her uncle, like her Papa, has compassion for the sailors he met whilst rigging the ships, concerned about their welfare. She can just remember Papa's voice telling Mama, who was protesting having so many mouths to feed. She would have been barely five years old.

'Catherine, you have to understand that these poor men have nowhere else to go. The Lascars are frequently abandoned in London. They have no way of returning to India or China and cannot earn a wage until they find another ship to take them on. They can pay for their meals by telling us stories. Now that I no longer sail on extended voyages, I love to hear them describe the exotic spices, teas and cloth they bring with them and the people they meet. I can almost smell the cardamon, see the deep orange colours of saffron, taste the exotic teas and feel the silk! I am always so shocked at the terrible conditions they experience when aboard ship.'

Her mama replied, 'But they could be bringing diseases and passing them on to us and our children. I understand it is our Christian duty to care for others, but not a day goes past when we have to provide for extra guests.'

Sadly, her mother's concerns were realised. How she misses her Mama, dead from consumption at forty-two, possibly caught from one of these sailors. It is increasingly difficult to recall her face, although she can still remember the scent of rose water that she always associated with her. Katherine was named after her mother and likes to think that is why her middle name is Rose.

She can hear the fishermen's cries as she turns the corner

'Fresh fish for sale. Nearly finished for the day. Good prices to be had.'

Almost in front of her are the darkly menacing hulks of prison ships where unfortunate prisoners are housed due to the overcrowded prisons. Their rotting masts rise like hands in prayer, silently beseeching an invisible God. Cries and screams are clearly audible, causing Katherine to shudder, wondering what ungodly punishments may be happening. Other boats are moored, stuck in the foul-smelling mud until the tide returns. It is almost possible to cross from one bank of the river to the other without touching the water as there are so many boats in this part of the Thames.

Steep, slippery, stone stairs lead down to the banks of the Thames beside the Prospect of Whitby public house,[40] rebuilt following a recent fire, and named after a local cargo ship that brought coal from Newcastle. She grips the cold metal rail tighter, worried that she might lose her footing. There are only two boats selling fish at this late hour. Avoiding taxes higher up the river enables them to compete with each other. Katherine appears to be the last customer for the day.

'Here, Miss, fresh fish, scaled and gutted or how you like it.'

'Come over here. Cheapest fish on the river. Just a few shillings. I'll clean them for you. They smell better than the Bermondsey abattoirs! Nothing like a cold southwest wind for bringing that stench free of charge!'

'I'll give you three large pieces and throw in a tail for free.'

Near the end of the day, Katherine pays only two shillings for the fish. Unlike the many obnoxious odours assaulting her nose they look and smell fresh and today it is her favourite fishmonger who attracts her custom.

'Here you are, Miss, freshly gutted and scaled, the bones left in to add to your stock.'

'Thank you,' says Katherine. She fumbles with her purse. 'Here is half a crown.'

'And your change.' The fishmonger passes her a sixpence.

The newspaper wrapping is inadequate, a pinkish red stain growing larger.

'Thank you,' she says, 'and good night.'

'Good night to you too, love, and I hope you enjoy the fish!'

Katherine goes back up the steps that are almost worn away in places and covered with a green seaweed that is very slippery. She clutches the packet of fish as she holds on to the metal handrail, trying her best to avoid the blood staining.

'Excuse me,' says Katherine.

She recognises the drunken sailors, one of whom has slumped to the ground. She steps over his legs, which are across the tops of the stairs.

She turns left, taking the most direct route to her home off Cable Street, wiping soot from her eye with a gloved hand. This evening, she needs to finish making a silk shirt for her uncle Peter's Christmas gift. Unlike many families she knows, celebrating the birth of Christ is always a special time in her family. They attend the Christmas Midnight Mass at St George-in-the-East and enjoy a rich meal on Christmas Day. Several horses passing cause her to pause as she approaches the corner of Cable Street. This long, local thoroughfare has traditionally been divided into sections with different names. It is sometimes necessary to wait several minutes in order to cross safely and avoid being hit by a horse or carriage, as they seem to pick up speed at this point as the road is so straight.[41]

Uncle Peter used to talk about the thousand-foot lengths of rope that were laid across these streets. They primarily supplied the myriad ships moored in the Pool of London. The younger men were employed to run from one end to the other, so he kept very fit. The rope was made into lines for rigging and mooring. It did not last for ever, so keeping up a supply meant plenty of work. The risk of fire was an ever-present hazard due to the hemp igniting easily, so smoking was strictly forbidden. Despite this, he witnessed several accidents where men were badly burned and died as a result of extensive skin damage. The remaining families often ended up in one of the local workhouses never to be seen again. At the far end of the street, starting at Rosemary Lane – the old Hoggestrete – and spreading into adjoining streets, is the Rag Fair, held from September to May each year, but closed on Saturdays and Sundays. It can be fun to make purchases there, but Katherine prefers to do this in the company of her older brother James as it is notorious for pickpockets.[42]

Katherine can hear the bells ringing from St George-in-the-East, practising for the Sunday service. When he was younger, Uncle Peter would often talk of the time he took leave from his rope making, in 1767. The Scottish reformation of 1560 had forbidden widespread ringing of bells due to Protestant reforms that were ridding the churches of Catholic influence, although handbells were rung at private gatherings. Peter and her papa were grateful that the tradition had continued in England, as they loved bellringing. As young men, soon after moving to London, they travelled to Debenham in Suffolk, where eight sturdy local lads had rung a particular sequence of peals in the English style, known as the Bob Major, at the Norman church of St Mary. The performance consisted of ten-thousand and eighty changes. The physical coordination required to ring the bells, combined with a sense of rhythm and good listening skills, had made the occasion momentous. The bellmen could barely stand at the conclusion of their heroic endeavour. Apart from a few sips of water and some pieces of bread fed to them as their hands remained on the ropes, they had not left their designated spots in the church tower for six hours. The brothers' journey home was not without incident, but Katherine was never quite sure whether her uncle embellished the dangers of horse travel at that time. He used to recite the nursery rhyme, Oranges and Lemons, when she was young. As a game, the family would add new rhyming couplets, to see how many churches and their bells they could name around London.

The house feels chilled when she arrives home. Uncle Peter does not notice the cold, and Aunt Margaret must have fallen asleep. Peter is sitting in his wooden chair knotting rope and making intricate patterns using the light from a tallow candle. His wiry body is muscular, with particularly strong arms and wrists. His hands, calloused from years of working with rope and making canvas sails, are slender and surprisingly delicate. Whilst twisting the strands he recites poetry. Most of the lines have been learned by heart over the years, the majority of poems, but not all, with a nautical theme. Katherine nods to him to continue, as she likes the rhythm of the 'Seafarer', although she cannot understand the words as they are in Anglo Saxon or mediaeval English. Traditionally, the sailmakers like Uncle Peter, would recite stanzas of poems as they stitched the sails, the words passed down through the generations as an oral tradition. Very few of the craftsmen or sailors could read or write.

'Good afternoon, Katherine,' says Uncle Peter. 'I trust you are well?'

'Yes, thank you Uncle Peter. I was able to get off work a little early and managed to buy some fish for our supper,' said Katherine. 'How is your back? It feels a little chilled in here.'

'It is still sore, so I am reluctant to return to work just yet. Margaret is having her rest. Could you please rake the coals in the fireplace, or we won't be able to eat. I brought some water in from the pump and boiled it earlier, so it is ready for you to use in the cooking. I have bought some vegetables from the market. I suggest you put some of that firewood onto the fire to get it going again.'

'I'm happy to do that, Uncle Peter. I'm unsure if James is coming for supper, but I managed to get several pieces of fish.'

'Thank you, Katherine, I am looking forward to dinner. I think it may be a little late for James to come around, but there will be plenty of food. I need to lie on my bed for an hour or so. After we eat, I have something to share with you.'

'Please, do go and rest. I will look forward to my surprise,' said Katherine, smiling.

As her uncle slowly moves upstairs, taking one step at a time whilst leaning heavily on the banister, Katherine puts some wood onto the coals which, luckily, are still glowing. The wood is tinder dry and quickly catches alight. Katherine selects a sharp knife and rinses carrots, potatoes, and cabbage, using some of the boiled water Peter has left in a large jug, then slices the vegetables. It is a rule of their home that all water is boiled before using it for drinking or cooking.

In the evening, her uncle prefers to drink ale, and occasionally both she and Aunt Margaret have a small glass, although more usually Katherine has a hot drink, using a few leaves of their specially conserved stock of precious tea. Peter has already put water into the large iron pot that is hung over the fireplace, so there should be sufficient water left in the jug for a quick wash in the morning.

Katherine reaches up to unhook her favourite wooden ladle with the extra-long handle that Peter made for her, and carefully places the vegetables into the now-boiling water. She will wait until the final ten minutes to put the fish in so as to not overcook it. She seasons the pot with salt and pepper and a blend of her favourite herbs that she buys at the Rag Fair, and plans to serve the supper about an hour later. She lays the table with the white linen tablecloth embroidered by her Aunt Margaret, on which she places the wooden bowls carved by her uncle. At times, Katherine finds caring for her aunt and uncle burdensome, something she rarely admits even to herself. They had been so generous and kind to her over the years, she perceives her occasional lack of grace is rather uncharacteristic. She identifies with the female characters from the novels she enjoys, secretly hoping that one day she might be swept off her feet by a handsome man, taken to live somewhere warm, with fresh sea air gently blowing from the ocean.

As a rope and sail maker, Uncle Peter was often required to go to sea, working to make new sails, or replace, or repair others as they wore out or were damaged. The bolts of canvas used for his work consisted of long strips of material about two foot in width, with different gradients and quality, depending on the type of sail required. The different pieces were stitched together to make the required size and shape of sail and had to fit the mast and rigging. Ships would typically have multiple sails, with the bigger ships needing several dozen, their huge total surface area measured in acres. His work was frequently undertaken when the ship hit rough seas, or on occasions, engaged in battle. He maintains that it is his deep faith that enabled him to return home safely on the completion of each voyage.

Katherine checks the stew once more, takes a sip, adds a little more salt, then places a lid on the pot. She has sufficient time to finish Uncle Peter's shirt, that is hanging in the room where her mother's old loom sits in the corner, alongside unused bolts of silk as well as ends of bolts. Each bolt has a standard length of 41 feet and a width of twenty-two inches. The cloth varies in colour and has been protected from sunlight, so has not faded over time. Katherine would like to make a fine dress with Mama's favourite colour, yellow, but she lacks an occasion to wear it.

She reflects how lucky she and her siblings were to have parents for whom education rated highly. Unlike Uncle Peter, normally a man of few words and little formal education as he found book learning difficult, her father was a master mariner and her mother was skilled at weaving silk. Both of them read widely. The money and directions left in their father's will ensured Katherine, like her brothers and sisters before her, was well educated in reading, writing, arithmetic, and Latin. Religious instruction was received at Sunday school, where she now assists. Other than the Bible – from habit she reads a passage each night just before retiring – she enjoys reading novels and poems, old copies of *The Female Spectator*, as well as women's accounts of travelling independently. Her two favourites, *Sense and Sensibility* 'by a lady', and Fanny Burney's *Camilla*, birthday gifts from her brothers, are read by candlelight once Uncle Peter retires to bed. She warms to the female characters in *Camilla* but finds the cold and judgemental Edgar Mandleburt to be of a superficial disposition. He is disinclined to probe for any deeper meaning in his encounters with the fairer sex.

As she places tiny stiches along the seams of the shirt from the rather uncertain light of a guttering candle, Katherine thinks about her sisters and how lucky they have been in their marriages. She is very fond of her three brothers-in-law, John Lindsay, James Halliburton and Adam Baildon, who are more like father figures to her.

Margaret married the distinguished and wealthy John Lindsay at St Pancras in Camden two years ago. John is twenty-four years older than Margaret and was a friend of their late Papa. He was particularly attentive to young Katherine at the wedding. Her brother James was one of the witnesses. John Lindsay has a splendid house at Laurence Pountney Hill that covers three floors and an attic space under the rafters. The home is notable for the rich wooden carving of the doorways. It has elaborate plaster cornices in all the main rooms that incorporate English roses in the design. The staircase has highly polished spiral balusters. Basements provide extensive storage space which is useful as the house doubles as a business premises for John and his brother. John is circumspect in regard to his employment. He tells the family:

'Laurence Pountney Hill was named after the local church that burned but was never rebuilt following the Great Fire of London in 1666. The Manor of the Rose, built in Tudor times, and dozens of houses, were also consumed by the fire. Local lore suggests that a witness, Thomas Middleton, and several of his friends felt the church was deliberately set on fire. In a published tract soon after the event, he claimed:

"I saw the fire break out from the inside of St Lawrence Pountney steeple when there was no fire near it. These and such like observations begat in me a persuasion that the fire was maintained by design."'[43]

Margaret and Katherine see each other regularly, but Katherine secretly finds her dull compared to their two older sisters and two brothers. She is rather plump and plain of face. Margaret has not been blessed with children, but it is obvious that she and John adore each other. She is a loyal wife and always defers to him at the table. On Sundays after church, the Lindsays regularly invite the extended family for a roast lunch. John sends a horse and trap which is large enough to accommodate all the proposed guests. Last Sunday, he announced that he and Margaret will be moving to Blackheath, just south of Greenwich, in early 1813. Their new home will have magnificent views of the surrounding countryside. Both of them are excited to escape the London fogs and odours.

Elizabeth is thirty-two. Her husband, James Halliburton, is fourteen years older than her, and for some years has been commander of the twelve-hundred-ton East Indiaman *Glatton* that regularly trades with India and China, calling in at St Helena, a tiny tropical island in the Tropic of Capricorn, about fifteen degrees south of the Equator, on the return journey. He can be away for up to eighteen months at a time. He has worked his way up through the ranks and spends most of his life at sea, but is well remunerated for his work. Katherine cannot remember a time when she did not know James Halliburton. Elizabeth lives in a fine house in Camden about five miles distant. Katherine makes a point of walking across the fields to visit her on the last Saturday of each month, enjoying the multiple fragrances of the country as she inhales deeply. She sleeps there overnight after a day spent playing with the girls. She supervises her nieces' bathtime in the downstairs tub that is placed by a roaring fire in winter. As a special treat, the children use Pears Soap, its scent reminiscent of an English garden. Katherine loves the smooth feel of her hands from the translucent brown glycerin bars that are delivered to Elizabeth's home from just off Oxford Street in London. Elizabeth's care for her three young daughters is a big responsibility, but she has a resident male servant, Matthew. He and his wife, Jane, do not have children of their own and undertake most of the domestic work. They purchase food, cook and serve the meals, and keep the back and front gardens in a good condition and clean the house. They have the attic rooms with sloping walls from the line of the roof. Matthew also fills and empties the bathtub each Saturday evening. After a leisurely Sunday lunch, he harnesses a horse and trap to take Katherine home. When Katherine's brother-in-law James Halliburton is in residence, he shares tales of his voyages. He frequently mentions St Helena, which is owned and governed by the Honourable East India Company.

'The island is a vitally important trading post for refuelling and restocking. Its steep cliffs and few beaches deter possible enemies. It is highly fortified. Over the years, I have befriended members of the Beale family who have lived there for generations. The surname Beale means "handsome man." Both the men and women in the extended family are blessed with good looks. I have made a habit of spending time with your sister Isabella, her husband, Adam, and their young daughters since they moved there in 1807. The ships anchor in the roadstead off Jamestown. Lighters take the passengers to the wharf. One time, there were more than twenty East Indiamen ships at anchor, that made for an impressive sight. The wharf is steep and slippery. On occasion, people greeting the ships fall into the sea, including, one memorable time, the Governor of the Island. Rarely, big rollers wash over the landing points. They are impressive to contemplate, but dangerous. It can be entertaining to watch the scarlet-coated soldiers engaging in exercises close to the landing area. There are many military installations throughout the island.'

'Can you tell us more about the town? Is it very hot?'

'Jamestown is built in a cleft between two mountain peaks. At the head of the town is a heart-shaped waterfall. Overall, the climate is mild and unlike what one might expect from its location north of the Tropic of Capricorn. The seas are full of turtles, whales, sharks, seals, and teeming with smaller, colourful fish. Unfortunately, the island is overrun with goats and wild boar. Whilst guaranteeing a constant supply of meat, they have caused a lot of damage to native plants and trees. Over the previous hundred years or so, valuable ebony trees have been almost completely destroyed. It is necessary to approach the island from the northwest and this requires precise navigation. Initially one is taken aback by the forbidding exterior of the island. The two main peaks are often covered in cloud. As one travels deeper into the island, one is struck by its lush, verdant interior and the different colours of the earth. The Island's steep hills are called knolls. Some have an elevation of over six thousand feet. The unique wildlife, flora and fauna, has attracted well known visitors to the Island, including Sir Joseph Banks, who partook in Captain James Cook's remarkable three-year voyage to the Pacific. The wealthy inhabitants of the island tend to go inland during summer.'

'Isabella tells me the island is full of guns, soldiers, and slaves,' says Katherine. 'Why is this?'

'The Honourable East India Company that governs St Helena has its own army and civil service. The elite British population is rather small. Domestic work and hard labour is undertaken by African slaves, or Chinese. The 1807 laws passed in England to outlaw the British Atlantic slave trade have made very little practical difference on the Island to date. The majority of households employ several slaves, but the total numbers are partly dependent on one's social standing on the Island.[44] The slaves' names are taken from their owners. Even relatively minor breaches by a slave may incur a severe punishment. Privately, the Islanders have expressed concern about emancipation. Some landowners are fearful for their safety. I assure you, I have never participated in slave transport, as I find it abhorrent. My greatest fear is that the Island will be used to illegally offload slaves who can no longer be taken to America.'[45]

At other times, James talks about his visits to Canton in China, to Java in the Dutch East Indies, and to parts of India:

'The most hazardous part of the voyage is between Canton and the Sundra strait.[46] Deaths amongst the crew are not uncommon, with sometimes one in ten men losing their lives. Through necessity, extra sailors come on board in China, Java, and India to supplement the numbers, many of whom elect to stay in the Cape of Good Hope to escape the cold of the Southern latitudes. It is relatively easy to recruit sailors wanting to go to London for the final legs of the voyages.'[47]

On occasions, he catches up with his old friend Colonel Mark Wilks, a longtime Resident of Mysore in India who sadly lost his wife some years ago. Wilks has made several voyages on East Indiaman ships. Katherine met him briefly at Elizabeth's house last April. James says:

'The Indian climate can be challenging for people of English backgrounds, due to the high prevalence of diseases and the unforgiving climate. I am thankful that I have escaped any serious afflictions such as cholera and typhus, but deadly fever caused by diseases is unfortunately not uncommon. I practise strict rules on the ships I command, that include meticulous attention to hygiene for all the sailors and any passengers that might be travelling with us. I insist that all who travel on my ships take lemon juice as a preventative for a horrible disease called scurvy, or in the absence of lemons, I ensure that oranges or other citrus are consumed.'

Elizabeth tells Katherine that James is unusual in his discipline, as many East Indiamen ships, including the English and Dutch, have unfortunate reputations amongst the sailors, with poor quality food, tainted water, and noisy, dark, unpleasantly moist and humid, cramped accommodation for the crew, that is infested with cockroaches and other insects. Other than infectious diseases that can be caught onshore, the journeys have other dangers, especially during the recent Napoleonic Wars. Although he does not dwell on such matters, James has been caught up in two potentially deadly skirmishes. Luckily the French ships turned around without incident. As well as acts of war, fires, storms, piracy, and the ever-present possibility of shipwreck due to lack of reliable navigation aids, discipline has to be maintained when men are in close confinement for months at a time. Elizabeth has recently confessed to Katherine that, whilst she is always enthralled by James's stories of his journeys, she hopes he is not tempting fate by continuing to go to sea. He only has another two years before he can retire on a handsome pension. She is looking forward to this, as her children barely know their father. She is hopeful they may have one more child together, as she would dearly love to have a son.

There is a loud bang followed by a cry. Katherine wakes with a start. She must have dozed briefly as the candle is low. She will need to trim the wick before using it again. She wipes the condensation away, then peers through the small window that looks out over the street, but cannot see anything. She quickly ties off the loose threads on the shirt seams, replaces the needle carefully on a piece of card, and hangs the shirt before returning to the kitchen. She removes the lid from the pot over the fire and checks the stew of vegetables and adds the fish. She will wake her uncle and aunt in five minutes if they do not appear. She was half expecting her brother James to call in, but as it is dark she assumes he has decided to wait until the family all meet on Christmas Day. Recently, he has been working long hours on the London Docks development east of Wapping.[48] Once the docks are fully functioning, James tells her that high value items such as ivory, spices, coffee, cocoa, wine, and wool will be regularly imported. Elegant warehouses and wine cellars are part of the construction.[49] James completed his apprenticeship with the Dagnell family of ropemakers but was tempted by the better money to be made in the Docks. Nowadays, he too is a mariner, following the family tradition, and has undertaken several extended voyages.

Christmas lunch will be served at Margaret and John's London home for the last time, before their move.[50] She is looking forward to seeing her brothers, hoping they might stay after the meal. James Halliburton is away, his latest voyage departing on the twenty-fifth of March, and is not expected to return for another six months. Elizabeth and her girls will be coming, accompanied by Matthew and Jane, her devoted husband-and-wife servants. The family are eternally thankful that both James and Charles managed to avoid being called up to fight in the various wars that have backgrounded their lives to date. They were fortunate to avoid conscription following the naval battle known as the Little Belt Affair last year, and the full-scale war with America that was declared barely six months ago, on the eighteenth of June. The English are fighting on all fronts. The news is all about America and Napoleon. His invasion of Russia last year has resulted in England being drawn into another conflict this month. The ripple effects from the French Revolution and the Reign of Terror, the awful spectre of Napoleon and the fear of invasion, has everyone looking over their shoulders, not quite sure who to trust. Despite England's maritime strengths, her armies would be no match for the combined armies of the self-styled French emperor.

No wonder the King has gone mad. The Town Crier announced his son George's appointment as Prince Regent last year. She shudders. Thank goodness there are no guillotines here, bloodied heads rolling into baskets, still blinking in surprise.

She can hear her uncle's footsteps overhead. Margaret appears from the gloom of the stairs.

'Hello, dear. Thank you for setting the table. We are so fortunate that you look after us in our older age.'

Katherine steps forward and kisses her aunt on her cheek. It feels cool. There is a scent of cloves.

'Has your tooth been bothering you?' enquires Katherine.

'Yes, that is why I decided to lie on my bed. I find chewing on the clove helps deaden the pain somewhat. I may have to make an appointment with Dr Fox in Carter Lane, if it does not settle. Perhaps he will need to remove the tooth. In the meantime, I will avoid harder foods. Our supper smells delicious.'

'I am sorry that you are still having pain. I would be happy to come with you to the dentist. I hope you enjoy the fish. I thought it looked fresh and Uncle Peter chose the vegetables well,' said Katherine.

She pulls the chair out for her aunt and helps her to sit at the table. The four wooden chairs were made by her uncle and smell of beeswax. They are comfortable to sit on and support their backs, which her aunt appreciates.

'Can I pass you anything?' asks Katherine.

'Perhaps a drop of ale,' says Margaret.

As Katherine pours out the drinks, Uncle Peter arrives. She serves the meal into deep wooden bowls. Once she has sat down and her uncle has taken his seat at the head of the table, he leads them in giving thanks for their meal, before they eat in companiable silence, as is their habit. Katherine wonders whether they have eaten anything since breakfast, as they seem to be hungry. She is curious to find out what her uncle was alluding to earlier.

As she prepares to leave the table at the conclusion of the meal, Uncle Peter says, 'Please stay for the moment.'

He brings out a thick letter with a broken seal.

'Please read this letter to us. I find I can no longer see clearly in poor light. James delivered it earlier this week and let me know the gist of the contents. I put it to one side and almost forgot it until this afternoon.' Peter passes the letter to Katherine.

'The seal and the paper look expensive. It is good quality linen,' observed Katherine.

Katherine reads:

Douglas, Isle of Man, 1 December, 1812

My Dear Peter,

This letter comes with many good wishes to you and your family for Christmas and New Year. Since my fleeting visit to James Halliburton in April last year, where I had the opportunity to meet your charming niece Katherine, and just prior to my return to India, I have made a decision to leave the country for good, resigning from my job in Mysoor. As you may know, on my prior trip in 1807, my daughter Laura travelled with me, starting school on the Isle of Man soon after our arrival at The Downs in April, 1807. The journey took almost six months from our departure from Saugor on 10 July. Laura showed considerable distress at having to farewell her ayah, who had cared for her since she was a baby, her mother Harriet sadly succumbing to fever in 1806. Laura was at a difficult age, turning ten, so it was with some relief, having endured unusually inclement weather, that we reached St Helena safely on 23 January. We were extremely fortunate to avoid the measles epidemic by a matter of days. During our voyage, I tutored her in Latin and encouraged her to read widely to ensure she did not fall too far behind in her schooling. I spent two days at Plantation House in intense discussions with the current Governor, Robert Patton. Our conversation was wide ranging.

On that occasion, I was introduced to young Anthony Beale, whose family has lived on St Helena for generations. Following family tradition, he wished to be employed, as are the majority of Islanders, by the Honourable East India Company, in their Pay Master's Office. On the recommendation of the Governor, and of James Halliburton who previously had dealings with the family, I had no hesitation in entrusting Laura to his care whilst we were on St Helena. His quiet demeanour and attentiveness to her needs was continued on the final leg of our voyage. Beale was travelling on the ship to attend the Honourable East India Company College at their purpose-built facility in Hertford. Despite the six-year gap in their ages, he was very tender with Laura, entertaining her for much of the time we were sailing. We spent two days anchored at Tenerife, and Beale continued to take care of Laura, whilst they explored the island. This enabled me to devote time to my writing, as I had a publishers' deadline to meet. By the time we reached The Downs on 12 April, Laura had recovered her usually sunny nature. I was saddened to leave Laura, but she settled happily with a family friend, Dorothy Taubman, in Douglas. The climate in India is not conducive to good health and the education opportunities for young women are limited.

My book Historical Sketches of the South of India *has been well received. I am delighted to advise you that the initial volume has been published, with the proposed second volume well under way. I accepted an invitation to address the young men training to be Writers – administrators – at the Honourable East India Company College, just prior to my return to India. I was impressed with the education curriculum for these young men. The content is broad, but detailed. In the course of my work, I have met many administrators, responsible for governing millions of people throughout Asia and the Indian subcontinent. Many had been appointed by patronage rather than training. On occasions this resulted in unfortunate and wide-ranging consequences.[51]*

I got to know Captain Henry Christopher very well during our journey from India, dining with him most evenings, and became reacquainted when we departed from Torbay on 12 May, 1810. He has captained Sir William Pulteney[52] since 1805. The ship is well appointed, and she operates under the charter of the East India trading companies. She carries a complement of fifty-five men who are well disciplined. She is armed with twelve strategically placed guns, but is primarily a cargo ship, with two decks of cabins. The usual complement of passengers includes missionaries and their families, as well as young, single men travelling to India, but rarely more than thirty paying passengers. The accommodation is basic, but adequate. As a matter of interest, Sir William Pulteney was one of the ships at the capture of the Dutch Cape Colony in 1806. I have also had the pleasure of travelling in the company of your nephew Charles Young aboard Earl Spencer, back in 1803/5, that was captained by no other than Charles Raitt, who I believe may be related to you through your wife?

In a roundabout way, this brings me to the main purpose of my letter to you. I was impressed when I became briefly acquainted with your niece Katherine whilst I was visiting Elizabeth Halliburton. Her comprehensive education and teaching role at the local school is admirable. We are fortunate in having some excellent schools on the English mainland, but Laura's experience of schooling on the Isle of Man has been disappointing. Girls' education in particular is neither robust nor especially useful for young women who may want to make their way in the world independently of the male sex.

I wish to put a proposition to you, that I hope you may be in a position to accept. I have been formally appointed to the position of Governor of

St Helena, commencing in June, 1813. It is my intention to travel on Sir William Pulteney once again. She departs Portsmouth on 18 March next year, bound for St Helena and Bengal, with a stopover at Tenerife planned for 12 April. My wedding to Dorothy Taubman is to take place early in the New Year in the city of Bath. Like my family, she is of Manx lineage. We have known each other for many years, and she is fond of my daughter. Laura has made the decision to discontinue her formal schooling and is eager to accompany us to St Helena. My son John Barry, who you may remember is very frail, lives permanently with a caring family on the Isle of Man, and will not be joining us.

I am likely to be fully occupied with preparation for my forthcoming wedding, but more particularly for my duties on St Helena, so will be unable to devote much time to Laura, either on the ship or when I start as Governor. There are many pressing problems already identified and formal engagements to attend, where my wife will be expected to accompany me. Laura would benefit from a companion/tutor close to her in age. As you know, your wife, Margaret, and her late sister Catherine were intimately involved in my late wife Harriet's first seven years when the family lived in Perth, after Harriet's mother, Laura's grandmother, died in childbirth. During our marriage, Harriet would frequently talk about her distant cousins, although it seems neither side of the family were quite sure of the exact kinship. Harriet was very distressed when she learned of Catherine's passing. Through her, my relationship with the Halliburtons, and the occasional crossing of my life with your late brother James Young, I feel your family is well known to us. I am also acquainted with the Baildons, and I understand Katherine and her sister Isabella were close to each other in their youth?

I am writing to ask whether Katherine would accept an initial twelve-month appointment as companion/tutor to Laura? I would of course be responsible for all of Katherine's expenses relating to the journey, including the purchase of appropriate clothing for a warmer climate, as well as the separate transport of any luggage, and for the voyage itself. A small retainer and appropriate housing – living with us at Plantation House, the Governor's country residence on St Helena, some three miles south of Jamestown – will be provided, and her everyday needs accommodated. A new stagecoach route to Portsmouth, by way of Guildford, can be taken from the Bolt and Tun at Fleet Street.[53] Limited luggage is permitted to be carried – more of an overnight bag – but local packet ships[54] run at regular intervals from the Thames to Portsmouth, where sea chests and other luggage can be transported reasonably quickly and then put directly onto the ship. I apologise for the short notice, but hope to hear from you shortly as to whether my proposal receives acceptance. I would require an affirmative answer no later than mid-January, in order to make the appropriate arrangements for travel.

Laura and I send our best wishes to you and Margaret. Please remember us to the rest of the family, who I understand will all be staying at St Laurence Poultney Lane for the festive occasion?

Yours very sincerely, Mark Wilks

When Katherine finishes the final page, she turns to Uncle Peter and notices he has tears in his eyes. Her aunt is looking at her with a quizzical expression. She feels a little overwhelmed but excited at the same time.

'How extraordinary. I was just thinking about Isabella and how I have not heard from her recently. It sounds like an exciting adventure. I'd love to give consideration to Colonel Wilks' request. I found him to be the very embodiment of a fine gentleman when I met him. But how could I possibly leave you and Margaret?'

Peter coughed, covering his face with a handkerchief, and Margaret answered:

'You are very young, with your life ahead of you. We have not shared this with you, but both of us are very keen to return to Inchture in Scotland, where we spent our childhood. We have sufficient money and would live very simply. Peter hurting his back has caused us to once again think how this might be possible. However, we were unsure how best to do this, as you have been so good to us and know no other home.'

'I see it is only for twelve months,' says Katherine, 'so the time would go quickly. I would miss you and Elizabeth and the girls. It might be difficult to get time away from teaching. What would happen if I accept this offer and find that Laura and I are not compatible? How on earth could I get ready to sail barely three months from now?'

'I would be happy to help you make suitable clothing, and I am sure Peter can find a wooden chest very easily. We could line it and protect against insects. What do you think, Peter?'

Her uncle sounds rather unlike his usual self and is a little gruff when he replies. 'I have an old wooden chest, and I can easily varnish it and add beckets on either end. It could be sent ahead by packet ship. A leather carry-all bag can be purchased from the Rag Fair for your overnight clothing. If you do decide to go ahead, we will miss you dreadfully.'

Her aunt adds, 'I suggest we put the letter away for a day or two so that we can all have time to think what it may mean for each of us. Now, I think it is time Peter that we both retire to bed and leave Katherine to have time for herself. Goodnight.'

'Goodnight and sleep well.'

As Katherine's uncle and aunt slowly make their way back upstairs, each wooden stair creaking loudly, she washes the dishes in rapidly cooling water, then also goes upstairs, carrying a candle carefully in one hand and grasping her skirt with the other.

She retires to bed, but her racing thoughts impact her ability to fall asleep as quickly as usual. She would not miss London, the fog, the smells, the cold, and the filth. She likes the sound of a tropical island. Isabella seems happier there since Adam stopped going to sea. Like her father, her uncle Peter, her brothers James and Charles, and brothers-in-law, James and Adam, she, too, can go on a long voyage and visit some of the places they have talked about so frequently. It will be so exciting to see Isabella, Adam, and Catherine again, and to meet their three youngest girls for the first time. Isabella is twenty-nine. Katherine was heartbroken when she and Adam moved to St Helena in 1807 with five-year-old Catherine. She falls into a deep sleep listening to the gentle pitter of the feet of the rats in the roof.

The following morning, Katherine pulls a bundle of letters that are tied together with string, out of her bedside drawer. She receives about two or three letters each year from Isabella describing her life on St Helena. Katherine selects one at random that happens to have been written by Adam.

'As you know, before being land-based, I had quite a few adventures when I was at sea. I was only twenty when I sailed on *Alfred*, captained by James Farquharson:

'As we left India bound for Canton in China, we were joined by five other East Indiamen, with Farquharson, as the most senior, assuming command of the six ships. By January, 1797, we were off Java when we encountered six French frigates during the height of the Napoleonic wars. In what became known as the Bali Strait incident, the French, thinking they were about to be attacked by a superior force that was fast advancing on them, retreated. One of the East Indiamen ships, *Ocean*, was wrecked by a storm the next day. The remaining five made it safely back to St Helena on the third of January, 1798, before arriving at Gravesend on the third of April. The Honourable East India Company recognised Commander Farquharson for his bravery, rewarding him with the considerable sum of 500[1] guineas.'[55]

Adam's third trip on *Alfred* was also memorable. She was about ten and had fallen asleep in a large chair at Isabella's home. Isabella had left the room for some reason and Adam was talking to his brothers-in-law with Katherine unnoticed as she snuggled into the chair. It must have been around Christmas, 1804, after he had been at sea for fifteen months and had not long returned home. The men were drinking and seemed to trying to outdo each other in their stories.

Katherine woke to hear Adam saying, 'The Napoleonic wars had resumed by that time, and once again *Alfred* faced a considerable threat. We exchanged fire for fifteen minutes with the French, albeit from a distance, before being safely escorted to St Helena by two British ships. By our actions, we saved the Honourable East India Company and the ship insurers, Lloyds of London, from likely financial ruin. Captain Farquharson and I both retired from *Alfred* after that occasion.'

---

1   £110,000 in today's money

Katherine choses another letter, this time from Isabella, written in late 1807:

'As you may recall, Adam's final voyage was on the new *Ocean* that sailed from Portsmouth in March, 1805, under the command of Captain Williamson. Once again, he witnessed combat, where they encountered three French warships on the outward journey to Penang. The skirmish was resolved after a brief exchange of fire with the French. He eventually returned to England, anchoring at the Downs on the third of September, 1806. At this point I begged him to consider a transfer to onshore employment. Unbeknown to me Adam was appointed to the medical establishment whilst anchored at St Helena in July, 1805, and he organised the purchase of a house. I was dreadfully upset when I learned of this.

'I was dreading going to St Helena and having to say goodbye to all the family. We were fortunate to escape the measles epidemic in early 1807. However, my opinion about our new home has softened in recent years, and after five years, I have grown to love it. I enjoy superior health that I attribute to the gentle breezes and mild climate. Our four daughters are happy and healthy.'

The most recent letter from Isabella was received about four weeks ago. Katherine smiles as she looks at some pictures drawn by the children. Her sister hints rather intriguingly about a few characters on the island, including the junior chaplain Reverend Richard Boys:

'Reverend Boys has recently taken over supervision of our newspaper the *St Helena Register,* after it was closed for seven months by Governor Beatson for printing "objectionable remarks." Adam was upset about the Governor's interference. He felt this cast aspersions on his character, as he had been acting in the editor's role. Since then, relations with Governor Beaston have improved and he has been very appreciative of Adam's support in various matters.'

Following this rather enigmatic statement, Isabella concludes that Reverend Boys is:

'A refreshing change to the senior chaplain Reverend Samuel Jones who enjoys insulting different members of the congregation during his sermons!

'Life on St Helena does not change very much, so occasional excitements get everyone on the Island talking, including a duel two years ago where the younger man was tragically killed, shot by a Captain Wright for insulting his sister. Perhaps one day you could consider visiting us if you have had enough of cold and dirty London?'

Chapter 3

Journal extracts
Sunday 14–Monday 15 March, 1813

This is my first entry in the new cream-coloured calfskin journal, given me by my sister Elizabeth as a farewell gift. I plan to use it as though I am talking to my closest friend. It has been embroidered with roses, using leftover silk from Mama's collection. On the eve of my departure to distant lands, most notably the island of St Helena in the South Atlantic off the west coast of Africa, I am reflecting on my life and my family. I wonder when I will see them all again. I received a gift of a sea chest from Uncle Peter and Aunt Margaret in which to store my clothes and belongings. Pens, ink, and pencils will be kept in a solid mahogany writing box, a gift from my brother James. Charles has given me a silver pocket timepiece hallmarked London 1811, but he assures me on board ship I will get used to the bells ringing to divide the day.

On 1 February, my belongings, along with other goods bound for India, were loaded onto *Sir William Pulteney*, whilst at anchor off the Downs.[56] The ship sailed to Portsmouth and departs on 18 March. I have sewn a selection of clothing suitable for a warmer climate including a yellow, short-sleeved, floor-length gown I made from Mama's silk bolt, now packed carefully into the sea chest. The chest is made of oak, its curved lid reinforced with metal bars, with a metal lock. I carry the heavy key on my person. Uncle Peter sanded, varnished, and waterproofed the entire chest, before carving two roses: the Tudor rose – an emblem of peace – and another to represent Katherine Rose, on the front. My initials KRY are below the lock along with the date: 1813. On either end of the chest, Uncle Peter has affixed rope handles or beckets that he made, to assist in carrying, as it is very heavy. The beckets are woven and smell faintly of grass and have a slight greenish tinge. I am not permitted to lift the chest. The interior is lined with a slightly padded satin material that Aunt Margaret worked on for several days.[57] I packed with care, with a rather tearful Margaret assisting me, in order to avoid crushing my dress and bonnets, and to ensure clothes for the long sea journey are easily accessible. Dried lavender and spearmint have been placed inside to discourage moths. Prior to packing the clothes, we ensured they were meticulously clean. Our accommodation will be on the upper deck in cabins that maximise exposure to fresh air and the sun. Other passengers' cabins are on the lower deck. The ship carries mail and cargo for islanders in the Atlantic before heading to Bombay. Coal will also be put onto the ship. The dust makes everything dirty, but I understand the ship is cleaned as best it can be before the passengers embark.

My sea chest and travel bag[58]

I have a cylindrical shaped, soft calf-leather bag for my travel to Portsmouth. The earthy and slightly sweet aroma is far from the sharp, stinging, acrid odours of the tannery. The bag is held together with three strong leather straps and was presented to me by my sister Margaret. Much to my surprise, I discovered a generous amount of money in an envelope inside from John Lindsay, and also some essential toiletries. A small amount of tooth powder is in a little porcelain pot. Used with clean rags, it assists in cleaning my teeth. A small bottle of Botot's Eau de Bouche scented with cloves, cinnamon, ginger, and anise keeps my mouth fresh. A luxury bar of Pear's soap from Elizabeth's supply 'to be used sparingly,' reminds me of the baths I gave my young nieces. I have dressed for the journey, with a high-waisted, thick cotton, cream-coloured dress for my travel, on top of which I wear a brown, woollen cape. I make most of my clothes myself, but occasionally visit the Rag Fair to supplement clothing. Underneath, I wear a chemise, a corset with a stay inserted and cotton drawers. A bonnet, made for me by Elizabeth, keeps my hair tidy and is replaced by a linen cap for overnight. My new sturdy leather boots are worn in, and I carry extra pairs of laces. I have a spare set of underclothes that I hope will not be needed.

My sea chest with initials, roses and becket handles visible on the left

Problems with a lame horse

We are spending two nights in Guildford on our way to Portsmouth.[59] The delay is due to a horse becoming lame. None of us were in a hurry to reach Portsmouth, and the New Inn had vacancies. Meanwhile, a farrier has been employed to examine the horse's foot and replace the horseshoe. The coach is a heavy affair drawn by four Cleveland Bay horses that are a reddish brown with large heads, long, well-muscled necks and shoulders. Their broad, deep chests, muscular legs, and a docile temperament, ensure they are well suited for their task. The stagecoach is modern. Safety has been improved to ensure the wheels cannot fall off, an all-too-common occurrence for unlucky travellers. We were informed that the turning capacity and braking system are also built to a high standard. We are kept warm by carriage rugs and, unusually for this time of the year, the weather is both dry and mild. Perhaps the least said about our London departure point from the Bolt in Tun in Fleet Street the better! I have tried to draw the building façade to remind myself of the start of the journey. It is probably relatively safe in daytime, but it would be a foolish person to be in the vicinity after dark. It marks the start of one of the new stagecoach routes from London that have been opened in recent times, that covers a distance of approximately seventy-two miles.[60]

Our coach is covered in a dull, black, leather, studded with nails, but the wheels are a bright scarlet and are kept surprisingly clean. The windows have leather curtains, that my three companions and I draw back so that we can watch the countryside pass by. I am glad that I brought a feather cushion with me as, despite the good condition of the road, every bump is felt deep within the bones. I imagine the extra passengers on the roof did not enjoy their journey as much as we did. They all had to jump off in rather a hurry once we reached the Inn, as the way into the cobbled courtyard was narrow with a low arch. I rather like this caricature of the Chelsea Stage Coach which I discovered in one of my magazines prior to leaving London, as our stagecoach is not dissimilar. I have pasted it in my journal.

It is the first time I have travelled out of London, and the countryside looks very green. During one of our stops, I spotted a lark high overhead.

Its song was so sweet that I envied its ability to escape the bonds of earth! We saw hares frolicking in fields and ducks swimming in village ponds. The air is fresh, with very little odour, such a contrast to the streets we live in every day. Even a trip to the local pump for water is a hazardous venture with obnoxious and foul-smelling puddles requiring many extra steps to be avoided.

Chelsea Stage Coach, Thomas Rowlandson[61].

A delicious meal

Last night I had to pay additional money, for candles to be brought to my room once it became dark; money for the evening meal and breakfast; and some local taxes. Luckily Uncle Mark has been very generous, so I am not short of funds. In our most recent correspondence, he invited me to address him in this familiar way, as we will be travelling companions for an extended period of time. His new wife will become Aunt Dorothy. We arrived too late yesterday to see anything other than this new Inn that is catty-corner to St Nicholas Church, overlooking the River Wey. Our average speed was around six miles per hour, allowing for some hygiene stops along the way! In the dying light, Guildford was bathed in gold, most notably along the High Street.

For dinner, we ate steaming hot vegetable Lenten pie, seasoned with herbs such as parsley, savoury, that gives a peppery taste, and rosemary. There was bread and cheese, and ale to quench our thirst. I was very hungry. Following this, treacle tart was served with a hot mug of aromatic bishop that warmed us in the cooling evening. The scents of oranges, lemons, and whole cloves, along with hints of cinnamon, allspice, and ginger, were heavenly. Each mug was sweetened, and none of us could stop at one. Even though we are in the second week of Lent, and in normal times I may consider fasting, I am making the most of the meals whilst I am here, as the food encountered along the way in coaching inns has been most unpalatable.

I slept surprisingly well despite the attentions of bed bugs, which normally keep me awake. The mattress, made from goose feathers – and the feather coverlet – ensured I remained very warm. A chamber pot was supplied to the room, as well as a jug and basin, the latter filled with hot water on my arrival. Following a breakfast of coddled eggs served with bacon, coffee, and a sweet pastry, and with assurances that it is safe to do so, I ventured into town and walked down the High Street to the Guildhall. It has three doors on the ground floor and three mullion windows above. An ornamental cupola graces the roof. The impressive clock, around 150 years old and built by John Aylward, projects out from the Guildhall.[62] It would be of great interest to Charles who, a few years ago, completed an apprenticeship to a maker of chronometers and clocks, Tobias and Co, based in Wapping.[63] We have been given food to take with us on the journey tomorrow so that we do not have to stop off at any Inns to eat. We will be leaving very early. I made a good start last night on my journal with the excellent light from the candles.

The Bolt in Tun Stage Coach departure point

The letter that prompted my journey

Uncle Mark's letter was discussed over Christmas, with robust debate from all present, as is customary in our family. We made a feast from two large geese, an unexpected treat from the farm adjacent to Margaret and John's new property at Lee. The geese were stuffed with softened onions and fresh breadcrumbs, to which cubes of quince grown on the estate were added. The birds were accompanied by roast potatoes, skirrets, cardoons and carrots, and spinach from their hothouse. A large cured ham was an alternative meat, for those who did not wish to eat goose, or were feeling particularly hungry. For dessert, we were served preserved fruits with fresh cream, followed by a selection of nuts, including walnuts and hazelnuts, gathered from the estate. I was the centre of attention with my news. I must confess I found this rather flattering. Whilst most of the family were encouraging, soothing my initial doubts somewhat, I was hurt that Elizabeth did not initially approve of my proposed odyssey. She said travelling by stagecoach was risky, ship voyages hazardous. Rats and other disease-causing vermin live on ships. Food is not fresh. She worries about Uncle and Aunt. Her eyes filled with tears and her daughter Elizabeth, a sensitive soul of six years, came over to hug her mother. They are very close. Her babies, Katherine and Isabella, were asleep in the nursery for most of the meal, but young Elizabeth had been permitted to stay up for the occasion. After my sister had exhausted what she had to say to me, our brother James, whose initial reservations about my proposed adventure have apparently softened, sought to calm the situation:

'I know Captain Henry Christopher well and I assure you he has an excellent reputation and high standards of safety. I believe this will be his last journey before retirement. His senior crew are also known to me: Samuel Bishop is the surgeon and an able, professional man if anyone chanced to become unwell on the voyage. The purser, James Thomson, will ensure you are able to travel in maximum comfort as the ship permits. He is attentive to the needs of passengers and crew. There are rules on board ship which will be explained to you, including when live flames are permitted. The main meal is generally held in the middle of the day. It is likely you will dine with the captain, other important passengers and the highest-ranking crew, given Colonel Wilks' seniority and deserved reputation within the East India establishment.'[64]

James had barely finished before Charles said:

'I have also had the pleasure of meeting Colonel Wilks in the early days of his travels to and from India, including following the tragic loss of his wife. As you may recall, I was fourth mate on *Earl Spencer* when she sailed to Bombay in June, 1803 and the captain was our cousin Charles Raitt. Wilks is a man of high integrity. His daughter Laura is beautiful and intelligent and perhaps three years younger than you. I believe you will get on splendidly. James Halliburton, our brother-in-law, is well acquainted with several of the families on St Helena, including the Beales. I think you will find the twelve months pass very quickly and you will be happy and fulfilled. However, the peregrination to St Helena will be challenging, as the East Indiamen ships are notably cramped. Voyages are not without risk because of Napoleon's ships, and it is usually the case that the East Indiamen travel in convoy for protection. Since Nelson's celebrated victory at Trafalgar, there had been very few encounters with French vessels in the Atlantic, other than the final confrontation in the 1806 Atlantic campaign. *Sir William Pulteney* has a full crew of fifty-five highly trained men, and it carries a dozen guns. It is smaller than many East Indiamen ships, as it was originally designed as a country ship that traded only east of the Cape of Good Hope, rather than proceeding to the Far East. Paradoxically, the worst part of the trip may be the English Channel. Occasional storms can cause discomfort as you approach the coast of Dorset. Navigating the Isles of Scilly off Cornwall requires both knowledge and skill.'

I was unsure if he was trying to frighten me, but on reflection, I felt the different perspectives on the voyage and St Helena itself were helpful to my decision making. At this point, Peter indicated he had something to say:

'As you all know Margaret has been unwell this year. We have decided to return to Inchture in the Spring.'

He turned to Katherine:

'We will miss you dreadfully but will always be grateful for the care and attention you have given us in recent years and our love and prayers are with you as you prepare to embark on your exciting journey.'

Margaret was nodding as Peter was speaking and I went and gave her and Peter a huge hug. I am too excited to be nervous or homesick. Tomorrow evening, I will be meeting Uncle Mark, Aunt Dorothy, and Laura in Portsmouth. Uncle Mark has sent a small portrait of himself in his most recent letter. He is a very distinguished looking gentleman, with thick, white, wavy hair covering his head.[65] It is time to get some rest, as we have a long journey ahead, with a very early start in the morning.

Chapter 4

Journal extracts
Early Friday morning, 19 March, 1813

The last 48 hours have passed in a blur of activity with no time to write in my journal. Time is different on-board ship, with the day divided into sections marked by the ringing of bells that also call us to meals. I am learning that historically the concept of time for mariners differs in many respects from their land-based cousins.[66] It is early Friday morning, and we have just passed Lyme Bay. The Devon coast is easily visible as we head towards Dartmouth. I spent the first night in my small cabin adjacent to one occupied by Laura. Uncle Mark and Aunt Dorothy have a large cabin with separate dining area. We will take many of our meals here, when not dining with the Captain in the wardroom. Breakfast can be taken in our own cabins, so we will be well nourished to start our day. I will set aside this time to read my Bible and write in my journal. To conserve valuable resources, and to minimise the risk of fire from unattended flames, we are not permitted to light our cabins after nine thirty at night.

I am envious of Laura's beautiful chestnut hair. Unlike her father who has striking grey curls that make him look very distinguished, her hair is straight and so long that she is able to sit on it. She has requested I assist her each night to wrap her tresses in rags, so that she can wear it down on occasions. Her usual preference is to wear her hair pulled up onto the crown of her head, fashioned into a loose bun. This morning, I am joining her in her cabin as I have offered to brush it for her. It will be an opportunity to get to know each other better. We are expected to keep our cabins clean and tidy, to discourage unwanted vermin. They are formally cleaned each week and on an 'as required' basis by members of the crew. On fine days we are encouraged to air our mattresses in the open air on the top deck.

Our sea legs are developing. We have felt mild nausea as we are not yet accustomed to the rolling of the boat. This was particularly noticeable when we hit choppy seas after emerging into the English Channel. We were escorted out of Portsmouth Harbour and the channel adjoining the Isle of Wight by a small ship, before passing the Needles and sailing due west. *Sir William Pulteney* is painted to resemble a warship, although we sincerely hope that we are not engaged in any form of battle during our planned journey. Our fellow passengers include two missionary families travelling with young children, as well as a few single gentlemen departing for service with the Honourable East India Company in varied parts of India, all accommodated on the lower deck.[67] I can see that I will have to develop a new vocabulary in order to appreciate more fully the various spaces on board ship. My first impression on boarding was needing to go around lots of rope that was coiled in piles. The complex rigging, with sails tightly furled, reminded me of Uncle Peter and his work in the rope and sail trade. Our cabins are located underneath the poop deck.[68] Cannons are arrayed beneath us, with the hull or sides of the ship inclining above the waterline, a feature referred to as tumblehome. The toilet facilities are basic but adequate. A small cupboard contains a deep-sided porcelain basin and pitcher with a lidded chamber pot in the lower space, that is emptied twice daily. Washing has to be accomplished judiciously to avoid spilling water on the floor.

Despite the relatively smooth passage along the English Channel, I did not sleep particularly well, feeling each movement of the ship. My bunk is quite short, made of wood, with raised sides and a horsehair-stuffed mattress, which will take time to accommodate my body shape. The sailors sleep in rope hammocks that I am told are quite comfortable, as they tilt in harmony with the ship. They sleep fully clothed, ready to assist in case of emergencies. Their duty span of a few hours at a time is marked by bells. A bell is struck every 30 minutes, with between 1 and 7 strokes that give the time. The crew are divided up between 2-4 groups called 'watches'. These watches each have their own names: for example, middle watch, forenoon watch, afternoon watch, first watch. The hours between 4 and 8 pm are divided into two called first and last dog watch.

SHIP'S BELL TIMES				
Number of bells	Pattern of bells	Hours (am and pm)		
One bell	o	12.30	4.30	8.30
Two bells	oo	1.00	5.00	9.00
Three bells	ooo	1.30	5.30	9.30
Four bells	oooo	2.00	6.00	10.00

I have my sea chest in my cabin. It is a tight fit, but it has enabled me to change my clothing and feel more comfortable. Laura tells me that there are basic laundering facilities on the ship, but I am unclear at present how one is able to access them. The ship is carrying cargo including large bales of woollen cloth, coal, and iron, all safely stored in the hold and bound for St Helena and Bombay. There are some live animals. Occasionally, the not unpleasant scent of their dung hangs in the air, before being swallowed by the briny odour of the sea. If permitted, I hope to explore the ship and sketch the boat for a letter to send home to Elizabeth. We will be able to leave letters with a homebound ship when we get to Tenerife.

The journey to Portsmouth from Guildford, though long, was largely uneventful. We left at the somewhat unearthly hour of seven in the morning. We were largely sustained on our journey with delicious provisions from the Inn. We made two stops to use crude facilities to accomplish necessary ablutions. There were Inns roughly every ten miles along the route. Approximately halfway, our horses were changed for the second time to a new team, enabling us to spend an hour or so enjoying the fresh air of the South Downs. Fortunately, we did not encounter any untoward events. The driver informed us that certain sections of the road are notorious, with stagecoaches not infrequently held to ransom by highway robbers. Regular milestones alongside the road, indicating distances between two points, enabled us to keep track of our journey. The other travellers were as appreciative of the fresh air as I was. My companions inside the stagecoach, well versed in the local history, had made the journey on many previous occasions and were able to point out features of interest. Portsdown Hill, a chalk ridge overlooking Portsmouth and its vast natural harbour, enabled a striking view.[69] Stone fortifications with mounted cannons surround the town, that is renowned for ship building using local oak trees, as well as boat repairs and maintenance. Different sized ships, sails tightly furled, were at anchor, both within and just outside the harbour. The stagecoach driver kindly agreed to a 30-minute stop, so the horses could enjoy a treat of carrots and apples and quench their thirst whilst we absorbed nature's bounty all around us. He is a Portsmouth native, and enjoys relating its history. I hope I have remembered what he told us as accurately as possible!

The town is built on Portsea Island, and is surrounded by water, with a very narrow harbour entrance. Along with the Isle of Wight that we could see clearly, these natural features have been a vital part of our country's defences for centuries, making an approach from the sea virtually impregnable. The Old Dock Mill on Portsea where Portsmouth lies is a flour mill with a domed cap and attached bakehouse. It was created to resolve a shortage of flour and bread as a consequence of the Napoleonic Wars and is just visible in the area known as Pestfields. At the head of the harbour to the north, is the mediaeval Porchester Castle.[70] There are currently over 7000 prisoners from the Napoleonic Wars incarcerated there. Burials for those who die in captivity take place on the mudflats to the south. It is said that, during bad storms, their bodies come to the surface and drift in the harbour. The driver explained that The Honourable East India Company and Hampshire more broadly have forged a mutually beneficial relationship over more than two centuries. Assets include a lengthy coastline, the availability of talented and experienced personnel as well as convenient port facilities located at Christchurch, Cowes, Lymington, and Southampton, in addition to Portsmouth. There are shipbuilding sites, a ready supply of timber, and well-developed overland communications, as well as extensive investment in capital and labour.[71]

The grasslands around us were full of colourful spring wildflowers, obviously loved by the bees, with their buzzing a backdrop to the sounds of the horses' hooves and bridles. We spotted orchids by the roadside, and also flax, hawthorn, and various herbs I was unable to identify. There were at least three species of butterflies, perhaps celebrating the early arrival of spring. The bright yellow-green of the male brimstone butterfly, whose wings resemble leaves, contrasted with the orange-tipped butterflies. The females of the latter species are largely white with black wingtips. Both male and female orange tips have mottled green underwings. Red admirals and peacock butterflies were also evident.[72] Yellowhammers and whitethroats were singing from the bushes, and skylarks floated gently above the waving grasslands, each lazy circuit seemingly drawing them ever higher into the sky, their song both distinctive and blending with other birdsong. Kestrels and peregrines were in abundance, finding plenty of prey in the extensive grasslands. We saw red-breasted robins, sparrows, and blackbirds with twigs in their beaks, preparing to build their nests. We could hear frogs croaking and spotted some frogspawn in a small stream. The array of hues and colours of the surrounding landscape were reflected in the sky. Overhead was a mixture of pinks, purples, oranges, and greys, with thin, wispy strands of cirrus cloud, the temperature continuing to be very mild for this time of year. I could not get enough of the fresh air, taking deep breaths at every opportunity, much to the amusement of my fellow travellers.

My cotton garments were looking rather the worse for wear, so I was impatiently waiting to be reacquainted with my sea chest once on board and donning fresh clothes. Drawing nearer to the town, windows shone with an orange glow from hundreds of oil lamps. A briny scent assailed our nostrils. My heart gave a huge leap, whether from excitement or pleasure or perhaps a little nervous beat or two, I was unsure, as I prepared to make my acquaintance with Uncle Mark and his family. On the way to the Harbour Inn, seagulls were shrieking, diving for fish heads, eating guts tossed from the jetty by fishwives wielding sharp knives as they prepared fish for salting in barrels. Teams of men carrying two-handled baskets full of medium-sized silver fish kept up a seemingly endless supply. A strong smell of tar mixed with the odour of the fish and the saltiness of the air, but it wasn't unpleasant. An array of ropes, bollards, and barrels almost covered the jetty.

My brother James and I would watch the lightermen[73] on the Thames and observe boat building when we were younger. I remember many of the ships from their shapes.[74] There were Blackwall frigates, three-masted full-rigged ships, built just down the river from our home; brigs of varying sizes, distinguished by their two square-rigged masts; smaller brigantines and three-masted barques. *Sir William Pulteney* is smaller than many of the East Indiamen, but I was unable to identify her with any accuracy. I am assuming the female gender: traditionally a female goddess or mother figure would guide and protect a ship along with its passengers and crew. No doubt she is somewhere in the harbour, perhaps still being loaded with goods for the long sea journey. There were strong looking men rowing a lighter barge and coordinating their strokes to move swiftly towards one of the ships, calling out to a person on the harbour wall. At the mole, the entrance to the harbour that forms a massive breakwater, are formidable-looking cannons, just visible in the dusk. Night was fast approaching by the time we reached the *Half Moon Street Inn*. Uncle Mark must have been listening out for us. As we emerged from the arch, he courteously raised his hat and bowed from the waist, before assisting me to exit the carriage. He offered his arm to traverse the cobbled courtyard after directing where my leather bag should be placed. I felt a sudden warmth in my face, and I was a little embarrassed about my dusty state. On my bodice I had observed a small stain, but he did not appear to notice, as the glow from the lanterns fixed to brackets around the courtyard did not penetrate the shadows.

'Welcome, Katherine. I am delighted that you accepted my offer. I will show you to your room, where hot water has been placed. When you are refreshed, I would be pleased if you could join me and my dear wife, Dorothy, and Laura in the dining room.'

My room was well appointed, with a curtained window facing away from the road. Good quality lamps with little odour ensured the room was well lit. The bed looked very comfortable. Feeling an overwhelming fatigue from the long journey, I was in no doubt that I would sleep soundly. I spent about ten minutes on my toilet, before emerging from my room and walking the short distance to the dining room. Uncle Mark stood as soon as he saw me.

'Please let me introduce you to my dear wife, Dorothy. And my beloved daughter, Laura.'

I gave a little curtsy, first to Dorothy and then to Laura, a beautiful statuesque young woman, with chestnut brown hair arranged in ringlets. Beside her and Dorothy, I feel quite undersized, with a clear disparity about our heights. We were shown to our table, resplendent with a white tablecloth and serviettes, before enjoying a meal of several courses. Uncle Mark asked after my uncle, aunt, and extended family. He trusted that my journey had been accomplished with very little discomfort. At my request, he regaled us with stories of visits he has previously made to St Helena, particularly his most recent sojourn.

'St Helena's beauty is at first hard to discern. The initial impressions of an inhospitable grey, rocky shore, apparent on one's approach from the northwest, give way to lush green pastures and remarkable landmarks as one travels further into the interior of the island. The Governor is accommodated in the main town Jamestown, in formal lodgings that include offices and reception rooms. That is where I will be staying initially, in order to receive a formal handover of responsibilities from Governor Beatson. The many-roomed Plantation House, whilst originally planned as a summer residence, is available to use year-round. Dorothy, Laura, and you will be taken there by bullock cart, and your luggage will accompany you. I hope to join you on the weekend. The interior of the island is rarely cold. Summer temperatures are tempered by the trade winds, so bely the expectation of extreme heat that one might expect at its latitude.'

My eyes were beginning to feel heavy, so the meal was concluded promptly with good wishes to sleep well. Tomorrow, I will be called in time for breakfast, before a carriage ride to the waterfront. Boarding *Sir William Pulteney* entails a short boat ride into the harbour. I was asleep as soon as my head lay on the soft pillow, full of goose feathers.

Chapter 5

Friday 19 March, 1813

Katherine knocks on Laura's door. She has accepted an invitation to join her, as she wants to get to know her better. They have both finished breakfast, which was served in their individual cabins. Laura's long hair is tightly bound with about twenty rags that she dampens before retiring to bed.

After exchanging information about how they slept, Katherine asks Laura, 'Would you like me to take out the rags and brush your hair?'

'Thank you, I would be delighted.'

'They must take a long time to put in?'

'Yes, but I am well practiced! However, I would be grateful for your assistance whilst we are on the ship. Dorothy usually does it for me, but she is busy with Papa. If you can, pass me that little box from the shelf and my hairbrush from under the basin?'

Katherine retrieves them, bracing herself at the slight swell from the boat. She has still not quite got used to the constant movement.

'Does your stepmother have any children of her own?' asks Katherine.

'No. She was not married prior to meeting Papa, but she worked as a midwife in Douglas. Despite our almost fifteen-year age difference, she seems more like an older sister than a mother. I lived with her when I returned to the Isle of Man in 1807. The Taubman family, like Papa's family, have lived on the Isle of Man for generations. Her father, Major John Taubman, is Speaker at our parliament, the House of Keys, and well acquainted with my father, despite their very different political points of view.'

'Why is that?'

'Dorothy's father was linked to several slave ships that left from Liverpool. He, like other Manx men, felt trading in slaves was justified and a necessary evil, to ensure that plantations in the Americas and West Indies could have a constant supply of labour.[75] Dorothy takes a more humane view. She and her father would engage in robust debates. Since he succeeded his father as Speaker in 1799, Taubman has raised the Douglas Volunteers and now has the rank of Major Commandant. The Volunteers' role is to defend the Island in the event of an invasion by Napoleon's forces, which luckily has not eventuated.'

'That was one of the things that frightened me before this voyage,' said Katherine. 'Several members of my family have had hostile engagements with French ships during voyages to China. Luckily, I believe we are well armed. What would you like me to do with the rags?'

'If you give them to me, I will roll them up and put them in the box,' Laura replied.

'Have you always had long hair?' asked Katherine.

'Yes, my mother did not like to cut it. She died when we lived in India and is buried at the foot of the hills in Mysoor. Dorothy has been like a second mother to me and indeed the women she looks after. She employs techniques in her midwifery practice that are used extensively in India. These include yoga and breathing, known as pranayama, to manage both the pain and duration of labour.[76] [77] Since Papa spent so much time in that country, he would send her information about local practices, and she has found this effective with the mothers she deals with. Occasionally I would accompany her on her visits. However, unlike Dorothy, I did not understand the Manx language, which is a form of Gaelic.'[78]

'I don't think I have heard of the Manx language,' said Katherine. 'I always assumed they spoke English.'

'I had not realised how common it was,' said Laura. 'The Isle of Man is one of six Celtic nations that include Cornwall, Britanny in France, Scotland, Ireland, and Wales. It was obvious Dorothy was well loved by all the mothers she cared for, many of whom were poor and did not speak English. Her views on childbirth are radical and unorthodox, and were not encouraged, particularly by the local doctors. She is in regular touch with a midwifery doctor called Samuel Merriman, who has written a useful book that she refers to. I can tell you more about Dorothy another time.[79]

'Would you like to brush my hair? Perhaps once you have finished, we can go for a walk on the deck?' asked Laura.

Laura folds the last few rags and places them carefully in a box on the end of the bunk. She hands Katherine a silver brush with boar bristles.

'Please use long strokes, as that avoids tangles,' requested Laura.

Katherine braces herself against the bunk as the ship is rolling.

Laura continues, 'When I was young, I didn't enjoy having my hair brushed. My ayah in India threatened to have it cut short!'

'I would love to learn more about your life and Uncle Mark,' said Katherine, pulling some hair out of the brush and placing it near the ribbons. 'Were you born in India? It sounds very exotic!'

'No. I was born in the Isle of Man in 1797. We travelled to India soon after the birth of my brother, initially returning to Fort St George, before moving when Papa was appointed as the Resident of Mysoor.'

'How did Uncle Mark meet your mother?'

'Papa met Mama in Madras, and they were married at Fort St George. Papa became ill, so was advised to take leave in 1795. He and Mama returned to the Isle of Man. My brother John Barry was born in 1798, but he was frail and did not return to India with us. He still lives with extended family in Michael, on the west side of the Island, and attends a local school when he is well enough.'

'Do you see your brother very often? That must be hard, being separated from your only sibling.'

'Sadly, I hardly know him. Papa spent many years in India, employed by the Company. He is fluent in Latin, Greek, and Persian, and was my first Latin teacher! We mostly lived in Mysoor in southwest India. Papa was always busy working or writing or translating books. Mama was delicate, but she used to tell me that the Indian climate suited her. Where we lived, the weather was quite pleasant throughout the year, with no extremes of temperature.'

'Your life sounds so different from my life in London. I cannot envisage a time when I have not been part of my siblings' lives. We are fortunate to live close to each other and were very sad when Isabella moved to St Helena in 1807. Where would you like me to put the hair from the brush?' asked Katherine.

'If you give it to me, I can throw it over the side of the ship later,' said Laura.

'Do you have many memories of India?' asked Katherine.

'I remember my ayah the best. She would play with me, take me outside, show me places in the town, introduce me to her family, and give me strange foods to try.'

'What is an ayah? I have heard of the term but never really understood it.'

'She was a bit like a nanny or a grandmother. She was unmarried, but so kind to me. I loved Mama, but her desire to support my father in his responsibilities meant our precious time together was limited. Her grave is in Mysoor, in the foothills of the Chamundi Hills, towards the southwest of Bangalore, although some of her ashes are also interred at Michael, in the family grave plot. I would like to return to Mysoor one day, as my memories of Mama and my ayah are fading. Father tells me our mothers knew each other as children?'

'Yes, that is what my sisters have told me,' said Katherine. 'I think they lived in the same village in Perthshire and may have been distant cousins, although the MacLeane family originally came from Coll, or another of the islands west of Scotland. Mama moved to London with her father, David, and her sister Margaret, marrying Papa when she was just twenty.'

'What is it like to live in London? Do you remember your mama?'

'The smell of London is indescribable. Clothes become impregnated with it. I could not go outside without a nosegay. It is dangerous to be out after dark. Pickpocketing and muggings are common. Just last year there were some dreadful murders. Regular public hangings attract huge crowds.'

'That must be horrible,' said Laura, wrinkling her nose.

'Sea fogs are frequent. Buildings are black with soot. Horses are everywhere. Abattoirs and factories discharge waste into the streets. Breathing is hard, as the air stings your nose or catches in your throat or makes your eyes water. On exposed areas of skin, dirt and a greasy feeling are common and not easily washed away. I frequently observed small boys known as mudlarks wade in knee-deep, odorous mud when the tide was out, trying, often by feeling with their feet, to find items dropped from ships that could be sold to pay for food or other necessities.'

'That sounds dreadful. The poor children. I imagine mudlarking could be very dangerous?'

'Yes,' said Katherine. 'It was not unknown for children to be swept away by the incoming tide, or sink in the mud, unable to be rescued.'

'I hope that one day I can make a difference to people living in poverty,' said Laura. 'I find it difficult to reconcile that people of great wealth can live alongside people who have such misfortune in their lives. Were you far from the river?'

'Our home in Three Colt Street is very close to the River Thames,' said Katherine.[80] 'It used to belong to my parents. It is built of brick, has a pitched roof, and is protected with weatherboards, but gets damp in winter. It was one of three in the street with gables on the roof, the purpose of which I am unclear. We sleep upstairs. My bedroom is over the room where Mama would sew goods made from fine silk. The material was sourced from Chinese workers employed by the Honourable English East India Company, who lived in nearby Limehouse.[81] Mama was always coughing and looked very pale. She taught my sisters to weave but sadly she, like many silk weavers, lost their work, due to various Acts passed in Parliament that became known as the Spitalfields Acts.'

'That is a very tragic story. Do you have anything your mother made from the silk?'

'She sold most of her work, but we kept the leftover silk and have used it over the years for rags, handkerchiefs, or nosegays. Most of it is now stored at my sister's home. We did not want to sell it because we felt it would be useful if we kept it carefully. The loom and some bolts are still in our home, but either Elizabeth or Margaret will take them. I have made a dress from yellow silk that is in my sea chest, that I will show you once we are at St Helena. Mama loved rose water, and if I smell it, I am instantly able to recall her face. Sadly, I cannot remember very much about Papa, as he was away on ships for most of my early life.'

'Do you have *any* memories of him?' asked Laura.

'Papa was dark haired with deep blue eyes reflecting his Gaelic heritage. I am told I have inherited his colouring. Like me, he was not very tall, but my memories are fading as, sadly, I was only five when he left. His ship was presumed lost at sea in 1801, and as far as we know there were no survivors. After Mama's death, my uncle Peter and aunt Margaret moved into our home, as their house was too small to house me and my siblings. Papa and Uncle Peter both started their working lives making rope.[82] Although Peter was Papa's brother, and Margaret Mama's sister, there is no family resemblance. My mama was delicate. Her sister Margaret has a good heart but is frail. She and Uncle Peter plan to return to Scotland, to their childhood home in Inchture, during the English spring or summer. It is hoped this will be more conducive to Margaret's health. They formally adopted me and my siblings in 1801. I will always be grateful to them for their kindness and love.

'Our church is St George-in-the-East. That is where we were baptised, our mother was buried, and from where my sisters married. Uncle Peter is a bell ringer. I love to hear him practice, and he tells me stories about bell ringing. I went to the local school and taught at Sunday school, all under the auspices of the church.'

'Our local church was also St George,' said Laura. 'But we would sometimes attend mediaeval churches in other parts of the Island, or St Matthew's on the quay in Douglas. Like you, I enjoy listening to the different peals of bells. Tell me more about your life?'

'Twice a week, I would buy fish from fishermen temporarily moored on the Thames. Despite my fervent hopes and prayers, I could not envisage how I could escape London. Unlike my sisters, opportunities to meet a future husband were limited. My school duties and care of Uncle and Aunt left little time. The arrival of the letter from your father was a prayer answered. I sincerely hope, like our mothers before us, we might become good friends.'

Katherine puts the brush down and sits on the end of the bunk as Laura stands up and stretches.

She grimaced. 'London sounds horrible, very different from the Isle of Man.'

'I don't know anything about the Isle of Man. Is it part of England?' asked Katherine.

'Douglas lies on the edge of a sweeping crescent-shaped bay. However, its reputation as a source of many diseases including cholera has resulted in many people moving away. The beaches on the Isle of Man, unlike many English beaches, are sandy. Our sunsets are magnificent, most famously in Peel, the main fishing town, that is overlooked by Peel Castle. Towards Port Erin are panoramic views of the Calf of Man, the stunning backdrop of the Irish mountains like exotic stage scenery. Fresh air and island life suit me.' Laura sits down again on the bunk.

'Papa and Dorothy are both from families who have contributed to the political life of the Island for generations. We have our own parliament, The House of Keys, and separate laws and traditions.'

'It sounds like a different country!' said Katherine. Following Laura's example, she too stretches to ease her back.

'In many ways the Isle of Man *is* different,' said Laura. 'The Island has its own character. I lived with Dorothy when I returned from India, in Castletown, our capital in the south of the island, that has an impressive mediaeval castle.'

'That's interesting. I wonder if it is as old as the Tower of London which was built about 1066 when we were invaded by the Normans?'

'I don't think it is quite that old. Castle Rushen is thought to have been built about two hundred years after that. It guards the entrance to the Silverburn River, where the Norse kings or Vikings had a strategic site.'

'With all the different peoples that have invaded our country, I find it surprising sometimes that we all speak the same language! Other than Latin, I am afraid I only speak English. What about you?'

'Dorothy is fluent in Manx, but I have only learned a few words that tend to get mixed up with the local Indian language I spoke when we lived in Mysoor. It was called Kannad, but people also spoke in Tamil, English, and a couple of other languages. I struggle with Latin, as I am sure Papa will tell you. However, I am reasonably fluent in French but cannot speak it like a native.'

'I think our roles may have to be reversed. I am sure I can learn much more from you than you can from me! May I sit on your bed again? We seem to have hit a rough patch of water.'

'Please do,' said Laura. 'I have found it necessary to brace oneself to avoid hitting one of the pegs in the wall. I suggest we exchange details about our lives for another ten minutes and then perhaps explore the ship if you are agreeable?'

'That would be lovely,' said Katherine. 'I am interested in learning more about religion in India?'

'The main religion where we lived in India was Hindu. There was no English church as such, but I think that might change one day. We would have informal services in each other's homes, often taken by an army chaplain. But the Hindu religion also affected the food that was eaten, as they do not eat meat. I loved the Indian food. We'd eat a fermented rice and lentil pancake called masala dosa that was often eaten with potato curry and chutneys. Potato was also used in a snack called bonda. There was a kind of spicy soup called rasam, made with tamarind, tomatoes, and herbs and spices, that we ate with rice and another vegetable dish.'

'What is tamarind?'

'The tamarind tree produces pods that contain a sweet, tangy pulp. It is delicious when used in traditional dishes.'

'Your descriptions bring back memories of the stories the Lascars used to tell when they came to our home when I was very young. Papa used to love their descriptions of spices, saying he could almost smell them. Very occasionally they would cook a typical Indian meal for us. I often wondered what became of the exotic goods that were imported to England in such great quantities! I am wondering whether you would brush *my* hair?' asked Katherine. 'I will fetch my brush from my cabin, unless you would like to continue the conversation in there?'

Laura nods her agreement. 'I would be happy to.'

They step over the plank at the bottom of the cabin door that ensures water does not easily enter the cabin. Both young women brace themselves as Laura starts to brush Katherine's hair.

'What did you drink in India?' asked Katherine. 'I occasionally have tea, but it is expensive, so I only use a few leaves at a time.'

'We would usually drink chai masala, a type of tea. Another drink that was delicious and refreshing was lime juice flavoured with mint. Would you mind if I have a glass of water?'

'Please do,' said Katherine. 'Luckily I still have some fresh water in the jug.' She passes a glass to Laura.

'Thank you,' said Laura. 'One thing I missed eating in India was fish. I do enjoy fish and seafood, and I have something to show you when we get to Tenerife!' She returns the glass to Katherine.

'I did not realise how thirsty I was,' said Laura. 'You had better make the most of our time in the Canaries. St Helena promises to be very different as it is a garrison town. Papa tells me one has to go into the interior to appreciate its beauty.'

'I'd love to hear more about St Helena.'

'I'm sure Papa will share his experiences. I will make sure to ask him to talk to us over dinner. Perhaps we should go up onto deck to continue our conversation and see if we can see anything of interest? I think we may just be able to see the coast of Cornwall in the far distance. I will go and freshen up and meet you in ten minutes.'

Katherine and Laura meet up on the deck and continue their conversation, leaning against a rail to counteract the motion of the ship. Katherine shades her eyes with her hand as the sea is reflecting the sunlight. She cannot see any land. She turns to Laura and asks, 'When did you leave India? Do you remember much about the ship journey?'

'We sailed on this ship! Papa has a great respect for the Captain Christopher's skills as a mariner. We joined her on the tenth of July, 1806, at Saugor, a city located on a huge river in India. As we approached the Cape of Good Hope, we had a violent storm, confining us to our cabins for days, which induced a feeling of claustrophobia. We slept a lot of the time. A sailor was washed overboard, after he slipped on the deck. I was very sick. I missed my ayah. I was conflicted about leaving India. I don't think I was very nice to Papa, I kept interrupting his work, as I was bored and frightened. I would wake from my sleep calling out as the storm induced nightmares. I soiled my clothes, and it was difficult for Papa to clean them. I did not like the food we were given.'

'It sounds a terrifying experience, and I cannot imagine being confined to a small space for such an extended period. How long did it continue?'

'I have forgotten much of the detail, but I remember stopping off at St Helena soon after Christmas, on the twenty-first of January, 1807, seeing all the soldiers marching in their scarlet coats near the harbour, thinking how bright they looked against the grey mountains. Many ships were in full sail, and either arriving or departing from the port at Jamestown. Thousands of fish were visible in the crystal-clear harbour waters.

'Papa had to spend time with the Governor, Colonel Robert Patton. He had two daughters and had built a walk for them leading upwards from the wharf that they showed me, but they seemed to lose interest in looking after me or had to attend school, I can't quite remember. I was then entrusted to the care of Mr Anthony Beale, an Island native. He travelled to England with us to attend the Honourable East India Company College,[83] so I got to know him quite well. It was agreed I would address him as Mr Anthony as that was the honorific to which he was accustomed, as the younger brother.' Laura turned to Katherine.

'Shall we move towards the other end of the deck for a change of scene?' she suggested. 'I will tell you more about Tenerife. It is a little early to enter Papa's cabin.' She starts to move but catches her foot on a coiled rope. Katherine put out her hand to prevent a fall.

'Thank you,' said Laura. 'That was careless of me.'

'The rule is to always have one hand on the rail or another anchor point,' said Katherine. 'I would hate for you to get washed overboard. Shall we stand here while you continue with your story? I would love to learn more about the Canary Islands.'

'We had two days at Tenerife. Mr Anthony offered to look after me whilst Papa was busy. We had such fun exploring the town. I remember lots of bananas, hands stacked high on roadside stalls. Mr Anthony told me Nelson had tried to conquer the Island in 1797, barely ten years previously, but failed. That was when he lost his arm.'

'I had not heard that story about Nelson. I am looking forward to stopping over on Tenerife. Can you remember anything else about it?'

'When on Tenerife, one's eyes are drawn to Mount Teide. Its barren grey-pink slopes are a stark contrast to the sandy beaches. The clear turquoise seas teem with exotic, brightly coloured fish that can be seen in flashes of light. Strange plants abound. A green cactus, with spikes on its fat paddle-shaped leaves, sprouting orange-yellow club-like protuberances, was widespread.'

'I think I have seen pictures of these cactus. I thought they were called prickly pear. I imagine it would be very unfortunate to be stabbed by these spikes?'

'Yes, very painful. The spines can be up to three inches long and they are also covered with tiny barbed hair, so best avoided. Hands have to be protected when harvesting them. We went for a walk and passed by a church that was in ruins following a fire, and were offered some of the peeled fruit from the cactus from a stall outside, but I cannot remember what it tasted like. I seem to remember we had to spit out the seeds. We then joined some local children collecting shells on a beach. The sand was very hot. Little cowrie shells are made into necklaces and sold to Island visitors. Mr Anthony gave me a necklace!'

'Do you still have it?'

'I think it must be at our home in the Isle of Man. I have not thought about it for years. After enjoying the beach for half an hour or so, we walked down to the harbour where we sampled some local seafood delicacies. I enjoyed charred octopus, whilst Anthony tried the ugliest dish I have seen in my life. Tenerife natives call them goose barnacles. Talon-like multi-coloured predatory "claws" are framed at their base by pearl-coloured "nails" that resemble baby teeth. Mr Anthony understands some Spanish. The old fisherman selling them, his face so deeply wrinkled that it appeared to be carved from wood, told him the barnacles are incredibly dangerous to harvest from surf-battered rocks near the base of cliffs. To eat them, one has to twist the tube part away from the shell, a manoeuvre that is not immediately intuitive.[84] It reminded me of the first time I tried whole prawns. Nobody told me to remove the shells or legs, so I crunched down on them, perhaps not appreciating the delicacy as I should!'

'I have never eaten prawns. I will have to get you to help me prepare them as I would like to try and eat the local food. The barnacles sound revolting! I cannot imagine why people would want to eat them. Where did you finally leave the ship?'

'We disembarked at The Downs on the twelfth of April. The ship's tender transferred us to the dock. Father took me directly to Dorothy's home, travelling by stagecoach and then a small ferry boat. I started school the day after we arrived, but I found the education offered on the Isle of Man disappointing. There was a strong focus on women's responsibilities in the home, but little emphasis on literacy and numeracy. Papa left soon afterwards, but not before I had settled comfortably in my new home. Papa supports my choice to leave school and accompany him and Dorothy to St Helena, but wishes my education to continue. I dream that one day I will return to the Isle of Man and endow schools that educate in the fullest sense of the word! How do you think it will work with you tutoring me?'

'Unlike you, I was fortunate to receive a good education from my local church school. There was no distinction between boys and girls. We were taught reading, writing and arithmetic and instructed in Latin. Sunday school classes ensured we had a good understanding of the Bible. When I turned fourteen, I was employed to teach younger children, but continued my own education, developing a close relationship with a lady called Mary Brown, who had been widowed, but did not have any children of her own. Mary became a good colleague and trusted friend.' Katherine's voice sounds wistful. 'I have been giving some thought to the structure of our learning but perhaps that is best left until we are more settled on the ship.'

'I think it is time to join Papa and Dorothy,' said Laura, letting go of the rail. 'I arranged yesterday evening to see them close to 10 am. I suggest we knock on the door of their cabin.'

The cabin is only a few yards away, located beneath the poop deck.

'Good morning, Papa, Dorothy,' says Laura as her father opens the door. Dorothy is looking over his shoulder.

'Good morning to you both,' says her father. 'I trust you slept well and are rested?'

'Very well, thank you,' replied Katherine. 'We are pleased we took up your suggestion of having our wooden chests in our cabins. The diminished space is more than compensated for by having our clothes and other items easy to access.'

'I am glad to hear it. I understand from Laura that you are keen to know a little more about our travelling companions? We had an extended conversation with Captain Christopher, who came to our cabin before we retired last night. Please, come in and sit down – I am sure our cabin is more comfortable than yours!'

Katherine and Laura sat down on the offered chairs but not before admiring the size of the room.

'Would you like some fresh water?' Dorothy asked. 'It is a precious commodity on board ship!'

Both girls accepted the drink that Dorothy served with a slice of lemon.

'I will let Mark tell you what we have learned about our travelling companions. Afterwards, perhaps you would like to share with us your thoughts about what you would like to learn or teach during our extended journey?'

'I would be very glad to do that,' said Katherine.

'As I explained to you in my letter to your uncle,' said Mark, 'the majority of passengers on *Sir William Pulteney* are on their way to India. There are three missionary families, two with young children. Lieutenant General John Skelton and his wife are also on board, and he will take up his posting at the same time as me. Their country home is at Longwood, some distance from Plantation House. Mrs Skelton is fluent in French and has agreed to deliver French lessons whilst on board. I am sure that will please you, Laura?'

'I will be delighted to make her acquaintance, as I need to practice my French, Papa.'

'The Skeltons have four children who will remain in England with relatives as they are still at school.[85] The Skeltons will disembark with us at St Helena, along with all kinds of goods for the Islanders, before the ship continues to Bombay with the remainder of the passengers. It is likely there will be some kind of ceremony before we are permitted to go aboard at St Helena. Additionally, we will be required to have a basic health check from the ship's surgeon. St Helena has absorbed its lesson from the disastrous measles outbreak that occurred six years ago which was thought to have been transmitted from one of the crew on a ship from South Africa, and no longer regards these checks as perfunctory as perhaps happened prior to that time.'

'I learned about that from my sister Isabella,' said Katherine. 'She and Adam were so thankful not to have arrived there until later in the year, especially as her oldest daughter, Catherine, has rather fragile health.'

'I am looking forward to becoming reacquainted with your sister and brother-in-law whose hospitality I enjoyed on a previous occasion,' said Mark. 'In the meantime, I have met several young gentlemen bound for Bombay and other parts of India. I have promised to talk to them about my tours of duty on the sub-continent, using my experiences as a Resident of Mysoor as a teaching example.'[86]

The remainder of the morning passes quickly. A substantial lunch is served on deck before Katherine excuses herself. She needs to rest and plan appropriate learning opportunities for Laura. She intends to adapt the provisional lesson plans she has prepared for Laura, so that she may also instruct the children travelling with them. Yesterday she approached one of the mothers, Rachel, who was most appreciative of her offer. As she lies down on her bunk, listening to the creaks of wooden beams she is gradually lulled into a deep sleep.

Chapter 6

Journal extracts
Sunday afternoon, 28 March, 1813–12 April, 1813
Heading South

Today is Laetare Sunday[87] – 28 March – marked with a service on the lower deck as it has been raining. One of the wives, Rachel, appears to be expecting a baby as her belly has grown remarkably in the last week or so. It is not good manners to mention such a thing, so until she is ready to share her happy news, I will not allude to it. Part of today's service was spent remembering our mothers. For Laura and me, Mothering Sunday evokes mixed feelings. I wonder what Mama would have thought about my new life. Whilst quietly remembering our loved ones, it is also an occasion to rejoice, as the date means we are halfway through Lent. Sunday services and readings will adhere to a timetable, weather permitting, as outlined below.

We have been reminded that structure and routine is important to maintain morale on board. An exception will be made for Good Friday and Easter Sunday that will be celebrated on Tenerife, God willing. An opportunity may arise to visit a local church. Uncle Mark also recommends spending time in the local markets. We need to ensure we take plenty of oranges, lemons and other fruit with us for the ongoing journey. He explained that the island, whilst similar in some respects to St Helena, is about four times larger in area. Tomorrow he is going to tell us some of the history of Tenerife that he has garnered from the various visits he has made in recent years.

Our Sunday services and weekly readings are marked as follows:		
Service on Poop	2 bells	10.00 am
Sunday School	4 bells	2.00 pm
Bible meeting lower deck salon	4 bells	6.00 pm
Wednesday		
Prayer meeting lower deck salon	4 bells	6.00 pm
Thursday		
Reading on Forecastle	4 bells	6.00 pm

We are now heading due south and are out of sight of land. I must confess to shedding a small tear in the privacy of my cabin when we could no longer see England's shores, the last sighting of the mainland a fast-disappearing Lizard Point. I am comforted that my appointment is for twelve months, which I am sure will pass only too quickly. Yesterday afternoon, we had dinner in the Captain's wardroom and were joined by the Skeltons. The Captain was talking about lighthouses. He told us that, whilst sailors preferred the coal-fired lighthouses for the much stronger light they projected, they had to be cleaned frequently as the windows used to blacken with soot. Approximately eighteen months ago, whale oil replaced coal as the source of power. The conversation moved to a discussion of sailing and the Trade Winds first discovered by the Captain's namesake, Christopher Columbus, as long ago as the fifteenth century. Captain Christopher, who has invited us to refer to him as such, drew a diagram on a piece of paper to show us the direction of the winds. He illustrated how they are influenced by a phenomenon known as the Hadley Cell, a model proposed by George Hadley, an English lawyer and amateur meteorologist, a mere eighty years ago. This causes the winds to have a westerly flow, rather than blowing straight to the Equator. He told us about the various winds that prevail on Earth, as well as currents, like undersea winds, that have influenced trade routes throughout the world.

Taking advantage of these can make a journey much faster. When we leave Tenerife, the Canary Current will influence our journey.

Captain Christopher informed us that a number of vital pieces of equipment assist in ensuring the ship travels in the correct direction. Hurricanes and storms start to appear in July and continue until October, so voyages are planned to avoid these where possible. He offered to show us some of the precision instruments after dinner. He explained the sextant is an astronomical instrument, used for calculating latitude by determining the height above the horizon of the Pole Star, in the Northern Hemisphere. It is made up of the following parts: a frame in the shape of one sixth of a circle; a pair of mirrors – an index mirror and a horizon mirror – and the index arm which moves the mirrors. These enable celestial objects to be measured relative to the horizon, rather than relative to the instrument. A beam of light extends from the measuring pointer, guaranteeing excellent precision even at night. We were permitted to hold the instrument and shown how observations are measured in degrees, then are recorded in the ship's log. For example, measurements for Portsmouth, our point of departure, are: Latitude: 50°47'56" N. Longitude: 1°05'28" W.[88]

Navigational charts that help with the calculations are kept in a large, highly buffed hardwood chart table with a polished glass top. Captain Christopher explained that, prior to the development of accurate chronometers, calculating longitude was harder, prone to error, relying on the sextant to calculate a lunar distance. He reassured us that the ship is now fitted with a marine chronometer, a timepiece mounted on a spring rather than pivots, that looks like a clock. The instrument keeps Greenwich Mean Time. On occasions, ships carry up to three marine chronometers, to compare findings in each, but they are very expensive. Longitude is determined by the difference between Greenwich Mean Time and local noon, when the sun reaches its daily zenith. I had a prior knowledge of chronometers from talking with Charles, who has always had a keen interest in mechanical objects, but until now I did not appreciate how important they were in preventing disasters such as shipwrecks. Captain Christopher said that he had to fight hard for the chronometer. Many of the East Indiamen ships are still not carrying them, but whether this is due to the expense, or the intransigent positions taken by experienced captains or owners of the ships, is unclear.

A nautical telescope and marine compass are also vital instruments to assist in safe passage. Captain Christopher's telescope is handheld with a tapered mahogany barrel and has brass fittings. He uses it to make general observations on the ship's deck, demonstrating that the telescope is made up of an objective lens that collects light from a far-off object, bringing it into focus. The bright light is magnified by an eyepiece lens that is on the narrowed part of the tube. The tube separates the two lenses to ensure proper spacing, but also acts to keep out dust, moisture, and unwanted light. He has promised to let us view the ship in the morning when the light is better.

The compass is kept in a wooden lidded box for safety. It is mounted on a gimbal, a pivoted support that allows it to rotate around two axes. One axis counteracts the ship's roll and the other the ship's pitch, so that the compass remains coplanar – on the same plane – with the horizon. A single iron needle sits on a weighted spike that projects from the bottom of the compass. The compass cards are made of paper and are beautifully illustrated. A star defines the four cardinal points of the compass as well as the intermediate directions such as northeast. A fleur-de-lys is used to illustrate the very important north. Captain Christopher explained that the ship my brother-in-law James is commanding is significantly larger than our vessel, but the principles of navigation would be the same. He believes it is likely James will be at St Helena any day now on the return leg of his journey from China. Sadly, we will most likely be ships passing in the night, as the schedule for *Glatton* does not include a stop at Tenerife.

Whilst we were drinking our early evening hot chocolate[89] prior to retiring to bed, Captain Christopher told us stories of peoples throughout history who have used all sorts of navigational aids to ensure they could complete their journeys safely, without the loss of people and ships. Ancient Norsemen, in the absence of stars during the summer months, would watch the behaviour of birds. Birds with full beaks after feeding at sea would head home to land. Some sailors would keep half-starved ravens on their ships, who would fly straight towards approaching land 'as the crow flies' in search of food, and the sailors would follow. In the Pacific

Ocean, Polynesians watched the direction and type of waves to assist in navigation. Islanders would build elaborate maps out of shells and palm tree twigs to identify the positions of islands and the direction of the sea swell.[90] Knowledge of the stars and their relative positions in the night sky served sailors well for centuries. Captain Christopher promised to spend time with us on the next clear night for a lesson on the sky. With a much better understanding of the workings of our ship, and greatly reassured by Captain Christopher's professionalism, we said our farewells. Nothing short of a disaster could have interrupted my sleep. The initial dinner conversation has given me several ideas on how to structure a learning program for Laura and the children on board. I will start work on it in the morning.

Afternoon, Monday 29 March

I have developed some ideas for our tuition. Laura agrees these sessions should be feasible and fun, with plenty of time left in the day for reading, sewing, conversing with other passengers, attending to personal hygiene, and basic cleaning of our cabins, whilst giving us ample opportunity to enjoy the voyage. Between them, Uncle Mark and Captain Christopher have a comprehensive knowledge of the world, of India, of ships, of Tenerife and St Helena, the night sky, ropes, ship building, winds and currents! If they are willing to share this knowledge, our lessons will be based around these topics, the exact content worked out as we go along.

The missionary families have agreed to take responsibility for organising Divine Services and providing additional Sunday school instruction for the children. Laura and I have offered our assistance if required. Between the crew and passengers, multiple Indian and Chinese languages, French, and Latin, as well as English, are spoken. Midweek singing sessions will be based around folk songs as well as hymns, with the young men encouraged to provide deeper voices for harmony. Several of the crew enjoy playing flutes and other instruments, so we will not lack appropriate accompaniment to ensure we remain in tune! The ship's cook has agreed to allow us time in the galley, weather permitting, to bake some favourite desserts so that we can mark children's birthdays. The young single men will organise some basic keep fit classes to be held each morning on the open deck as long as it is fine. The women will spend regular time with each other, exchanging information, sewing, knitting, or working on other craft, reading, and recounting our life stories. Meantime, the men seem happy to play chess or discuss 'men's business.' Uncle Mark has been asked to develop a series of talks on India for the young gentlemen about to take up positions in colonial outposts throughout that country. They have been beneficiaries of the training offered by the East India Company college. The school recently relocated to new purpose-built buildings on Hertford Heath. The young men report that formalised training has given them confidence, enabling a more consistent approach to duties wherever they may be posted to work for the Company. Their education is impressive: targeted classes and lectures focus on history, mathematics, the classics, the political economy, and the law. Arabic, Urdu, and Bengali are amongst the wide range of languages offered. The young men appear to have had no difficulty absorbing the basic structures of the language that will predominate in the area of proposed service.

Captain Christopher has given us permission to look around the ship in the company of the second mate, Charles Le Gaillais, who has been directed to answer our questions and show us how to use the telescope. He has a pronounced French accent, so we will have to listen carefully. Unless we hit inclement weather overnight, we hope to do this tomorrow. We have been advised to select appropriate footwear and reminded that when on exposed decks, to prevent accidental slips and falls, we need to keep one hand on the ship at all times. Whilst attending any or all of these events is not mandated, Laura and I find that it gives structure to the day. Any 'homework' as a result of information we have received from the various experts travelling on this craft, can most easily be completed in the morning immediately after breakfast.

Thursday 1 April, 1813

Today is April Fool's Day, traditionally a day for practical jokes and hoaxes. However, I feel I have been the fool. Laura and I had a little tiff earlier in the week, over something so minor I have forgotten what started it. As far as we are able on a relatively small ship, we have elected to spend a couple of days undertaking separate activities. Uncle Mark and Aunt Dorothy have wisely left us to resolve our quarrel. I have spent the last two days on my own, with meals brought to my cabin, as I feel unable to join anyone to engage in idle chatter. I am missing Elizabeth's wise counsel. Even when we did not agree on certain matters, we know each other so well that we rarely retired before agreeing on a way forward. Unfortunately, Laura's constitution is of a different nature, so that we were unable to reconcile immediately.

I have been thinking about my family every time I open my sea chest and use the writing box or my timepiece. I need time alone to nourish my spirit and am thankful that I am not sharing a cabin. My lack of gratitude is something I need to work on. It does not accurately reflect on the person I believe that I am. This afternoon I plan to go on deck and find somewhere sheltered so that I can read a chapter or two from *Pride and Prejudice*. As with the contents of the books, the author's pseudonym is likely ironic, as most books are authored by men. I have been remiss in writing my journal. We are now two weeks into our voyage and establishing a routine of sorts. After breakfast I spend some time cleaning my cabin. We have been able to wash our shifts and rags. They dried much faster than I had anticipated, in no small part due to the excellent winds we have been experiencing over the last couple of days. I feel as though I am getting my sea legs. Until now, we have been fortunate to have experienced a steady passage with no storms or excessive swelling of the sea.

Sunday 4 April, 1813

My prayers have been answered. Laura and I are again on good terms and ready to continue with our learning in the morning. Time away from each other will be built into the lesson plans.

Early evening, Monday 12 April, 1813

This morning, I had an experience like no other. My new friend, Rachel, a missionary travelling to India with her husband and young children, gave birth to a baby before time. The baby's arrival was explosive and shocking, and my first experience of a birth. There was a suddenness to the event that caused difficulty realizing it, giving it an air of dreadful mystery. The baby gasped twice and died. I held Rachel's hand and gently swept the hair away from her eyes. I gave her a towel so she could cry into it. There were practicalities involved in getting rid of all the water and wet towels and taking out the bedding to be washed and dried on deck. I found some dry clothing and assisted Rachel to put on fresh clothes. As the cabin is used by several families and there is only a small partition separating it from the single men's cabin, I was also watching to ensure no one entered whilst all this was occurring. Dorothy was practical, wrapping up the baby and giving it to Rachel whilst waiting for the afterbirth to be delivered. Rather than Rachel delivering a beautiful child to be loved, birth and death were almost simultaneous.

I was trying to comfort Rachel by holding her hand, but realised in the moment that this was totally inadequate. I felt that I had not earned the trust Rachel had placed in me to be present. It opened my eyes to the harsh reality of giving birth on a ship, with so little privacy and lack of dignity. A time for joy was a cause of deep sadness. I reflected that essentially good people are not immune from harsh lessons. I thought about the fleeting, arbitrary nature of life and how we need to trust in something bigger than ourselves to give meaning to the event. Until now, I had not given much consideration to people outside my own family. I had not recognised the practicalities, possible dangers and unknowns associated with carrying and delivering a baby. I had not thought how a death at sea condemns that person to be returned to the sea, so that there is no physical grave one can visit or mourn. I could not imagine how to explain a dead baby, who may have been longed for, to its brothers and sisters. I feel I need to spend some time with Dorothy, a woman who possesses great wisdom despite her relative youth. I realize how little life experience I have had with grief and loss as an adult. Losing Mama as a child was different as I was largely shielded from it by my older siblings. Seeing the hanged men and hearing about public executions and even the murders of the Marr family were all somewhat removed from me.

I offered to sit with Rachel in silent vigil and to let her speak if and when she wished. I was able to bring her nourishment that was specially prepared in the galley. Rachel is appreciative of my offer to care for her older children, as it will enable her to have some private time with her husband. Later this morning, the children will be able to look at and touch the baby who has been named William Henry. His birth and death have been reported to Captain Christopher, who is responsible for recording in the ship's log the exact position of the ship at the time of death. There will be a small solemn service for the infant tomorrow before he is consigned to the sea.

This evening, in the privacy of my cabin, I take out my new book of 'Practical Prayers and the Gospels,' a generous farewell gift from the St George-in-the-East parishioners. There is a bell embossed on the leather cover and an extensive index at the back.

I reflect on Matthew 5:4:

'Blessed are they that mourn: for they shall be comforted.'

Chapter 7

Letter to Elizabeth
Tuesday 13 April, 1813

My dear Elizabeth,

I am writing to tell you that I am well. My days have been filled with activities, so I have neglected to write before this. There are ships leaving Tenerife for England, so this letter will be put into a mail bag for you. I am hopeful that you will receive it in the not-too-distant future. Our estimated date of arrival in Tenerife is in two days' time, on Maundy Thursday. It has been the most extraordinary experience of Lent. The journal you gifted to me has been a most useful way to keep a record of, and reflection on, all we have been doing, although recent days have been tinged with sadness.

There are only a small number of women on board the ship. Yesterday, early in the morning, I was asked by one of the young mothers I have befriended, Rachel, to come to her cabin that she shares with many others on the lower deck. She requested that I hold her hand, as she expected to deliver a baby. It was my first experience of a birth and a rather shocking one for all present. Aunt Dorothy took charge of the event, as she is experienced in attending labouring mothers on the Isle of Man. She ensured there was plenty of hot boiled water and soap. She lathered her hands up to the elbows, asking me to take care of her new wedding ring. A length of oiled cloth was placed under a clean bed sheet to protect the mattress. The lack of space was challenging, with only a crude partition separating the family area from the single men's quarters. Despite the swelling of Rachel's abdomen suggesting she was well advanced with her child, this was not actually the case. After a very short while, she gave a loud cry, whilst gripping my hand tightly. This was almost immediately followed by an explosive push, expelling without warning, a tiny infant covered in a caul. His birth was accompanied by a huge volume of fluid that soaked all the available sheets and towels. I had not realised the human body could contain so much water. Such was the force by which the baby was born, the cord was torn from his body. Thankfully, the afterbirth was expelled soon afterward without incident. We were fortunate the ship was experiencing a period of calm, as I cannot imagine the chaos if we had been in roiling seas, or in total darkness.

The poor baby took a couple of gasps before lying still, any sign of life abandoning it in a moment. It was a perfectly formed little boy, but so tiny. His nails were like small pearls. Blue veins were visible on his body. His eyes were tightly closed. He was covered in a white waxy substance Dorothy calls vernix, that protects the skin and a very fine hair that Dorothy explained is lanugo. Its purpose is to keep the vernix in place, and it ensures that the baby stays warm whilst still inside its mother. Dorothy explained that it usually disappears before birth in mature babies. His head seemed disproportionately large, due to his early birth. Rachel was understandably dreadfully upset. She will have to wear binding to ensure her milk does not come through. Between us, we spent time comforting her, encouraging her to hold her small son. As is the custom, he has been named William, after the ship, and Henry his middle name, after the captain. He was washed before being wrapped in a white muslin cloth with just his face visible, so that his older brothers and sisters were permitted to look at him prior to the funeral service.

William's funeral was a solemn occasion. His body was wrapped in a small sail, with weights sewn into the cloth. The crew and passengers gathered on the upper deck, Rachel being supported by her husband, whilst I ensured her young children did not get into mischief. The service followed the Book of Common Prayer, with words modified to reflect the burial at sea:

We therefore commit his body to the deep, to be turned into corruption, looking for the resurrection of the body (when the sea shall give up her dead,) and the life of the world to come, through our Lord Jesus Christ; who at his coming shall change our vile body, that it may be like his glorious body, according to the mighty working whereby he is able to subdue all things unto himself.

At this moment, William's body travelled from under the flag into the sea with all on deck bowing their heads.

I know this is not something we would customarily discuss, but our distance compels me to put things in writing that perhaps are more appropriately shared as part of delicate conversation. On a happier note, I was pleased and grateful that you were able to overcome your initial opposition to my travels, and hope that you are now fully recovered from your sickness. I enjoyed the company on the stagecoach journey, but was thankful I remembered the feather cushion that you kindly gave to me, as one feels every single bump on the road. My position within the carriage was superior to the travel conditions experienced by the hardy travellers on the top of the coach. I ate some delicious meals in Guildford, and Portsmouth, all the more enjoyed as they were prepared by someone else. Once Lent concludes, I am assured our diet will contain meat as well as fish, although Uncle Mark has warned me that the further from land we travel, the less variety will be on offer, with a reliance on salted meat. Our breakfast on Easter Sunday will include dyed boiled eggs, as was the custom for early Christians of Mesopotamia. Uncle Mark has previously visited the Church of the Immaculate Conception: Iglesia de Nuestra Senora de la Concepcion, on Tenerife. It has an impressive bell tower. The original building dates back to the 16th century, but several earthquakes meant the church had to be reconstructed with completion a mere 24 years ago. We intend to take part in a service on Easter Sunday.

My cabin is small but sufficient for my needs. It is vastly superior to the accommodation provided for lower deck passengers. I have a single wooden bunk with raised sides. There is space underneath it for storage. When the weather is fine, we take mattresses out to air on the deck. Ship's rules require regular cleaning of the cabin to discourage vermin, bed bugs and other parasites. The crew try to keep the ship smelling as fresh as possible. A red-hot iron is dipped in a pail of tar, causing smoke and steam to make the worst odours less apparent. Different areas of the ship are cleaned daily, with the lower deck scraped twice a week. Sea water is made available for all lower deck passengers. They – and the crew – are encouraged to wash their clothes weekly. It is advisable for the lower deck passengers and the sailors to have a spare set of clothing at the time of boarding, as access to sea chests is only possible when the ship is at anchor. When the ship is at full capacity, belongings cannot be retrieved until the final port of disembarkation is reached.

Despite the long voyages, with limited chances for personal hygiene, the sailors maintain a smart appearance. The majority are clean shaven or have very neatly trimmed facial hair. The discipline on board is strict, but the crew appears to respect the captain. The surgeon, Samuel Bishop, is a good friend of Adam and Isabella. He also has skills as a carpenter and can easily adapt to either role, if anyone is unfortunate enough to require his services. Although we have seen a few ships in the distance, we have not encountered or been apprehended by any who do not have our welfare at heart. However, *Sir William Pulteney* is painted like a warship and carries many guns secured behind gunports that emerge from the lower deck. During the height of the Napoleonic wars, ships would usually travel in a group, so I am a little unclear as to why we seem to be travelling without this additional protection. It is something

I will ask Captain Christopher when we next dine with him. The ship curves inwards as it narrows towards the highest deck for added stability. Captain Christopher told us that this feature is known as a tumblehome.

At one end of my cabin are two small shelves with a crude plank placed horizontally in place of battens. I can put my books and journal in this space. There is a tiny window, more of a porthole, that lets in natural light, but it cannot be opened. Small vents permit fresh air and light to enter. During turbulence or storms, they are tightly shut to prevent seawater from coming in. This immediately plunges anyone without a porthole into complete darkness. I can usually read and write my journal without needing extra light. The use of oil lamps in the cabins is strictly limited. In rough weather we are not permitted to use them because of the danger of fire. My sea chest takes up considerable room, but it is placed so that it resists moving when the ship rolls. To have access to a change of clothes if required, is much appreciated. Getting dressed can be difficult with the need to brace oneself in the space between the bunk bed and the small door. If the ship encounters a decent swell, bracing minimises tipping onto the floor or becoming entangled in clothing.

At the other end of the cabin, is a small cupboard containing a chamber pot with a lid. It is officially emptied twice daily. If I choose to empty it myself, it is a chore that requires discretion and an appreciation of the wind direction! Above this cupboard is a triangular shaped piece of wood that fits into the corner of the cabin. There is a large, circular hole in the wood for a small porcelain basin with deep sides. A smaller hole accommodates a mug. I rarely use soap as it is difficult to achieve an adequate lather. The pitcher of water sits just above on a small shelf, with two horizontal wooden bars keeping the jug in place. We are given two generous allocations of sea water per day that suffices for both washing one's person and cleaning teeth and items of clothing. Sea water is also used to wash dishes. Fresh water is allocated sparingly and can only be used for drinking. When it rains, buckets and other containers are placed strategically around the deck to collect the fresh water.

There are wooden pegs affixed to my cabin wall where one may hang garments. It is also advisable to spare a hand to hold onto a bolt when washing to prevent an accidental fall. Drying of garments is permitted on areas of the deck if fine. To exit the cabin, one is required to step over a horizontal beam which also serves to keep water out in the event of poor weather, although I have yet to test its adequacy. We have to provide our own bed linen which is something I had not considered. However, Uncle Mark had anticipated this and has given me sufficient for my needs.

Our meals are eaten at odd times. A light breakfast of freshly made bread or biscuit served with butter and jam is followed by a more substantial lunch which is served either on the deck or in Uncle Mark's cabin. Dinner, which can be as early as four o'clock in the afternoon, depending somewhat on the weather conditions, is also taken in Uncle Mark's generous sized cabin where he has access to a dining table. Once or twice a week, the meal is served in the officer's wardroom. The ship has livestock, and animals will be killed to provide meat after Lent. Our food was relatively fresh for the first few days after leaving England, but is becoming less palatable as we are now more dependent on dried foods. We eat cheese, salted fish, dried peas and beans, and on occasion oats and a ship's biscuit. Occasionally, a sailor will catch a fresh fish, which we have enjoyed. Passengers on the lower deck are responsible for cooking their own meals in the galley, as well as bringing their own provisions on board ship. The further we get from land, the poorer the quality of food. We have been advised to stock up with fresh oranges when we get to Tenerife. I am thankful that we are only going as far as St Helena, as I cannot imagine travelling to India or China, particularly on the lower deck.

Our speed is approximately 4-5 knots averaging 120 miles a day, but that is dependent on weather conditions. After passing the Straits of Gibraltar, the Canary Current pushed us southwest towards Tenerife. Once we depart from the Canary Islands, the trade winds will assist our passage. Captain Christopher has been generous with his time, giving Laura and me a lesson on basic navigation skills, that have been acquired over the centuries by sailors crossing the world's oceans. He is going to teach us about the night sky, when there is a clear night. The millions of stars and the brilliant moon, that seems so close sometimes that you feel you could touch it, are a nightly miracle of which I will never tire. The weather on board ship has been kind to us so far, with the exception of our journey through the English Channel, where the swell of the sea made for an uncomfortable first night. The prevailing winds that blow around Dorset and Devon have caused ships to be wrecked on the rocks closer to shore. We navigated this part of the journey without incident as far as I am aware, although the crew may have had a different interpretation of events. The weather is getting hotter as we travel further south, exceeding the temperatures we experience in mid-summer in London, but the air is fresh with a cool breeze that blows after dark. We are adjusting to the warmer temperatures by shedding some of our underclothing. On occasions, in the privacy of our cabins, Laura and I just wear a simple shift so that we do not overheat.

Captain Christopher is a great raconteur, so Laura and I are being educated daily on the finer points of sailing on a comparatively small vessel. We have great confidence that we will be safely delivered to St Helena, although I do not envy the remainder of the passengers who have many more weeks to go, before reaching their final destinations. I will write to you again once we have crossed the Equator. Our daily routine does not permit much variation, and I do not wish to bore you with repetition.

Please give my good wishes to all the family.

I remain, your loving sister,

Katherine.

Chapter 8

Journal extracts
Wednesday 27 May, 1813

Today is my 19th birthday. This time last year, barely two weeks had passed since the assassination of our prime minister, Spencer Percival. He had entered the lobby of the House of Commons when a man – John Bellingham – pulled out a pistol and shot him. It was a shocking event that overshadowed any other news. Twelve children became fatherless that day. Two days before my birthday, another disaster was announced by the town crier and published in all the London newspapers. The Felling mine explosion in northern England left 96 people dead. The explosion was attributed to firedamp, but whether the event encouraged a review of safety at the mine is doubtful. I am hopeful that this year will be memorable for many positive reasons, where I sense I am at the start of a completely different life.

Laura and I have been given permission to use the galley and want to try and be as creative as possible with our limited fare. We are approximately 5 days from passing Ascension Island. The occasional monotony of our sea voyage was considerably relieved when we reached Tenerife. We arrived very late on Maundy Thursday, 15 April, and departed on Easter Monday. I was able to ensure my letter to Elizabeth was safely in the mail bag of a ship that left for England late on Easter Sunday. We were given some liberty to explore the Island of Tenerife in the company of Uncle Mark and Aunt Dorothy, and learned some of its recent history.

The resident population observes Holy Week – Semana Santa – with various processions and gatherings. We enjoyed watching the religious ceremony on Good Friday, with Tenerife natives dressed in colourful costumes. Mount Teide was impressive. Just over a hundred years ago, in 1706, an eruption destroyed the main port of Garachico. A smaller eruption in 1789 left a black magma carpet of ropey lava on its south side. The native population have great respect for the mountain, never able to be sure that it won't once again come to life. A local tradition is to regard Teide as the prison of Guyaota, the devil, with eruptions attributed to him trying to get free. We obviously hoped there would be no such eruptions whilst we were enjoying the island. Uncle Mark spent time educating us on the newer theories, known as Plutonism, that are gaining more credibility in clarifying how islands such as the Canaries and St Helena were formed by underwater volcanos. The old beliefs in Neputism, where the earth was covered with a great sea from which it gradually emerged, as for example in the Noah's flood traditionally taught in churches, are losing favour.

Laura and I spent an hour at the beach, enjoying the warm water and looking at the fish. We took off our shoes and enjoyed the feeling of walking on hot sand. I had never before seen fish in such glorious colours and could have watched them for hours. We ate meals of local seafood and purchased bags of oranges and lemons for our onward voyage. I declined to eat goose barnacles, but enjoyed Uncle Mark's recounting of the legends associated with this delicacy. Shipwrecked sailors have been sustained by eating barnacles, sometimes scraping them off the backs of dead whales. Bearing in mind Laura's first encounter with the seafood, I had no hesitation in asking Uncle Mark how best to remove the legs and shells from prawns before eating! To experience the sun and fresh air was a great pleasure, especially after a month of mixed weather on a constantly rolling boat. Rachel, who lost her baby in such tragic circumstances, felt well enough to leave the ship with her husband and engage in the pleasures of the beach with their three children.

Our departure from the Canary Islands invoked mixed feelings. For the first time, I had a real sense of having left England behind. The different languages, the warm to hot weather, the fresh seafood and the beautiful fish, all contributed to a feeling of lightness and relief. London is a world away, but so is my family. We continued our journey, before anchoring at the tropical paradise of Cape Verde, an archipelago in the mid-Atlantic, on Wednesday 5 May. The white sand was dazzling. Combined with the deep blue azure of the sea, it was a rich palette of colour unsurpassed in my life until now. As we approached the islands, Aunt Dorothy pointed out an enormous turtle. We followed its path for quite a few minutes in the clear sea. Our ship was at anchor for about 72 hours, before leaving the isles early on the morning of Friday 7 May. We were accompanied by a pod of dolphins that alternately swam in parallel to us or rushed ahead, their graceful bodies a series of silver arcs over the waves. Captain Christopher told us we were roughly 350 miles from mainland Africa and 1000 miles north of the Equator. The sun was very hot. To prevent sunburn, parading on deck in the middle of the day is discouraged. I was more than happy to return to my cabin, as I find the sun also induces a sense of stupor or insensibility that can only be relieved by a period of sleep. Further supplies of drinking water were brought on board whilst we were anchored off Cape Verde, so our daily allocation was increased. Our diet has also become more interesting now that we can once again partake of meat.

Captain Christopher took advantage of the Canary Current on the approach to Cape Verde. Due to his navigational skills, we were able to avoid the worst effects of the Doldrums as we approached the Equator, by sailing further west. We will not see land now until our approach to Ascension Island.[91] Uncle Mark, Lieutenant Colonel Skelton, and Captain Christopher have kept us entertained in the evenings, when we sit down for an early dinner.

Before reaching Cape Verde, Captain Christopher permitted us to view the night sky through his telescope. He pointed out the main stars and planets. The Big Dipper constellation looks like a large saucepan. Tracing its line of pointer stars, one locates the North Star, or Polaris, at the tip of the handle of the smaller Little Dipper constellation. He permitted us to take a reckoning using his sextant. Following the curve of the handle of the Big Dipper, Captain Christopher showed us Arcturus, the brightest star in the sky. He said that Native Americans believe the bowl of the Big Dipper is a giant bear, the hunters chasing it formed by the stars of the handle. Other cultures identify it as a wagon or plough. He showed us diamonds and kites and many other constellations whose names were not familiar. The beauty of the stars in the midnight blue of the sky is something rarely seen in London. Even the moon is hard pressed to make much of an impression. On this voyage, we have watched the moon rise as the sun sets, images I will remember for the remainder of my life.

We reached the Equator on 15 May. We were invited to participate in what was referred to as an Equatorial baptism. At noon, Neptune, graced by a long, white beard, with flowing robes and a trident in hand, arrived on deck. He was accompanied by a retinue of dishevelled-looking characters with their faces painted red. His bedraggled wife had blackened teeth, but took little part in the proceedings. Those sailors who had not previously 'crossed the line' were brought one by one to the deck. They were obliged to sit on a plank that straddled a large tub filled with seawater. Their faces were covered in tar and grease, then scraped with a metal hook in place of a razor. At the conclusion of this 'shave,' the hapless novice was immersed in the sea water until his struggles quietened, by which time he was hauled out of the tub and lay on the deck, in some cases vomiting sea water that had been inadvertently swallowed during his ordeal. The drama was performed to beating 'drums.' Sailors had sets of saucepans and their lids for the purpose, commandeered from the galley or ship's kitchen, that produced a cacophony of sound painful to the ears. Whilst the tradition is intended to be humorous, one could not help feeling that the reluctant participants were relieved to survive the initiation. Laura and I found the whole ceremony rather distasteful. Indeed, Captain Christopher barely tolerates it, as he recalled a similar incident resulted in damages being paid to an irate gentleman, who sued once he reached Bombay in 1802. Whilst the sum was nominal, culpability was not.

Chapter 9

Letter to Elizabeth
Wednesday 14 June – continued on 28 June, 1813

Dear Elizabeth,

Last night we had a full moon that seemed enormous over the sea. It was not so much the man in the moon but his entire extended family. The reflected light was so bright I was able to write an entry in my journal using its illumination alone. We are a week away from arriving at St Helena. The weather has been very hot, and at times all I have worn in my cabin is my shift. I will start this letter whilst we are still sailing, but plan to finish it on land. Mr and Mrs Neptune appeared when we crossed the Equator on 15 May. The celebrations were enjoyed by the children, despite the loudness of the affair. Sailors crossing for the first time had their beards removed and were soaked by buckets of sea water. They then underwent ear piercing to mark the occasion, and received a gold hoop earring. I think the majority of paying passengers were relieved when it was over and that all appeared to survive the experience!

Since leaving the Cape Verde Islands, we have seen an extraordinary variety of fish. Just as we passed Santo Antao with its rocky shore, a fin-backed whale breached the water. A flock of petrels, or Mother Carey's chickens, were spotted flying in formation. Sailors believe these birds are a portent of storms and it is unlucky to kill them as each carries the soul of a drowned sailor.

This superstition is extended to a belief Mother Carey's husband is Davy Jones, a metaphor for the oceanic abyss and final resting place of drowned sailors and travellers. A few days later, we did indeed encounter a heavy storm and were quite concerned about the bolts of lightning, as they appeared very close. The decks were cleared, and we were confined to our cabins for a couple of days. On emerging, we saw an extraordinary sight: hundreds of flying fish took off almost in front of us. We could see dark fast-moving shadows under the water that occasionally breached the surface, returning below the waves so quickly we could not identify the species. The wings of the flying fish are distinctive. Many are tinged with pink. Sadly, for some of the fish, escaping the underwater hunters pushed them into the path of Man of War birds. These creatures are predominantly black, but with deeply forked tails and long, hooked beaks. They take the fish on the wing. Other birds we spotted included albatross and different species of boobies, some with vivid, coral-red feet and bright-blue beaks. The sailors caught a bonito that was cooked and served to try a mouthful. I found the flavour too fishy for my palate. Two days later, one of the young boys managed to land a juvenile shark. We were all given a small piece. The texture was firm, but tasty, and a welcome change from salted meats. At various times we have seen dolphins and tuna. Yesterday – 11 June – our boat sailed into a mass of Portuguese men of war. These jellyfish-like creatures have long tendrils that can inflict a painful sting. A few were a great deal larger than the others, and tinged pink.

Laura and I are much more knowledgeable about the finer points of sailing than when we set off, but we both long to see land again. Uncle Mark spent one evening telling us about exotic animals that have visited St Helena over the years, as well as endemic species, and pest animals. There was a brief visit from a rhinoceros in 1515, en route from India to Lisbon, but whether it landed on the Island is unknown. It was later immortalised in a woodcut by the artist Durer. Imported feral goats run wild, eating and destroying native flora. The Island also has more than its fair share of rats. Thankfully there are no snakes. Interesting species of bugs and insects with colourful names include a blushing snail, a spiky yellow woodlouse, and a vibrant blue leafhopper. The seas around St Helena are full of fish. Large numbers of whales provide fuel for lighting, soap, and candles. The oil is also used to lubricate machines, in making varnish, and in the manufacture of textiles and rope. Whalebone is used to make stays, chess pieces, keys for pianos and even some children's toys. Since 1802, license fees for whalers were abandoned and St Helena became a free port for the industry.[92] Donkeys are widespread since their introduction just over a hundred years ago. They are used for transport of people and goods, as are yoked bullock carts, the latter harnessed for heavier goods and travel into the interior. Many of the wealthier islanders travel by horse, but an eccentric, Miss Polly Mason, rides on an ox!

Chapter 10

**Letter to Elizabeth
Tuesday 28 September, 1813**

Dear Elizabeth,

It has been three months since we landed on St Helena and my life has been a whirl of activity. I have scarcely had time to put pen to paper. Writing has been neglected, apart from copying some favourite passages from the bible into my journal, to aid in prayer and reflection. It is my hope that this extremely long letter will go some way to assure you that I am settling well into my new home. I continue to enjoy Laura's companionship, which I believe to be reciprocated. Any education she and I may partake in is entirely focused on learning more about the history, geography, geology, the flora and fauna on land and in the sea, as well as Island politics and everyday life in this extraordinary place. St Helena is unique in its location, with no other island so isolated from any continent. Different worlds come together in a tiny package: whether it be the east meeting the west as evidenced by the different races that make up the resident and visiting population; the exotic goods that are available; the different foods; the military versus civilians; the class system which mirrors but is fundamentally different from the England we are familiar with; slavery – one could go on for ever! Please share all, or part of my letter, with anyone in the family who may show an interest. Give your girls lots of hugs and kisses from me. This afternoon the weather is quite unpleasant and not likely to clear for a couple of days. Laura is accompanying her father and Aunt Dorothy on some official duties for the remainder of the week. Isabella and her children (more later) are indisposed, and Adam's services are very much in demand. I have plenty of time on my hands to bring you up to date with my life!

The final and longest leg of our journey, far from Europe and the African continents, was in many respects, the most interesting. As we travelled alongside exotic creatures that make their homes in tropical waters, I was astounded by the exquisite range of colours to be found in Nature's palette. The silvery hues of flying fish with strange wings, pink-tinged, are an extraordinary sight. They leap out of the water in their hundreds, to escape sea dwelling predators that are visible only as dark shadows. Their freedom is an illusion, with many birds just waiting to catch them on the wing. The purples and pinks of men-of-war jellyfish, with their deadly tentacles like strings of pearls, contrast with drab-coloured but curiously named Mother Carey's chickens or the flashing silver of dolphins racing our ship. The magnificent white albatross, with their massive wingspan, command seas that are turquoise or aquamarine closer to land, shading to the deeper blue, green, and occasionally black expanse of the ocean. The gamut of colour continues with the verdant green of tropical islands fringed by dazzling white sand. The millions of stars that light up the night, like diamonds lying on black velvet, are becoming more familiar, as are the myths and legends associated with the night sky. Whilst rarely visible in polluted London, the deep orange-red of the rising or setting moon, viewed when we were closer to land, at times feels as though you could stretch out an arm and touch it. The purples, pinks, oranges, mauves, reds, and navy-blue colours of the sunrise and sunsets we have seen have brought home to me how of all the possible senses one might lose, to be blind would be truly confronting. The other remarkable thing is how quickly darkness comes upon one in the tropics. We do not have the hours of twilight that we experience in London.

Sir William Pulteney arrived at St Helena in the late afternoon of 22 June, 1813. On our approach to St Helena from the northwest, the immediate impression was of a place devoid of colour. The sea had a noticeable swell, with brightly coloured fish in a range of hues and sizes, clearly visible. Hundreds of seabirds added to the cacophony of sound that was almost overwhelming after our relatively silent voyage. The birds are predominantly white, but several have darker colours on their heads and wings. The different sizes suggest a variety of species. Unfortunately, the wind carried a disagreeable odour that seemed to emerge from the mist. It brought to mind the London fogs rising from the Thames and the darkly brooding hulks of ships holding unfortunate prisoners, before their transport to the other end of the world. I cannot begin to imagine what their journeys would be like, compared to the relative comforts we have experienced aboard *Sir William Pulteney*. I was momentarily sorry that I no longer had my nosegay!

Perpendicular cliffs hang precariously. Vertical thousand-foot drops finish as black and grey rocks pounded by angry, grey and white seas. I have since learned that, in the early days of settlement, rocks were rolled from the tops of these cliffs as a very effective deterrent to any persons who thought to invade the Island! There are no gently shelving beaches to offset the starkness and terror of unleashed forces, where waves travel uninterrupted for thousands of miles, before smashing on the shores. Traditionally our church teaches that rocks, compromising most of the Earth's surface, were formed from the crystallisation of minerals in the early Earth's oceans, such as occurred following Noah's flood. During the voyage, Uncle Mark introduced us to the modern theory, that Earth's rocks were formed through magmatic or volcanic activity. The seas are rich with dozens of species of exotic and edible fish, as well as whales and turtles. The islanders enjoy meals of fish and rice as part of their regular repast. Whale oil is used as fuel, as wood is scarce. Some fish can be caught from land, but a larger catch is guaranteed when using small boats to reach deeper water. The largest fish, a whale shark, is a gentle creature that survives on minute sea creatures. We must wait until December to see one. No-one knows where they go when they leave the seas surrounding the Island.

As the ship came around a point to the northwest of the Island, we had our first view of Jamestown that is seated in a narrow V-shaped valley. It sits between two lofty mountains I learned are Rupert and Ladder Hills. As we travelled towards the half-moon-shaped bay, one of the very few landing areas on the entire Island, the settlement emerged in a cluster of white buildings with red rooves. Grey stone buildings on the harbour became apparent. A church spire was visible. Even at this late hour, soldiers were parading in bright scarlet jackets close to the wharf. Cannon and other iron weaponry were clearly visible on prominent rocks, contributing to the impressive and formidable fortifications. The wharf is a continuous wall, strewn with gun emplacements. Dorothy and Laura were yet to join us, hence Uncle Mark continued to point out features of interest. The most direct approach to the Ladder Fort from the town is via an almost vertical plane. This holds a rope ladder that fit, young military men are to be seen ascending and descending, frequently carrying supplies, as though it is no more challenge than a few stairs.

We anchored approximately a cable's length from the shore and were treated to a remarkable sunset. The buildings and surrounding hills were bathed in hues of gold and rose that illuminated the harbour and softened its outline. A decision was made to disembark the following morning due to the lateness of the hour. With the sails furled and the two anchors located in the bow and stern holding fast, we were invited for our final meal with Captain Christopher.

The sun was still low in the sky the following morning, when I took the opportunity to walk on the deck and take in what I could see of St Helena. I was soon joined by other passengers, equally excited to have arrived at our destination. The island gives the impression of a giant figure lying in repose: two peaks represent its feet on the left. A central peak, that suggests folded hands, marks the middle. Its head is another massive rock. A less kind interpretation, as expressed by another passenger who is to continue his journey to India, is that the island resembles a forbidding castle, arising from a perpendicular rugged rock; a barren wasteland, endlessly battered by large waves, denuded of trees, shrubs, or herbage. It brought to mind a vaguely remembered story about St Barbara in 3rd century Italy, who was imprisoned in a tower. The story has been rewritten by the Brothers Grimm in their book *Children's and Household Tales* that Laura received as a first-edition gift at Christmas last year after its formal publication on 20 December. She has generously loaned me the book and I am enjoying reading a tale each day. Some of the stories are quite shocking and are possibly more suited to adults than children![93] I have since learned that St Helena has a rich mould of soil. It sustains a great number and variety of exotic plants that have been augmented by introduced species, some of which thrive. Others have been more challenging to sustain, because of the somewhat unusual climate. Defying the latitude, the tropical temperatures are modified by the southeast trade winds and ocean currents from the Antarctic. Captain Christopher advised that the temperature is benign, with little variation between the seasons, or even days and nighttime. As a consequence, I have started making clothes that are more appropriate to the climate and prevailing fashions.

A gentle rain started to fall, but did not diminish our excitement at the prospect of stepping out on land for the first time in many weeks. Other ships were lying at anchor in the harbour, their rigging making a rhythmic sound in the gentle wind. The temperature of the air was mild, but not as warm as I had expected from a tropical island. I was glad to be wearing my cape. The mist had yet to clear, and the higher parts of the island were not visible. As we prepared to farewell *Sir William Pulteney*, I observed much activity at the wharf, with several boats or tenders approaching our ship. Before we were permitted to leave our home of the past several months, various personages were piped aboard, with their arrival marked by a shrill whistle from the crew, who were dressed in formal clothing and formed two parallel lines. The welcoming party approached Uncle Mark and Lieutenant Skelton, both of whom were in ceremonial dress, as the initial formalities of greeting the new governor of St Helena were undertaken. The current governor, Sir Alexander Beatson, welcomed Uncle Mark and Aunt Dorothy, Laura, me, and the Skeltons. Before any of us were permitted to disembark, the main medical officer checked the papers supplied by Captain Christopher and Dr Samuel Bishop, the ship's surgeon. Each individual on board needed to be of sound health and unlikely to bring disease to the Island. The boatmen who came out to greet us landed us at the Lower Steps on the wharf with remarkable skill. We stepped ashore confidently with dry feet and in an orderly fashion, whilst preserving our modesty. Uncle Mark had indicated he would lodge at Government House in the town. It was likely the intensive handover of duties from Sir Alexander would require working sessions that went well into the night. Aunt Dorothy, Laura, and I, and all our baggage, were conveyed to Plantation House, some three miles inland. The Skeltons remained in Jamestown.

There is a suggestion a ball may be held at Plantation House which has filled Laura and me with great excitement! However, it will no doubt have to be planned carefully. As recently as April 12, Rev Jones, speaking from the pulpit, complained of profanation of the Sabbath on 4 April. On board the East Indiaman *Arniston*,[94] an elegant tiffin was given and a splendid dance held in the evening. There was an exhibition of conjurers and other entertainment, that the Chaplain denounced as being attended by an alarming number of respectable inhabitants.

After disembarking, we crossed over a moat via a drawbridge, travelling along behind defences and so into town. We declined a lift in a horse and trap as it was good to stretch our legs after such a long voyage, and the slower pace enabled us to take in our surroundings. We were then transferred to a heavy cart drawn by yoked bullocks, the principal beasts of burden of the Island. Our belongings had been placed inside it by a small posse of muscular-looking black men that Laura whispered were slaves. Our way up the hill was through a double row of brilliant green trees, before we reached an arched gateway under a terrace that formed one side of a parade ground. Numerous soldiers in smart red jackets were parading around the large square, muskets held stiffly by their sides. We passed several important looking buildings before approaching The Castle, the government headquarters and administrative offices. The Governor's formal lodging is here also. Next door is the church of St. James. Towards the upper part of the valley, we passed the barracks and a hospital, as well as shops and a series of neatly constructed houses. A dramatic waterfall appeared under the arc of a rainbow. From a certain angle, it is heart-shaped.

Plantation House is the Governor's 'country residence.' It is a further two or three miles inland from Jamestown. Uncle Mark will join us on weekends and at other times. We were fortunate to have fine weather for our arrival. When wet, roads are a quagmire due to the presence of claylike marl that would seriously curtail our getting to know the island. I learned later that in his rare spare time, Adam is interested in discovering more about the properties of this clay to see whether it may be developed into something useful. He has also analysed the properties of lime that is quarried in various parts of the Island. Governor Beatson is preparing to write a book about his time on St Helena and hopes to publish his *Tracts* next year that will include an acknowledgement of Adam.[95]

I was disappointed that Isabella was unable to greet me as I arrived on St Helena. As you know, she had written to me on many occasions suggesting I come out to join her. However, I had the opportunity to visit her and Adam and their four girls for the first time in late June. Unfortunately, they had been unwell. The three girls born on St Helena have an appearance of robustness, but Catherine looks delicate. Isabella sends her love to you and apologises for her tardiness in exchanging letters, but her girls keep her very busy.

I was a little shocked to see Adam. He has aged significantly and looks much older than his thirty-six years. His fair hair has faded to white at his temples, and he has a pronounced bald spot reminiscent of a monk's tonsure, and a slight limp he attributes to an old injury incurred during a long voyage, where their ship was tossed at sea by a violent storm. Fortunately, he no longer has to embark on the challenging sea voyages that your James is still obliged to undertake. As a senior surgeon on the island, his work is diverse, but presumably not without risk. Luckily the Baildon family's move to St Helena was after the measles outbreak of 1807, as the disease did not discriminate by status on the Island. It was thought to have been brought from Cape Town. At least 160 deaths were recorded from 1 March to 1 May, although the true rate was thought to be much higher amongst the slave population. Isabella tells me there were many cases where the individuals have been left permanently incapacitated.

Catherine is now 11, dark haired and olive skinned like her mother, but frail and prone to catching colds. She has a loving personality and takes her responsibilities as the eldest child very seriously. She appears particularly close to her baby sister, Adamina, who at 18 months old is still chubby but running all over the place and keeping Isabella on her toes. Elizabeth will be five on 20 October and is fair like Adam, her hair a mass of untidy curls. She is looking forward to starting school under the auspices of Rev Wilkinson before progressing to the Head School of the East India Company.[96] This school is fee-paying. Elizabeth appears to have an outgoing, dare I say, bold approach to life, and nothing appears to disconcert her. Perhaps not unlike her namesake?! She is quite a chatterbox. Little Isabella, aged 3, enjoys her own company and happily plays in the garden for hours, requiring very little entertainment. She has inherited her mother's dark hair and her father's bright blue eyes which is a striking combination. She is possibly a little delayed in learning to speak in full sentences, but has to compete with her older sisters to be heard!

As an aside about the schools, and more generally about St Helena, occupants are identified as whites, enslaved, and free, as well as Chinese. The stratification of the population has some similarities to the English class system. It is perhaps more conscious, as everyone knows their place in this relatively small society. Formal learning on St Helena has historically been given a high priority. The church was originally responsible for all schooling, with a particular focus on religious education, although I am told that is slowly lessening in influence. Uncle Mark has wasted no time officially establishing a library of which he is the patron. It is for 'the dissemination of information and mass enlightenment of the people,' and will be formally opened on 11 October, and a large crowd will likely attend.

Plantation House is surrounded by fields and hills, and is the finest property on the island. It contains about forty rooms. It was built in 1791, and is surrounded by almost 180 acres of parkland. As we approached it, we observed many of the strange tree-like plants with bunched, fleshy leaves reminding one of cabbages that grow prolifically. Ferns are plentiful. A tree branch with several orange fruits and a few pink blossoms had a grey and red bird sitting on one part of the branch. There are many species of trees, including ones familiar to us: oaks, Scotch firs, and cedars, but also trees from more temperate or tropic climes including Norfolk and Chilean pines. Its elevation above the sea is about 1800 feet, from which there are beautiful views that may be seen from many vantage points as is possible to walk within the grounds shaded from the heat of the tropical sun. Behind the main building is the outline of a church, the 'Country Church,' with its steeple supporting a cross at the top, just visible through the trees.

Land animals include goats, hogs, and sheep. The former have overrun the island and destroyed much of the native vegetation. There is an urgent need to control them. We have seen oxen, cattle, donkeys, pheasants and partridges, turkeys, geese, ducks, and fowls. We spotted a strange black and white native bird that is called a wire bird on account of its legs that are very thin and look like wires. To deter predators from attacking their eggs, which are laid on the ground, they pretend to have a broken wing, to get the attention of a predator and lead them away from the eggs or young. This is a behaviour I have only observed once before in an English peewit. The islanders are very proud of this bird. A variety of colourful but harmless insects, and the cabbage trees, add to the exotic feel. Most larger animals, edible crops, fruit trees, and other farmed produce, were brought onto the island from elsewhere.

Governor Beatson will remain on St Helena for a further three months, to ensure a smooth handover of the duties and responsibilities incumbent upon the Governor. Despite being appointed by the Honourable East India Company, invariably shortened to 'The Company' or even 'Uncle John,' Uncle Mark is required to take an oath of allegiance to the King of England, as part of the elaborate handover from Governor Beatson.

You are never far from my thoughts. I will continue to write this long letter to you after lunch as I am being called to the dining room.

I remain your affectionate sister,

Katherine Rose

Chapter 11

Letter to Elizabeth
Tuesday 28 September, 1813 (continued)

Dear Elizabeth,

I have enjoyed some soup and fresh bread, with fruit for dessert. Laura has not yet returned so I will continue with this letter to you. As with previous letters, please share with any member of the family who may be interested in hearing my news.

That first weekend, after an intensive three days, Uncle Mark joined us as he wished to look at Plantation House and ensure we were comfortable. Even though the residence is barely 20 years old, the construction was not of the standard one might expect for such an important building, partly due to the limited availability of suitable building materials and skills on the Island. He was looking remarkably fresh despite commencing his duties at daybreak and continuing well into the night. I was unsure if it was my imagination, but there was also a sadness present in his demeanour. Laura told me later that Uncle Mark had just learned of the death of a dear friend of his, Major General Sir Barry Close, who had been created a baronet after his return from India. He died a month after *Sir William Pulteney* left Portsmouth. Laura explained that her brother John Barry had been named after him:

'He was a mentor to Father, who acknowledges him in his recently published book on the history of Mysore, India. I was privileged to meet him on several occasions in India as a young child. He was a highly intelligent and ethical man who was very much loved in both his professional and private life and always took my childish engagements with him very seriously.'[97]

Over dinner prepared for us by the resident domestic staff – I am reluctant to call them slaves but sadly that is their status – Uncle Mark told us of some of the most immediate and pressing problems that he will need to prioritise as Governor. He has asked for 150 additional Chinese from the East India Company's factory in that country, as the prohibition on importing slaves has led to a shortage of labour. This will augment the existing numbers of the 650 Chinese who arrived in 1810. A previous governor, Patton, had recommended the Company import Chinese labourers to grow the rural workforce, but understandably the process has been quite slow and has not always progressed smoothly. A little over 18 months ago, in November, 1811, a curfew was imposed on the Chinese labourers, supposedly to control petty crime.

Uncle Mark needs to tighten the regulations regarding feral sheep and goats – the latter potentially overrunning the island – and to discontinue the resident population's reliance on imported food at discounted prices that are expensive and of poorer quality. For example, part of the cargo from our ship was salted beef contained in large barrels in the hold. He gave us a broad overview of his considerable responsibilities and stated he felt his many years of working in India had been an excellent preparation for the role. He is hoping to build on recent initiatives to encourage more production on farming lands. He is petitioning the Honourable East India Company to repeal ancient laws to assist in this. With the Island surrounded by fish, he would like to formalise the fishing industry to ensure that a regular supply of fresh fish is available for all Islanders, including ex-slaves or others currently subject to indentured labour. He thinks the Chinese population would be eager to support this initiative.

A widespread dependence on cheap or illicit alcohol has played no small part in recent social unrest. Uncle Mark has to approach the problems delicately, with a serious rebellion against proposed changes happening as recently as the year before last. The previous governor – Beatson – was forced to inflict severe punishment, including the execution of ring leaders, to regain civil order. In his report about the events in December, 1811, Uncle Mark showed us the extract where Beatson singled out Adam Baildon in despatches as:

'a valuable friend who voluntarily came forward to support me in the hour of danger: and on whose zeal for the public service, as well as personal attachment, I had the most perfect reliance. Doctor Baildon had been on duty in the fort: and had opportunities, some days before the mutiny broke out, of hearing what was going forward. He had, indeed, reason to imagine the danger to which my person was exposed, was greater than I apprehended, for I declined Captain Pritchard's offer to accompany me, and left the fort, on the evening of the mutiny, unarmed, and attended singly by my groom: but the Doctor, suspecting some of those desperate mutineers might attempt my life, armed himself (although, for some days, he had been extremely ill), and, unknown to me, followed; keeping at some distance, and carefully watching if any persons approached me. Nothing, however, occurred; and he arrived at Plantation-house about sun-set, on the 23d of December.

'From this moment, until the termination of the mutiny, he was constantly with me, employed in aiding in preparations for defence, in communicating my orders, in collecting information, and, in short, in discharging, in the most able manner, all the duties of a zealous friend, and an active staff officer. For such distinguished services I feel great pleasure in thus recording my best acknowledgments and thanks; and whilst I discharge this public duty, it is due to Doctor Baildon, that I should recommend him, in the strongest manner to the favour and notice of your Honourable Court. '[98]

Our conversation at the dinner table then turned to the welfare of the slaves and their descendants, whose lives are wretched. The importation of the enslaved was made illegal in 1792. Ten years later, the March 1802 census identified 893 military personnel, 122 families and civil servants, 241 Planters, 227 formerly-enslaved, and 1,029 enslaved: a total population of 2,512. The regular census information is kept in a designated book that enables a quick reference to measure progress on St Helena on a range of measures, including the emancipation of slaves.[99] As the progressive freeing of slaves and the prohibition on slavery takes effect – albeit very slowly, as reliance on slaves is entrenched on the Island – labour shortages are apparent. Older slaves who die or become incapacitated are not replaced. People who seem decent in many other respects, do not appear to have any qualms about owning ex-slaves, or treating them poorly, whereas newcomers to the Island like us have a very different perspective. Isabella and Adam secretly agree with me, but are circumspect due to their social standing. Part of their household includes two black married couples, who between them have three children. One of the larger landowners of the Island, Miss Polly Mason, is known to own six.

Penalties are excessive for even minor transgressions from any slave aged 16 or older.[100] We were horrified to learn that mandated, incremental punishments for men include hundreds of lashes, branding on the forehead, and wearing a 30-pound ball and chain for 12 months. Women receive similar penalties, but face having their ears cut off and branding on the cheeks in addition to the forehead. Repeat offences for both sexes are punishable by death. Governor Beatson had proposed to Council the abolition of slavery on St Helena, but his enlightened move was opposed by the landowners, led by Sir William Doveton. Uncle Mark stated he will be presiding over a trial of Mary Braid next month for the 'wilful murder' of one of her slaves.[101] Aunt Dorothy, Laura, and I were rendered speechless on account of these cruelties. I began to wonder what other kinds of hellish punishments, aided by current laws, would be permitted on St Helena. For the first time, I was having serious doubts as to my wisdom in accepting my new role, as these were issues that never crossed my mind when agreeing to travel to the Island. Just before retiring to bed, Uncle Mark advised us that he has made arrangements with the Company Paymaster, to release Captain Anthony Beale from his clerical duties for one month. Captain Beale, whose family have lived on the Island since colonisation, will be tasked with the responsibility of showing us around the Island. He will facilitate introductions to families that we will be mixing with socially. As an accomplished horse rider, he may also be persuaded to give lessons in the art of staying attached to one's horse, or possibly donkey, particularly when traversing slopes.

And so began our first weekend in our new home!

The following day, we were formally introduced to Captain Anthony Beale, recently promoted from Writer to Factor within the Paymaster's Office. As Laura had already intimated, he gives the appearance of being a kind and thoughtful young man who has only our best interests at heart. What Laura neglected to say is how handsome he is! As the weather was somewhat inclement, Captain Beale asked us whether we would be interested in learning some of the recent history of the Island. We were in agreement, and if my memory serves me correctly, the gist of what we were told is as follows.

Captain Beale was born in 1790 to a family who have lived on the Island since his great, great, great grandfather Anthony – born 1640 – arrived as a young man from England. This Anthony had worked as a carpenter in his youth. In 1659, The Honourable East India Company occupied the Island following discovery by the Portuguese, and Anthony was appointed Governor in 1672. The Dutch briefly recaptured the Island before the Company retook it, augmenting its military power by 250 troops. Anthony was reappointed as Deputy Governor before being poisoned by his own (black) servant in 1685. Throughout the subsequent generations, the Beales named many of their sons Anthony or Onesiphorus or Richard. Girls' names included Margaret and Eleanor.

Captain Beale is the youngest of four surviving children. Two younger siblings died in infancy. He was five when his father died. His mother remarried in 1804 to a widower, Major Smith. Mrs Smith, now 52, is not in the best of health, having recently suffered from an incident of apoplexy that has confined her to bed and significantly weakened her left side. His older brother Onesiphorus is engaged to be married. The wedding is planned for 9 November at St James Church. Traditionally, Governors are in attendance, and an invitation has been extended to Uncle Mark for the four of us. It promises to be a grand affair, with many society people from the Island expected to be present. Soldiers in scarlet jackets will form a guard of honour at the entry to the church. Fortunately, any dancing will not occur on a Sunday, as Captain Beale told us the senior chaplain, Rev Jones, holds strong views. As recently as April, he complained that the Sabbath was profaned when Governor Beatson and others attended a dance on board a visiting ship!

To return to my description of the Island – my own education is progressing fast – as is my ability to control a horse! There are at least three different species of gum trees, including one that Islanders can tap overnight. They are rewarded in the morning with a sweet-tasting liqueur. Vines are widespread, along with figs, and many varieties of citrus fruit that include oranges, lemons, limes, and citrons. The latter looks like a huge, rough lemon, but it is mainly used for its zest as any juice is sparse and the pulp is rather dry and inedible. Other plentiful fruit include bananas and plantains, peaches, tamarinds, quinces, pomegranates, melons, pumpkins, and mulberries. Blackberries have unfortunately run wild and are now regarded as a pest. Within the town itself are many shady spots with groves and gardens filled with trees, including the oddly named Peepal trees or sacred figs, originating in India. They offer a pleasant contrast to the many military installations and strategically placed cannon. The Peepal trees are where slaves are auctioned, whereas the Sisters Walk is a path cut from the hillside and built for Governor Patton, who preceded Governor Beatson, for his daughters to enjoy. The three highest mountains on the island are Mount Actaeon to the south-east, Diana's Peak in the middle, and Cuckold's Point to the north-west.

As one approaches the interior of the island, the overall impression is of a lush green, with many steep, narrow valleys or guts that host waterfalls and rivers or springs. The Island receives plenty of rain and many of the higher peaks frequently appear shrouded in misty cloud. If one is mindful to explore the soil or rock faces in more detail, they reveal some extraordinary colours and textures. During our riding lessons, Captain Beale has shown us how one can see lava, cinders, and vitrified stone alternating with layers of basalt and bright red volcanic piles of earth and clays. He explained that an army surgeon, Francis Duncan, visited the island over a five-week period in 1801 and came up with an astonishing theory, namely that the island must have been the result of subterranean fire, with the land being pushed up above the sea as a result of volcanic activity. He published his book in 1805, and Captain Beale and his brother Lieutenant Beale have a copy as they are fascinated by the information. Captain Beale had shared his copy with Uncle Mark on the voyage to England where he was caring for Laura back in 1807. It turns our understanding of how these islands formed in a completely different direction from the prevailing wisdom, sometimes referred to as Neptunism.[102] Uncle Mark is keen to add to the geological record of the Island that was started by the previous governor, Alexander Beatson, with whom Uncle Mark has spent many hours since our arrival in June. There are several areas of open and relatively flat grasslands including Deadwood, below Sugarloaf Peak, and Francis Plain, some of which accommodate the military. The knolls - small hills or mounds – and unusual rock formations, are distinctive features. Higher hills are known as mounts. In an area known as Long Wood, Uncle Mark is enclosing land to form a plantation of some thirty-six acres. He is also effecting repairs and improvements of barracks, guardrooms, government houses, the hospital and other buildings, aqueducts, and reservoirs. The estimated cost is nearly thirteen thousand pounds. Dorothy, Laura, and I are hoping that some of this largesse might be extended to improving the

Plantation House drains.[103]

Captain Beale has a house called Terrace Knoll. Lieutenant Beale's adjacent property is called Sunnyside. Both properties are close to Plantation House. One of Captain Beale's tasks, when he is not seconded to take care of two young ladies – he refers to us as Miss Young and Miss Wilks, a formality we hope may be dropped during private discourse once we are better known to him – is to monitor the arrival and departure of ships. His office has to check on the condition of the Honourable East India Company's cargoes from the east, as it is mainly on the return journey from India and China that the ships call at St Helena. Responsibilities for monitoring the Island's affairs are strictly regulated and are roughly shared between the military and civilian officials. Information to be reported includes land tenure, distribution of land afforestation, exploitation of local resources, and agricultural development.

His office is run with military precision, with the clerks, known as Factors or Writers, assigned military equivalent ranks, namely Subalterns or Captains. The junior merchants are Majors, and the senior merchants are Lieutenant Colonels. There are four persons assigned to each rank. Weekly reports are submitted to their superiors: judges and magistrates, who are members of the Council, that in turn report to the Governor. The Paymaster's Office maintains the accounts and inventories of the Company stores, to ensure all military and civilian employees of the Company, are paid correctly.[104] The Governor's office is responsible for the laws of the Island. The Governor has to have a working knowledge of everyday life and activities, and any health concerns brewing on the Island, such as epidemics. He has to informally monitor the local newspaper and gossip to measure the residents' morale. He is required to attend official events including regular church services and ceremonious occasions on the Island. Lieutenant Onesiphorus Beale expects to be promoted to Captain before the end of the year. He serves in the St Helena Foot Regiment, a longstanding family tradition. His department is also required to report to the Governor of the day, with a focus on muster rolls of the island troops as well as the state, armaments, and condition of the Defence's roads.

The Island population is close to three and a half thousand souls, with another census to be undertaken next year. The wealthier European families are all known to each other, attending weddings and other celebrations and making social calls. Many are regular parishioners at St James Church. Next year will mark 40 years since the current edifice replaced an even older church, built more than one hundred years previously. The heat takes its toll on the Island's properties, and the soft red stone of its construction is not really robust enough for such a large building.

Captain Beale has now been formally seconded to the Governor's Office for three months. During this time, he has been charged with ensuring Aunt Dorothy, Laura, and I are introduced to the European settlers, taken around the Island to get a better idea of its geography, topography, flora, and fauna, and informed of the history and culture of St Helena. I do not wish to bore you in this letter, but I will return to it over a space of several weeks so that I can share with you details of my new life! We have certainly met some characters along the way, including Miss Polly Mason, who owns a number of properties, has at least six slaves, and favours riding an ox, although she is invariably polite, bowing deeply on our initial introduction.

There are various modes of transport. Oxen are used to draw heavy carts and traverse greater distances. The roads are steep and potentially hazardous. Donkeys are used as beasts of burden for relatively lighter loads but can be used instead of horses, particularly when traversing rough terrain. Horses are the primary mode of transport for speed, so Laura, Dorothy, and I have been taking lessons on horse riding. Dorothy has indicated a preference for Captain Beale's small, well-tamed donkey she has christened Maughold. I am undecided in regard to either beast, whereas Laura appears to be a natural horsewoman. Horses are used pull light carriages particularly on the main roads.

There are many grand buildings both within Jamestown and

also in the interior of the Island. Plantation House is in the lee of a hill and about three miles from the centre of the town. Apart from the main building, there are ancillary houses and graves. Horses are kept in paddocks, but there are plans to eventually build stables as part of an overall upgrade to the estate. The house is surrounded by closely tended gardens. There is a Country Church further up the hill, its steeple emerging from the trees when one views both buildings from the front of Plantation House. Unfortunately, it does not seem to have been constructed with as much care as one would have expected, with pieces of masonry, particularly following high winds, at times to be found smashed on the nearby grounds and headstones. Captain Beale has hinted that the two main chaplains on the Island are renowned for outspoken views delivered from the pulpit! Each man appears to try to outdo the other for seemingly outrageous comments. No doubt before long I will be able to judge this for myself.

I enjoy hearing the sound of the clock bell from the tall, square church tower when we visit Jamestown. The clock was made in London for the Company at the request of the Governor at that time and put into the church tower in 1787. It has massive weights that govern its movements. It makes me a little homesick for Uncle Peter. I trust that he and Aunt Margaret are happy living back in Scotland?

Uncle Mark lives at The Castle, the official residence in Jamestown. The entrance to the walled complex is through an arch that displays the arms of the Honourable East India Company. He joins us on weekends at Plantation House and adds to our knowledge of St Helena. He greatly respects Lieutenant Governor Skelton who travelled with us on *Sir William Pulteney*. He was present for Uncle Mark's formal commission into the position of Governor on 21 August, and this was the last formal role for Colonel Beatson who plans to return to England shortly.

The Bible, or stories arising from it, has given birth to many unusual names on St Helena. Captain Beale intends to show us Lot and Lot's wife, ancient volcanic cones, in the Sandy Bay area of the island. He enjoys bathing in the Lot's Wife Ponds, a series of rockpools. He has informed us with no hint of irony that it is possible to visit Purgatory, the Gates of Chaos, the Devil's Cap, the Devil's Hole, the Devil's backbone, and the Devil's Garden, and that slaves are buried in Mount Eternity. One only hopes that in death they find a freedom and peace not accorded to them in their lifetimes. The Asses Ears and the Chimney are volcanic cones, and a brilliantly green area in dry Sandy Bay is known as Fairyland. The Bell Stone, a volcanic rock, makes a clear, ringing sound when struck. Captain Beale will accompany Laura and me to visit this stone.

I feel the length of this letter may be more than can be comfortably posted, and a ship is leaving tomorrow. Uncle Mark is agreeable to take it with him when he returns to Jamestown later this afternoon. As always, I send my love to you, to your husband, James, and to your girls.

I remain your affectionate sister,

Katherine Rose.

Chapter 12

Saturday 9–Sunday 10 October, 1813

Katherine and Laura are dressed in their riding habit and are sitting outside in the gardens of Plantation House. It promises to be a fine day. Fortunately, there is little wind. Their clothing is loose and comfortable. Whilst retaining their modesty, they designed and made it from material purchased at Solomon's emporium in Jamestown. Katherine can hear the faint sound of horses' hooves. She feels slightly nervous as she still has occasional doubts about her riding ability, and she fears that the day's planned journey might be more of a challenge than previous outings. Captain Beale appears, mounted on his horse that has been affectionately renamed Colonel Brandon. He is leading their favourites: Elinor and Marianne. The names are a nod to characters in *Sense and Sensibility,* as early in the days of their acquaintance, Katherine enthusiastically shared her passion for the book, much to Laura's and Captain Beale's amusement.

In the three and a half months since their arrival, both young women have received intensive riding lessons and now feel more confident tackling the many bridlepaths and other tracks around the Island. Laura is more proficient, in part due to her previous riding experiences on the Isle of Man. Her horse, Elinor, is a deep chestnut colour, and Marianne is a dapple grey. Both animals are gentle and placid. Dorothy abandoned her riding lessons soon after their move to Plantation House, preferring to use a horse and trap for her errands. After a frank discussion with the Governor and Mrs Wilks, and with an agreement that correct forms of address will be continued, it has been agreed that Captain Beale may continue to escort the two young ladies around the Island without the benefit of a formal chaperone.

Horses' hooves sound louder. Captain Beale dismounts and greets them with a small bow:

'Good morning, ladies. I trust that you are well this beautiful day?'

'We are,' responds Laura. 'We look forward to meeting your brother Lieutenant Beale and Miss Desfountain.'

'They will be joining us in Jamestown,' replied Captain Beale. 'Miss Ann Margaret Desfountain will be bringing a delicious picnic. As you know, she is to be married to my brother Onesiphorus, in November. Her father, John de Fountain (who favours the French spelling of his surname) is a senior merchant with the rank of Lieutenant Colonel in the Paymaster's Office.'

Captain Beale turns to Katherine. 'Miss Young, if I may I would like to adjust your stirrup slightly?'

As Captain Beale checks that Katherine is comfortable, he continues. 'If you are agreeable, the plan is to take the ride at a walking pace so that you may appreciate the view. From Jamestown, we will ride to Ruperts to see the cannon, and perhaps a brief walk on the beach before progressing to a pretty picnic spot. At times it may be necessary to ride single file when the paths are narrow. That may make conversation difficult.'

'That sounds wonderful,' said Laura. 'It would be nice to spend a few minutes paddling in the water and seeing if we can spot any fish.'

They set off at a gentle walk, riding three abreast towards Jamestown, passing High Knoll Fort with its defensive tower to their right. Captain Beale explained, 'The bluestone used for its construction was excavated from a local quarry.'

Twenty minutes later they approach the round magazine tower.

'This tower was built in 1797 to cover the rear of Ladder Hill Fort. Its gun platform is a circular space constructed from coarse, unmortared rubble, with local soft red stone forming the supporting block. As you can see, this gun is relatively small.'

'For such a little island, the number of munitions seems extraordinary,' said Katherine. Laura nodded in agreement.

'It has always been highly fortified, as it is of critical strategic importance to the Honourable East India Company. That is why they pay for the St Helena Artillery and St Helena Regiment which require a considerable outlay of funds, and that does not include the corps of militia and the soldiers' wives and children,' said Captain Beale. 'My work in the Paymaster's Office gives me a good overview of the costs of maintaining St Helena. My brother can give you more detailed information relating to military matters.'

Various walls alongside their pathway act as boundaries. As they approach Ladder Hill, Captain Beale indicates a wall that appears very well constructed.

'Different materials are used, depending on the function or purpose of the wall. This one is important and has been built from a mixture of mud mortar, lime, and random rubble, using high-quality white lime mortar. The lime is extracted from quarries, but is in short supply so it is only used for specified buildings or structures. The wall's function is to protect the southern side of the Ladder Hill Fort.'

When they arrive at the barracks in Jamestown, Lieutenant Onesiphorus is holding two horses.

'Welcome to Jamestown and St Helena. Let me introduce my fiancée, Miss Desfountain.'

'How do you do,' said Laura. 'I am Miss Wilks, and Miss Young is my companion. We are delighted to meet you and are looking forward to learning more about the Island and partaking of your picnic.'

'Thank you,' said Miss Desfountain. 'We are pleased that you are to join us today and most appreciative of the positive changes Colonel Mark Wilks has already made to our welfare in the short time he has been here. Lieutenant Onesiphorus will lead the way. We are going to Rupert's first, where many slaves live, and my fiancée will point out features of interest.'

The horses pick their way, avoiding the worst bumps in the road. Lieutenant Beale points out the Two Gun Battery, where two twelve-pounder guns are situated on the ridge between James's and Rupert's valleys, protected by a low wall. He later points out Sampson's Battery, a gun platform designed to cover Rupert's valley, that complements the Saddle Battery.

'We will ride down to the harbour, where we can dismount and stop briefly to paddle in the shallows. You should be able to see shoals of fish that customarily swim close to shore at this time of day. It is an opportunity for the horses to nibble on the grassy verge or void their bowels.'

'I have a couple of towels in my saddle bags that you are welcome to use once you have finished paddling,' offers Miss Desfountain.

'I think we should continue our journey to get to our picnic spot,' said Lieutenant Beale, after fifteen minutes had elapsed. 'We will follow the coast path to the battlements and cannons of Banks Battery. The path will be steep in places, but we will take it slowly.'

'Please call out if you need assistance,' added Captain Beale. 'The route is well known to the horses, so you will be quite safe.'

Lieutenant Beale points out a hauling eye – a round, metallic structure made from wrought iron that is fixed securely into the rockface by drilling a hole into the rock.

'These are used to haul cannon and other heavy, but necessary, equipment into place and are an essential part of all the battlements around the Island. The design and method of fixing them into the bedrock or natural rockface might vary.[105] 'On another occasion, we can stop at the forge and the blacksmith can show you how he makes them.'

'I think that would be very interesting,' said Katherine. 'I would also like to learn more about the harnesses and yokes we have observed that are used on your bullocks. They appear to be well constructed.'

'I am sure the blacksmith would be very happy to show you, as he is proud of his work. I know his brother well,' said Lieutenant Beale. 'We are about to make a second stop so that the horses can graze. You will see that there is an excellent view down into Jamestown.'

'I am sure our guests would like to join me in using this small cliff-top privy,' said Miss Desfountain. 'If you would like to follow me?'

The privy is attached to the tower, and does not appear to have a roof.

'It is very close to the cliff edge,' said Laura. 'Is it safe to use?'

'If you walk up these blue stone steps you will be fine. It has been here for a long time. But only one of us can use it at a time.'

'Please, Miss Desfountain, use it first. We will have a look over there, as I think I can hear fowls,' said Laura.

'Over here, Laura,' said Katherine. 'See that low wall with the box-shaped enclosures of flat, stone slabs? Half a dozen chickens are pecking the dust. But I cannot see a rooster.'

'That is interesting. Perhaps they are kept for their eggs. We will have to ask Miss Desfountain, as there does not appear to be anyone else here.'

A few minutes elapse, and the ladies rejoin their companions.

'If you are happy to continue the journey, I will point out some further landmarks,' said Lieutenant Beale. 'The buildings over there on Crown Point also include a signal flag system. It is based on a system introduced by a Frenchman, Claude Chappe d'Auteroche, during the Napoleonic Wars.[106]

'We will be taking this bridlepath to our right that traverses the Sugar Loaf Ridge, heading south. I think my brother wants to say something – you have been very quiet this last half hour, Anthony,' he teased.

'The path is quite narrow, as it has been cut into the side of the ridge, and is partially retained by a revetment wall. At this point we have to travel in single file. I suggest my brother leads and I bring up the rear. That will ensure I can quickly intervene if you are experiencing difficulty.'

'Is it safe?' asked Laura. 'Katherine and I are still relative novices at riding on such paths.'

'It has been used without incident for decades,' reassured Anthony. 'I suggest we cross it now, and we will be at our picnic spot in a few minutes.'

Katherine grits her teeth but does not say anything, content to let her horse do the hard work whilst she focuses on its ears and the rider ahead of her. She is conscious she might appear a little flustered. However, Marianne is firm-footed in picking her way, which she does without missing a step. They arrive a few minutes later at their picnic spot. Laura has taken the narrow pathway in her stride. Miss Desfountain is very confident on her horse, but she explains she has been riding since early childhood:

'Father always insisted we were comfortable in the saddle, and we started riding ponies when we were three or four.'

'Whilst we hobble the horses and get out the rugs, if you look towards the north-east you will see Flagstaff Hill. Beyond that is Flagstaff Bay, clearly visible with white tipped waves,' says Lieutenant Beale.

'Many places on St Helena are traditionally named after military, geographic, or geological features, or sometimes for their unusual shape. We will have to show you Lot and his wife on another occasion when you are more confident riding your horses, as the access is very steep. Jamestown was founded in 1659 by the Company and is named after James, Duke of York, the future King James II of England. Rupert's origin is more obscure, but possibly was inspired by Prince Rupert of the Rhine who fought in the English Civil War. Lemon Valley marks where lemon trees were planted, to supply sailors with citrus fruit to prevent scurvy,' adds Captain Beale.

'I hope the food prepared for today is acceptable to you. There is plenty of variety, so please help yourselves,' says Miss Desfountain, spreading her skirts as she sits down.

They start eating their picnic, content to be silent whilst admiring the view and listening to the bird song. Katherine offers a few crumbs to a little yellow green canary with a fringe of feathers, like a cap on its head. Once it finished swallowing the small morsels of food, it burst out into what could best be described as a song of praise. He appeared very tame and was not intimidated by the giants in his presence, even settling briefly on one of the horse's ears before the beast engaged in a violent twitching, whereupon the canary flew downwards towards the valley. From their vantage point, they look down over Jamestown.

Lieutenant Beale turns towards the ladies. 'The principal fort of the island, Ladder Hill, can accommodate up to two hundred soldiers and is accessed by a rope ladder, although there are plans to build a structure that makes it easier to navigate. I lived there briefly before purchasing Sunnyside. Half Tree Hollow overlooks Ladder Hill. The original trees were killed by feral goats or hogs, with only tree stumps remaining. Such was the destruction that, approximately one hundred years ago, this roughly three-mile circular area was designated a common, where the East India Company could corral its cattle, hogs, and goats.

'That small speck in the distance is Egg Island, beyond which you can trace the coastline to South West Point. Egg Island guards the entrance to both Swanley Valley and Old Woman's Valley, the latter ironically named for a very steep part of the Island. It has been the home of millions of seabirds for centuries, and when the winds blow from the sea the odour from the guano is distinctly unpleasant, although fortunately there are very few homes in the area.[107] Immediately below us is Dead Wood, now almost a desert since most cabbage trees have been cut down to provide timber rafters for many homes.'

'I think we may have had a small sample of the odour the night before we came ashore in June,' said Katherine. 'For a moment, I was reminded of the noisome vapours that arise from the Thames near where I used to live.'

'I am afraid I have not had the chance to travel to England, although Anthony tells me he enjoyed his two years there,' said Lieutenant Beale. 'However, I like to think I am knowledgeable about different facets of this island, and I am in my spare time an amateur botanist.'

'I would love to learn more about the plants here,' says Laura, 'particularly your unusual cabbage trees. I believe three species are growing here?'

'"He" cabbage trees are hairy, "She" cabbage trees are not, and then you have black cabbage trees. At first sight, the black cabbage tree flowers look like daisies, but if you examine them closely they are much more complex, as they are a composite of much smaller flowers. The cabbage trees are also related to other native trees known locally as gumwoods. These trees have been used for fuel since St Helena was first settled, and are related to sunflowers, the seeds of which were probably born on the wind across the Atlantic.'[108]

From behind his back, Lieutenant Beale presents Miss Desfountain with a beautiful white flower. She accepts it with a little curtsy.

'This is the flower of the scrub wood plant. As you can see, it has soft, furry leaves and dozens of long, white petals. Whilst many flowers have a delicate perfume or none during the daytime, on a moonlit night the different scents from the myriad plants on the Island intermingle into a sweet-smelling fragrance that is quite delightful.'

He then produces a second flower.

His brother teases him. 'Always the gentleman.'

'This is the flower from the redwood tree. That wood has been used for the frames of buildings for generations as it is also generally resistant to termites. As you can see, the flower is delicate, with five main petals that are striated and creamy-coloured. This colouring deepens to an orange-yellow in the centre, that contrasts with this odd little patch of fuzzy red hairs just off centre. When it ages, the petals turn pink. Here you can see that the green stamen projects from the centre of a five-petalled star of a purple-black hue. Its dark green leaves have pronounced veins on their underside. Miss Wilks.'

He presents it to Laura, with a small bow from his waist.

'Why, thank you, kind sir.'

Finally, with a flourish, he gives Katherine a delicate, white, bell-shaped flower that reminds her of the snowdrops in England. She is momentarily homesick.

'This plant is common in rocky areas and is known locally as the small bellflower.'

'That is so thoughtful of you. Perhaps you do not know how important bells are to me, and this flower is one of my favourites to appear in the English spring.'

Captain Beale says, 'Make the most of the view to the southwest, as we need to get going. The horses are getting restless.' He packs up the picnic, handing items to Miss Desfountain to put in her saddle bags.

Laura turns to Miss Desfountain. 'Thank you so much for arranging such a delicious picnic. Katherine and I trust all will be well as you prepare for your wedding to Lieutenant Beale.'

'I have enjoyed meeting you and will look forward to your attending. I suggest we get back on our horses as we will take this narrow track that wends its way south before it joins a wider road that leads back to Jamestown. Lieutenant Beale and I will leave you there.'

Captain Beale, Laura, and Katherine are soon back at Plantation House.

'Thank you. We have enjoyed our day,' says Laura. 'I am sure we will sleep well with all the fresh air.'

Katherine nods in agreement, almost too weary to speak. 'Yes, and we are relieved the horses were so well disciplined.'

'That's a pleasure,' says Anthony. 'I look forward to seeing you again before too long. Goodnight.' He remounts his horse, takes the reins of the other two, and heads towards home.

The next morning, Katherine wakes feeling the after-effects of yesterday's excursion. There is no time to dwell on the enjoyable day they had yesterday. She and Laura are attending a service at the Country Church at the back of Plantation House following breakfast. Uncle Mark and Aunt Dorothy will be joining them for what may be a controversial sermon preached by the always unpredictable Reverend Boys.

Chapter 13

Journal extracts
Sunday 17 October, 1813

I have had an exciting first few months in St Helena. Captain Beale, Laura, and I have been exploring the island to the best of our abilities. He was granted leave, so with a combination of horse riding and Shanks's pony, I feel I have a much better grasp of my new home.

Last week we visited two homes that are situated in Lemon Valley. The approach was steep, and one thing we did not see was lemons. Our reward for the effort involved was sighting a group of extraordinary birds that appeared to use the cliffs as nesting sites. The birds were pure white, with orange curved beaks. Their tails were remarkable – at least twice the length of their bodies – with a suggestion of a fork at the tip. Captain Beale says they are often called bosun birds.

Their cry is shrill, almost harsh, at odds with their beauty. There may have been up to twenty circling each other in tall vertical columns, with their long tail feathers waving in the wind.

Other birds we have seen on our visits have included the native wire bird.[109]

I received a letter from Elizabeth this morning – the first since my arrival in St. Helena. I postponed reading it until this evening to reflect on her words in private. I shed a tear or two when she described her children.

I have changed the focus of my bible reading to read about the women of the New Testament.

It seems fitting that I start reading about Elizabeth and reflect on the extraordinary gift bestowed upon her in her later life.

The light is poor so I will have an early night.

Chapter 14

9 am, Saturday 6 November, 1813

Katherine wakes early. Captain Beale has suggested a trip to the Bell Stone to mark his recent twenty-third birthday. Since returning to his post in late September, it has been difficult for him to visit regularly, so Katherine and Laura have taken to walking around the local area of Plantation House and also going into Jamestown, particularly to shop at Solomon's store. On one of these excursions to Jamestown, they chanced on a replica painting of Terrace Knoll that was nicely framed with an inscription below. Captain Beale has described the cut and dressed stone pillars or gateposts that mark his property, topped with pyramidal shaped bluestone. Pintles, a type of bolt inserted into a gudgeon, form the hinges of the hardwood timber gates. She cannot see these in the picture and wonders if they were added at a later date. She and Laura decided to purchase it for Captain Beale as a thank you present, and plan to give it to him tomorrow when he has invited them to have a look at his property. The storekeeper assures them he was well acquainted with William Burchell and his work. Burchell was an important early naturalist, explorer, ethnographer, and linguist, as well as being a talented artist.[110]

The inscription says:

'Terrace Knoll: A view in St. Helena. "In looking inland you have this view and turning towards the sea you have the view of the Friar. This was drawn and coloured on the spot and is very correct. In the winter the hills are much greener. The bamboo is not finished but correctly shows its growth. The yams grow along a stream of water." 16 February 1807'

Captain Beale will bring their favourite horses from the Plantation House paddock already saddled. Katherine and their resident domestic servant, prepared the picnic earlier this morning. It can be placed inside the attached saddlebags along with personal items. She has selected pork meat enclosed in pastry, scotch eggs, a freshly baked loaf of bread, some cheese, and salad items. There is a colourful mixture of fresh fruits, along with lemonade and spring water to quench their thirst. Suitable plates and cutlery and serviettes dampened with water are also packed. A small bottle of eau de cologne is stored alongside a picnic rug.[111]

She was a little disappointed not to have observed Guy Fawkes Night yesterday. At home the dastardly plot is remembered with bonfires to burn the guy, church bells ringing out, official artillery salutes and fireworks. Despite St Helena's shared English heritage, observing Guy Fawkes night is muted, so there was no reason not to retire at a reasonable hour. The trip to the Bell Stone may be the last horse ride with Captain Beale for the remainder of the year. Lieutenant Beale and Miss Desfountain get married next week. Once Captain Beale has honoured his necessary duties in support of his brother, he is eager to get his house in order. Aunt Dorothy chaperoned their various sojourns with Captain Beale in the earlier weeks, before she became busy with the obligations required of the Governor's wife. She has hosted regular dinner parties at Plantation House to ensure that the most senior men and their wives, of both the civilian and military establishments, have had the opportunity to meet her and Uncle Mark in a social setting. Important visitors to St Helena also receive invitations to dine with the Governor. Laura and Katherine frequently join these guests for the meal. Several have caused Laura to blush when they remarked on her great beauty, often in an aside to her father.

It seems extraordinary to Katherine that she and Laura, whose homes are so distant, now mingle with native-born islanders, many of whom prefer or are forced by circumstances to live out their lives within an easy walking distance of where they were born. Unless there is an exceptional or compelling reason to do so, they rarely venture further than a five-mile radius of their homes. For those with means, bullocks may be harnessed. The beasts can proceed along the main routes of St Helena with their passengers travelling in relative comfort. Alternatively, a smaller horse and trap can progress faster. For the more adventurous or intrepid traveller, a humble donkey, or a docile but sure-footed horse, enables a freedom to travel along bridlepaths and enjoy Nature's gifts. Laura has observed a not dissimilar divide occurring on the Isle of Man: most of the population, whether it be due to poverty or other reasons, rarely ventures outside known areas. Consequently, local dialects can sound like different languages, potentially creating communication difficulties that are compounded by large segments of the population who cannot read or write. On the other hand, there are people such as Laura and Uncle Mark, as well as Katherine's late father, her uncle, brothers, and brothers-in-law who regularly voyage to the far ends of the earth, working with men from multiple nations, with regular exposure to risks as well as diverse cultures and all the richness that brings to their lives and the stories they can relate. Katherine has reflected on many occasions how the opportunity to participate in education as a child has lifelong benefits.

She finds it difficult to articulate the yearning she had to venture out of England. She would be the first to acknowledge that her life, too, was largely spent within a small, circumscribed area of East London. Perhaps it is still the newness of St Helena, but the beauty of the island, its mild climate, its military history, and the congenial people that she has met, have satisfied her need to experience something very different from her childhood home. She feels her happiness will be complete if, like her favourite characters in her books, she can find a soulmate. She is content to make her home here for the foreseeable future, her initial homesickness having largely abated since reestablishing her relationship with Isabella and her children and meeting many new people on the Island.

Laura interrupts Katherine's reverie with a light touch on her shoulder, and then they hear:

'Good morning, Miss Wilks and Miss Young.'

'Good morning, Captain Beale,' they quickly respond, with Katherine adding, 'And many good wishes for your birthday!'

'Why, thank you, ladies. Are you prepared to visit the famous Bell Stone?'

'We are.'

They mount their horses and head south, with Captain Beale taking the lead and pointing out places of interest:

'The first part of our journey will take us past Luffkins Tower to Cason's Forest, where we will turn east and head towards Diana's Peak,' said Captain Beale.

Before long, they reach Luffkins Tower, a secluded manor house that rewards them with a magnificent panoramic view.

'That is Mount Aceton and Diana's Peak. Beyond that, just visible, is Flagstaff, where we were the other day, and The Barn.' Captain Beale points to each landmark in turn.

'What is the Barn?' asks Laura.

'As you may know, St Helena was thought to have been created by two separate volcanic eruptions. The Barn is a capping of younger lavas upon weaker rocks. On the seaward side it forms cliffs.'

'The Island has a fascinating geological history,' observes Katherine.

'As you know, we had a visiting geologist Francis Duncan visit the island in 1801. He wrote a book about the structure and formation of St Helena. My brother and I were fortunate in that he took an interest in us as we were so familiar with the Island's geography. We accompanied him on many of his site visits, and he explained the different types of rock structures, earth, and other information to us in detail. Later, we were able to purchase a copy of his book to consolidate our learning.'

'I would be interested in reading it,' said Katherine.

'His research, built on the work of an Italian abbot, Abbe Anton Moro, originally theorized that islands, such as the Canaries, were created by volcanic activity. James Hutton, a Scottish geologist, debunked the theories of an earlier geologist, Abraham Werner, who subscribed to the Neptunism view of the world.'

'Papa is very interested in learning more about the geology of St Helena,' said Laura. 'He would like to expand the work of Alexander Beatson. Papa intends to send geological specimens to London, but he will maintain a duplicate copy in St Helena.'

'That is a splendid idea,' said Captain Beale. 'Next time we will continue south towards Lemon Valley Head. On the far side of the forest is Horse Pasture, an enclosed space for horses, where we will likely see a wire bird.'

Today, we will pass Diana's Peak on our left, before heading south and then southeast. When we reach the Castle of Otranto you should be able to see both the Peak – if it is not shrouded in mist – and Mount Acteon and Sandy Bay to the south.'

'Why has the house such an extraordinary name?' asked Laura.

'My brother Onesiphorus and Francis Seale serve together in the St Helena Foot Regiment. His brother Robert Seale is employed in the Pay Master's office, so we know them both well. The brothers thought their home, Wrangham's, had nightmarish aspects to it and with a bit of a stretch resembled a Gothic castle. They had a wager with their father about something lost to history, but in an ironic nod to the book by Horace Walpole, the name stuck.'

'The Island certainly has some fascinating names,' observed Katherine. 'Particularly the biblical names.'[112]

'Yes, they are quite extraordinary,' said Anthony. 'People or events characterise many of the names on St Helena, other than the geographical features or biblical references I have already mentioned. Jamestown was originally Chapel Valley when the Portuguese discovered the island in 1502. A small wooden chapel was built that was eventually replaced by a stone chapel. Major Seale has a battery point named after him. Peaks, plains, and valleys are self-evident. Mason's is called after the owner. The Bell Stone is the most famous, but other phonolite stones on the island are difficult to access. The name is derived from ancient Greek meaning sounding stone.'

'What is that house over there, Captain Beale?' said Katherine, pointing to the south.

'Rock Rose. It was built by Governor Robert Brooke in 1789 which was quite a feat because the roads to the area were even less developed than today. It is used as a summer house and is built in a C shape with the servants' quarters located at the rear.

'This road takes us north and east for about a mile and then we will arrive at the bridle path to the Stone Top Ridge where I suggest we have our picnic. I will leave you for about fifteen minutes so that you may attend to any personal business.'

'Thank you,' says Laura. 'We are finding this information most interesting.'

Captain Beale leads their horses to a patch of grass some distance away.

'Captain Beale is very considerate. I have some water in a bottle we can use to wash our hands, and a spare towel,' says Katherine.

'That is very thoughtful of you. I suggest we put our rug here in the shelter of the rocks. I cannot see any insects, so hopefully we will have a peaceful picnic.'

They eat in companionable silence, all three appreciating the picnic, while the horses nibble on the long grass. There are barely any crumbs left over for some opportunistic birds. Captain Beale selects a rock.

'This will be suitable to show you one of the most famous landmarks on St Helena.'

As Anthony struck the stone, producing a dull clanging noise, something changed within Katherine. She had not been indifferent to his good looks, but thought perhaps he had set his heart on wooing Laura. Her face felt suddenly warm, so she turned away. Captain Beale offered the stone to Laura.

'Miss Wilks.'

'Thank you.'

'And Miss Young?'

Something imperceptible and gone in a fleeting moment seemed to cross Captain Beale's face as he handed the stone to Katherine. His voice sounded unusually gruff when a few minutes later he stated it was time to return to Plantation House.

'We will take a more direct route home. Please follow me.'

That evening Katherine pleads a headache and advises those present that she needs to retire to bed.

'It has been a most enjoyable day, but I hope you will excuse me if I leave the table.'

'Goodnight, Katherine,' Laura and Aunt Dorothy chorused. 'We trust that you will sleep well.'

On reaching her bedroom and following a quick wash, Katherine kneels by her bed. She opens her book 'Practical Prayers' which she last consulted following baby William's birth and death aboard *Sir William Pulteney*. Using the light from her fast-disappearing candle, she prays for wisdom and guidance as she reads the following prayer:

'O Jesus, lover of the young, the dearest Friend I have, in all confidence I open my heart to You to beg Your light and assistance in the important task of planning my future. Give me the light of Your grace, that I may decide wisely concerning the person who is to be my partner through life.'[113]

Katherine crosses herself before snuffing out the guttering candle. She briefly enjoys the waxy scent, before quickly getting under the bed covers. She is in a deep sleep within minutes.

Chapter 15

Sunday 7 November, 1813

A large party from Plantation House, along with Captain Beale and Lieutenant Beale, are in the Country Church and suffering through another upbraiding and uncompromising sermon delivered from the pulpit by the Reverend Richard Boys, appointed chaplain by the East India Company three years previously. As the Junior Chaplain, he is known to have a fractious relationship with the Senior Chaplain, Reverend Samuel Jones. The latter has been living at Terrace Knoll, but is in the process of vacating the property. It is almost a relief to exit the church.[114]

Miss Desfountain is busy with her wedding preparations and declined to attend the church service. The two Beale brothers have offered to take Mrs Wilks, Miss Young, and Miss Wilks on a local tour.

'My brother and I hope that you will be comfortable in your transport,' said Captain Beale. 'I am afraid that the barouche has seen better days, but we have placed cushions on the four seats to lessen the discomfort from the bumps on the road.'

'We are most appreciative, Captain Beale, that you and Lieutenant Beale are taking the time to show us places of interest,' replied Dorothy. 'We are getting used to many new ways of transport since coming to St Helena and have mostly enjoyed our novel experiences.'

'My brother Onesipherus will sit on the high seat to control the four horses, and I will join you on the two double seats that face each other. Do you have any preference to travel facing the way we are going or looking backwards?'

'It would give me great pleasure if you can take your seat beside me, Captain Beale, and I believe I will find it preferable to look backwards, so may I suggest, Laura, that you sit opposite me, and Katherine sit opposite Captain Beale.'

Once the ladies are settled, Lieutenant Beale taps the horses, and they progress slowly along the road.

'If we could pause here briefly, please,' Captain Beale requests. 'If you look over there, you can see a distant view of Sunnyside, where my brother lives, and Terrace Knoll, my property, currently occupied by Reverend Jones. We can show you a better view a little later.'

'The knoll on which your property sits appears very steep,' observed Laura.

'It is, indeed. To traverse it safely, the paths travel diagonally across the hill. You can just see the large Cedar of Lebanon to the front of the house. It is one of my favourite places to relax in the garden.'

The journey continues and Captain Beale points out various items of interest as they progress slowly along the road. After riding in relative comfort for a mile or so and basking in the sunshine, Katherine shares with her congenial companions how she misses her church of St George-in-the-East. She is thinking about the shocking sermon they had listened to this morning.

'We were very fortunate with our ministers.'

Rather unexpectedly, Aunt Dorothy mildly rebukes her:

'I understand Reverend Boys' bark may be worse than his bite. In some neighbourhoods of St Helena, he is held in high regard.'

She does not elaborate further. As the Governor's wife, she may need to provide an alternative point of view.

'I apologise for my remarks. I am sometimes given to making too hasty a judgement,' says Katherine. 'It is an area of my life that I need to work on.'

'I am afraid that our Island does tend to attract some rather outspoken men of the cloth,' said Anthony. 'But as Mrs Wilks stated, I have been fortunate to see a different side to Reverand Boys. Many young soldiers posted to the island regard him as a father figure. He regularly invites them into his home, particularly if they are having difficulty adjusting to a very different life so far from loved ones.'

With impeccable timing, Lieutenant Beale brings the horses to a halt near an area with generous grass coverage. He dismounts and then attaches the horses' reins to a nearby post before he assists the ladies out of the carriage. After a few moments, the party walks along a path bordered on one side by a stone wall constructed without mortar. It reminds Katherine of English dry-stone walls. There is a significant falling away of the land on the other side of it. She and Captain Beale are in the lead, with Lieutenant Beale gallantly offering his arms to Mrs and Miss Wilks. Behind them is a tree with globular yellow fruits hanging from most of its branches. To their left is a stand of bamboo. A convenient pile of boulders warmed by the sun make a not uncomfortable seat. Whether the boulders are naturally occurring or have been put there for the relief of travellers is unclear.

Captain Beale points towards the north.

'If you look to the middle distance, there is a small stand of trees that resemble poplars. Alongside them are giant fern-like plants. That house that from this perspective appears to be perched almost precariously on the top of the knoll is Terrace Knoll. As you can see more clearly from here, the pathways from the house cross the hill in a zig zag pattern as it is too steep to go directly downwards. Once we reach the house, you will have a closer view of some of the shrubs and trees that grow on the property, including the agaves on the lower slopes.'

'I am interested in learning more about herbs and other plants that can be used to promote health,' said Dorothy. 'I understand that agaves can be used in such a way?'

'Yes, that is the case here,' said Anthony. 'Each of these plants, when mature, produces several pounds of edible flowers. The stalks that appear before the blossom are ready to harvest in the summer. The Islanders like to roast them as they are sweet. They are chewed to extract the honeylike sap and are believed to have medicinal properties that reduce inflammation. The roots are also used, but care has to be taken as some people develop allergies if the sap comes into contact with the skin.'

'I was always keen to explore complementary treatments in my midwifery practice,' explained Dorothy, 'but I don't think I have come across these before.'

'I believe they originate in Mexico, where they are a symbol of purity, strength, and health,' said Lieutenant Beale. 'They are succulents, and come in possibly as many as two hundred different species. I believe you have some specimens at Plantation House, so I am very willing to show you them.'

He adds, 'We plan to grow coffee trees, as visiting botanists suggest the climate is particularly suitable. Not all trees on the island are natives. Much of the introduced flora and fauna may have been brought by the winds, or possibly generated from seeds dropped by birds, or even carried on the sea. Where exotic species have been deliberately introduced the results are mixed. Whilst some plants thrive, many die on the voyage from India. Others have flourished with specimens exported to England. Goats have been a disaster and are responsible for the near extinction of several valuable tree species native to St Helena including the St Helena ebony.'

Captain Beale and his brother assist the ladies back into the barouche. As they get closer to Terrace Knoll, Captain Beale indicates two mature figs.

'These trees provide abundant fruit in the summer. That tree over there, with the broad canopy and twisted trunk, is a Cedar of Lebanon. It has stood as a sentinel for generations of our family.'

Katherine likes the biblical symbolism of this tree that stands for protection, wisdom, and strength, qualities she is secretly beginning to attribute to Captain Beale. The Beale ancestral house itself is white, two-storeyed, and of a generous size.

'We are not permitted to invite guests to enter the house until Reverend Jones moves, although he has facilitated several of my visits. He has acquired some rooms over a shop in Jamestown. As you can see, the house has five windows in the upper storey that command a magnificent view of the surrounding countryside. They are duplicated downstairs and on the rear of the building. One can take a boat out and view the estate from the sea to gain a different perspective. That forest of trees over there is cool in all seasons, but is occasionally covered in a misty cloud. In the middle distance you can see stands of cabbage trees as well as the area overrun by furze that has been spread by the goats. Over there, to the right on that hill, is Rosemary Hall.'

Lieutenant Beale stops the horses momentarily. 'That road leads to my home, Sunnyside. If you do not wish to alight again, we will continue to Plantation House.'

When the ladies are assisted out of the carriage ten minutes later, Aunt Dorothy acknowledges both men. 'On behalf of Miss Wilks, Miss Young, and myself, we thank you for a most enjoyable day.'

Both brothers give a little bow to her. 'It was our pleasure.'

As the ladies disappear inside the building, the brothers return the barouche to its home near the Plantation House stables and release the horses into a nearby field. With the women clearly out of earshot, Onesiphorus turns to Anthony.

'Mrs Wilks and the young ladies are charming, Anthony. It would be my dearest wish that you can find a soul mate like Miss Desfountain has become for me.'

'I met Miss Wilks as a young child,' replied Anthony. 'I believe our friendship will endure, but more in the sense of an older brother and younger sister. In confidence, I find Miss Young intriguing and would like to get to know her better. I observe we share many values that I consider to be important. I am a little unclear whether she intends to return to England next year, as she has indicated that her employment is for twelve months.'

'If that is the case, Anthony, it may be timely to use every opportunity to change that. Miss Young would be entirely suitable as a future wife for you. I am well acquainted with her brother-in-law Dr Adam Baildon, who provides us with medical services, and have met his wife and delightful daughters on many occasions. I have also engaged with her other brother-in-law Commander James Halliburton during his stopovers at St Helena. I have learned much about the Youngs and their extended family, most of whom are master mariners. I think you are well suited to each other, and I shall watch your progress with interest!'

Chapter 16

**Journal extracts
22 November, 1813
St Cecelia's Day**

*'The Patron Saint of Musicians and Church music, preached
Christianity and was martyred for her beliefs, but at her wedding
she sang her heart to the Lord.'*

I have copied this passage into my journal from a small leatherbound book I discovered in the informal library at Plantation House. It reminds me of the beautiful wedding I attended with Uncle Mark, Aunt Dorothy, and Laura on Tuesday 9 November. Captain Beale stood by his brother Onesiphorus, who was resplendent in scarlet as he pledged himself to his future wife at St James' Church. The music from the organ and the accompanying choir, made up of men and women, made the occasion memorable. Even the church bell managed a few notes as the bride and groom prepared to depart. The day more than made up for my disappointment on 5 November. I may have to let go of some of the traditions that marked my childhood. It would be faintly ridiculous to light a huge bonfire in the equivalent of a late English spring.

The inside of the garrison church of St James' is impressive, with wooden struts crisscrossing the vaulted ceiling. The striking baptismal font is located at the rear of the building where the congregation enters.

The font is sculpted from white marble, with its supporting stand and plinth made from black marble. Isabella's three youngest daughters were baptised here. Our seats were close to the highly polished teak wood altar rail, with its beautifully carved arch-like pattern. The altar was draped with a gold cloth. Six white candles in gleaming brass candlesticks were on top, three on each side of the central cross.[115] As guests of honour, we were formally shown to designated pews, some of which are specified for military use. The internal church walls are painted a brilliant white. At regular intervals, display plaques commemorate past lives. The choir stalls are at the front of the church, Opposite them is a small but powerful organ. The altar stands in front of a white, bas-relief, arch-shaped, marble wall that reflects the pattern in the altar rail, whilst drawing one's eyes to the three arch-shaped stained-glass windows above.[116] The light streamed in during the wedding service, making the words of the hymns easy to read.

The wedding breakfast was a sumptuous affair held in the officers' barracks: a long two-storey building constructed from undressed rough stone with a double pitched roof. At one end of the building is a single-storey cook house. Wisps of smoke or steam emerged from the chimney set into the south wall. There were occasions for dancing, and I confess, I could hardly take my eyes off Captain Beale. His gentle, rounded face is framed by wavy hair a few shades darker than my own. He is of medium height and slim build. His deep, grey-blue eyes sparkle with mischief. His fingers are long and narrow, with short, but shaped, nails. He has been so kind to Laura and me. I was most flattered to be invited to be his dance partner on more than two occasions, and Laura also appeared to enjoy his company.

Uncle Mark did not remain for the wedding breakfast, as strict protocols govern what social occasions the Governor is permitted to attend. However, he read the well-known passage from Corinthians 13:4-8 during the marriage ceremony, and he and Aunt Dorothy appeared to enjoy the wedding service as much as anyone. Aunt Dorothy was a most obliging chaperone for the remainder of the evening.

Later that night, Laura and I reflected on the people we had engaged with at the wedding reception whilst I brushed her hair. This is a duty I have taken on willingly since our first night aboard *Sir William Pulteney*. Our conversation turned to the previous Wednesday and the time we spent with Captain Beale. I asked Laura if she would mind my being bold. She half turned towards me and gave a small smile. I felt my face becoming a little hot and was glad that I was standing behind her.

'Captain Beale has been very generous with his time since our arrival on St Helena. I know that you are very fond of him. Do you think he might become your beau?' asked Laura.

'Why, whatever makes you think that?' said Katherine. 'I know you have known him a long time. He is a very handsome man, and courteous in all his dealings with us. Your father respects him.'

'In truth, I do care for Captain Beale,' said Laura, 'but in the way a sister might care for her brother. As you know, I have barely seen my brother since he was very young. Sometimes I imagine he could have had many of the traits we see in Captain Beale, his generosity of spirit, his courteous manner, his good looks! But I have no passion for him. I hope to marry one day, but my personal preference is for a man of mature years, who has had the opportunity to travel the world. I have no great desire to have children, but if that were to happen, then I should let Nature take its course.'

Katherine feels a strange sensation inside and her cheeks feel even hotter. She pauses briefly and then continues to brush Laura's hair.

Laura adds, 'Whilst I am content to live on St Helena whilst Papa is the Governor, I find I am missing living on the Isle of Man. It is my dearest wish that at some time in the future I can do something to improve the opportunities for girls on the Island. I would start by ensuring they have an appropriate education, so that they can make choices about their lives and may live independently of marriage, if that is their choice.'[117]

'That sounds a wonderful idea, Laura. Education for girls is so important and I will always be grateful for my opportunities.'

Laura stifles a yawn. 'And now, my dear friend, I feel the need for sleep, and I think it is way past our bedtime.'

'Goodnight, Laura, and I wish you pleasant dreams.'

Chapter 17

Journal extracts
1 January, 1814
My first Christmas and New Year on St Helena

Today is the day after *Old Year's Night,* as the last day of the year is called locally. The bell at the Country Church was rung at midnight, but otherwise we have had a quiet few days in contrast to the Christmas festivities. Tomorrow we will attend the Country Church for the usual Sunday service. We observed an extraordinary Christmas season, with various festive engagements hosted at Plantation House. There were street parties in Jamestown where the agapanthus flowers, sometimes called Lily of the Nile or African lily, were resplendent; their purple, blue, or white flowers contrasting with the lush, green foliage of their strap-like leaves. Traditional carols such as 'Holly and The Ivy', 'Good King Wenceslas', and 'While Shepherds Watched Their Flocks by Night', were sung without any sense of irony, as well as carols that were new to me, but more appropriate to the warmer climate. Many people were holding candles, and we were fortunate that the night was still with little wind.

In mid-December, a nativity play was performed by local children in St James' Church. Catherine proudly played the role of Mary in a simple costume sewn by her mother, and her three sisters had some minor parts. There was even a real baby in the crib that behaved very well. Flowers called St John's, also known as Easter Lilies, or White Heaven Lilies – names possibly bestowed because of the heady perfume – were placed around the church in vases. Some were almost three foot tall, with clusters of up to nine buds. Adam, Isabella, and their four girls joined us on Christmas Day for a delicious lunch at Plantation House. Captain Beale also attended, so we were quite a large party of eleven. We exchanged presents after lunch, as has always been the custom in our family, before Captain Beale and I, along with Isabella's three oldest girls, went down to the horse paddock with carrots and apples to give to the animals. Whilst the girls were focused on giving our mounts – Marianne, Elinor, and Maughold the donkey – their treats, Captain Beale turned to me:

'Since I first set eyes on you at the Plantation House Ball, you have constantly been in my thoughts. I truly believe that we should be two souls joined together.'

He then knelt on the ground in front of me asking:

'Will you give me your hand in marriage?'

He presented me with a small, dark velvet-lined box, inside of which was a tiny silver cross on a delicate chain. My body responded with a feeling of warmth as we looked directly into each other's eyes. I allowed him to fasten the cross around my neck. The horses had finished their treats, and the girls turned towards us. I just managed to let Captain Beale know that he should formally ask Adam, as the oldest male in the family on St Helena, for permission to marry me. I am still officially underage. I explained that Uncle Mark and Aunt Dorothy are honorific titles agreed to by us, rather than an indication of kinship. We will keep our engagement a secret until Captain Beale has had the opportunity to talk to Adam. With no reason to believe the permission will not be forthcoming, we will then agree on a date on which to make our betrothal public knowledge.

At Christmas, I was delighted to have news from Isabella that our brother James Young married Elizabeth Edsall Biggs on 16 September at St George-in-the-East. Witnesses to the wedding included Elizabeth's husband, James Halliburton. Peter and Margaret Young had already moved back to Scotland.

Chapter 18

Mid-January, 1814
Visiting Solomon's emporium
to prepare Katherine's bridal trousseau

Katherine and her sister Isabella have agreed to meet in Jamestown to purchase appropriate materials to prepare for Katherine's forthcoming wedding, that has now been formally announced. The Wilks, Baildon, and Beale families were delighted with the news, and Katherine wrote a quick letter to Elizabeth in early January to share the excitement, using Solomon's postal service to facilitate its delivery.

The women read the poster in the front window detailing the wares that are available, before entering Solomon's store through the main door, looking around to orientate themselves. There is stationery displayed to the left and haberdashery is visible towards the rear of the floor. The shop accepts its own copper ha'penny or the East India Company guinea, and Isabella and Katherine are carrying money in both currencies. Katherine is struck by the many different aromas that appear to overlay each other but are not unpleasant. There is a hint of spice, a slight mustiness, lingering body odour, a suggestion of fish or salted meat, and a yeasty odour from barrels of ale.

'Where would you like to start?' asks Isabella.

'I am not sure. There are some very unusual goods for sale. Many names are unfamiliar to me so I hope we will get an opportunity to talk to Mr Solomon. In the meantime, I would like to look at sets of stationery that may be suitable for formal wedding invitations.' As they move closer to the stationery there is a distinctive smell of wax.

'I expect Solomon's will be able to print out to any design you like,' suggested Isabella. 'The bolts of cloth are through here. Is there any particular design or texture that appeals to you? I could help you make some things, if you like?'

'That's a kind offer, Isabella, but I am sure you will be busy making outfits for your girls and Adam. Laura and Dorothy have both said they will help me prepare my bridal wear, as have various members of the domestic staff. They are very excited about the forthcoming wedding as they know the Beale family well.'

'Is Captain Beale still busy getting his house in order?'

'Yes,' said Katherine. 'But I will not be permitted to look inside Terrace Knoll whilst work is in progress, as he wants it to be a surprise. I think that is Mr Solomon approaching – I have questions to ask him.'

'Good morning, Mrs Baildon. Who is this young lady with you?' greets Mr Solomon.

'I would like to introduce my sister Miss Katherine Young, who is soon to be married to Captain Anthony Beale. The wedding is planned for June.'

'I am delighted to make your acquaintance.' Mr Solomon bows towards Katherine. 'How may I best assist you?' he asks.

'My sister is very keen to learn more about the exotic goods in your store, Mr Solomon,' says Isabella. 'If you would be so kind as to give a little explanation of them, we would appreciate it very much. Many of the names of goods are not familiar to Katherine.'

'If you would like to follow me to this other room, ladies.' Mr Solomon moves quickly. 'This is the area where I store the casks. The contents are either wet or dry cooperage. Contents range from sugar to rum, fish or salted beef, with a capacity of between 22–44 gallons.'

'And all these goods are imported?' asks Katherine.

'We receive goods from India, China, Java, and also from the Americas, so can offer a wide choice, as you can see. If you come over here, I will show you samples of stationery and what we can print for you. We have wafers of sealing wax in tin boxes that I suggest you use to seal the wedding invitations.'

'I particularly like this pale blue paper,' said Katherine.

CATALOGUE OF GOODS, &c.

FOR SALE AT

S. Solomon's

WARE-HOUSE,

Corner of LADDER-HILL, ST. HELENA.

Confectionary.

Comfits in Decanters
Scotch Carraways in Decanters
Peppermint Lozenges
Raspberry and Strawberry Jams
Currant Jellies and Marmalades
Cherry and Raspberry Ratafia
Bottled Fruit and Currants

Cutlery.

Scissars and Pen Knives
Clasp Knives
Knives and Forks
Razors and cases, complete

Tin Furniture.

Sauce Pans and Stew Pans
Tea Kettles and Coffee Pots
Tureens, Dish covers, and Patty Pans
Japanned Tumblers and Pots
Table and Tea-Spoons
Jacks
Cullenders and Fish Kettles
Pudding Pans and Tea-Pots
Ink Stands
Candlesticks and Lanthorns
Wash-Hand Basons

Oilmen's Stores.

Mustard, in Pounds and Half Pounds
French Olives
Mushrooms and Capers
Vinegar
Sweet Oil and Florence Ditto
Fish Sauces of different Sorts
Europe and India Pickles
Soap, Starch, and Blue

India Goods.

Fine Worked Muslin for Gowns
Coarse Ditto
Coarse coloured Handkerchiefs
Bandanas Ditto

Muslin Neck and Pocket Handkerchiefs
Chintz of various Patterns
Chopper coloured Handkerchiefs
Long and Short Brown Nankeen
White Nankeen and Black Ditto
Hyson Tea, in Ten Caddy Boxes
Ditto, Quarter Chests
Gunpowder Ditto
Sonchong Ditto, in Quarter Chests
Wax, Tallow, and Mould Candles
Almonds and Sugar
Black Silk Handkerchiefs
White Shirts and Coarse Cloth
Sewing Silk, different colours
Ribbons and Sarsnets
Nankeen Jackets and Trowsers
Ivory, Sandle-Wood, and Horn Fans
Mother-of-Pearl Fish Counters
Japanned Ware
Large and Small Palampores
Lutestrings and Cornelian Necklaces
Cornelian Stones, Harts, Drops, and Crosses
Table Cloths and Towels
Men's and Woman's Shoes
Camel Hair Shawls
Preserved China Ginger and Oranges
.... Chow Chow
Arrow Root and Nutmegs
Cheroots
Cayenne and Black Pepper
Dried Ginger and Allspice
Madras Pocket Handkerchiefs
China Flannel

Stationary.

Demy and Foolscap Paper
Gilt, Letter, and Note Paper
Red and Black Sealing Wax
Black Lead Pencils
Black and Red Ink Powder
Wafers, in Tin Boxes
Quills, Blotting Paper, and Playing Cards

Hosiery.

Men's and Women's fine Cotton Hosiery
-------------- coarse Ditto

Ladies' and Gentlemen's Silk Hosiery
Men's Buckskin, Doeskin, and Buff Gloves

Haberdashery.

White and Nankeen Thread, in Pounds
Blue Nankeen Thread, in Ditto
White Ounce Thread
Black, White, and Red Tapes
Button Moulds, Ribbons, Lace, & Bobbins
Thimbles, Bodkins, Pins, and Needles

Sundries.

Cottons of various Fashionable Patterns
Broad Cloth and Europe Flannel
Beef, Pork, and Flour, in Tieres & Barrels
Hams, Cheese Butter, Beer, and Ale
Canvas, Quadrants, Saxtons, & Compasses
Powder and Shot
Decanters, Tumblers, Wine, Rummers, and Finger Glasses
Hair and Tooth Powder
Pomatum and Essence of Peppermint
Eau de Luc and Aromatic Vinegar
Eau de Colonge and Arquebusade
Lavender, Honey, Hungary, & Rose Waters
Hair and Comb Brushes
Shoe and Clothes Brushes
Fine Tooth, coarse, and Dressing Combs
Perfumed Soaps and Stoughton's Bitters
Cake Blacking
Plates, Dishes, Tureens, Cups and Saucers, Mugs, Basons, Guglets, & Chamber Pots
Port, Sherry, Claret, and Madeira Wines
Men's, Woman's, & Children's Europe Shoes
Boat Cloaks, Worsted Hose, Flannel Shirts, Guernsey Frocks, Duck Drawers, Blue Jackets, and Frocks
Men's fine, plated, and coarse Hats
Ladies' Straw Bonnets and Beaver Hats
Pipes, Pig-Tail, Shag, Brazil, Leaf Tobacco and Snuff
Fish Hooks of various sorts; Log, Deep-Sea, and Fishing Lines
Velno's Vegetable Syrup
Medicines of different sorts

*** GENTLEMEN SUPPLIED WITH CASH FOR GOOD BILLS.

‡‡‡ SHIPS supplied with Vegetables, and all kinds of Stock, on the shortest Notice.

‡‡‡ INDIA GOODS, OF EVERY DESCRIPTION, PURCHASED.

N. B. Board and Lodging.

☞ PRINTING in all its various Branches, with Neatness, Accuracy, and Dispatch.

St. Helena: Printed for S. SOLOMON, by J. COUPLAND.

Solomon's Emporium 1811 Catalogue of goods[118]

'Then may I suggest that you choose these seals, as they are elegant and stand out?'

'There are a couple of other things I would like to purchase today, other than suitable materials for garments – which perhaps we can do at the end. I see you have a good selection of herbal waters? Captain Beale is suffering from a skin condition that I believe could be treated thus.'

'I would recommend trying a small bottle of Arquebusade. It is a distilled water infused with such herbs as rosemary and milfoil and it is effective for a wide range of skin conditions.'

'Thank you, Mr Solomon,' said Katherine. 'I will take a bottle. Mrs Baildon and I would like you to show us the different cloth you have in your store and to discuss what is appropriate for a wedding.'[119]

Katherine's brother-in-law Adam had given the necessary formal permission for Captain Beale to marry her. He has agreed to walk down the aisle with Katherine at the wedding on 15 June at St James' Church. The formal ceremony will be followed by a wedding breakfast at Plantation House. The logistics of getting the guests from the church to Plantation House following the wedding will be worked out by Captain and Lieutenant Beale. Aunt Dorothy and Laura will organise the flowers, the menu, and the place settings for the reception.

Chapter 19

Journal extracts
2 May, 1814

A very brief journal entry. I was invited by Isabella and Adam for lunch today. To my great excitement there were other guests: our brother-in-law Commander James Halliburton, and the ship's surgeon, William Jardine. They are stopping off in St Helena for two days whilst the East Indiaman *Glatton* is off-loading and on-loading goods. James has delegated responsibilities for this to his deputy, first mate Henry Upton, and the second mate, Alexander Lindsay, explaining that the deputies need to learn to do these tasks before they can command a ship. They work together with the purser Robert Miles. *Glatton* will progress to Benkulen on the Island of Sumatra and then onwards to Penang in China, with an expected date of arrival towards the end of August. William and James have known each other for a long time, first serving together on *Glatton* in May, 1806, when the first, second, third, and fourth mates, as well as the surgeon, were all named William!

Glatton left Portsmouth on 22 February, 1814, and is not expected to return to Long Reach until around 22 August, 1815. James assures us that Elizabeth and the girls are well and was excited to inform us that Elizabeth is expecting another baby. They hope it might be a boy, as they would like Captain Charles Drummond, with whom James has made many voyages, to be the godfather and namesake. She is well advanced in her pregnancy and hopes to deliver the baby in late July. James brought a letter from Elizabeth for me that I opened at the meal, as Isabella and Adam were also interested to hear her news.

Elizabeth continues to be supported by the resident domestic couple, Matthew and Jane, who have become more like family. James stated that he will be calling at St Helena on 12 May next year, almost exactly twelve months from today, and hopes to stay for a little longer than the forty-eight hours on this occasion. He continued to regale us with his stories about his voyages, but was unable to persuade Adam to return to sea. We were quite emotional saying our farewells, as we feel that life can sometimes be so unpredictable. Despite James using humour when describing his voyages, the risk of dangerous diseases and other hazards remain very high.

14 May, 1814

Yet again I have been neglecting my journal. I can only put it down to the state of my excitement about our planned wedding next month. Captain Beale and I have been a little nervous, as the banns in relation to our forthcoming marriage have been read aloud in St James' Church for the last three Sundays. As well as being an announcement in church of our intention to marry, it is a chance for anyone to put forward a reason why the marriage may not lawfully take place. We are fortunate that no-one has been inclined to do this. I think it would be a brave person who may be tempted to challenge or question either of the Island chaplains. One can never be sure that the pulpit will not be used the following Sunday for the expression of very strong views. On one occasion, another couple recently arrived from England, Mr Joseph Solomon and Miss Hannah Moss, who are betrothed and will be married on 7 July, also had their banns read immediately after ours. The congregation have been praying for us, which we find very moving.

Captain Beale and I have been receiving marriage guidance from Rev Boys. I need to acknowledge, at least in my journal, that Rev Boys' demeanour in private is very different from his public persona. Despite his somewhat rigid and uncompromising divine, he presents as an honest individual, and Captain Beale and I believe him to be a man of wisdom and experience. On occasions we pass each other on our walks past his property at Smiths Gate, that is close to Plantation House. He presides over the services at the Country Church that we attend at least two Sundays in every four. It has been said that the Reverend Boys does not hesitate to use the pulpit for damaging disclosures of the moral depravities to be found in all levels of St Helena society, including irregular unions between men and women.[120] There have been reported instances where the baptism records of illegitimate children born to women slaves have been accessed without authority, and the names of the fathers obscured by ink blots, or on occasions completely erased by a sharp instrument. It is presumed this was undertaken by the fathers who wished to remain anonymous. More than once in his sermons, the Reverend Boys has referred to this 'abandoned and profligate Isle.'[121] Captain Beale informs me that his older brother Lieutenant Beale and his fellow military officers have encountered a completely different aspect of Reverend Boys' character. For many deployed military men without family for many thousands of miles, he has become a peculiar blessing, acting as a surrogate father. On occasions when their health is compromised, he has taken them into his home and, with the able ministrations of his wife, has nursed them back to full physical and spiritual health.

Although I have been pre-occupied with my wedding preparations, we continue to have our regular meals with Uncle Mark when he returns to Plantation House on weekends. He is in the process of establishing a Benevolent Society 'for the education and relief of the poor.' The library that he set up last year is flourishing. In talking to the various ladies on the Island, he is held in very high esteem by all levels of society, including the slaves, as he has a particular interest in improving their lives as much as it is in his power to do so. Unlike many in the Establishment, Uncle Mark is also highly regarded by the Rev Boys and there appears to be a mutual respect between the two men. The Country Church is well patronised by residents and guests at Plantation House.

Late last year and earlier this year, Uncle Mark hosted meals for his long-time friend the botanist Dr Roxburgh[122] and his family prior to their departure for England on 1st March. They arrived from India barely two weeks before we reached St Helena. Roxburgh's health had been poor and he believed the climate on St Helena would be conducive to his recovery.

The shock of returning to England's cold, damp climate directly from India was not appealing. Dr Roxburgh, whom we had the pleasure of meeting on several formal and informal occasions, made good progress in his botanical review of the Island, creating an alphabetical list of all the plants that were identified with their common as well as scientific names.

He recommended the introduction of the Cinchona officinalis plant from South America, advising that the plants would flourish here and could be raised for transmission to India, thereby generating some income for the Island. He informed us that people use the bark to make medicine, and the plant itself, Cinchona, is used for increasing appetite, promoting the release of digestive juices, and treating bloating, fullness, and other stomach problems. It is also used for blood vessel disorders including haemorrhoids, varicose veins, and leg cramps. On his return to London, Dr Roxburgh will submit a formal report to the former Governor Beatson to include in his book on St Helena that is due to be published in approximately 18 months' time.[123]

Another guest who makes a regular appearance at Plantation House is Lt Colonel John Skelton and his wife, who arrived on St Helena at the same time as us. We got to know them quite well on *Sir William Pulteney*. The Skeltons live at Longwood. Mrs Skelton is fluent in French and on occasions the conversational exchange at meals is conducted in this language. I struggle a little with following the flow of a foreign tongue despite the closeness to some Latin phrases, but Uncle Mark and Laura have an enviable fluency and a natural talent for languages.

In conversation with various long-term residents we have learned that, over the years since its discovery, St Helena has hosted many famous visitors. The astronomer Edmund Halley stayed for approximately twelve months from February 1677. My sister Margaret tells me that he is buried at their local and appropriately named church St Margaret's at Lee Terrace, Blackheath. Captain Beale took Laura, Aunt Dorothy, and me to see the stone building that held his observatory that is now sadly ruined and slowly disappearing.[124]

Captain Cook visited twice. His first visit in 1771, when he captained the barque *Endeavour,* caused quite a furore on the Island, due to reported words that appeared to cast a slur on the inhabitants and the treatment meted out to slaves. There have been other botanists and artists and cartographers whose names I have forgotten.

Chapter 20

Journal extracts
Early September 1814

It is three months since our wedding. Anthony and I are preparing to move into Terrace Knoll, which has been vacated by Rev Jones who it is rumoured may be about to leave St Helena altogether. I think most people will give a sigh of relief. The bad relations between the two chaplains on St Helena are extraordinary and unbefitting to men of the cloth. His pension will amount to six shillings per diem.[125]

For our marriage, I gave Anthony a bible. It has an embossed leather cover with strong hinges. It is illustrated throughout with black and white pictures, such as Daniel interpreting the handwriting on the wall from the book of *Daniel,* and Jesus blessing little children from *Mark.* Anthony has placed our certificate of marriage inside the front cover. If we are blessed with children, it may be used to record their baptisms and perhaps, when they are grown, for their weddings! We would be doubly blessed if we can also record the names of our grandchildren. Soon after our wedding Anthony had to ask for our marriage record to be amended, so that my middle name was included, as the entry shows below. On occasions he likes to call me Rose and that was Mama's pet name for me. We noticed other errors, including the use of an apostrophe with marriages, the misspelling of my name with an 'a' instead of an 'e' and the original record starting my name with a C but crossed out. The Rev Boys blamed his clerk for the mistakes. It is rather disappointing, but I have been assured it will not affect the legality of our marriage.

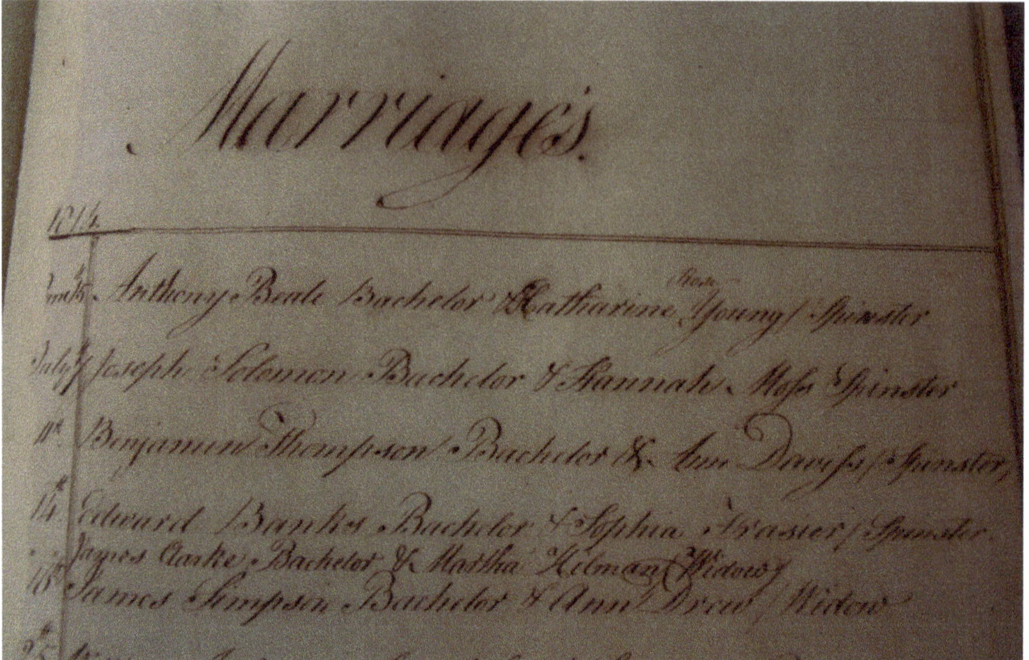

The marriage register at St James

Anthony knows that I love bells. Accordingly, my wedding present was a sterling silver bell in a box lined with blue silk, the same shade as the satin lining of my sea chest. It is about four inches high and was crafted and hallmarked by London silversmiths in 1813, an auspicious date that marks the year I left London. It has a beautiful tone when rung, and the handle fits into the palm of my hand. The circular rings on its base signify unity, infinity and perfection. I believe it was chosen by Elizabeth and carefully transported to St Helena by James Halliburton.[126]

I believe I am with child. Nature's monthly inconvenience having been absent, I have had no use for the silk rags. It is difficult to enjoy my usual breakfast due to strange feelings of sickness. A piece of dry toast is all I am able to retain. I have experienced such tiredness that I need to take to my bed for an hour in the afternoon. Aunt Dorothy is to visit later this morning. She is such a wise woman and a source of quiet strength for Uncle

Mark, in his many complex interactions with the British Government, the Company, the native islanders, and the slave population. I am not yet ready to share this news with Anthony as I do not want to raise his expectations. It is customary for slave women to assist in delivery on St Helena, but I have such trust in Aunt Dorothy that, for my first child, I cannot think of anyone I would rather have to support me.

Extracts from KRB journal
Late afternoon, Mid-September, 1814

Anthony is due to arrive home at any minute. Aunt Dorothy has given me a number of instructions on how to care for myself over the next few months and suggests that it is time to share the exciting news with Anthony. Firstly, I am to ensure that each day I get plenty of sunlight, fresh air, and exercise. I need to eat fresh fruit, especially oranges; vegetables; fresh and oily fish including tuna (albacore); eggs; seeds and nuts; and a small amount of meat. I should drink milk and clean water, but avoid drinking ales or wine. A few small meals throughout the day are preferable to overindulging at dinner. Aunt Dorothy suggests taking in a little fresh ginger to manage the nausea. Alternatively, a few powdered cloves may be dissolved in water for 30 mins, strained, and sipped as needed. She asked me if I had ever taken sick as a child. I assured her that I have always been fit. My aunt Margaret insisted we drink plenty of milk purchased from the 'milk below' maids who carried buckets attached to a yoke around their necks.[127] Margaret served eggs and fish twice or three times a week.

I answered questions about Mama and my sisters and their pregnancies to the best of my knowledge. Whilst my sister Margaret has sadly been unable to conceive a child, I was able to reassure Aunt Dorothy that Mama, Elizabeth, and Isabella had good-sized, healthy babies. As far as I am aware, very few infants were lost. Aunt Dorothy has told me she will check my baby is growing each month. I am to let her know when I feel the baby move, or if I am concerned. She estimates the baby will be born in the middle of March. Nearer the time, she will explain to me what to expect when the baby is about to be born. In the meantime, she suggests I put together a layette. She is agreeable to come shopping with me at Solomon's emporium as there is never a shortage of stock. She suggests infant gowns made from Egyptian cotton or muslin, little bonnets, and wraps and napkins made from muslin.

Extracts from KRB journal
November, 1814

This morning I felt a little flutter, like a butterfly gently beating its wings. I have developed a slight swelling in my belly just above the naval. Apart from Anthony who showed great excitement when I told him our news, Aunt Dorothy is the only other person on St Helena party to our secret. If I am successfully delivered of a son, his name will be Onesiphorus as is the tradition for the oldest Beale son. Onesiphorus was a good friend to the apostle Paul and is a good, strong name. According to tradition, St Onesiphorus was one of seventy disciples chosen by Jesus to preach, following on from the twelve apostles. He became a bishop, and was known for his hospitality, courage, and kindness.

Aunt Dorothy is pleased and happy for me. Each time I visit her she is measuring my progress. Each finger width is about a week in the baby's life. She is happy for me to drop the 'Aunt' when we are together. My nausea and fatigue have disappeared. I am feeling a new contentment and happiness, which is a prompt to write another letter to Elizabeth. We eat fresh fish most days and pick oranges from a tree in the garden. Anthony has recently received another promotion. Our marriage is very blessed.

Chapter 21

Letter to Elizabeth
Early November, 1814
Terrace Knoll, St Helena

My dear Elizabeth,

I trust this letter finds you in excellent health? I am writing to you at some length as, for reasons that will become apparent, I may not have the liberty to write as frequently from the new year. We are delighted to hear of the safe arrival of your newborn son on 3 August in your recently received letter, and that you have settled into your new home at Ramsgate. James told us that it commands a magnificent view of the sea and that you have a large garden and local schools for your girls. It must be pleasing to you that Matthew and Jane still wish to be part of your household and that they have also purchased a small home close by?

Charles Drummond Halliburton is a distinctive name. I understand that his godfather is Captain Charles Drummond that James served with in his early days on *Glatton*? What a pity that James is yet to meet his baby son. He was very excited about the prospect of another child and was convinced it would be a boy. I am sure Isabella will agree with me that we are all looking forward to James's two-day planned visit on his return to St Helena. He hinted that this may be his last voyage, so obviously we wished him well. He is greatly looking forward to spending more time with you and the children. He and Adam are good friends. It is pleasing to reflect that on past occasions both my brothers-in-law were serving on the same East Indiaman ship at the same time. There is never a shortage of stories over the dinner table, the recounting of which goes well into the night. I sense that Adam and Isabella may one day return to his native Scotland with their girls. He misses his family. He says it should be straightforward to find employment as a doctor in Midlothian.

James spoke very fondly of Captain Charles Drummond. The Captain commanded a tight and well-disciplined ship, including maintaining a meticulous ships' log, when James first joined *Glatton*, lessons he has taken on for his own command of the East Indiaman. As you may remember, they had two extended voyages together, to China and Benkulen respectively, in 1795/6 and 1798/9. As per James's account, the first voyage unusually was diverted to Cork on its onward journey from St Helena, their ship having narrowly avoided becoming embroiled in the Atlantic Raid, where the French incurred heavy casualties. The British declared a victory and captured three frigates and a corvette with only a loss of four men compared to 99 French.[128] James told us this was his first visit to Ireland and the seas around Cork were regularly patrolled by the Royal Navy in order to reduce the damaging effects on trade caused by French raiders. That small victory was to be overshadowed in December 1796 when:

'a large French invasion fleet slipped past the Royal Navy and moored off the South-West coast of Ireland at Bantry Bay.'

The weather defeated them, as storms did not permit them to land, so they returned to France where Wolfe Tone, an Irishman who felt the French were allies in their war against the English, wrote:

'we were close enough to toss a ship's biscuit ashore.'[129]

At Anthony's request, James showed us the manifest of officers and seamen from the log that is headed 'List of Officers and Seamen aboard *Glatton*.' The information commences with the captain or commander and senior crew, purser, surgeon, sailmakers, carpenters, gunners, cooks, boatswain, midshipman, to ordinary seamen, with details listed in columns. The sailor's name, his station, where he entered the ship. His wage and his fate: died, ran away, or discharged. For example, Enoch Jarvis, Seaman, Bengal, 2 March, 1785, died at sea 29 June, 1785. James said all the ports the ship calls at, together with the dates, are recorded, as are the passenger manifest, including the East India Company recruits bound for India. For example, passengers travelling from Europe to Bombay, from Bombay to Bengal, from Bengal to Madras, are listed in sections on a page. Another page details the departure from Deptford on Friday December 13, 1782:

'First part moderate breezes from the southwest. Fair weather – the latter part fresh gales … Afternoon, Mr Neale the Company's surveyor came on board and surveyed all the ship.'

Some of the writing is fading, making it harder to read, but we appreciated that overall it is very clear, particularly when one might consider the inherent instability of ships sailing on the high seas.[130] Anthony was fascinated with the logbook as it also gave him ideas for laying out his own journals.

James told us he supervises the loading of the ship with goods that are again meticulously recorded, as required by the East India Company. They have to be loaded in a particular order with designated weights for items. He showed us the inventory sheets for his ship. Every piece good has to be calculated carefully in terms of tonnage. For example, calico sheets (for beds) 80 pieces to the ton. At the back of the goods list is a page of items that may be taken on board by Commanders and Officers of East India ships outward.[131]

Anthony and I like to imagine where James is on his journey. We think by now he must be on his way to Whampoa, that we understand is roughly equidistant from the western Portuguese Macau and Chinese Canton on the extensive river system of the Canton or Pearl River in southern China. We have tried to follow his progress using a newly published map called 'The World On Mercator's Projection' that James generously gifted us for our wedding. It is an engraved map spread over two sheets that includes explorer's routes. It was created by a cartographer, John Pinkerton, in 1812 and drawn by L Herbert under Mr Pinkerton's direction. Much of southern Africa remains unexplored, and New Holland or, to use its newer name, Australia, has an almost blank interior. I can never look at a picture of this country without thinking about the prison ships in the Thames. I imagine that many lives are lost in transit and the voyage would be one of misery and despair. We live in a cruel world where transportation of desperate women or young children is considered acceptable.[132]

James told us how much he enjoys the time they spend at anchorage at Whampoa as it gives him many chances to observe life in the Far East. There are three famous pagodas that are used as navigation points. At any given time, there will be a mix of East Indiamen ships or junks and sampans at anchor, waiting to trade. The sampans ferry the offloaded goods to Canton about fifteen miles further up the river and return with goods to be loaded. Tea accounts for a significant amount of the load. He explained that crossing the Second Bar[133] refers to a sand bar about twenty miles down river from Whampoa and is usually included in the ship's log when identifying places on the return voyage from China.[134] Whampoa is surrounded by mountains and is picturesque.[135] He showed us a picture he has that was drawn by one of the many artists to be found in the area. It was indeed beautiful, and in its way quite different from anything I had seen before. The oriental architecture was particularly striking.

He loves the richly ornamented smock-like outfits worn by men and women alike. Although loose-fitting and usually simple in design, he tells us the embroidery or applique or woven designs are exquisite and often include seasonal or symbolic motifs, that convey the status of the wearer. Many different types of birds may be embroidered, such as cranes, golden pheasants, peacocks, wild geese, or peacocks; heavenly symbols such as the moon and stars or clouds and waves; Chinese symbols and mythical creatures such as dragons, the latter usually reserved for members of the imperial family or high-ranking court officials.[136] He is also fascinated by the ducks that are cultivated in the local ponds and surrounding fields. The Pekin duck has very soft, white and cream feathers and is much more upright than the ducks we are familiar with. He says he enjoys looking at the paddies planted with rice and the bamboo hats that protect the wearers against the powerful sun and rain. Apparently, it is common to dip the hats in water for the cooling effect. Heavy pails are carried using a yoke across the shoulders to balance the weight, not unlike the milk below maids if you remember them? James says he gets pleasure from informally trading directly with local people for fresh food. I am sure there must be many risks, particularly of disease and accidents, shipwrecks or fires on board, but he never dwells on these, merely acknowledging that is the price that has to be paid for trade between nations. You are never far from my mind when James is talking, and I think it must take great courage on your part to continue your life when he is absent for years at a time! James explained the high heat and humidity and the necessity to anchor for weeks if not months, can take its toll on sailors who are often poorly nourished, with typhus and other fevers prevalent and illnesses such as smallpox and leprosy commonplace. Piracy and accidently falling overboard, particularly if the sailor has overindulged in alcohol, are everyday perils. He told us there is a Christian cemetery for foreigners at Whampoa as well as a Muslim burial ground. His reasonable command of the local Chinese dialects and Portuguese languages, and a good understanding of the strict rules that underpin interactions between the English and Chinese, serve him well.

I take great pleasure in hearing the poetic names of the Chinese goods that he carries on *Glatton* and can well imagine the scent of the spices that he describes. At various times the goods in the ship's hold include silk, lacquer, porcelain, furniture; tea, both black and green; spices such as peppercorns, cinnamon, nutmeg and cloves, ginger, mace, saffron, anise, and turmeric. The names frankincense, spikenard, grains of paradise — a rare peppercorn from Africa that is occasionally found in our main goods store, bring to mind stories in the New Testament. One of the wonderful things about living here is our access to so many exotic spices. James says the places where they trade are always rich with artists capturing the different types of ships, the views, and the unique buildings that are so different from European architecture and other scenes of port life in exotic locations. Non-Company ships' passengers and crew include explorers, resident botanists, and artists.

Our known world is gradually increasing in size as distances appear to diminish. When I shared with James that I cannot envisage what the journey to the colonies that are forming in New South Wales and Van Diemen's Land must be like, or the complete loss of hope despairing convicts must feel, as thousands of miles of dangerous sea journeys and unknown punishments await them, his response was a surprise. He said reports are coming through that in many cases the food appears to be much better than what is offered to prisoners in England, and because of this, the population appears to be growing at a faster rate, at least amongst the free settlers, than perhaps would have been expected.

Anthony records all ships that dock at St Helena, the dates of arrival and departure, the names of the captains, and the temperature and weather for each day, in a large, leather-bound journal embossed with the stamp of the Honourable East India Company. His proudest moment was when a fleet of 22 East Indiamen ships arrived in James Bay on 12 May, 1810. He also maintains a private journal 'for his descendants', in case they should ever show an interest in his life! In a roundabout way, this brings me to some news I would like to share with you. We are expecting our firstborn in March next year, so I will be proud to show our new baby to James. As I told you in my previous letter, the occasion of our wedding was one of great excitement, although it seemed to pass too quickly. I love the silver bell Anthony gave me and use it to summon our domestic help if we require assistance. Several members of the Yon family work for us, as Anthony eschews the use of slaves. Even yesterday, there was a slave auction under the Peepal trees in town, advertising three slaves for sale and a further dozen to be let. Without any sense of irony, the poster continued to outline goods and livestock that would also be traded later that morning.[137]

The Palampore bed cover we received from the Wilks' family for our wedding is exquisite. It portrays a very complex and elaborate design of a central tree laden with fruits and birds, rather as I would imagine the Garden of Eden.[138] Occasionally I tutor Laura in her studies as she and I both enjoy the experience and opportunity to share our news. However, she is taking on more duties relating to Uncle Mark's role as Governor, filling in when required for Aunt Dorothy. My remuneration from Uncle Mark officially ceased at the time of our wedding. Laura is receiving lessons in French from Mrs Skelton. Like most of the wealthy white families on St Helena, the Skeltons have a house in Jamestown, and a country property at Longwood that is approximately 3.7 miles from Jamestown and a similar distance from Plantation House.

In his role as Governor, Uncle Mark continues to work extremely hard and is highly respected by all echelons of St Helena society. He has informally adopted a slave, which raises a few eyebrows.[139] On 4 June, eleven days before our wedding, Laura told me her father received the brevet rank of colonel from the Company, a more senior rank that entails some modification of his formal uniform, but without a commensurate raise in his remuneration for the role. This year he founded the Benevolent Society to 'relieve pecuniary distress and for the education of slaves, free blacks, and the poorer children of the community, with a particular focus on religion and morality.' Attendance at schools for slaves is only permitted if their owners give them time off.

Uncle Mark has continued to add to the geological collection of the Island that was started by Governor Beatson four years ago. I imagine this is quite fascinating, as the range of colours one observes in the rocks in the interior of the Island must be unique and entirely at odds with one's first views of St Helena that are overwhelmingly grey and depressing. Whilst the official samples have to be sent to London, he has organised a duplicate set to be carefully preserved and formally catalogued and kept on St Helena. He has also begun a series of extensions and repairs to Plantation House, that will include a more reliable water supply. Even though the property was only completed by a previous Governor, Brooke, in 1792, the unsuitable materials used, and obvious insect damage has necessitated considerable work to be done to bring it up to the standard required for the Governor's residence. When we first arrived last year, we experienced several episodes of water leaking in through the ceiling and unsealed windows, but luckily any damage was minimal, and carpets will be replaced as part of the planned work. On occasions the open drains, cess pits, and earth closets leave much to be desired, and brings back unwanted memories of London.

I have been reflecting on the momentous changes that have occurred in my life in less than twenty-four months. Two years ago, I was buying fish from boats moored on the River Thames. My nosegay could scarcely mask the obnoxious smells. Grease impregnated the pores of my face. A focus on the prison hulks blanketed by a rapidly approaching sea fog, the hanged men, and the impoverished mudlarks, was more immediate than the romance of tall ships bringing exotic goods from all over the world, or the new docks' development. I had never really considered the Thames as flowing with possibilities that could literally transport me to a different world. Our trip down the English Channel, particularly off the Dorset, Devon, and Cornish coasts with dangers from sudden winds, currents, or rocks, could potentially have ended in disaster were it not for the skills of Captain Christopher. In contrast, the Atlantic Ocean was vast, isolating, and dangerous, the uppermost concern that we may encounter ships from the French Imperial Navy. We only had glimpses of what lay underneath the hull of *Sir William Pulteney* through fast-moving shadows, but it caused us to reflect on the lonely fate of people who die aboard ship, their bodies consigned to the sea, or those who have the misfortune to fall overboard through an act of momentary carelessness.

I have met people and had so many different experiences

that never would have been available to me if I had remained in London. Likewise, I have had to remind myself that, whilst it is tempting to think of the islands we encountered on our journey to St Helena are some modern-day Garden of Eden, this is a simplistic perspective. After all, what started as innocence and bliss in Paradise, resulted in the present human condition of knowledge of sin, misery, and death. I have been rereading Milton's *Paradise Lost*, the extraordinary poem that I first read a few years ago. Uncle Mark is agreeable to my borrowing any book from the library at Plantation House. Once the initial shock of seeing St Helena's imposing cliffs and raging seas wears off – such a contrast to Tenerife and Cape Verde Islands – one does discover a softer interior. With the opening of my mind to new ways of looking at things, I wonder whether the biblical names that are widely used within St Helena may be ironic in a way that the 'lady' author of my favourite books would have appreciated. Now that I have made the acquaintance of many of the inhabitants, worshipped regularly at St James and the Country Church, and explored the physical environment of the island, several things have occurred to me. I am reluctant to share my observations with Anthony because the native St Helenians cannot regard the Island with the fresh eyes of someone from England, even from a relatively small area of London such as St George-in-the-East. Anthony states St George-in-the-East covers a mere 244 acres whereas St Helena has 28,000 acres, although he concedes not all of the latter is habitable.

The 'blacks,' or slaves, are largely confined to the next valley along from Jamestown – Ruperts Valley – if they do not live on the premises of their 'owners'. Their lives are miserable, with little, if any, freedom. They are still forbidden to enter certain buildings. Whilst their owners order them to attend church, they are usually forbidden to partake in the sacraments.[140] Despite slavery now being illegal under British law, it seems to thrive on St Helena. The Chinese are not much better off.

The military include two regiments which are governed by strict hierarchies and conventions. One cannot visit Jamestown without observing soldiers engaged in military activities. Possibly because there is very little practical work for the men to engage in, they too have been subject to unrest. In 1811, Governor Beatson banned soldiers from using the many inns and taverns, restricting their drinking to the army canteen. This provocation echoed an earlier ban in 1783 and predictably resulted in another rebellion, luckily with minimal loss of life. The 'Spirits Rebellion' resulted in seven men being hanged. A longer-term effect of the widespread restrictions on drinking freed up needed hospital beds.[141]

The civilian population, most of whom are employed by the Honourable East India Company, likewise have strict rules governing conduct and seniority. Even the senior members of council who meet weekly with the Governor need to follow strict protocols and ensure information is sent regularly to the Company headquarters in Leadenhall Street, London, close to where John Lindsay and Margaret were living. A census earlier this year showed the official population of St Helena is 3587 inhabitants, an increase of almost a thousand residents in twelve years, that is attributed to a mixture of reasons, including the importation of more Chinese workers. No wonder Solomon's emporium is flourishing! This year has also been remarkable as the first post office was established on the wharf. It may eventually lessen dependence on Solomon's postal service, or more informal delivery methods that have prevailed until recently. We were able to obtain a copy of the Census that listed the families and cattle upon the Island of St Helena taken 30 September, 1814.[142]

Please give my love to your beautiful daughters and your baby son. I hope that you have a wonderful Christmas and that from next year you will be able to enjoy James's company and celebrate all the important family events together. Please share my news with Margaret and John when you next see them, and also with James, Charles, and their families!

Affectionately,

Katherine Rose.

Chapter 22

Journal extracts
Sunday 19 February, 1815

I write this in my journal with a heavy heart. Isabella's husband Adam succumbed to an unknown illness yesterday morning. He had been feeling unwell during the week, but did not appear to have any rashes or other physical manifestations of illness, apart from feeling, as he expressed it, 'as weak as a kitten.' On Friday night he retired to bed early. Isabella woke at about 5 am yesterday and found Adam not breathing and cold to the touch. He was scarcely a month on from his thirty-ninth birthday. Due to the advanced state of my pregnancy, I have been unable to offer any practical help with the girls. They are being looked after by another family that are close to the Baildon's. Adam's funeral is to be held tomorrow, with the military forming a guard of honour at St James' Church. He will be buried in the Country Church cemetery with a small family burial service. I have agreed to look after the girls with the assistance of Peggy Yon, as Isabella is keen to attend.

Anthony spent the day with Isabella. He states she is very pale, but in control of herself and remaining strong for her children. She and Adam had only been married fourteen years. They have some assets other than their slaves, owning 15 cattle and 10 swine. His parents, William and Elizabeth, still live in Larbert, near Stirling in Scotland. I imagine his early death will come as a great shock to them. It was his intention to return to Scotland with Isabella once his contract at St Helena was completed. He had been held in very high regard by the highest echelons of the Honourable East India Company, especially since his bravery in ensuring

Governor Beatson's safety during the 1811 mutiny. Whilst it is perhaps not something that one ought to be thinking about at this time, the Company will be under an obligation to award Isabella a generous widow's pension. If she chooses to return home to England or Scotland to fulfil Adam's wishes, I will miss her dreadfully.

26 February, 1815

I have been struggling with walking for a week or two, unable to mount stairs without great difficulty. Dorothy visited yesterday and gave me a massage. Whether it was that or my baby moving further downwards, I feel I can breathe much better today and no longer experience the pain in my legs.

Thursday was a momentous day. The first post office opened on the wharf with the postmark of St Helena Packet Letter. This event followed a formal proclamation delivered by Uncle Mark as Governor on Monday 20 February. Certain rates of postage were agreed to be paid for letters that were transmitted from or brought to our Island. William Brabazon has been appointed as the postmaster. The new service is likely to be very expensive. Continuing with the informal method of getting letters delivered is a cheaper option. Our current system has been to give a letter to a captain or passenger on a ship, even one that may not be travelling directly to England, and trust that they then post the letter using the English postal service once they arrive at their final port. Written messages, to facilitate communication between ships at anchor in Jamestown Harbour, are taken by rowboat. Anthony has worked out that I would have been charged 1s 8d for the letters to Elizabeth — 8d shipping rate and 1s inland rate from e.g. Portsmouth or Falmouth to Blackheath. From 11 July, 1815, the official packet rate for letters will increase to 3s 6d.

One excitement last month was the arrival of the schooner *Saint Helena* from England on 16 January, for use by the St Helena Government. It is the first island ship to carry this name, but we are unsure exactly how the government will be using her. There has also been a 'riot' among the Chinese, eventually quelled by the military who used extreme measures.

Several soldiers were subsequently disciplined for using excessive force. The Yons were not involved in this, but some of their friends received injuries and they are understandably upset.

215

Chapter 23

22 March, 1815
Katherine becomes a mother

Katherine rises early, around 5 am, after a sleepless night, distracted by thoughts of giving birth to her baby. She goes out into the garden, as she does not want to wake Anthony. She inhales the scents of citrus, rosemary, and orange blossom that are carried on the air by gentle breezes, then exhales slowly. There is low cloud over Diana's Peak, but it looks as though the day will turn out to be fine. Water trickles from a nearby stream; strands of green weed just below the surface are pulled in the direction of the flow. Reaching down, she places her hand into the brown water, supporting herself by holding onto a nearby branch. It is colder than she had anticipated, but she enjoys the coolness. Tiny fish swim in the depths.

The noise the birds make at dawn is deafening. Katherine spots a native wire bird. Her plump body is barely supported by stilt-like legs, her eye overlarge in a round head. A yellow male canary, green helmeted, trills with ever higher notes, revelling in its joy of music, perhaps looking to attract a mate. Various sea birds are howling protests, sounding like tomcats fighting. Cattle are lowing, sheep bleating. There is a faint greasy odour, suggestive of goats, that she finds nauseating. It is almost impossible to avoid the animals on St Helena, but the smell of billy goats is repugnant. All her senses seem sharper. She gently touches an elaborate cobweb hanging from one of the bushes, drops of dew trembling from the horizontal strands. It feels slightly sticky. A small fly is trapped in the upper corner. The spider is absent, most likely still foraging for food.

She replaces a rock that looks out of place. A tiny false scorpion scurries away. Overnight her abdomen squeezed tightly. It was difficult to get comfortable.

Katherine likes to talk to her unborn baby, telling him stories. She is convinced she will deliver a son and privately she calls him Christopher. Anthony is excited about the prospect of becoming a father. On frequent occasions, when he wakes in the morning, he puts his ear to her belly, to listen to the baby's heartbeat. Yesterday, she had felt restless and full of energy. She spent some hours cleaning the house and preparing the room where the baby will be born, although Peggy and Sarah Yon between them had left very little to be done. In the evening, Anthony suggested to Katherine that they go out for a walk. They watched the sun setting over the sea, reminding her of the beautiful sunsets experienced when *Sir William Pulteney* was anchored at Tenerife. The hues of purple, orange, pink, violet, and navy blue gradually disappeared as the sun sunk beneath the horizon.

There is a wooden seat in the garden and Katherine sits down. Her baby's foot pokes out from under her left rib, and she strokes it gently. The views from this part of their property are primarily to the west and south. One time, Anthony took a boat out and at a prearranged time she was able to wave to him from the garden.

Katherine was longing to see another sunrise, but in almost two years living on St Helena she has only seen one, as it is more challenging to observe because of the topography of the Island. Anthony had taken Dorothy, Laura, and Katherine very early one morning soon after they arrived in St Helena to Longwood, at the invitation of the Skeltons, who were staying at their country property. At an elevation of approximately 1700 feet, they had an excellent view of the rising sun that started to appear just before 6 am. The colours were most unusual. The sky briefly developed a distinct greenish tinge before the sun fully emerged from the distant sea and the colours settled into a more conventional violet, deep pink, and orange-yellow. Following on from the shared wonder, the Skeltons had served a substantial but very welcome breakfast, and part of conversation at the meal was conducted in French. Katherine had been impressed with Laura's command of the language, a skill no doubt inherited from her father Mark, a polyglot. Katherine wonders whether her baby will be good at languages, or what kind of life he may lead. Many native-born St Helenians have worked for generations for the Honourable East India Company and are content to live out their lives on the small island, but Katherine secretly hopes that her son will wish to explore the world like so many males in her family. In the meantime, she appreciates her beautiful house with its many bedrooms she dreams will eventually be filled with their children.

Katherine frequently gives praise for the life she is living on St Helena and how fortunate she was to meet Anthony so soon after her arrival on the Island. Each weekend, they spend time together, finding a sunny but private place in their garden at Terrace Knoll. They place a mat on the grass, often under the distinctive horizontal branches of the Cedar of Lebanon. The tree seemingly embraces them, whilst offering strength and protection. They both like the spicy aromatic scent of the wood with its undertones of camphor and citrus. In many cultures, the cedar is a symbol of eternity and immortality, and it has been revered throughout the ages. One of Anthony's favourite bible passages is from the Song of Solomon. He likes to read aloud from the illustrated King James Version Katherine gave him, to hear the poetry of the words:

'His eyes are as the eyes of doves by the rivers of waters, washed with milk, and fitly set.

His cheeks are as a bed of spices, as sweet flowers:

His lips like lilies, dropping sweet smelling myrrh.

His hands are as gold rings set with the beryl:

His belly is as bright ivory overlaid with sapphires.

His legs are as pillars of marble, set upon sockets of fine gold:

His countenance is as Lebanon, excellent as the cedars.'[143]

Occasionally she responds with her own favourite passage:

'As the apple tree among the trees of the wood,

So is my beloved among the sons.

I sat down under his shadow with great delight,

And his fruit was sweet to my taste.

He brought me to the banqueting house,

And his banner over me was love. [144]

Lying in the shade of the tree, each recalls a favourite place. Anthony not infrequently rides his horse to Lots Wife's pools, a dramatic series of rockpools where he swims alongside small sea creatures such as sea urchin, eels, or crab, that make their homes there. The waves crash over the edges of the pools. He imagines the scene as he inhales through his nose, follows the breath down the length of his body, then exhales, visibly relaxing.

Katherine is reminded of a recent conversation with Uncle Mark. His experiences in India led him to interact with devotees of Yoga, who practise breathing techniques to achieve a sense of wellbeing. He had instructed Dorothy in these practices, as he thought she would be interested in using them with expectant mothers. With the sun gentle on her face, Katherine dreams of Tenerife, her first experience of a sub-tropical paradise. How long ago that seems. Turquoise seas, with gentle waves, break on the beach before retreating with a little rush of sound, gathering strength for the next wave. Hot, white sand feels gritty under her feet. She picks up little cowrie shells, the white remains of cuttlefish, and small pieces of seaweed that pop underfoot, releasing the faint odour of brine. She espies fishermen with freshly caught fish, the creatures flashing silver and green as their scales catch the sunlight. In the distance the sea is gathering strength. She follows the bigger waves until they crash into the cliffs in a shower of white foam. At the end of this vision, as she exhales, she deliberately turns her face to the sun, taking in its rays. She imagines her newborn baby on the beach beside her, also enjoying the warmth and the water.

A loud knocking from the kitchen window startles Katherine, abruptly waking from her reverie. Peggy Yon is calling her in for breakfast. She gets up slowly, unsure whether she wants to eat anything, although Peggy usually has something to tempt her.

As she enters the house, Peggy greets her. 'Good morning, Katherine. You are up early.'

'I could not sleep. I believe my baby is about to arrive. I have been experiencing strange pains in my stomach, so I don't feel hungry.'

'Can I offer you some raspberry leaf tea? It is important that you keep drinking. Perhaps you can eat something small to keep up your strength?'

'The tea and a couple of dry biscuits may settle my stomach. I can smell Sarah's bread baking, but I do not want to eat that today.'

'Don't forget, I have assisted at many births in the Chinese community,' says Peggy. 'Dorothy is keen for you to go about your normal business as long as possible and to drink plenty. Perhaps later, you might enjoy some of Sarah's lemonade?'

Katherine particularly enjoys the drink Peggy's sister makes from an old Chinese recipe using lemons, Chinese barley, and raw cane sugar. The lemonade, being sweet, as well as having additional herbs such as lemongrass added, will sustain her over the next few hours.

'Yes, please Peggy, if Sarah is able to make some more. I think I finished what was in the jug last night. I am a little tired, so I may return to the garden after I have spoken to Captain Beale.'

As Katherine heads down the corridor, she is greeted by Anthony leaving his bedroom.

'Good morning, my love. You are up early. How are you feeling?'

'A little tired, so I am planning to return to the garden and doze in the sun's warmth. I am getting more frequent muscle contractions that I feel in my belly and my back, requiring me to stop what I am doing for a few seconds.'

'I am sorry to hear that. I have to leave for work now, but I will ride over to Plantation House and request Dorothy comes over as soon as she is able to do so. In the meantime, I am sure Peggy and Sarah can attend to your needs. I am so excited that we may soon be meeting our newborn baby. One of the Yon men can come and get me from town if you need me sooner than the usual time I return home.'

'It will be a comfort having Dorothy here.'

Anthony kisses his wife gently on the cheek before going out of the door. Katherine walks down the corridor to the back exit. A clean, slightly yeasty and sweet aroma permeates the house, but Katherine does not feel hungry. She is so fortunate that Dorothy is able to be present for the delivery of her baby. When she arrives, she and Peggy will prepare the front room.

Katherine closes the door behind her and heads for the flower beds where she has left some garden scissors and a flat wicker basket. She plans to pick some flowers, whilst using the breathing exercises that Dorothy has taught her. The sun is starting to feel hot, so she turns to it and tries again to imagine she is back on the beach at Tenerife. Nothing feels quite real, as though she is experiencing a dream, and she has a sense of being outside her body as an observer. She cuts some flowers, keen to avoid ones with too strong a perfume in case they set off her nausea.

She hears Dorothy's voice 'Katherine, I've arrived.'

Dorothy waves from the house, having ridden her little donkey, Maughold, from Plantation House. The name is of the patron saint of the Isle of Man and is pronounced similar to 'mild.' She jokes that Maughold is both old and with a mild temperament – for a donkey. She has found it difficult to master the art of horse riding.

Katherine brings the flowers into the kitchen and places them in a vase before returning to her room. Dorothy comes towards her and Katherine leans on her, almost doubling over. The belly tightenings are now much more frequent.

'Let me help you to get onto your bed,' says Dorothy. 'It is best to do it between contractions.'

'Thank you,' gasps Katherine.

She lies on her bed facing the window. She draws up her knees as her body is swept along by a wave of intense pain. She is drowning in wild seas. Squeezed. Dragged downwards. An unrelenting current. Gasping. Her tummy rises, tight as a drum. Intense pressure, blocks out thoughts. A rolling pain goes from her belly to her back, pulling her down the bed. Barely seconds elapse before the pressure builds again, making her gasp and call out.

'Ow, ow, ow!'

A few seconds respite.

'You are doing fine, Katherine,' says Dorothy, rubbing her back in circular motions. 'Peggy is here, too, and will bathe your face to make you more comfortable, and then we will both help you off the bed.'

Katherine nods her thanks.

She is assisted off the bed. Her belly squeezes, throbbing, all consuming, a hard ball. Dorothy and Peggy hold her as she crouches, her nails digging into the backs of their hands, half-moons drawing blood. Deep inside her belly, something pulls and snaps, a hot rush of fluid gushes. Cramping gives way to burning, stinging, pressure: she urgently needs to evacuate her bowels. Bearing down with all her strength when the waves of pain return, she wants it all to go away. Her hair is wet, the floor is wet. She is passing a large melon, too big to be a human baby. Dorothy shouts:

'Stop pushing. Take little breaths through your mouth.'

Belatedly remembering their practice sessions, Katherine does her best to follow Dorothy as they pant in unison. She looks down. She thinks she can see a bit of dark hair. She is panting like a rabid dog. Her birth passage is burning, her body cleaving. Dorothy is gently pressing downwards on the baby's head, so that it is born slowly. Numbness replaces burning. A sudden relief of pressure. Katherine lifts her shoulders. The baby's head turns to the left. She has another strong pain. Yet another hot rush of fluid, followed by a curious emptiness.

'It's a boy.'

Dorothy holds up the baby by his feet. He is crying. A fat purple cord is looped around his neck like rope. Dorothy quickly slips it over his head, wipes his mouth. Miraculously, Katherine's pain disappears. She is exhausted, but feels triumphant, as though she can do anything she needs to do in life. Peggy assists her back to bed. She holds her son, taking in the smell of him, silently thanking God for this miracle. She relaxes into the bed, the first time she has held a newborn baby. They look at each other uncomprehendingly, their faces both foreign, yet strangely familiar. She touches her son's tiny hand. The miniature starfish-like fingers with almost impossibly small nails curl around her fingertip. Tiny veins on the back of his hand are just visible beneath the skin. His eyes are a deep blue. All the colour of the world's oceans are captured in his intense gaze. He is all knowing. Suddenly, a small triangular pink tongue appears between his lips. She laughs. His fingers uncurl. He places his two middle fingers into his mouth, sucking gently. Katherine strokes Onesiphorus' head, breathing in his scent. She can feel ridges on his skull. Gently touching the soft spot that is shaped like a diamond, she notices it is pulsating slightly. The baby's head is damp, elongated, mottled with blood. His soft ears are moulded close to his skull. In the crease of his elbows, under his arms and behind his knees, are patches of a creamy white substance like lanolin. He has fine hair on his back. His legs are plump, red, and smooth and drawn up to his belly, from where a fat, whiteish-purple tube tied with string dangles. As Katherine inspects his private parts, a stream of water hits her nose.

'Onesiphorus!' The name sounds strange.

The baby turns his head slightly as his mother's finger brushes his cheek. She needs to nurse him. Dorothy helps attach him to her breast. There are little snuffling sounds as he breathes through his nose. His sucking brings on a strange sensation. Her whole body relaxes. She feels another urge to push, a slight pressure, and a sudden warmth. Dorothy cradles a purple-white coloured, dinner plate sized, fat disc of the afterbirth.

'Here you are, Katherine. You wanted me to show you the placenta. As you can see, it is shaped like a cake. The umbilical cord has three little tubes inside that kept your baby alive when he was inside you. The baby's side of the afterbirth resembles the back of an autumn leaf.'

'How extraordinary.'

'On the reverse side you can see that it is quite different. It has liver-coloured cups of fissured flesh. I check it to make sure that it is not damaged.'

'Which part is the caul?' asks Katherine.

'These are the membranes that protected Onesiphorus and kept your waters in place. Now, I am going to give the afterbirth to Peggy, and I need to rub the top of your belly to check that it is remaining hard. Would you like me to help attach Onesiphorus to your other breast?'

'That would be wonderful. He still seems to be hungry,' said Katherine. Dorothy assists her and the baby sucks vigorously before releasing the nipple, grunting and falling into a deep sleep. He has evacuated his bowels, producing a black, viscous-like fluid. Although there is no odour, Katherine is slightly repulsed.

'I assure you, Katherine, this is normal and a good sign that everything is working as it should. Would you like a drink of lemonade?'

'Yes please.'

Sarah Yon knocks on the door and enters. There is a pleasant smell coming from the laden tray she is carrying. 'I have brought you some steamed chicken with mushrooms and dried lily flowers and some *tang yuan* – sweet rice balls with black sesame filling – and some ginger tea. In our community we offer these to new mothers to ensure they return to full health.'

'Thank you, Sarah,' says Katherine. 'I am very hungry, so I hope you do not expect me to leave anything.'

'Please call me if you need anything further,' says Sarah, before leaving the room.

Whilst Katherine is eating her lunch, which is as delicious as Sarah promised, Peggy wraps Onesiphorus in a warm towel, quickly washing his head and body in cooled boiled water. Just before he is dressed in swaddling clothes, Katherine catches a glimpse of thick fair hair that had been almost invisible moments before. She is assisted to wash and change into fresh clothing. Dorothy and Peggy clean up the room. Sarah's husband is sent to fetch Anthony from the Paymaster Office near the barracks.

Katherine is dozing when Anthony enters and is invited to hold his small son. He is entranced. 'Welcome to the world, Onesiphorus.'

The curtains of the room have been drawn back and the beams from the setting sun penetrate far inside the room, showing dust motes dancing. Katherine's face feels wet. They are tears of joy, not sadness, as Anthony and she celebrate this miracle of new life. Onesiphorus will be baptised at St James' Church by the Rev Richard Boys approximately four weeks from his birthday. Sarah Yon offers her a tisane made from the Balm of Gilead – a perennial herb – and infused lemongrass that Dorothy assures her is safe to drink. The mixture is used in the Chinese community as a pick-me-up after giving birth. It tastes refreshing and palatable.

The Yon family use a variety of native-grown products in their cooking that are believed to be both delicious and good for health. The pigweed – *Amaranthus Lividus* – grows in warm, shady, and damp places and in taste is similar to spinach and goes well with diced pork or bacon. A different species of pigweed can be used to treat ulcers of the mouth or elsewhere on the body when the juice is extracted from the plant or roots. Water mint is found all over St Helena, growing near or in fresh water or marshy areas, and has a range of health benefits including treating fevers and digestive disorders when taken as a tea, and the wonderfully named donkey ears can be used in salads as well as medicinally. The Yons gather purslane that grows well in dry and poor soil, grinding the seeds to make flour, whilst the blacks eat it as a vegetable. Katherine is finding the locally grown and prepared foods delicious and is slowly learning how to cook both native and exotic dishes. Anthony not infrequently remarks on her skills as a cook. The Yons have promised to cook her a special dish made from pig's trotters that the Chinese traditionally prepare for new mothers.

Chapter 24

Journal extracts
May, 1815
Death of a second brother-in- law

We have been visited by a second great sadness in as many months. *Glatton* has arrived in port – on 12 May – with a hastily promoted Commander. Isabella and I learned subsequently that James Halliburton died at sea on 10 April, most likely from a tropical disease. He was fifty years old. A faster ship has already been dispatched to England from South Africa. No doubt Elizabeth has been informed of the tragic news that she will never see her husband again. Their infant son Charles will never meet his father. Anthony and his brother Onesiphorus received James's body that had been preserved for the remainder of the journey in a vat of arrack, as is the custom for a commander who dies at sea. His cask was lashed to the main mast of *Glatton* and guarded day and night in the manner that Admiral Nelson was cared for post death at sea.[145] Soon after reaching Jamestown, James's body was wrapped in a canvas sail, before he was speedily transferred via oxen cart and formally interred on 16 May, in the same grave as Adam Baildon at the Country Church. Anthony spoke with Rev Boys following the interment in order to organise a memorial service the following day. *Glatton* was due to depart that afternoon, but various crew were interested in attending the funeral to pay their respects to a popular commander. Uncle Mark acknowledged James's significant career with the Honourable East India Company and various tributes were given by Henry Upton on behalf of the Honourable East India Company. If there is any comfort to be had, Elizabeth will receive a generous widow's pension on account of the length of time James served with the Company, commensurate with his seniority. His second in command, Henry Upton, will sail *Glatton* back to Long Reach, and expects to arrive in England around the middle of August.

Isabella has told me that she is planning to return to England as there is no longer any reason for her to remain on St Helena. It will take several months for Adam's affairs to be finally settled. She has worked with Anthony to ensure her widow's pension will be organised as soon as possible. She is ably supported by her servants and the wives of officers serving in the Company. Her girls are understandably missing their father. Isabella has written to Margaret and John Lindsay enquiring about a property in Lee. Our brother James has recently purchased a house close by at Hither Green. Isabella and I have selected a headstone for the grave to commemorate both men. I have promised to visit the graves regularly once she has departed from the Island. The inscription reads:

In memory of Adam BAILDON M.D. Head Surgeon on this establishment. Born Jan 13th 1776, Died Feb 20th 1815. Also, of James HALLIBURTON Commander of the Hon E.I. Compys ship Glatton, Born Sept 24th 1764, Died April 10th 1815 on board that ship on the passage from China. Interred here May 16th by their widows, by whom this memorial is erected.[146]

<u>Postscript</u> (15 June – our first wedding anniversary): Anthony tells me his office has received sad news. *Arniston* has been wrecked during a storm on 30 May off South Africa, with the loss of 372 lives. There were only six survivors. It was the same ship where a notorious party was held in the April before I arrived on St Helena. Apparently, the Captain or the owner could not afford a marine chronometer.

July, 1815

I have only time for a brief journal entry. My day is planned around Onesiphorus's needs, as he still requires frequent feeding. Anthony and I try to have a quiet dinner together most nights, when he brings me up to date with the latest happenings on St Helena.

The Reverend Boys continues to upset his parishioners. On 15 April he apparently refused to admit into church the body of an Islander for a funeral, claiming that the funeral attendees were pagans who did not respect his church. What the final outcome was is shrouded in mystery.

Shockingly, on 22 May, again one believes instigated by Reverend Boys, the following notice was published including the words:

'No Slaves or Free Blacks are to occupy any of the Pews.'

On 11 July, our formal packet service for letters commenced from Britain to St Helena, with the St Helena Packet letter date stamp.

Country Church headstone for Adam Baildon and James Halliburton

Chapter 25

17–18 October, 1815
An unexpected visitor – a second baby expected

Katherine is carrying her small son, Onesiphorus, in a sling that she made. It is late in the afternoon, but the weather is mild. Like most of the other inhabitants on St Helena, she is heading down to the harbour, near the quay. For the last two days, there have been rumours of a number of vessels approaching Jamestown, including one with an important personage, travelling on a 74-gun third-rate ship of the Royal Navy. Faster ships have brought the news of Napoleon's defeat at the Battle of Waterloo and his abdication as Emperor. He was held under tight guard at Torquay, then Plymouth in Devon, before it was announced that he would be sent in exile to St Helena. Several ships are anchored, and their sails have been furled, but the largest ship is still displaying some of its sails.

She shifts the baby slightly, as her right shoulder is aching. Onesiphorus is gaining weight rapidly. In his seven months, he has brought great joy to both his parents. He has settled into his own routine. His overnight sleep is supplemented by a short nap of about an hour in the morning and a two-hour sleep after lunch. His cot was made for them by James and John Yon, using cedar wood harvested from the property at Terrace Knoll. The top rails can be removed to make a small bed. James and John also built a matching dresser with changing table. Onesiphorus is starting to eat solid food to supplement his milk diet. Katherine steams vegetables to make them soft and encourages him to feed himself. He likes fish and rice and is gradually expanding what he eats with no discomfort. After overcoming some initial difficulties, Katherine enjoys nursing Onesiphorus, producing prolific amounts of milk. She will always be grateful to Dorothy and Peggy for their care of her and her baby.

For the cooler months, the Beales have been living in a small house in town. The weather is warming, so they plan to return to Terrace Knoll soon. Peggy and Sarah Yon live on the top floor of the town residence, whilst their husbands have remained at Terrace Knoll, as there is always a considerable amount of work to do on the property.

Half the island must have descended on the Harbour, thinks Katherine, as the news has spread about an exciting event. It is hard to move with the crowd unpleasantly close at times. She cannot see Anthony but expects he is here somewhere. The largest of the flotilla is *HMS Northumberland*. It is lying deep in the harbour with huge white sails. There are many sailors in the rigging, suggesting the sails are being taken down. A lighter with oarsmen is making its way out to the ship. Governor Mark Wilks is a passenger and is dressed in his uniform of Colonel. Katherine espies Laura and Dorothy in the distance, and skirts around the crowd to make her way over to them. Meanwhile, the crew are now standing to attention. A high-pitched whistle sounds and a smallish man in a triangular shaped hat is assisted onto the boat. Others follow, including two women in splendid gowns, the likes of which have never before graced this island. The harbourside crowd is growing. Soldiers in scarlet coats are standing to attention, muskets by their sides.

Women with small children hiding behind their skirts whisper to each other.

'They say it's Emperor Napoleon, Bogey – the Bogeyman. He was defeated at Waterloo on the eighteenth of June and the British don't want him, and neither do the Prussians.'[147]

I have reached Laura and Dorothy. The latter whispers in my ear, 'This is an act of great discourtesy. Mark has been surprised as the rest of us. He had no advance warning that *HMS Northumberland* had been sent out from England with its famous prisoner. There is no place to accommodate him, nor the people that have sailed with him. We believe there are other vessels making their way to St Helena. Mark was formally received by the Emperor in the company of several other gentlemen aboard *HMS Northumberland* on the fifteenth of October, but Napoleon elected to remain on board until this evening. He will spend his first night in Jamestown at Mr Porteous' house, as he is anxious to avoid the crowds.'

The entourage of perhaps twenty persons has docked in several boats at the harbour. It is beginning to get dark. A small procession moves up from the water. The watching crowd parts to enable passage of the visitors. Mrs James Bennett happens to be at a vantage point near the steps of the Glacis and is the first lady to receive a bow from the Emperor Napoleon. His landing at the upper stairs, rather than the usual and most frequently-used lower steps, was a surprise to many in the crowd, not least to Mrs Bennett. In formation, the procession makes its way, military fashion, up the main and only street. A whistle is blown, a command given, and the line of people stop in front of the government buildings. The few steps leading to the main door are ascended by a small party that disappears indoors. Accompanying soldiers from the St Helena militia peel off to either side, proceeding at a quick march to return to their parade ground. From the ship in the harbour, the sounds of a military anthem carry over the still water. It is unfamiliar to most of the shore-based observers, although it is not completely strange.

The harbourside is gradually emptying as the crowd moves further up the street.

Katherine turns to Dorothy and Laura. 'I had better leave you now as Onesiphorus is getting restless. He needs to be fed and bathed before I get him ready for bed.'

'We are happy to walk with you as far as your house. We are planning to return to Plantation House, as Mark will be fully occupied.'

They arrive at Katherine's house in less than five minutes.

'Good night and thank you for seeing me home safely.'

'Good night. We will be in touch,' chorused Dorothy and Laura.

The fresh air has been good for Onesiphorus, and the time passes fast. Katherine puts him in his cot, and he is soon asleep. She just has time to freshen up and ensure Peggy and Sarah have prepared an evening meal when Anthony returns home about 7.30 pm.

Over their dinner, they talk about the most exciting event on St Helena within living memory.

'I'm sorry I was unable to find you at the harbour, Katherine, but as you may imagine we have also been very busy in the Pay Master's Office, including finding suitable accommodation for Napoleon's first night ashore. Mr Porteus and his family agreed to vacate their home at very short notice and with not a little inconvenience. Tomorrow, an urgent review of suitable accommodation will be undertaken, not only for Napoleon, his immediate family, and supporters, but also for the many soldiers that have accompanied him to ensure he does not escape his island prison.'

'I gather that Uncle Mark is very upset about the failure of the British government to give him any notice. I managed to find Laura and Dorothy in the crowd, and I am sure we will hear more about it in coming days,' said Katherine.

'I'm afraid these events will mean that I will likely need to work many extra hours,' said Anthony. 'It might be safer if you, Onesiphorus, Peggy, and Sarah return to Terrace Knoll sooner than we had planned. It may be necessary to accommodate some of the visitors in this house.'

'I will speak to Peggy and Sarah in the morning and ask them to let their husbands know to start preparing for us to return to Terrace Knoll. I will see if we can return before the end of the week.'

'I would be most appreciative,' said Anthony. 'I think it is time for us both to retire to bed after such an exciting day.'

The next afternoon, Katherine receives a visit from the two Balcombe girls, Jane and Betsy, their younger brothers, William, Thomas, and Alexander, and their mother, Jane. They have travelled in a carriage from their home *The Briars*. Their father, William Balcombe, a colonial administrator with the Honourable East India Company, is rumoured to be an illegitimate son of the Prince Regent. It seems Mr Balcombe does not discourage this rumour. [148]

'Good afternoon, Katherine,' said Jane, a little red in the face. Her usually immaculately groomed hair is somewhat array. 'It is sweet of you to look after the girls for me when you are so busy with the baby. As you know, I need to take the boys to Solomon's. They are growing so fast their shoes no longer fit. I am sure the girls can fill you in with the news.'

'That is a pleasure. Onesiphorus will be pleased to have someone to play with.'

'My husband has been called to an urgent meeting by Colonel Mark Wilks and Admiral Cockburn, who travelled with Napoleon. Come on, boys, we need to leave. Girls, be polite and please assist Mrs Beale in any way you can. I hope to be back within the hour, Katherine.'

'That is perfectly fine. I will see you to the door.'

'Mrs Beale, we have something exciting to tell you,' the girls cried in unison.

'Please come and sit at the kitchen table where we can have a drink, and you can tell me your news. Onesiphorus is asleep but I expect him to start waking soon. Perhaps you could start to tell me what has been happening Jane?'

'It seems that Napoleon may be coming to live in our garden!' explained Jane. She is fifteen and takes her responsibilities as the oldest child very seriously. 'On the way home from a visit to Longwood, which is barely habitable except for the few rooms occupied by the Skeltons, Napoleon asked about the Pavilion. It seems it can quickly be cleaned to accommodate him and his immediate family. That is why our father is in this important meeting. I fear he will find the Pavilion not to his liking, as there is only one main room and an even smaller room above the Pavilion.'

'*C'est fantastique*,' said Betsy, who at thirteen is a lively girl and an excellent French speaker. She tends to revert to the language when excited. 'I will be able to talk to him *en francais tous les jours. Parlez-vous,* Madame Beale?'

'*Un petit peu*,' responds Katherine, 'but I think it is better to speak in English so we can all understand your news.'

'Apparently, Napoleon wants to get away from the heat and the crowds in Jamestown,' said Jane. 'He plans to move as early as this evening. It will be temporary accommodation whilst soldiers are deployed to make Longwood more suitable. The latter property has been chosen as it is relatively easy to secure in case any attempts are made to escape.'

A loud wailing interrupts their conversation.

'Would you like to come with me to get Onesiphorus?' asks Katherine.

'Yes please.'

'*Oui, s'il vous plait.*' Betsy cannot help herself.

The remainder of the afternoon passes quickly. Such is the Island's informal communication, that barely twenty-four hours elapse before it is confirmed in everyone's minds: the self-styled Emperor has been banished to St Helena following his defeat at the Battle of Waterloo and his subsequent abdication. Anthony returns home that evening with further news. Nothing remains a secret for long on St Helena.

'Good evening, my love. Hello, Onesiphorus. Supper smells good. I have not had the chance to eat lunch,' exclaims Anthony.

'Welcome home! Give a kiss to Daddy before you go to bed, Onesiphorus,' says Katherine. 'Onesiphorus has had some steamed fish and vegetables. Perhaps you would like to hold him whilst I check that Peggy and Sarah are ready to serve the evening meal?'

'Hello, little man,' says Anthony, kissing the top of his son's head. 'How about I take you upstairs to bed and read you a story? I will be down in ten minutes, Katherine,' he calls out.

'Supper will be ready when you are.'

Anthony reappears wearing an old, comfortable jacket. He and Katherine sit down and start eating the white fish with a spicy sauce and fresh vegetables that Sarah Yon has served.

'I believe it is local fish, but I am unsure of the name,' said Katherine. 'The green vegetables are freshly picked from the garden. How was your day at work?'

'I expect you heard some of the news from the Balcombe girls?' said Anthony. 'Napoleon was brought to St Helena as part of the fleet commanded by Rear Admiral Cockburn. He and Mark Wilks have visited Longwood with Napoleon today, who has stated he will not move in until the accommodation is brought up to the standard required for someone of his status. It seems the Skeltons have been prepared to put up with many more inconveniences than Napoleon and his entourage will accept. The house is cold, damp, and infested with rats. The work at Longwood will necessarily include such additions to the house as will render it, if not as good as one might have wished, yet at least as commodious as necessary. It is possible that up to forty rooms will be required, such are the numbers that have accompanied the deposed Emperor into exile. The carpenters from *HMS Northumberland* will be employed to do this. It seems that a British-appointed governor of greater seniority may be deemed necessary, but it is too early to say how this might affect Uncle Mark's position as the incumbent governor.'

'It seems extraordinary that Uncle Mark has had to be put to so much trouble,' said Katherine. 'It will be interesting to hear regular updates from Betsy as to how he has settled in the Briars Pavilion, which I understand is very small?'

'I think we may find that Napoleon's arrival will change the nature of our society in ways it has never been challenged before,' said Anthony. 'I have heard rumours that the British are planning to occupy Ascension Island and claim it as a British territory. I am wondering if that is also their intention for St Helena.'

'Dorothy was saying how discourteous it was to Uncle Mark that he was not given advance warning. She wonders whether they will have to return to England much sooner than they had planned.'

'That is quite likely. There are rumours that such an important visitor will require a British soldier of higher rank than Colonel, but we will just have to see what eventuates. Napoleon is fortunate in that both Rear Admiral Cockburn and Colonel Mark Wilks speak excellent French. To change the subject briefly, this fish tastes excellent.'

'We are so fortunate, having Peggy and Sarah cook our meals,' said Katherine. 'I find I enjoy the oriental touches much more than our rather mundane English cuisine. What else have you been doing today?'

'I have been busy documenting the names of the ships that are a part of the official fleet from England, as the Honourable East India Company wishes us to continue to do this. As well as *HMS Northumberland*, I have recorded that the following ships lie at anchor as part of the official fleet from England: *HMS Icarus, HMS Havannah, HMS Peruvian, HMS Zenobia, HMS Red Pole, HMS Bucephalus,* and *HMS Ceylon*. The last two ships transported the fifty-third Regiment.'

'That sounds as though our population will be double the usual number. Where will all these men be accommodated?' asked Katherine.

'That is still to be decided, but most likely the soldiers will have to sleep on the ground using a blanket until sufficient tents can be sourced and erected. At least it is warmer here than England. Napoleon's personal entourage numbers some twenty-eight persons. It is probable they will be accommodated in Jamestown, and possibly in this house, so we will need to prioritise our return to Terrace Knoll. A census of available rooms is already underway. I understand Rear Admiral Cockburn will continue to live on board *HMS Northumberland* but will eventually live at The Castle.'

'You said you think Napoleon's arrival will change St Helena's character significantly?' asked Katherine.

'It is not generally known, but from now onwards, the island will be under the control of Rear Admiral Cockburn until a replacement may be found for him. Any current residents believed to be undesirable will be sent to South Africa. Soldiers will be stationed at all landing places. Very few ships will be permitted to land, and then only for the purpose of supplying water and provisions under strict conditions of monitoring. Any foreign ships will not be permitted to land. We will be virtually sealed off and prisoners on our own island.'

'I hope you are wrong, Anthony. I imagine all sorts of essential items we need for daily living will become scarce. If all the newcomers are reliant on Solomon's store for their supplies, it will be chaotic. Although, no doubt he will welcome the extra custom!'

'Unfortunately, I have also heard one will need a special pass to leave Jamestown after dark, which is all the more reason to return to the relative freedom of Terrace Knoll. The semaphore system will be employed to send signals around the Island to ensure Napoleon and his family's whereabouts are known at all times. It is also rumoured in the office that the Cape may be able to supply such things as bullocks, sheep, poultry, salt pork, wheat, forage, soap, salt, candles, and fruit, and even building materials, as it is unlikely there would be such surplus items on St Helena. The ships that will take the foreigners and others to the Cape could be used to bring these goods to St Helena.'

'It sounds as though you will be fully employed for the foreseeable future,' said Katherine, hastily stifling a yawn. 'I am feeling extraordinarily tired tonight, so I will take my leave and retire to the bedroom.'

'Good night, Mrs B. I will stay up for a little longer, as I have so much to think about, I doubt whether I will be able to sleep, at least for a couple of hours.'

Journal Extract
Late October, 1815

Although it is very early days, I believe I may be with child. I shared the news with Anthony yesterday. We moved back to Terrace Knoll earlier in the week and we were sitting under our favourite Cedar of Lebanon, something we have not had an opportunity to do for several months. I am pleased to say he is delighted as I am. We have agreed to keep it quiet for a few weeks, as the baby is not due until around my birthday next May.

We recently learned that James Halliburton's ship, *Glatton,* was unceremoniously sold by its owner, Sir Robert Wigram, Bart, for a hulk. This was shortly after anchoring at Long Reach in Dartford, on the south side of the Thames, on the 22 August, 1815, under the command of the hastily-promoted Henry Upton.

I have decided that writing long letters and extensive entries into my journal will not be possible once our second baby is born. I will try to correspond at least annually with Elizabeth, requesting that she share my news with the rest of the family, and focus on recording brief, factual information. It will preserve the remaining pages and ensure that I am prompted to recall events if asked. Anthony will continue to enter daily information into his official journal. The birthdates and baptism details of Onesiphorus and his unborn sibling will be recorded in the family bible, as is tradition in the Beale family.

Anthony is much busier at work than prior to Napoleon's arrival. Thankfully, our lives have not yet changed in any significant way, and we are still able to purchase necessary food. I have bought more cloth from Solomon's, as Onesiphorus is growing out of all his clothes, and I want to prepare some new items for the baby.

Chapter 26

Journal extracts
April 1816

Onesiphorus is now thirteen months old. For the last three months he has been crawling and pulling himself up on furniture. We have placed precious items out of his reach. He is walking a few steps independently, but can suddenly sit down on his rear, so he needs to be closely watched. Only yesterday, he took off at such a pace when crawling that his limbs got out of sequence and he toppled sideways, hitting his head on the hard floor. A second later he produced a roar of such volume that it echoed around the house, but he was soon comforted. I get great pleasure watching his development. He is a dear little boy with a sense of mischief and a deep belly laugh. He rarely cries. His eyes are a deep blue-grey shade, and his hair is thick and fair. Whilst I continue to nurse him before settling him to sleep at night, he joins us for the main meals of the day. It can be a messy business if I encourage him to feed himself. He is frequently vocal, with most of the words unintelligible, although rising and falling like speech. His first words of Mama and Papa are becoming more distinct and make us very proud. He still tends to put things in his mouth. I had to scoop out some dirt yesterday, but it does not seem to have harmed him. James and John Yon have cleverly made a chair out of wood that can reach the height of our regular table. By the innovative use of hinges, it can be folded to use as a little table with a seat on either side.

My pregnancy continues to go well. Dorothy has been able to reassure me about this. However, she told me in secret a few weeks ago, that she, Uncle Mark, and Laura will likely be returning to the Isle of Man, due to the appointment of a new Governor who is not an employee of the Company. This appears to confirm Anthony's suspicions. She has asked me to keep the information to myself until it is formally announced. Anthony has been quite depressed. He feels our future has suddenly become very uncertain. The Company has had to cede control of St Helena to the British Government for as long as Napoleon is in residence. Anthony says that Napoleon has a high regard for Uncle Mark, but things are expected to change quickly. Sir William Webber Doveton, the Paymaster, has become tight lipped and circumspect in his behaviour. Sir William has had a long career with the Company's service, entering employment aged 15, in June, 1769. He has a distinguished background as a magistrate, judge, President of Council, and was a popular Commandant of the St Helena Volunteers during the Napoleonic wars. In 1810, he was rewarded with a Sword of Honour. The Beales and Dovetons are related by marriage. Both families have lived for generations on St Helena, and are closely involved with the Company, in both civilian and military capacities.

We are still reeling from the shock of Napoleon's arrival. The population on St Helena increased significantly. This included 2,000 troops. By all accounts they have very little to do, which is of concern. Idleness leads to trouble. It is proposed that the soldiers not already involved in rebuilding Longwood be put to work improving St Helena's defences and its roads. Such upgrading will ultimately be of benefit to us all. When it is wet, many roads that are barely more than paths become a quagmire, very greasy and impassable, due to the presence of marl, a sort of sticky clay that covers a lot of the Island's surface. Occasionally, broken stone is placed over the worst sections. The steep drops on either side of some roads present a challenge to horseback riding, but my own skills in controlling a horse quickly improved with early lessons soon after our arrival on St Helena. Anthony's present for our son's first birthday is a little pony that we can lead around the grounds of Terrace Knoll.

The Balcombe girls came to Onesiphorus's 1st birthday party. Betsy was full of news about her visits to Napoleon. She has had many conversations with him conducted in French. She also wanted to talk about her recent visit to Plantation House:

'I had but just recovered from a slight attack of *coup de soleil* and he was quite cheering in his sympathy. I told him it had been occasioned by my walking with Captain Mackey and my sister to call on Mrs Wilks, and that our way led over the high mountain at the back of The Briars, called Peak Hill. It was certainly a tremendous undertaking for one so young to attempt. The mountain is not accessible to four-footed animals, and is two thousand feet in height, nearly perpendicular. Imagine, therefore, our toiling to its summit, and descending to the deep valley beneath, crossing Francis Plain, and ascending two mountain ridges, before terminating our expedition! We arrived at Plantation House worn and weary, but when once there, the kindness of the lady governess and the care and attention of her amiable and lovely daughter soon made us forget our fatigue. At noon of that same day, we started for Sir William Doveton's lovely valley of "Fairy Land."'[149]

I was delighted to receive a visit from Laura yesterday. We have rarely managed to see each other, since the arrival of the Emperor. She told me about her visit to Napoleon on 21 April, the day before, accompanied by her father and another lady who has been accommodated at Plantation House and was to act as her chaperone for the occasion:

'This was the third time Papa has made a formal visit to Longwood,[150] although we attended Admiral Sir George Cockburn's ball at Maldivia house on 20 November, when Napoleon was in attendance. On two previous occasions, Papa has been invited to make a formal visit to Napoleon, the first on 12 December, two days after he moved into Longwood. At this time, Papa agreed to procure a horse and carriage for Napoleon, as close to Christmas as possible. His second visit on 20 January, was the occasion of a spirited debate with Napoleon, carried on over a game of chess.

'We proceeded from Plantation House, in a huge vehicle recently made for travelling around St Helena. It was drawn by six bullocks that were driven by three men, each responsible for two bullocks. Luckily the animals were placid. It took some hours to cross the narrow roads and paths, with sharp turnings and precipitous drops, before we arrived at Longwood. The journey appeared to upset my chaperone, who was using her fan to ensure her face remained cool, as it filled with colour. Captain Younghusband of 53rd regiment travelled with us, and three other ladies.[151]

'Napoleon was formally dressed in a green coat with his stars and orders, wearing ribbon-silk stockings, small shoes with gold buckles, and a distinctive cocked hat of beaver fur, that is designed to be held under the arm without losing its shape. He was standing to receive Papa, who was also in his formal dress. Although neither Papa nor I needed the assistance of an interpreter, we were introduced to his secretary Count Las Cases who will perform that service if required.

'Papa formally presented me to Napoleon, who smiled at me and said (in French), "I have long heard from various quarters of the superior elegance and beauty of Miss Wilks; but now I am convinced from my own eyes that the report has scarcely done her sufficient justice." He then bowed to me, as I curtseyed to him and he proceeded to say, "You must be very glad to leave the island," to which I replied, "Oh no, sire, I am very sorry to go away." Napoleon answered, "Oh, mademoiselle, I wish I could change places with you." He then presented me with a bracelet.'

Laura showed me her bracelet that I admired.

'I am sorry to hear that you are leaving the Island,' said Katherine. 'You will be greatly missed.'[152]

'Papa tells me his replacement, Sir Hudson Lowe, arrived on board *HMS Phaeton* on 15 April. He is to take over as governor. Father, Dorothy, and I will be leaving on *HMS Havannah,* a fifth-rate navy frigate, a glamour ship that is built for speed. It will be interesting to compare against our journey on *Sir William Pulteney*! *HMS Havannah* was part of the squadron that accompanied *HMS Northumberland* last October. Papa was able to meet with Captain Hamilton at that time, to ensure the dates of our proposed travel would fit in with the planned voyages. Our belongings are being loaded today, and we leave tomorrow, 23 April. I will write to you once we are settled at home in Douglas.'

Laura and I kissed goodbye. Once again, my heart is heavy, as Isabella and her children also left for England this week, sailing on the East Indiaman *Carnatic* that anchored in Jamestown Harbour on 23 April. It is due to arrive in Purfleet about 20 June. She and her girls came to Onesiphorus's birthday party, and I went to see them for the last time a week ago. She is looking forward to meeting the family after a nine-year absence. I am glad that Onesiphorus demands much of my time, otherwise I fear my grief might be overwhelming, but I have a new baby to look forward to and no doubt there will be little time for letter writing, journal entries, or indulging in sadness.

Anthony and I celebrated my 22nd birthday on 28 May with a picnic, sitting on a woollen rug under our favourite Cedar of Lebanon tree, at Terrace Knoll. The weather was a little on the cool side, but it was a gloriously sunny day with deep blue skies. We gave Onesiphorus several rides on his little pony. Anthony says he has the potential to be an accomplished equestrian! Even to my untrained eye, he does appear to have a good sense of balance and no fear when he is seated on his pony. Our new baby is due to arrive tomorrow. There are already some early signs of his or her pending arrival. Peggy and Sarah will both be assisting me this time. They have delivered several Chinese babies without any adverse events over the last twelve months, and I have full confidence in their midwifery skills.

Betsy and her sister, Jane paid a call yesterday, as they were missing Onesiphorus. I requested they limit their visit to an hour due to my fatigue. As before, Betsy is full of news about Boney, as she calls him. He has now procured a Phaeton from the Cape. It is considerably lighter than the old barouche Uncle Mark gave him from Plantation House. Stables have been constructed at Longwood, and Napoleon has been seen on frequent occasions atop a horse. However, Napoleon's freedom to go anywhere is likely to be severely curtailed by Sir Hudson Lowe, who reportedly intends to implement his responsibilities as Governor to the letter.

Betsy says Napoleon has confided in her that he has great respect for Colonel Mark Wilks, and he likes to hear stories about him, but Napoleon is also concerned for Betsy's welfare, as she proceeded to tell me.

'I described all our adventure, and the kindness we had received from Mrs Wilks at Plantation House and from Miss D at Fairy Land during our visit in March. A few days after, Napoleon invited the former lady, with her husband and daughter, to Longwood, but from political reasons the honour of the interview was declined, until the twentieth of April when

Miss Wilks was formally presented to him. Seeing me one day unusually low-spirited, Napoleon inquired what could possibly have happened to drive away the dimples from my usually radiant face. "Has anyone run away with a favourite protégé or is the pet black nurse, old Sarah, dead! What can have occurred?"

'I told him it was neither one thing nor the other, but simply that our kind lady governess, Mrs Wilks, had left the island, and such demonstrations of grief had never before been seen at St Helena. She was so beloved, people of all ranks and ages crowded to the Castle to say, "God bless you, and a safe and happy voyage home." I told Boney, not a dry eye was to be seen amongst the crowd then collected. That leave-taking of our much loved and respected governor and his family resembled more a funeral than a levee, so sad and solemn was every face. I fancy I can see them now, following the party to the beach as they embarked in the barge that conducted them on board *Havannah*; and when the noble frigate spread her canvass to the swelling breeze that bore from the little rock, those who had contributed so much to the happiness of its gratefully impressed inhabitants, groups of sorrow-stricken ladies were seen wandering under the peepal trees of the Sisters' Walk watching the vessel as she lessened from their tearful gaze, bearing on board a family who had rendered themselves so popular by their urbanity and kindness, which is even remembered to this day. I recounted the scene we had witnessed (and suffered with the rest) to the emperor. He was quite interested in the recital and regretted much not having been acquainted with the lady governess, as she must have been so very amiable.'[153]

Anthony tells me that one of the ships he logged on 18 May was carrying Sir Thomas Stamford Bingley Raffles. He is the Lieutenant-Governor of Java and has been recalled to London to report on some local issues. He sailed from Batavia on 25 March. He visited Napoleon on 19 May, but reportedly he was less than impressed with the Emperor. The Skeltons have also left St Helena, sailing on 14 May. No doubt they will be missed by Napoleon. They were generous in letting him stay at Longwood, but work will soon commence on a new Longwood property. Materials have arrived to enable this. It will be known as Longwood New House.

I was able to send a letter to Elizabeth which the Skeltons promised to post once they reach England. The cost of postage from St Helena is becoming prohibitive. On 23 May, the Paymaster's office required a double packet letter to be sent to Scotland to be charged thus: the total cost was 9s 4d – 2 x 3s 6d packet rate + 2 x 1s 2d double inland rate from London to Ayr, plus Scottish toll of ½ d. By September it is estimated that the following costs will be incurred for a single packet letter to Scotland: 4s 8d (3s 6d packet rate + 1s 2d inland rate London to Ayr plus Scottish toll of ½ d). 3d was charged by the St Helena post office for handling the mail, before any of the actual postage charges were incurred.[154]

Chapter 27

Journal extracts
January 1817

My journal is like an old friend – loyal, even if our paths do not cross very often. Last year turned out to be eventful. Anthony was promoted from Writer to Factor in October 1815. His quarterly salary was £45 for his Factor responsibilities and a further £15 as assistant in the secretary's office.[155] His total annual remuneration was £240. It was useful to have the extra money. Young children are expensive. I spend hours making baby clothes, or feeding the baby, who has a voracious appetite. From later this year, Anthony will become a Junior Merchant, First Assistant Paymaster, earning £350 per year and with the rank of Major. He believes his training at the East India College in Hertford prepared him well for this role, and his promotion has been quicker than some of his peers.[156] Despite the extra work following the arrival of Napoleon, his office remains small, with four men at any time occupying a given rank. He tells me that Law Offices and Courts are to be built by Sir Hudson Lowe, on the site of the main guard room in Jamestown. The Civil Administration of the Island is vested in the hands of the Governor and two Members of Council, but in addition there are 'ex officio' members. The two most lucrative posts in the administration under the Company, viz Paymaster and Accountant, each carry a salary of £1400. The other salaried positions in the East India Company's service are held by officials who are divided into four grades: Senior Merchants, Junior Merchants, Factors, and Writers.[157]

I received a letter from Laura at Christmas, with the splendid news that she will be marrying Sir John Buchan, a distinguished army officer, in Scotland later this year. He is some years older than her and an old friend of Uncle Mark. Sadly, her brother, John Barry Wilks, died on 5 September, 1816. He is buried in the family grave at Michael on the Isle of Man.[158] Laura says he was always frail, and struggled to speak or walk, but was cared for beautifully by members of her extended family. Whenever she saw him, he appeared delighted to see her. By all accounts he led a simple but happy life, nursed in a bath chair. She tells me that England has had one of the coldest, wettest summers on record, with widespread crop failures. Unusually, they have had to light fires to keep warm in July.

Our second son, Edward, is now six months old. His birth on 1 June was exciting, but a much calmer affair than the arrival of his older brother. Onesiphorus is not quite sure about the baby. He appears disappointed when they cannot play together. This week, Edward has started learning to throw a small ball. Onesiphorus is happy to play that game with him and keep him occupied. Both boys have plenty of energy. Edward moves remarkably fast, propping himself up on his elbows and moving his body forward, whilst dragging his tummy and legs against the floor, not unlike a porpoise. It is a very different crawling style from Onesiphorus, who used to extend one leg out and propel himself forwards, whilst still sitting on the floor.

Last August, we heard that Tristan da Cunha has also been claimed as a British Territory and occupied by troops. Anthony thinks the Company will be unlikely to relinquish control of St Helena, although the reality is that, for the foreseeable future, we are under British Government control.

On 21 November last year, The New Theatre opened in mid Jamestown with a performance of *John Bull*. The comedy was first performed at Covent Garden in March 1803. John Bull became the national symbol of freedom, of loyalty to king and country, and of resistance to French aggression during the Napoleonic Wars. He was the ordinary man in the street, who would fight Napoleon with his bare hands if necessary. I cannot imagine that Napoleon would be permitted to watch the play! Elizabeth informed me that she, her husband, James Halliburton, and our brother James, went to a performance later that year (1803) after her husband had returned from the Far East in late April. The occasion had coincided with my 9th birthday, and I was disappointed not to see them. Our production was managed by Denzil Ibbetson who also performed on stage. He is developing quite a reputation for his drawings of Napoleon when he is not engaged in his work in accounting as the Chief Commissary Officer, responsible for feeding the regiments.

Chapter 28

**Journal extracts
January 1818–August, 1820**

It may give an indication of how our lives have changed. I have not had the time or energy to commit to my journal for a full twelve months. We have been blessed with a third healthy son. Anthony was born on 24 November, two months ago. This time the labour was very quick, and I held him within an hour or two of my pains starting. Unusually, St Helena experienced an earthquake on 21 September, but luckily it caused no damage. We were preparing to go to bed about 10 pm when the floor rippled underfoot. Some tremor was felt for a few seconds. It was all over before we realised what was happening.

There have been occasional shortages of paper. As a consequence, my long letters to Elizabeth are considerably curtailed. At times, we receive a letter that has been turned inside out and reused, with two postmarks apparent. The cost of official posting is becoming even more expensive, particularly if there is insufficient packet mail. This means the full cost of inland and ship rate may have to be taken on. The only relief is for soldiers who have concession rates of 1d, but these letters have to be prepaid and signed by the commanding officer. The courtesy has not yet been extended to the Company Pay Office. It is likely that the informal method of posting mail via a trusted traveller, successfully employed over many years, will continue.

Sir Hudson Lowe has not wasted any time building the law offices and courts above The Castle on the site of the main guard room. He has kept the garden above the buildings for his use when he is residing there.

We believe the Balcombe family have fallen foul of this gentleman in no small way because of their ongoing friendship with Napoleon. Anthony thinks Sir William Balcombe's position is no longer tenable. The visits from the Balcombe girls have been less frequent since the Wilks returned to England. People are wary of the new powers invested in the Governor.

I will be reduced to making small entries only in this journal, with three babies. I find I am thoroughly enjoying being a mother, and Anthony is proud of his small sons. However, his sometimes variable moods give me cause for concern. The children and I frequently visit their little cousins, with Peggy and/or Sarah accompanying me. Their husbands take turns driving the bullock cart.

December, 1819

We were blessed with a son, Robert, who sadly arrived before his time on 3 January this year. At first, he could barely take milk, which had to be administered in a little dropper. Peggy would spend many hours at night with him. Sadly, our baby died on 17 January, barely two weeks old. It brought back the memories of young William aboard *Sir William Pulteney*. I often wonder how Rachel and her family fared in India, but sadly we have not kept in touch. I am now well-advanced into a new pregnancy, and this baby is due in February. The Greentree family have become close to us, and Mrs Greentree was also delivered of a son who she has named John Charles. Sadly, she was unable to nurse him, but as I had plenty of milk, I was able to maintain a supply to give to her to nurture her small son.

The Balcombes left last year on 18 March. I receive regular letters from Betsy. She tells me she is developing into a competent pianist and is maintaining her French connections through a friendship with a local French family. This enables her to continue to speak French fluently.

We had a second earthquake on 12 August last year. Luckily, no one was injured, but a few people are concerned about the recurrence of such a phenomenon in less than twelve months. I am not superstitious, but I do sometimes get a sense that the many changes on St Helena have had an equally upsetting effect on Anthony, although it is nothing that I can explain rationally. Twelve days later, a momentous decision was taken at a public meeting. Anthony tells me that the significant change in opinion of the St Helena establishment can be credited to Sir Hudson Lowe. He is apparently indifferent to the conservative points of view long-held by many of the older and influential families on the Island. It was agreed that all children, born to the enslaved on or after Christmas Day last year, will be considered free. I hope to share this with Laura. She and Uncle Mark will be delighted to hear this news. Laura tells me that Samuel Ally, the slave who travelled back to the Isle of Man with them, is now fifteen, thriving, and devoted to Uncle Mark.

In July, Anthony recorded the visit of *HMS Trincomalee*. The cargo included bullocks and other supplies for the squadron based on St Helena, to assist in fulfilling its duties guarding Napoleon. She had stopped by during her maiden voyage in January. Anthony befriended the captain, who showed him around the impressive frigate, built with teak in Bombay, due to oak shortages in Britain following the Napoleonic wars. More worrying, in July, was the unrest between the Chinese in Upper Jamestown. Soldiers shot dead two Chinese. Peggy and Sarah were very upset. The two victims were family friends. In Anthony's view, the soldiers should be charged with murder. Such is the disruption on the Island since the huge population increase occasioned by Napoleon's arrival, that Anthony is concerned there may be no consequences for the soldiers. Following on from the visit by Sir Stamford Raffles three years ago, we learned that the Company have established a trading port on the island of Singapura. Anthony explained this move is highly significant, given the geographical location of the island on the tip of the Malay peninsula, with its strategic location between the Pacific and Indian oceans. The 'white' population on St Helena has increased to more than three thousand five hundred, so we can no longer say that we know everyone on the island! We hope to add to the population in early February, as once again I am with child.

August, 1820

Our grief is overwhelming. Our beloved baby Robert arrived on 20 February. Unlike his namesake Robert, who died last year, he appeared to be thriving. On 10 August he developed an unknown fever. Less than twenty-four hours later, he was taken. Both of the babies we lost were baptised and then buried with Rev Boys officiating.

The three oldest boys are now five, four, and two. Onesiphorus has started school and is enjoying the company of other children, including his cousins. Many adults on the Island still cannot read or write. It is unlikely this unfortunate state of affairs will be put to rights any time soon. School fees act as an impediment. It is to Rev Boys's credit that he spends many hours supervising the education and religious instruction of the children from poorer families. Clara George, who was born into slavery, has started teaching her own young children in her home and is now offering to teach the children of other slaves.

We recently had an unexpected visit from Miss Mason, for whom I have had a soft spot following our first meeting soon after I arrived in St Helena. She was very kind to me and expressed her sadness at the loss of our two babies. She tells me she is friends with Napoleon, and occasionally takes tea with him under a Cape Yew tree at the bottom of the garden. She often signals to him using a lamp, from one of the back windows of her house that looks straight towards Longwood. All this presumably without coming to the notice of Sir Hudson Lowe, whose attempts to enforce strict rules around his famous prisoner has led to what may amount to civil disobedience amongst some of the Islanders.

It seems our world is constantly expanding. News reached us recently that an English man, William Smith, discovered land south of the 60 degrees south latitude late last year, that he has christened the South Shetland Islands. Two expeditions earlier this year, the first led by Russians and the second led by an Irishman, claim to have found what they believe to be an enormous icesheet and possibly a whole new country. Since Captain Christopher spent so much of our journey to St Helena discussing navigation with Laura and myself, I find I have maintained a keen interest in better understanding measurements of latitude and longitude. With so many men in my immediate family employed as master mariners, I also find myself hungry for news about new discoveries made by brave seafaring men.

Chapter 29

Journal extracts
Christmas, 1821

Anthony and I have been blessed with a daughter. Katherine Ann Sibella Beale was born on 13 April. She has quickly become known to all of us as Kas. She is named after me and Anthony's mother, Anne. Her third name is after Sibella, the wife of the chaplain Reverend Bowater Vernon. He and his wife have become our good friends since they arrived on St Helena three years ago. Their daughter, also Sibella, is six months older than our son Anthony, and a regular playmate. Katherine's three older brothers are delighted with their baby sister and spend hours entertaining her. She is petite, and has been crawling for several weeks now and doing her best to stand, holding onto furniture and moving in a sideways motion. Her eyes are a deep charcoal, and she has the appearance of a much older child due to her fine features. God willing, she will have a younger brother or sister, about six months from now. Anthony and I are truly fortunate with all our children. We have planted a crepe myrtle tree in our garden in memory of both our baby sons. The plant comes from a not dissimilar climate in India. When it matures, it will produce scarlet flowers.

5 May was a momentous occasion when Napoleon unexpectedly died. I was still confined to our home, nursing the baby. Anthony attended the funeral, which took place on Wednesday 9 May on a beautiful, sunny day. I had spread a picnic rug outside our home at Terrace Knoll and was enjoying my time with Kas, listening to the birds singing, before my peace was rudely interrupted by the sound of guns discharging.

Napoleon's death was only two months after it was declared that Longwood New House had been completed. Unfortunately for him, he was not well enough to move into his new home. Captain Bennett, a friend of Anthony's brother Onesiphorus, confided that he sacrificed his dining room table to make one of the four coffins that Napoleon was buried in, due to a shortage of wood on the Island. Reportedly, Napoleon was buried in an inner layer of tin, then a coffin of pine, a third coffin made from lead, and an outer mahogany shell.

> 'Tap! Tap! Tap!
>
> Haste indeed!
>
> So great is the need
>
> That carpenters have been taken from the new church,
>
> Joiners have been called from shaping pews and lecterns
>
> To work of greater urgency.
>
> Coffins!
>
> Coffins is what they are making this bright Summer morning.
>
> Coffins–and all to measurement.
>
> There is a tin coffin,
>
> A deal coffin,
>
> A lead coffin,
>
> And Captain Bennett's best mahogany dining-table
>
> Has been sawed up for the grand outer coffin.'[159]

The St Helena Infantry Regiment and St Helena Artillery provided detachments to Napoleon's funeral.[160] Altogether, there were 24 coffin bearers selected from the Corps that carried Napoleon's coffin down the hill, in turns of eight, due to the extreme weight and challenging terrain. The main body of the garrison remained on the road above. A battery of eleven guns was posted at Hutts Gate. His burial was in the Valley of the Willows, or as Napoleon apparently preferred to call it, the Valley of the Geraniums. Many, if not all of the household of the late Emperor, subsequently sailed for England in the store ship *Camel*.[161]

It is almost twelve months since a review was held on Deadwood Plain, to mark the first anniversary of King George IV's accession. The death of George III and the end of the Regency period was a time when I felt a little conflicted. George III, who had come to the throne when my mother was an infant and whose long reign of 60 years covered my entire early life in England, died on 29 Jan 1820, barely three weeks before our second Robert was born. Sadly, King George's only daughter Charlotte died in childbirth in 1817. She was only twenty-one. Her mother, Caroline of Brunswick, died on 7 August this year, but it was an open secret that the marriage was experiencing difficulties. She was unable to attend her husband's coronation on 19 July, but whether this was because her husband did not want her, or she was too unwell to be present on such a demanding occasion, perhaps we will never know. We are a little uncertain about the governance of St Helena. Sir Hudson Lowe finished his role on 25 July. No doubt he and his family are looking forward greatly to returning to England. His time as Governor was controversial. He did not generate the loyalty for which Uncle Mark was renown.

We had some dramatic surf in March that caused serious damage to properties along the wharf. We watched from a distance, as Anthony said it was too dangerous to go any closer. He continues to maintain his journals of important events that affect the island. We are recording our children's births, baptisms, and, sadly for two babies, their death dates, in the Bible I gave him before our marriage. There is talk on the Island that the Ladder may be replaced with an inclined plane, a horse-powered machine that travels on rails. By employing pulleys, it will be capable of hauling goods to the top of the hill. It is unlikely to carry passengers, as it would be too dangerous. For the foreseeable future, the rope ladder will remain. It is quite astonishing how fast the soldiers can travel up and down this ladder, with seemingly no fear of falling. Anthony is unaware of any accidents relating to the Ladder. There is some disquiet in town. Traders have, for years, set up their stalls in front of the Government Gardens. Access will now be restricted, as the acting governor, Thomas Brooke, has erected new iron railings – originally proposed by Sir Hudson Lowe

– thereby forming a barrier to the Gardens. It was possible to purchase items of good quality much cheaper than at Solomon's store, so whether the stall holders will be permitted to sell their items elsewhere is no doubt still being debated.

Governor Brooke, the nephew of Robert Brooke, an earlier governor, has built himself a new home in Jamestown called Prospect House. He wrote a book about the history of St Helena that was published in 1808, and Anthony informs me that he is updating it to include the most recent history from 1808 to the present day. I am sure the information about Napoleon will make fascinating reading. He has already spoken to Anthony, as he plans to include a letter from Uncle Mark to the Honourable Court of Directors which was written in 1815 about the lands and tenures of St Helena. In the absence of anyone else, we are considered to be the closest 'family' connections that Uncle Mark has left on the Island.

It is rumoured that a large part of the Great Wood wall at Longwood has disappeared, with the stones used in building the Longwood New House. Urgent repairs are needed, and the military will be employed to do this work. Finding the culprits responsible might be harder, as it is thought that many would have left the Island altogether. There is also talk that the Country Church might be redesignated a cathedral.[162] From next year it will permit baptisms. Sadly, termites – the Islanders call them white worms – have damaged a significant number of trees at Plantation House. Laura and I used to enjoy collecting acorns and sitting under the magnificent oak trees around the property. One tree in particular stands out as a venue for a picnic soon after I arrived on St Helena, with none other than Captain and Lieutenant Beale invited to attend, under the supervision of Aunt Dorothy.

Chapter 30

Journal extracts
Mid-1823

I have been unable to maintain a regular entry in my journal. Despite this, I have almost reached the end of the book of blank pages given to me by Elizabeth, even though most of my writing has been as concise as possible. Anthony has promised to obtain another book of blank pages for me. We talked about whether the approach offered by a commonplace book might be more appropriate. My journal may become such, but I find value in writing about events as they happen, even if the entries are by necessity infrequent. I have always regarded my journal as a trusty friend. Reflecting on things that I consider to be of interest is as important to me as recording objective matters. Nevertheless, I am guided by the mores of the times. My most intimate thoughts and concerns form the basis for my silent prayers, shared between my God and me, that remain private.

Laura writes to tell me the sad news that Samuel Ally, the slave who returned to England with her family, sadly died last May, aged 18. Her father is very distressed, but fortunately both he and Aunt Dorothy remain in good health. The epitaph reads:

An African and native of St Helena. Died the 28th of May 1822 aged 18 years. Born a slave, and exposed to the corrupt influences of that unhappy state, he became a model of TRUTH and PROBITY for the more fortunate of any country or condition. This stone is erected by a grateful master to the memory of a faithful servant who repaid the boon of Liberty with unbounded attachment.[163]

Following her marriage to Sir John Buchan on 22 July, 1817, Laura says they spend some of summertime in Edrom, Berwickshire, and Scotland, and in the colder months they live in London. They were unexpectedly blessed with a son, Mark Wilks Buchan, who was named after his maternal grandfather. He was born on 23 August, 1819, in London, when Laura was 22 and her husband 37. On 6 June last year, we too were blessed with a second daughter when Isabella Margaret Beale arrived rather earlier than we expected. Issy is much fairer than her older sister but is determined to try and keep up with Kas's activities.

<u>Post script</u>: we have recently received a letter from my sister Isabella to say that her beloved oldest daughter, Catherine Anna Baildon, died on 27 January this year. Obituaries will be appearing in *Blackwood's Edinburgh Magazine* for January–June, 1823, in the *Gentlemen's Magazine*, and *The Asiatic Journal* and *Monthly Register for British India and its Dependencies*.

The notice will read:

> *At Lee in Kent, aged 20, Catherine Anna, eldest daughter of the late*
> *Adam Baildon, M.D. of the Honourable East*
> *India Company's Service, St Helena.*

We know no more than this, as Isabella had given no indication in her somewhat infrequent letters that Catherine was unwell, although she was always frail. It is possible that moving to such a cold climate after St Helena may have contributed to her malaise.

Christmas, 1823

We welcomed our third daughter on 2 October. Bessy's full name is Elizabeth Maria, named for my older sister Elizabeth and Anthony's late sister Maria Mills, who sadly died aged 35 two years ago. Maria's husband, Captain Moses Mills, had been a widower when they married. He also died at the very young age of 28 in 1810, so I never knew him. Their son, Samuel, is a frequent visitor to our home and regards Anthony as a father figure.

I am extremely fortunate with my pregnancies and the births of my babies, as to date they have been largely uneventful. We now have 6 children under eight. Despite welcome help from Peggy and Sarah, most of my day is spent in caring for the children, cooking meals, or making and repairing clothes. Sarah has offered to take charge of the cooking, but I find it relaxes me and I like to try new dishes that are unknown to me. We include Chinese and African foods in our daily repast. I encourage Sarah or the several black women I have befriended, to tell me more about the individual dishes and how they might be served in their native countries. We talk about rituals or other meanings associated with their special fare. As my knowledge increases, I find I look at plants differently. We are surrounded by nutritious foods, without necessarily understanding how to prepare and serve them.

The Governor, Alexander Walker, was sworn in on 11 March. He has proposed building an Observatory at Ladder Hill. This will enable a more accurate use of Greenwich Mean Time so that ships may reliably correct their chronometers that are essential for determination of longitude. The observatory will also be available for St Helenians to observe the night sky, although I feel it is only necessary to go outside on a cloudless, cool night, and we are rewarded with a firmament shining with stars. I love to watch with the little boys and try to be the first to see a shooting star. Sometimes we talk about the man in the moon and make up stories. At other times, particularly on a fine night, we will watch the sun sink beneath the horizon.

A new market has been established on the wharf, but I am yet to pay it a visit. As long as we do not experience a repeat episode of the violent rollers from some years ago, I imagine it will be a success, as previous – but informal – markets have been. Its location on the wharf will be convenient for ships unloading their exotic goods. Anthony is about to take on new responsibilities as deputy paymaster, with the rank of senior merchant. Additionally, he has been appointed purveyor to the hospital.[164] The extra income will be much appreciated by us all.

Late January 1825

Our dear son Adam was born on 3 January and is named after Adam Baildon. We plan to hold his Baptism at the Country Church on 13 March. In his early behaviours he is not unlike our two precious babies that were not destined to remain in this world. Unfortunately, he does not appear to have the robustness of his older brothers and sisters at a similar age.

Clara George's school is now a large and flourishing school in Jamestown, with too many children enrolled to possibly continue in her own home.

On 3 April last year, 151 of the Chinese labourers left on the East Indiaman *General Harris,* and apparently further repatriations to China are planned. However, the Yons have indicated to us that they have no wish to leave St Helena and nor does their extended family, so we are delighted with this news. The vessel had arrived on 6 March, 1824. Captain George Welstead, who knew both Adam Baildon and James Halliburton, having made several voyages with them, was delighted to take up the offer of staying at Terrace Knoll when he was not supervising the unloading and loading of the East Indiaman. *General Harris* was due to arrive at Benkulen in late May, before continuing to Penang with an estimated arrival of mid-August. Captain Welstead assured us that he would be agreeable to staying with us for a couple of nights on his return journey, which will be sometime towards the end of March this year (1825). We are hoping he can help us celebrate Onesiphorus's 10th birthday.[165]

Christmas, 1826

On 11 April we joyfully welcomed our tenth child, Rose Eleanor Beale, named after me and Anthony's older sister Eleanora, who recently celebrated her fortieth birthday. My sister-in-law has been present at the births of several of my children, including Rose. She joins her four older brothers: Onesiphorus, Edward, Anthony, and Adam, and three older sisters: Kas, Issy, and Bessy. Whilst I love all my children equally, there is something about Rose that awakens feelings of protectiveness in me.

My marriage to Anthony feels stronger than ever, and his overall mood has improved since the birth of Rose. There is something about this child that sets her apart from her brothers and sisters, and she is universally adored. We never stop thanking God for his generosity in giving us so many children. We are so fortunate to live in a large home with plenty of space for the children to play, and with weather that enables them to be outside most days. We have several ponies and two placid, small mares that the children share. The older boys in particular are becoming very comfortable riding the horses.

A notable change on the Island has been occurring. The rate of slaves being emancipated is growing faster. Nevertheless, there are still many slaves on the Island who are not yet free. Anthony and I think this is a shameful state of affairs. More and more children in these families are receiving an education. Thankfully, St Helena values educating its children. Clara George's school now comes under the auspices of the Benevolent Society, that should ensure its longevity. Uncle Mark would be very proud to know that the Society he started, plays such an important part in the lives of slaves.

In September, Anthony attended the ceremony for the laying of the foundation stone for the proposed Ladder Hill Observatory. If all goes to plan, the observatory will be opened the year after next.

Chapter 31

**Journal extracts
Early February, 1828**

Our fifth daughter, Margaret, was born on 16 December last. She is unlike her older sister Rose in temperament and colouring. She is a difficult, fussy baby who is unable to hold onto her feeds, so her feeding times extend to several hours over the course of the day. It is challenging to keep up with all the washing necessitated by her vomiting. I must confess I find the odour repugnant. Peggy has offered to look after her, so that I can attend to the other children. I pray each evening that God will find me a way to love poor little Margaret, rather more than I feel able to do at the moment. It is uncharitable of me to feel this way. Anthony is kinder to her, for which I am very grateful.

Last year, we had an extraordinary weather event that started on 24 July at 8 am.[166] Anthony recorded it at length in his official journal. It started with heavy surf and the wind blowing from a southeasterly direction, before it moved to the southwest, causing the sea to become very rough and the surf even higher than the rollers we experienced in March, 1821.[167] Several boats, including a valuable fishing boat, were driven onto the wharf and smashed. A coal bunker was breached, and its contents spilled into the sea. Several roads and tracks were damaged near Sandy Bay. At nightfall, we experienced lightning and thunder that upset several of our children, who all ended up in our bedroom. The water seemed to be pulled out of Jamestown Bay. Sadly, a woman fell into the water. Whether she was there for a purpose could not be determined. Her rescuer, a Lascar, also died from his injuries.[168] All this information was recorded over several editions of the St Helena Gazette. As can be imagined, the tragedy was talked about on the Island for many weeks.[169]

It is hard to say how things have changed since the death of Napoleon, but overall people seem more tense and nervous and less friendly than when I first arrived here. Anthony is not immune from this. He not infrequently expresses concern about how the Island will survive. There is a sense in his office that the Company is losing interest in what had been a very valuable asset. Our population has decreased markedly from its peak when Napoleon was here, now roughly half of what it was. There is less of everything: food, fabrics, variety in the goods. The prices have gone up significantly. The churches are still hostile to blacks and slaves. Indeed, slaves are still being sold under the peepul trees in town. Anthony states that, whilst the money is still being received from the Company, there have been instances where, unusually, some administrative matters have not been performed to the normally high standard expected. Unfortunately, it seems we have all become increasingly dependent on the Company to provide for whatever we require. The soldiers are less disciplined. There have been several instances of cannon being fired on ships entering James Bay that had not sought prior permission to enter. We hope that the changes to Ladder Hill might provide gainful employment to the military, who appear to be underutilised. The sense of purpose that prevailed during Napoleon's imprisonment seems to have abated. There are no longer the regular formal occasions such as balls and dances that used to be a source of weeks of anticipation and activity, to produce the most beautiful of gowns.

I was able to write a brief letter to Betsy Balcombe, with whom I maintain a semi-regular correspondence. She had a short-lived marriage in 1822 and gave birth to a daughter. Her father moved to the Colony of New South Wales with all the family in 1824 when he was appointed Colonial Treasurer. The family are living on a 6,000-acre estate, Molonglo, near Bungonia, County Argyle, New South Wales. Sadly, her sister Jane did not survive the voyage on *Hibernia*. Betsy tells me that her father is seriously ill. She and her daughter are planning to return to England with her younger brother William. They did not find the country appealed to them. I informed her that the Briars has now been purchased by the

Company, who intend to start a silkworm industry. Longwood itself, has become a farm. Napoleon's grave at Sane Valley attracts regular visitors.

Anthony came home last night more animated than when he left in the morning. He said it has been formally announced that, over the next five years, the Company will purchase any remaining slaves from their owners and declare them free. This will no doubt cause upset amongst some of the elites on the Island. With the repatriation of the Chinese, domestic assistance is becoming increasingly hard to obtain. We are to have a new governor: Brigadier Charles Dallas has recently retired from the army in Madras and will take up his post in late April. In the meantime, Mr Brooke will again resume his post as Acting Governor.

December, 1828

We have once again been visited by great sadness. Our beloved youngest son, Adam, succumbed to a mysterious illness overnight on 23 September. He was a dear little boy, quite different in colouring from Anthony and me, with very fair hair and a placid nature. Unusually, he had complained of a sore throat and aching legs, but was able to eat his supper before being put to bed. He did not appear in our bedroom in the morning as was his custom. Anthony entered his room to find him cold to touch. He was three and a half years old. Our hearts are broken. The children begged to be part of his funeral service. With the three older boys assisting Anthony to carry his small coffin, Peggy and Sarah supervising the little girls and looking after Margaret, me carrying Rose, we laid Adam to rest. May his dear soul rest in peace.

'How far from St. Helena to the Gate of Heaven's Grace?'

That no one knows--that no one knows--and no one ever will.

But fold your hands across your heart and cover up your face,

And after all your trapesings, child, lie still![170]

December, 1829

On 13 March this year, Adam Beale was born without incident. He has been named after his recently deceased brother as is the custom in our family. He is more robust than his namesake. Once again, I find I am with child, and our next baby will be born in early April. Last week, I received a letter from Betsy to say her father died in February, 1828. She and her brother William are planning to return to New South Wales to take up a land grant adjoining his property. Their brother Alexander wants to travel to Port Phillip and explore options for purchasing land further south.

The replacement incline at Ladder Hill has been completed, and Anthony tells me it is functioning as it should. A deep well of more than eighty feet is being sunk in Ruperts Valley, where the majority of slaves and ex-slaves live. It is hoped this well will provide them with regular fresh water close to hand and the water can be used to hydrate their crops, with a completion date early in the new year. Cattle ticks have become a problem. Sucking the blood causes the herds to lose weight and affects the milk production. Some islanders have lost most of their herds to the scourge. A radical solution needed to be found. The government has recommended introducing myna birds from India. They are brown birds, related to starlings. Their beaks are bright yellow, they have a yellow patch near their eye, and their sturdy legs are also yellow. Just how many will be captured and transported is not yet known.

I must confess, there are times when I miss my brothers and sisters so much that, if Anthony was prepared to leave St Helena and settle in England, it would make me very happy. Even though our relationship with Isabella was prickly at times, I miss her girls and also Elizabeth's daughters. Elizabeth's son Charles is 15 now, a strong, strapping lad who, Elizabeth writes, looks like his late father and has a similar temperament. I try to visit Adam Baildon and James Halliburton's grave regularly. My sister Isabella Baildon moved to Scotland to be close to her parents-in-law following the sad death of her oldest daughter, Catherine Anne, at Lee in late January, 1823. She writes that she returned briefly to witness her daughter Isabella's wedding in September, 1829, to Frederick Halliburton, a nephew of our late brother-in-law James. We were delighted to receive the news just before Christmas.

On 18 May, Anthony brought home a copy of a printed public notice on display in town. It advertised three slaves for sale and their current owners. A further eleven slaves were advertised as being available for hire or rent. The remainder of the notice featured domestic goods for purchase. It was printed by the government office …

Chapter 32

Journal extracts
December, 1831

It is extraordinary that two years have passed since my last formal entry into my journal. I have copied out some favourite recipes, but plan to make a dedicated book for these. I would like to pass them down to one of my daughters when the time is right. I continue to exchange letters with Elizabeth approximately twice a year. I request that she read them to family who live in Lee and Blackheath, so that they may be appraised of our life on this remote island. We have marked the births of two more sons: John Lindsay Beale was born on 4 April, 1830, and James Young Beale on 6 October this year. John Lindsay has been named after my sister Margaret's husband, and James Young after my older brother.

Much has happened on St Helena in the last two years. Our silkworms are producing silk that is sold in the London markets and generates some income for the Island. Anthony tells me that the outlay from the Company is still in the region of £90,000 per annum. A large proportion of this is maintaining the 700 or more soldiers and their families. We continue to have three companies of artillery, and the St Helena Regiment has four companies plus a corps of militia. Until recently, it seems no one has questioned why such a remote island requires so many men to defend it when, sadly, it appears there is very little that needs defending. Rather, it would appear that we are much more vulnerable offshore. Shockingly, we learned that the island ship that travels to and from the Cape of Good Hope was attacked by pirates. Most of the islanders who were crewing the boat were murdered. We held a memorial service for them and their families mid-way through the year.

Another memorial service was held for little John Greentree who sadly died in May last year, following an accident. He was the little boy born at the same time as our first son named Robert. He has been buried at the Country Church, not far from the Baildon/Halliburton grave. We continue to worship regularly there.

I was dismayed to learn of Elizabeth's youngest daughter Isabella's death on 18 September at Ramsgate in Kent.[171] She was twenty. I do not yet know what was the cause. By a very sad coincidence, she died on the same day as Uncle Mark. Anthony has found out from the current governor that Uncle Mark died as a result of apoplexy.[172] The announcements will be placed in the usual papers, including the *Asiatic Journal*. As Uncle Mark is still remembered very fondly by all sections of St Helena society, it is planned to hold a formal ceremony honouring his contributions to the Island, in the New Year.

On 15 July, the main theatre in Jamestown was destroyed by fire, the cause of which has not been discovered. We hope that it is not an omen of things to come. Anthony is uncharacteristically moody and appears to be taking less interest in his younger children. Onesiphorus is nearly seventeen but is showing no inclination to leave home. He provides great practical support to Anthony around the homestead. A gentle soul, he is very good with his small sisters and brothers. Edward is fifteen and a strong, fit lad who takes a great interest in his Uncle Onesiphorus's responsibilities in the military. Young Anthony has just turned fourteen and continues to build on his love of painting. He presented us with a beautiful watercolour of Terrace Knoll for Christmas, with prominence given to the Cedar of Lebanon.

Kas, Issy, and Bessy all enjoy each other's company. They share a large, bright, and airy room on the second floor of our home. We often hear peals of laughter from them. Rose, at five years old, is striking in her beauty, her baby features now more or less disappeared. Her dark, almost black, hair contrasts with her blue-grey eyes. She shares a smaller room with Margaret who has just turned four and is yet to lose her infant plumpness. She was eventually able to retain her milk feeds, but not before

I developed an uncharacteristic resentment towards her, something I find painful to admit to myself. She did not walk until she was nearly two. She is still content to sit on a rug in the garden making daisy chains out of flowers and making very little demands on anyone. Her namesake, my sister Margaret, is not unalike in her disposition. Despite my, at times, difficult relationship with Margaret when we were younger, we will always be appreciative of her and John Lindsay's generosity, as they have sent gifts on the birth of each of our children. They continue to host family Christmases at their home in Lee.

For Anthony's fortieth birthday last year, I put in an order to purchase a print of East Indiaman ships leaving St Helena in 1830 that will have pride of place on our dining room wall. No doubt the names of the individual ships are part of his journal.[173]

Chapter 33

Journal extracts
January, 1834

Halliburton Beale was born on 30 March last year, another healthy little boy, named after Elizabeth's late husband, James Halliburton. I am also expecting another baby in a few weeks from now. Anthony and I have agreed that our very large family should not be added to after that. It takes longer to recover from the births, and I will be forty at the end of May. He is also starting to express concerns about our future on the Island. I am worried that he may once again sink into a mood where he appears distracted and irritable. We love all our children dearly and thank God that they all appear healthy as they bring us great joy. We received very sad news at Christmas that my sister Margaret died on 8 October. She had been unwell for a few months, but her end was peaceful. Nevertheless, I was very shocked and sad for her husband, John Lindsay, who is 24 years her senior. She was barely eighteen months older than Anthony.

On 21st January this year, the parish committee put out the following announcement in relation to non-payment of taxes:[174]

The subject of parish and county taxes, having been frequently brought to the notice of the vestry committee, owing to the reduced state of the funds for the disbursement of the present year's current expenses, it has been deemed proper to refer to the list of in habitants with a view of ascertaining who does and who does not pay parish taxes.

By which it appears, to the astonishment of the committee, that there is a large portion of the inhabitants, many of whom amongst the most affluent and many receiving large salaries, who do not contribute anything towards the parish expenses …

We the members of the vestry and parish committee presume that every member of our community must feel a disposition to share in common with his neighbour the burden of taxation …

Proposed that the following plan be adopted as likely to equalize the burden of taxation and produce a sum annually sufficient to meet all exigencies viz the persons at present taxed for houses to continue to pay at the rate of 3s 6d per 100 value, and all other persons to be assessed at per cent or 5s per 100 of their annual income or salary …

Whenever a larger sum than what may be thus raised shall be required for the exigencies of the parish, that the increase be assessed in the following proportions. For example, if one half more is required, the house tax will be 5s 3d per 100 value, and the income tax or poor rate & per cent, or 7s 6d per 100 of the annual income or salary and so on.

Parish committee announcement re non-payment of taxes

We were also very disturbed, but not entirely surprised when the *St Helena Act 1833* was passed in August last year.[175] The Honourable East India Company sold the Island, its assets, and its inhabitants it would seem, to the British Crown. The various regiments have been dispersed, and many soldiers have left for South Africa. Families who have lived on the Island for generations are trying to decide whether to remain or move. Some of the civilian employees have been pensioned off, with others remaining, but on a much-reduced salary. The Governor will not be spared: his remuneration under the Company was as much as £9,000 a year. It will be reduced to about a quarter of that amount. Even Plantation House has suffered. Governor Dallas has moved to Longwood New House. He claims the drains around Plantation House have caused disease in his family. I am glad that Uncle Mark did not live to hear this news. Changes will start to take effect from 2 April, but may not be fully felt for another two years. Regrettably, from 4 September last year, we are completely owned by England. Administration of the Island will remain the responsibility of the Company for a further twelve months. As Anthony puts it: 30 pieces of silver has a current value of £100,000. The mood on St Helena is one of overwhelming grief and despair. Anthony and I have been discussing what it might mean for our family. Early last year, he wrote to my brother James, asking whether he might be in a position to be a guarantor for Edward and Anthony. Both boys decided they would like to go to England and train in the military and medicine respectively. They left St Helena last year. Anthony's brother Onesiphorus has decided to take his family to South Africa. He has requested Anthony look after Sunnyside to the best of his ability.

We had great pleasure meeting our nephew Charles Halliburton, who was 4th mate on *Canning* when it called at St Helena on 22 January last year, bound for England from a port in China. The ship was huge, displacing some 1,320 tons. Charles had disliked his earlier employment as an articled clerk. He was apprenticed from November, 1830, to William Bramley, attorney of the Court of the Kings Bench and Solicitor. He had discontinued the apprenticeship, much to the disappointment of his mother, Elizabeth, who had made use of her private contacts to secure the position for him. Anthony made a point of taking Charles to the joint graves of his father, James Halliburton, and uncle, Adam Baildon. The memorial headstone was erected by his Aunt Isabella at the Country Church, before she left the island. The two men enjoyed each other's company, with Charles viewing Anthony as a father figure.[176]

On occasions, when I am feeling less than charitable towards Anthony, I cannot help comparing him to Charles's father, James Halliburton.

James's stories of the places he visited and the people he met used to enthral me as a child and during the early days on St Helena. I am proud to have come from a family of master mariners whose lives were so different from the Beales. The latter have lived for generations on a small volcanic rock that seems reluctant to release them. Secretly, I believe Anthony would have preferred Edward and Anthony to remain on St Helena, but I fully supported their desire to lead their lives across a broader canvas. My brother James is providing practical and financial support to both boys. Edward has already enrolled in the Greenwich and Military Seminary. He commences at Addiscombe later this year. His twelve-month cadetship will equip him to become a soldier with the Company. Anthony is training to be a doctor. He plans to become a surgeon with the British India Office once he is qualified. He also wishes to develop his skills as a watercolour artist.

My older brothers, James and Charles Cobb Young, also left home as boys, to become apprenticed to a rope maker and a clock maker respectively from the age of fourteen.[177] On completing his apprenticeship, James decided to follow in our late father's footsteps to become a master mariner. He married Elizabeth Edsall Biggs six months after I left England, so I have not met her. I used to enjoy seeing James on the various occasions that his ship berthed at St Helena. Unfortunately, he and Anthony never developed a close relationship. There was always a certain amount of tension present whenever the two were together.

Charles abandoned his apprenticeship as a clockmaker after three years. He wanted to go to sea, like so many other males in my family. His first voyage was in 1803, when he served as 4th mate with a distant relative, Charles Raitt, commanding *Earl Spencer*. That voyage was characterised by a dispute between the commander and William Balcombe, Betsy's father, who was the second mate![178]

My brother Charles had been fortunate in 1809 to survive unscathed, when two East Indiamen ships that had departed with a large group from Portsmouth on 7 July were taken by the French. I was reminded of the event by Captain Christopher when we were sailing to St Helena, as *Sir William Pulteney* had also been part of that group of ships. Charles's last voyage on an East Indiaman was in 1815. Since then, he has preferred to serve on smaller ships.

Christmas, 1834

We grieve the loss of our fourth infant son on 3 April. Charles Cobb was named for my brother, but he was a sickly, jaundiced baby from birth and unable to suckle. As with our son Robert, we had to feed him by a dropper. Peggy spent many hours during the day and night ensuring he took some milk. Sadly, he failed to thrive. Following his baptism on 30 March, he barely woke. He was unable to take nourishment before passing away on 3 April. He is buried beside his three older brothers, Robert, Robert, and Adam.

On the death of an infant[179]

Sleep, little baby! Sleep!
Not in thy cradle bed,
Not on thy mother's breast
Henceforth shall be thy rest,
But with the quiet dead.

Anthony is under great pressure at work and looks exhausted. Following the cessation of the Company's trade, the commanders and officers of the East Indiamen ships consider themselves very much aggrieved, having found themselves without a job that they thought had been guaranteed for life. Many of them have spent almost their entire lives as employees of the Company. In July, they banded together and sent a letter to the directors of the East India Company, appealing for compensation in the shape of pensions. As a result of this petition and other appeals, the civil service will also be pensioned off. Anthony, as Paymaster, is responsible for allocating these pensions. He advised me that he may be eligible for about £500 per annum. Somehow, this will have to support a large family with possibly no home to live in. So many other families have already left or are planning to do so. Many of his siblings have gone to South Africa.[180] Anthony says it is entirely possible we may have to abandon both properties, Terrace Knoll and Sunnyside, for ever.

January, 1836

I received a sad letter from Laura to tell me that her son Mark Wilks Buchan, her only surviving child, died on 10 September, 1834 aged 17, and was buried in London. She is understandably heartbroken. Laura tells me she and her husband are raising funds to endow various education establishments on the Isle of Man, with a particular focus on girls' education. This is a realisation of a passion she shared with me on our original journey to St Helena almost 23 years ago. She continues to live in the Royal borough of Kensington and Chelsea. Two years ago, in 1832, she attended a ceremony on the Isle of Man where the foundation stone of a Tower of Refuge, built in the style of Castle Rushen, was laid on St Mary's Isle or Coniston Rock in Douglas Bay. It will provide a refuge for shipwrecked sailors. Many well-known Manx families contributed to the building.

Earlier in the year, 3 April, 1834, she was part of the wedding party when Dorothy Wilks married her cousin William Blamire, a farmer by profession, but now a member of Parliament for Cumberland. Laura says Dorothy continued to work as a midwife for several years after their return to the Isle of Man. An approach was made to her father, Mark Wilks, following the death of Napoleon, to see whether he would be interested in resuming as Governor of St Helena, but he declined the request. Correspondence relating to this were found in her father's papers following his death. In 1826, he was elected a Fellow of the Royal Society, a significant honour.[181] She said his death was a shock. Mercifully, it occurred in his sleep whilst on a visit to her and John Buchan at their country property, Kelloe House, in Berwickshire on the English–Scottish border. His grave is in the Grosvenor chapel, in Mayfair, London. The inscription on his memorial stone reads:[182]

Sacred to the memory of Col. Mark Wilks, of the Honble.

East India Company's Service; late Governor of St. Helena:

who departed this life 19th. Septr. 1831, aged 73 years.

Also of his grandson Mark Wilks Buchan, the beloved and only

surviving child of Major General Sir John and Lady Buchan: who

died on the 10th. Septr. 1834, aged 17 years.

Laura tells me there have been significant changes in England since we left in 1813. An Act in 1833 no longer permits children under nine to work. Children aged 13 and over can only work a maximum of 69 hours per week. Steam ships are gradually replacing sailing ships, with a greatly increased speed. The first public railway opened in 1830. The Poor Law Amendment Act of 1834 forces the poor into workhouses, no longer providing parish relief in private homes.

In keeping with the decline of many aspects of St Helena society, the spire on St James' Church has been pulled down. It has been deemed dangerous due to damage from insects. Possibly the material it was made from was unsuitable. We hardly recognise the church. The Ladder Hill Observatory, another institution that has become beloved by the Islanders, is also to be dismantled. Most of its contents have been sold to an observatory in Canada. The role and significance of the observatory in showing true mean time at St Helena and thirteen other locations including Amsterdam, Calcutta, Petersburgh, and Rio de Janeiro, was published in the Asiatic Journal.[183]

St Helena True Mean Time

The following plan for shewing the true mean time at this island and at Greenwich has been published by authority.

To prevent mistakes, a White Ball hoisted upon a staff over the observatory will denote the time agreeably to the following instructions:

- The ball will be hoisted half-mast at five minutes and close up at two minutes before twelve o clock.

- At the instant of the mean time at noon of St Helena the ball will drop from the top of the staff when the gun will be fired at High Knoll.

- The signal will be repeated at one o clock at the instant of Greenwich mean time for the benefit of the shipping.

A ship wishing to correct her chronometers and arriving after one pm and not likely to remain the twenty-four hours may hoist the Blue Peter at the main top gallant mast head when the same method will be adopted at the next ensuing hour after the signal. Foreign ships to substitute their ensign for the Blue Peter.

Should there be any uncertainty and the ship wishes to have the signal repeated she will dip the flag and re hoist it on observing the ball half-mast. The ball will again drop at the ensuing of the last hour.

Ships concealed from a view of the observatory will attend to the repeating ball at Ladder Hill and in neither case is any allowance to be made for loss of time since the astronomer will make the calculation of the few tenths required.

Life continues to take a backward step, with much bitterness on the Island. Many abandoned buildings are gradually being reclaimed by the land. All male inhabitants remaining on the Island will have to serve in a local Volunteer Corps from mid-year, to replace the soldiers departing from the Island. It is likely that Governor Dallas will have to relinquish his position.

Setting right the status of slaves is seemingly at a snail's pace. Whilst some are officially 'free,' many are still indentured to their owners, who are increasingly desperate for labour to keep their properties under a semblance of control. We have had many late nights trying to plan the best way forward. To this end, we have decided to call upon the generosity of John Lindsay, fully disclose all the issues and problems, seek his advice and possibly accept financial support, for any move from St Helena. Anthony will receive a pension as per his equivalent rank of Lieutenant Colonel. According to a private letter (an extract appears below) Anthony understands will be published in the *Asiatic Journal,* the following rates have been agreed:

> *From St Helena we learn by a private letter that the East India Company's establishment is dissolved the corps of artillery and infantry having been disbanded most of the men sent to their own parishes others having enlisted as volunteers for His Majesty's service in the East Indies. The officers are all pensioned on the following scale viz Lieut Colonels 460 per annum Majors 365 Captains 255 and Subalterns from 90 to 120. The civilians have likewise been provided for but not to the extent it was expected. A few are re-employed by His Majesty's Government.*[184]

The very poor way the Company have treated its employees will be the subject of a debate by the Honourable East India Company in September.[185]

My brother Charles spent two days with us on his way to Bombay, captaining *Justina,* a 410-ton ship. He has agreed that we should travel on the ship with him on the return journey from Bombay when he will dock at St Helena for approximately one week. His ship will eventually berth at Rotherhithe on the south bank of the Thames. This is only a short distance, approximately four miles, from Blackheath and Lee, and easily travelled in an hour. A large carriage and four horses will be provided by John Lindsay, with further transport put in place for our belongings.

From somewhere, and Anthony is a little vague about this, he has acquired a rather splendid bell, which he has wrapped carefully in blankets and placed inside one of our rooms. He has stated he will be bringing the bell with us, wherever we go. For the last two years, he has been harvesting various seeds, including from local willows and our Cedar of

Our most recent voyage was enabled by the generosity of our recently-widowed brother-in-law, John Lindsay. He paid the passage for Anthony and me, our ten children, as well as the ongoing transport of our worldly goods. When we disembarked at Rotherhithe Dock on the south side of the Thames, our large carriage took us directly to Blackheath, a distance of some 3.5 miles. Our goods were transported separately but arrived within 24 hours of reaching Blackheath. It took a couple of days before we were free from the sensation of rolling as on a boat. My English family, now largely settled just south of London, had begged us to come and live with them whilst a decision was made about our future. Sadly, it is unlikely we will get to see Isabella. She, and her now-eldest daughter, Elizabeth, are living in Scotland. Her daughter Isabella married Frederick Halliburton in 1829 in Lee, before moving to Devon. Adamina, her youngest child, who was barely five when she left St Helena with her widowed mother and older sisters, married William Owen on 13 April last year. They live near Blackheath.

With the help of my two oldest girls and the tearful Yon women, I packed up our home at Terrace Knoll. Onesiphorus, with the younger male members of the Yon family, helped Anthony with the heavier pieces. We left with all our worldly goods, including the bell, packed into the ship's hold. The majority of the voyage was spent below deck, where the five girls, four younger boys, and me were accommodated, although we were permitted on deck to take in fresh air. The crude tables and cooking arrangements were decidedly less comfortable than the initial journey I had taken to St Helena. Our lives had already started to change irrevocably.

The children enjoyed catching sight of fish and dolphins in the sea and watching birds flying in formation. We ensured that a strict timetable of events aboard the ship was observed, keeping the children occupied as much as possible. Each day we would start with a bible reading and a short period of prayers, before eating a simple breakfast. Each twenty-four-hour period was marked by bells, a novelty for the children, that helped break up the long days. We brought maps so that the children could follow where we were travelling and would be living in England; puzzles and books. I spent many hours mending and washing clothes, at times assisted by the girls, as the little boys frequently managed to tear or soil their clothing. We took turns to prepare treats in the galley, and marked Halliburton's third birthday on 30 March, which coincided with crossing the equator, and John Lindsay's sixth birthday on 4 April.

Prior to leaving St Helena, we paired each of our older daughters with their younger brothers to supervise them for the duration of the voyage. We had many discussions with Onesiphorus, Kas, Issy, and Bessy about what to expect on board the ship and how England differs from St Helena. I shared with them as much family information as possible. Anthony and I tried to allay any understandable concerns that the children had expressed, including the sadness at leaving friends and family behind on St Helena. They are looking forward to meeting their English aunts, uncles, and cousins.

Kas, at 14, was given responsibility for 2-year-old Halliburton, who is full of energy, running everywhere and turning into quite a mischievous boy; Issy, 13, looked after James, 4. Bessy, aged 12, looked after John Lindsay, 5. Rose, aged 10, Margaret, 8, and Adam, 7, were to look out for each other. I was responsible for overseeing each child and ensuring meals were available to be eaten, assisting as necessary with cooking or serving. Our accommodation was lighted with candles and oil-lamps. They had to be extinguished safely and relatively early each evening. Our eyes had to learn to adjust to the darkness. We relied on our hands and sense of smell to guide us to the secured bucket used in lieu of a chamber pot, if needing to visit it overnight.

Anthony told us that the ship was loaded with ale, beer, and wine that was carried in casks or bottles. There was beef, pork, bacon, suet, tongues, bread, butter, cheese, flour, fish including herrings and salmon, and some local fish purchased when the ship was in Jamestown harbour; lime juice, citrus fruits, oatmeal, potatoes, vinegar, various groceries and confectionary, and, most importantly, fresh drinking water. Non-potable items included coal, gunpowder, iron and lead shot, pitch, rosin, spare cordage, sheet lead, tobacco, tar, turpentine, and quantities of wood for the boatswain's, gunner's and carpenters' stores. The majority of these goods had to be loaded in such a way as to be accessible on the journey from St Helena to London. The ship was also carrying tons of tea, spices, and other exotic goods from India.

Onesiphorus and Anthony worked with Charles to oversee the loading of our goods and chattels. We were permitted four tons or twenty-four feet of baggage. These primarily consisted of small items of furniture, including a wash-hand stand and two porcelain chamber pots, as well as bedding and clothing, the latter most likely inadequate for the English climate but required for the ship. Each of the older children was allowed to select up to six possessions they wished to bring with them, including books. Anthony brought several of his journals, the bell, which was carefully padded with goat hair and wrapped in outer linen cloth secured with rope, and his precious seeds. He and Onesiphorus shared a cabin space with other men.

The rest of us travelled below deck, sleeping on an arrangement of tiered wooden beds, joined at either end. It was close to the water line. Several of the children were quite sick before they developed their sea legs after about three days. Dining was at a central table made from oak. It was bolted to the deck, as were the bench seats. Privacy, such as it was, consisted of curtains that could be unrolled to cover the bed space. Washing, of body and clothing, and toileting, was accomplished as discreetly as possible in the corner of our allocated space.

Before leaving St Helena, we secured both Sunnyside and Terrace Knoll as best we could, as we were unable to sell either house. We assume the properties will eventually be acquired by the British Government, but it is unlikely that Anthony or his brother will receive any financial compensation. The Yons, meanwhile, had to make their own living arrangements, with their future no less uncertain than our own. The children enjoyed watching the sailors prepare the ship prior to departure from St Helena, where cables were put away and anchors stowed for bad weather. Sails were set and brave sailors were sent aloft to take in sail as needed and trim sheets and braces. Unloading and reloading of the ship had taken several days. We observed some of this from the Wharf, as we had been spending our final hours on St Helena in town. Anthony was uncharacteristically dour and out of sorts, already grieving the loss of his home and heritage.

The sailors started work at 6.30 am, washing down the decks and stowing their hammocks, before breakfast was served at 8 am. The crew were divided into two watches, with four hours on duty and four off duty. They would scrub the decks twice a week using sandstone and dilute solutions of sweet-smelling vinegar to keep rats, lice, bedbugs, and cockroaches at tolerably low levels. We were fascinated to learn that this was referred to as holy stoning. The stones used were called prayer books or bibles, depending on their size.[187] Charles told us that sailors' lore attributes the sandstone having its origin at a church on the Isle of Wight near Portsmouth, and possibly from another church in Great Yarmouth, and that it was illicitly removed. On the main deck, there was a prevailing smell of tar and fish which was not unpleasant. However, the odour emanating from the various animals carried aboard the ship occasionally overwhelmed one's senses. Livestock, including two cows and several goats, were carried below deck, along with live fowls, so we could obtain milk for the younger children. Eggs from the fowls were a welcome source of food when our fresh supplies ran low. Ablutions and clothes washing were attended using sea water, or occasionally urine. The latrine used by women and children emptied directly into the sea and was flushed several times a day with sea water, weather permitting.

We tried to air our bedding at least weekly to keep down the level of insect infestation. Prior to leaving St Helena, we purchased several bottles of camphor that we kept with us. It was reasonably effective to treat insect bites if used several times a day. The distinctive smell went some way to ameliorate the stuffy and unpleasant odours that permeate every space below deck. The children spent hours watching the sailors splice rope or repair their heavy canvas sails using huge needles, which made me think of Uncle Peter and Aunt Margaret. Both of them had enjoyed a few years living back in Scotland, before dying within weeks of each other.

At mealtimes, the sailors ate in groups of eight men in a space between the guns. On Saturday evenings, they entertained us with singing and dancing. Sundays were set aside as a day of rest and prayer, and the whole family joined in the two Divine services held on the top deck. A generous dinner of three courses and dessert was served at noon. Anthony and Onesiphorus usually drank ale or wine. The older children would also have ale if they liked, or drink the water, which had an acquired taste.

Chapter 35

Journal extracts
December, 1837

We have a new Queen! On 20 June, Queen Victoria, who was born 24 May, 1819, just before my 25th birthday, has ascended to the throne at the tender age of 18. She will be crowned on 28 June next year. She is the granddaughter of George III, and the niece of George IV and William IV. Her three paternal uncles, including the brother of George IV and William IV, Prince Frederick, Duke of York, predeceased her without legitimate issue. We narrowly avoided having another regent appointed, as King William died a mere four weeks after Queen Victoria came of age.

Our first Christmas last year (1836),[188] twenty-four years after that earlier fateful Christmas, was in an England much changed, in no large part due to manufacturing transformation. Just up the road, work is well underway building the London and Greenwich railway, which is due to be completed next year. John Lindsay says he will treat us to a ride on it once it is formally opened. He is impressed by the elevated brick arches. The steam locomotive will run south of the Thames, between Tooley Street and Greenwich.[189]

We initially lodged with my brother James, meeting his wife Elizabeth Young, nee Edsall Biggs, and their children for the first time. Their oldest son, James Halliburton Young, is a few months older than young Anthony, born on 28 March, 1817. He is named after his deceased brother who died in the autumn of 1815, aged 8 months. Lindsay Buckle Young is 8, and Katherine Elizabeth has recently turned 5. I was overjoyed when our sons Edward and Anthony took leave and joined us for a few days. They have both matured into good-looking young men, aged 20 and 19. Edward told us that he has been promoted to ensign.[190] They currently share lodgings in Plumpton, about eleven miles from Lee. In the morning, most of the family took part in a church service at St Margaret's in Lee Terrace in Blackheath. Since then, we have attended services regularly on Sundays and, once again, I have been savouring the sounds of church bells. I had forgotten that St Margaret is often portrayed as a shepherdess, loving and kind. My late sister Margaret had given me a picture of St Margaret when I left for St Helena, but until now I did not really appreciate the significance of her gift. Perhaps all those years ago, I was insensitive to such subtleties. Indeed, I often dismissed Margaret as someone who lived in the shadows of her older sisters, Elizabeth and Isabella. I deeply regret that I was never to meet her in person again.

We were introduced to Charles's delightful wife, Elizabeth Young, nee Hay. She, Charles, their twelve-year-old son Charles, his sister Georgina, ten, and the newborn baby, Margaret, all arrived on Christmas Eve. Elizabeth grew up in the West Indies and she met Charles on one of his many voyages. She confessed she has still not got used to the cold weather in England. They stayed with our sister Elizabeth Halliburton, before returning to London in the New Year of 1837. Charles sailed to Bengal as Captain of *Justina,* which is owned by our brother James, on 1 December this year.

The Christmas was memorable, not least because we were introduced to James's daughter Isabella, born out of wedlock in the West Indies in 1810, who met her father for the first time on her 21st birthday. James supports her financially, and he hosted the wedding breakfast for her marriage to Joseph Mitchell the previous year, on 4 April, 1835. She gets on well with Charles's wife, Elizabeth, as they share a similar heritage, growing up in the Caribbean. We are fortunate that our family has traditionally marked Christmas, by preparing special foods and sharing gifts. This is not the case for many people who do not observe particular customs, although Queen Charlotte, the wife of George III, introduced the idea of the decorated Christmas tree to Queen's Lodge, Windsor, in December, 1800.[191] In our family we also like to acknowledge St Nicholas on 6 December, as the patron saint of sailors.

Our young children were accommodated in a dormitory-type sleeping arrangement, and enjoyed getting to know all their cousins. The women and older girls helped with the cooking, whilst the men and older male children discussed business. A large pile of logs was lit in the huge fireplace, its gleaming copper cover ensuring the smoke went straight up the chimney, with the warmth causing faces to turn red. Mistletoe and holly were hung from various points, the white and red berries making a striking contrast of colour against the green leaves. Additional pieces decorated the dining tables, which were covered with white linen tablecloths and white serviettes and gleaming silver cutlery. Bowls containing nuts harvested from the estate were also placed at intervals on the table. The decorative tableware, James informed me, is hand-painted bone china, sourced from Minton's pottery in Staffordshire.

Two especially large turkeys were carefully nurtured in the lead up to the festival. The turkeys were cooked in huge ovens fuelled with wood gathered on the estate, stuffed with sausage meat and sweet chestnut puree, before being served with bread sauce, gravy, steamed Brussels sprouts, carrots, roast parsnips, and potatoes. For those preferring plainer fare, hot sausages were served alongside cold, cured ham. The turkey bones were made into a flavoursome strained stock that was used to make hearty soups over the next few days. A delicious Punch Royal was served as an alternative to ale and enjoyed by all who tried it![192] A loud handbell was rung to ensure all the family were gathered in time to give thanks before the meal. Several tables were laid, and the dining room was large enough for us all to eat at the one time. Adamina and her charming husband, William, were able to join the family. With John Lindsay and all the children, we numbered 32 plus Charles's baby, Margaret.

The next course was rich plum puddings that had hung in muslin cloth for months. As is our family tradition, new silver coins that have been cleaned in boiling water were inserted into the moist fruit. The puddings were decorated with holly, the green leaves dark against the red berries. Our brother James, as the host, pretended to choke on the coins, which made the children laugh. Following the meal, the coins were washed, and one given to each child.

Before serving the rich fruit dessert, French brandy was poured over and lit at the last minute, the blue-yellow flame curling and flicking over the surface of the puddings. The puddings were served with brandy-flavoured custard or rich cream, fresh from the cows on an adjacent farm. There were hot mince pies, star-shaped shortbreads, and a decorated gingerbread house, the tradition stemming from Grimms' fairy tale about Hansel and Gretel. I had enjoyed reading the Grimms' fairy tales to our children after my first introduction to the tales through Laura. She had an original first edition that was published in December, 1812. Last Christmas, I was delighted to be given a gift of fairy tales written by a Danish man, Hans Christian Andersen. The first two booklets have been published. I am hoping I may be lucky enough to receive the third for a Christmas gift this year. Anthony and I both love reading. For his first English Christmas, I gave him a copy of Geoffrey Chaucer's *The Canterbury Tales*. This year he has been exploring two works from a new novelist, Charles Dickens. *The Pickwick Papers* addresses the injustice of the justice system. It was serialised last year, with the final instalment last month. Episodic publication of *Oliver Twist* commenced in February and will likely continue for another twelve months. The children each received small gifts that included books, wooden or mechanical toys, and a rattle for Margaret.

Last Christmas was also a white Christmas. It was the first time any of my children had seen snow, or felt the cold of an English winter. Christmas Eve had been quite frightening, with a huge storm blowing up over southern England that caused massive snow drifts. On Boxing Day, whilst the weather had calmed somewhat, the children wrapped up warmly and played outside, making snowmen or throwing snowballs, following the tracks of small birds or animals imprinted in the virgin snow. The men cut down any dead trees on the property, storing the logs carefully alongside others in the woodpile, whilst the women shared stories in the kitchen. Sweet chestnuts, collected from trees by Anthony on his daily perambulations, were roasted over the open fire. It was not until several days later that we learned about the terrible avalanche in Lewes, 60 miles south of Blackheath. Eight people were suffocated. A further seven had been lucky to escape with their lives two days after Christmas, when a wall of snow that had built up on a nearby cliff collapsed on their homes.[193]

On Ascension Day, 4 May this year, the parishioners were permitted to go into St Margaret's church tower, climbing steep stone steps to emerge at the top. We were rewarded with magnificent views of the surrounding countryside, with London visible in the distance. Anthony marvelled at the sights, but I have no desire to revisit London. I am enjoying the company of my sister Elizabeth and sister-in-law, Elizabeth, and their families in Blackheath and Lee. On our frequent visits to St Margaret's, we have taken the opportunity to learn more of the church history.[194] Apart from the remaining tower, the mediaeval church has largely been rebuilt on the original foundations, some twenty years ago. It is famous for being the burial place of two Royal astronomers, Halley and Bliss, and a third astronomer, Pond, who died earlier this year. When Laura and I first arrived on St Helena, Anthony took us to where Halley would look into the heavens. Stargazing was very much enjoyed by St Helena residents. It was such a pity that the Observatory at Ladder Hill, was recently dismantled. Halley sailed to St Helena in November, 1676, with a letter of introduction to the Honourable East India Company signed by King Charles II. He built an observatory to map the stars of the southern skies. Over two years he was able to catalogue 341 southern hemisphere stars, discovered a star cluster, and observed the complete transit of the planet Mercury.

We were horrified, whilst out walking and enjoying the sun's warmth on 24 July, to observe a fatal parachute descent where a man fell from the sky and landed in the adjacent farm at Lee Green. This followed an ill-fated balloon flight launched at Vauxhall Gardens. Our son Anthony knew of the victim, Robert Cocking, who was a professional watercolourist. His passing has left his wife and children in dire financial straits. The inquest was held at the Tigers Head at Lee Green, and the poor man has been buried at St Margaret's, close to Halley's grave.[195]

Anthony has been rambling around the countryside, as he is restless and unsettled. On one occasion, he was absent for several days as he wanted to journey to Maidstone, some thirty miles to the southeast of Blackheath and Lee, and then continue to Canterbury to visit the cathedral, returning along the old pilgrim way via Lesnes Abbey. The mediaeval town of Maidstone is famous for its palace that was the home of the Archbishops of Canterbury from King John to Henry VIII. Of particular interest to Anthony was the All Saints Church. In the east corner of St Thomas Becket Chapel, located within the church and named after the martyred 'turbulent priest,'[196] is the Beale memorial. Anthony believes his family may be distantly related to the Maidstone Beales commemorated here, whose descendants emigrated to Virginia in America.[197]

Walking from Blackheath to Lesnes Abbey and back is a fifteen-mile trek, through wood and grassland, heath, streams, bogs, and ponds.[198] In the spring, extensive bluebells in ancient woodlands spread like a carpet as far as the eye can see. Anthony, as an avid student of English history and respectful of family heritage, loves visiting the magnificent but ruined old abbey and reflecting on its past. It was founded in 1178, built as a penance by the chief executioner of England to try to relieve his guilt after the murder of St Thomas a Becket, Archbishop of Canterbury, in 1170, in which he was involved. The abbey was closed by the Cardinal Wolsey in 1525, predating the dissolution of the monasteries by eleven years. Wolsey was arrested and died on his way to the Tower of London in 1530. He had fallen out of favour with Henry VIII for his failure to arrange an annulment with the Pope, of the King's first marriage.

Anthony tells me he runs his hands over the ancient bricks to feel their retained warmth from the sun. He always takes his book of *The Canterbury Tales* alongside a simple meal of bread and cheese for his day. Being a man of habit, he eats his repast sitting on a rotting trunk of a fallen oak tree at the Abbey. He quenches his thirst with water from the spring-filled pond. Sometimes he finds bits of bone, seashells, or other fossils he believes are remnants of ancient fish, birds, and mammals. They are displayed on the mantelpiece above the woodfire in our bedroom. Anthony is comforted by being close to nature. He often describes the soft, white and purple heather, the brown furls of bracken, and the green fiddleheads of younger growth that can be safely eaten as a vegetable, and the sharp-thorned, yellow gorse that provides shelter for animals. He follows badger tracks and enjoys watching the playful red squirrels with their bright, white chests and tufted ears, running up and down the trees and hanging by their fuzzy tails. One day he stopped to let a family of stoats cross his path, the several babies miniature replicas of their parents and seemingly unalarmed by this giant towering above them. On another occasion, on a hot but humid day, he told me he encountered a flutter of butterflies that had formed a conical mass just in front of him. They briefly dispersed before once again reforming as he looked backwards, a shimmering vertical column of black and orange. Each evening, he relates different stories about his day over the dinner table and it seems to be calming for him.

Meanwhile, Elizabeth and I have had much to talk about. I have been getting reacquainted with her daughters Elizabeth and Katherine, who had been small children when I departed for St Helena in 1813. Their mother chose not to remarry after James's death, as there was no financial imperative to do so. She misses her oldest daughter, Isabella, her grief as raw at times as it was six years ago. The widow's pension from the Honourable East India Company based on James Halliburton's service and seniority was generous. She said that, whilst James's death had come as a great shock and she had been deeply saddened that he did not get to meet their son Charles, his voyages had meant he was away from the family home for eighteen months at a time, so she had adapted to a life where she needed to be self-reliant. We have made several visits to St Luke's church, where her daughter Isabella is buried and a memorial has been erected to her father. Our sister Margaret's remains lie in a nearby vault. The family usually alternate between St Luke's and St Margaret's to partake in the Sunday services, as they like both churches.

The landscape around Blackheath and Lee is distinguished by magnificent oaks, ancient trees with individual stands or groups known as a quercetum. Their thick trunks and spreading branches are an embrace offering shelter and protection, symbolic of strength and endurance and wisdom. The tannins in their wood make them resistant to insect and fungal infestations. I love the feel of the rounded rough or smooth leaves and the tiny acorns that eventually turn into such majestic trees. Anthony thinks many are likely hundreds of years old, putting the relatively short history of the colonisation of St Helena into perspective. He sometimes collects acorns as he gets pleasure from their cup shape. As long as they are soaked or boiled to get rid of their toxic tannins, they can be roasted and sprinkled with salt for a snack, or ground into flour. In season, he also brings home sweet chestnuts, that we roast over an open fire.

Anthony tells me he has seen hares leaping across fields, and rabbits with their kittens, bobbing white tails disappearing down burrows as he approaches. There are different types of deer in the woods. On one occasion, he spotted a magnificent stag with huge antlers. He had no fear, gazing at Anthony for several minutes before leisurely departing into the wood from which he emerged. Anthony has seen otters, with short necks and long tails, swimming belly-down in rivers. He is slowly learning the names of other trees in the woodlands, including beech, hazel, and hawthorn. He loves the pale-yellow primroses and the hint of garlic from the wild ramsons growing beside the narrow woodland paths. Parts of the woods he travels are coppiced, named after an ancient woodland management technique. It encourages tree growth so that they can be more quickly harvested for timber and firewood. The original tree is cut to the stump, from where new shoots grow. This technique is particularly adaptable to sweet chestnut, hazel, lime, and ash trees. John Lindsay has told him that these trees are cut in rotation. The number of years' growth depends on the type of tree. Sections of the trees are known as coupes or cants. Hazel grows more quickly, and is usually coppiced every eight years, whereas it may take 15–20 years before the wood of the chestnut can be usefully harvested. An oak tree may be coppiced over a fifty-year cycle for poles or firewood.[199]

Around the Lee estate, John Lindsay has shown both Anthony and me a stand of birch that is the basis for heating his home. The bark of the tree is an excellent fire starter, and faggots can be harvested on a three-to-four-year cycle. Because birch burns quickly, it is used with a longer-burning wood such as elm, or oak. John said that different species of wood burn at different rates. Some wood is much more effective at producing heat, whereas other wood can be burned for its pleasant aromas. For instance, ash wood has a low moisture content whilst still green. When the seasoned wood is used, it burns slowly producing heat over a long time. Apple or cherry wood, provided they are well seasoned, produce a pleasant scent. John made it clear that he is still learning about the properties and potential uses for the trees and their fruits, bark, and other parts, on his estate. Whilst he has both sweet and horse chestnut trees, he dislikes them for firewood as they spit continuously, raising the risk of starting an unintentional fire. He has been experimenting with using the inedible conkers from his horse chestnut trees. They appear effective at keeping clothes moths away if placed in drawers. He is also experimenting to see if he can produce a soap from the conkers to use for cleaning clothes.

He explained the purpose of hedgerows that Anthony has seen on his travels. As well as marking field boundaries, they provide wind breaks and important shelter for small animals and insects. They tend to be a mixture of shrubs, trees, and flowers that are sources of nectar, berries, and nuts. Birds build their nests deep inside, seeking a safe haven from other more aggressive species or land-based animals. Some of the shrubs and trees include hazel, which produces yellow catkins in late winter. These are important sources of pollen, but also herald the start of spring and brighten fresh flower arrangements. Blackthorn can be distinguished by its tiny stars of white flowers. It provides a good stock barrier as it has spiny branches and twigs; likewise hawthorn, that produces red berries known as haws in late August. John smiled and said:

'Margaret used these berries to make chutneys and wines, but she always left sufficient numbers behind for the birds. These berries should not be confused with the berries from the cuckoo pint that cannot be eaten but are enjoyed by small creatures like mice and voles. Blackthorn berries can be harvested to flavour gin, and we have several bottles put away if you would like to sample some! Or perhaps Katherine might prefer rose hip cordial from the pink dog rose? Margaret would carefully pick blackberries from the brambles that thread themselves through the hedges, before turning them into delicious desserts. She would also make elderberry tea that has a sweet, tart taste despite its rather musky odour.[200] I miss her very much.'

Chapter 36

Journal extracts
28 May, 1838

Yesterday Anthony invited me to take a walk with him to celebrate my 44th birthday. I had previously declined to accompany him as he needed to spend time alone. For a reason I could not quite determine, this time felt different. Anthony's mood is lighter than in the past several years. He has lost some weight and gained some colour in his face. It reminds me of the early days on St Helena, when he and his brother Onesiphorus took pleasure in showing off their island home to Laura, Dorothy, and me. He is smiling more and appears to be enjoying the company of our children once again.

We requested a fresh loaf of bread from Elizabeth's faithful servants, Matthew and Jane, who are now quite elderly but once again live in the same house as Elizabeth, and some preserved, smoked ham and cheeses from the estate. We took bottles of elderberry cordial and two glasses, carefully wrapped in newspaper. Anthony put them in a leather bag he placed over his shoulder. On his recommendation, we both wore sturdy boots. We each selected a strong stick from the garden. Anthony chose beech, but I found a hawthorn one more to my liking. There was a lingering earthy scent from a recent rain shower, but the sun was now bright in the sky and producing considerable warmth. I could hear a lark, its delicate musical song barely audible. It was just visible, rising as a dark speck in the sky.

Trees looked resplendent with their scented blossoms in various shades of pink and white. Insects were buzzing, and a few butterflies and damsel flies were also making the best of the sunny, late-spring day. John Lindsay has been proud to show us a glass-fronted cabinet. Each drawer is full of butterflies affixed with a pin, many unfamiliar to me. They are carefully preserved, with each specimen labelled in small, neat handwriting. My preference is to let all small creatures enjoy a natural life. I am particularly fond of butterflies with a more subtle colour, such as brimstones. We saw a male brimstone with its yellow wings outstretched against the blue sky, a small red dot on each wing clearly visible, and later a much paler female, balanced on a primrose. Anthony said his favourite is the speckled wood butterfly. It has chocolate brown wings with cream patches and black eye markings, and appears to favour the shady woodland. There were still carpets of bluebells in the woods, although their season is nearly over.

Our early perambulations took us past strange mounds of earth that Anthony believes are ancient burial grounds. They are most likely thousands of years old, possibly dating to the Bronze Age, some seven hundred to two thousand years before the birth of Christ. We climbed a steep hill that reminded me of Ladder Hill on St Helena. We enjoyed the commanding view. In the distance the Thames was visible. I tried to remember how I felt when I lived there. The good things were the many occasions I had contact with my family. Making a life away from them was one of the heavier burdens that I would pray about as it was not something Anthony felt comfortable discussing. I was usually able to bring myself out of introspection by focusing on the children. It was sad to be orphaned so young, but we were blessed with our adoptive parents. The poverty and filth of London is best forgotten. I have been enjoying our time in England, particularly spending time with Elizabeth once again, and I was dreading what Anthony might have to say. We were sitting on the chalky grass, when he turned to me:

'My Dear, I have decided that our future will be in Australia where we can live as free settlers. There is land to be purchased near Melbourne. We will farm the lands, selling any excess produce, whilst ensuring we have plenty to eat. My plan is to make a prefabricated house, availing myself of an old barn on John Lindsay's property to build and store it. Onesiphorus can assist me to erect it once we arrive in the new country. I have already spoken to John, and he has offered to be guarantor once again for our venture. Whilst I am most appreciative of his generosity, it is my preference to sell my Company pension to give us sufficient money to be independent. I do not see any future for myself in England. I do not find the climate agreeable. I cannot see an opportunity to be employed in a position that gives sufficient remuneration to support our family.'

For a minute or two, a great silence engulfed us as I was unable to speak. My heart gave a large thump in my chest. My hands were trembling, my voice a little uncertain as I said:

'I am begging you to let me speak to my sister Elizabeth about this, and also Edward and Anthony, to establish their views? And, if we are to go ahead with this proposal, please let me speak to our girls? The boys are too young, but the girls are enjoying the time they are spending with their cousins, and I would hate to once again uproot them from all that is familiar.'

'Of course, Mrs B. I have already spoken to Onesiphorus, but requested he did not share the information until you and I have had the chance to talk.'

Anthony's plans were further along than I imagined, as he then said:

'I have spoken to Captain Waddell of a square-rigged ship known as a barque of 247 tons. *Cecelia* will be sailing next Spring and can accommodate a large family and their possessions including a prefabricated home. She was built in 1832, in Nova Scotia, and on 23 February underwent a detailed inspection and was signed off as being in good condition. Lodgings are readily available either in George Town or Launceston in Van Diemen's Land. The family can live there, whilst Onesiphorus and I travel to Melbourne to purchase land and erect the house. I intend to apply for a government grant, but I am unclear of our eligibility.'

We completed our walk in silence that was hardly companionable. I cannot bear to think about travelling to the other end of the earth and once again, saying goodbye to my family. This time it will surely be for ever. Unbidden, the memory of the black hulks of prison ships on the Thames emerged. The impression of beseeching hands makes more sense now. I feel the time for our departure will come around quickly. I must ensure I choose an appropriate time to talk to Elizabeth and the girls. For the moment, I will have to keep my thoughts and feelings to myself and try to act as though nothing has changed. The next few weeks are likely to be busy, as we are planning to celebrate the coronation of Queen Victoria with a huge street party. It will be hosted by John Lindsay in Lee. The notion of a street party is causing us great excitement as it brings back memories of the celebrations around Admiral Nelson's victory at Trafalgar. The sound of the bells ringing from all the churches around London is something I will never forget.

Chapter 37

Journal extracts
27 May, 1839

'I saw the long line of the vacant shore,
    The sea-weed and the shells upon the sand,
    And the brown rocks left bare on every hand,
    As if the ebbing tide would flow no more.

Then heard I, more distinctly than before,
    The ocean breathe and its great breast expand,
    And hurrying came on the defenceless land
    The insurgent waters with tumultuous roar.

All thought and feeling and desire, I said,
    Love, laughter, and the exultant joy of song
    Have ebbed from me forever! Suddenly o'er me

They swept again from their deep ocean bed,
    And in a tumult of delight, and strong
    As youth, and beautiful as youth, upbore me.'[201]

My forty-fifth birthday is today. We are approaching South Africa, where we will take on fresh water and citrus fruits and further supplies of livestock. We left England in early spring. Despite praying, reading the bible, receiving comforting words from my girls, and watching the amusing antics of our small boys once they had found their sea legs, my heart is a block of wood. At times, my breath, far from being a natural and gentle act, is squeezed reluctantly from my body. My usual energy and ability to express gratitude or receive grace has left me. Our journey began with much seasickness, with the little boys in particular 'just like a lot of sick little monkeys … discharging their rebellious dinners in all directions with two using a hat as a sort of spittoon.'[202]

Onesiphorus is a great help distracting the younger children. He has developed a close friendship with Captain Waddell. *Cecelia* is principally a cargo ship and has a relatively small crew. This is fortunate, as we rarely have to queue to use the cooking facilities. I try to prepare nourishing soups as the principal meal of the day, which we eat around two in the afternoon. Ships' times are very different from our usual routines. We had to make some hard decisions about what to bring to Australia, as we were limited to twenty cubic feet of free luggage space in the hold. We were permitted to keep a month's supply of clothing and essential items, as well as our eating utensils and food chest, containing basic provisions, that is stored under the lower bunks. Continuing the children's education, as far as was possible on the long voyage, required careful planning and packing of appropriate books to support this. The older girls have assisted me, and we have focused on having small, daily classes to teach reading, writing, and simple arithmetic. We have been joined in the lessons by Catherine Monk and her daughter, who are travelling to Australia to meet up with her husband, who left several months ago. The only other passenger, apart from the Monks and our family, is John Burt of the East India Company. He is a handsome man, closer to me in age, and he, Anthony, and Onesiphorus enjoy each other's company. He is unmarried.

Just before leaving for Australia, I was fortunate in finding a new edition of the complete set of *Hans Christian Andersen Fairy Tales*. They have been easy to read on our long voyage to Australia, and worked their magic not only on me, but also my travel companions, when at times our homesickness has been overwhelming. We also received an advance copy of Captain Frederick Marryat's *The Phantom Ship* which is to be published in May this year. The children are enjoying the stories. Anthony befriended the author, and indeed he lodged with us during our time in St Helena. In 1820, Captain Marryat was temporarily in command of *HMS Rosario* in order to carry despatches to England announcing the death of Napoleon. He is 18 months younger than Anthony and has already had a distinguished career as a Royal Naval officer and novelist. Like Anthony, he enjoys sketching and he showed us several of his pictures of shipboard life above and below deck, detailing the cramped conditions many people are forced to endure for months on end, with no guarantee of a safe passage. It never occurred to us that one day we would be travelling in very similar fashion.[203]

Our living conditions in steerage leave much to be desired. When I first saw them, I was filled with dread, as we are so cramped that I fear the outbreak of disease. I decided it is essential that we all maintain the strictest level of hygiene. The wooden bunks are made from rough boards and are arranged in upper and lower layers, fore-and-aft, to try and minimise the effects of rough seas. They are lined with straw filled mattresses that we try to air each day. We have had to bring our own pillows and bedding. Unfortunately, we rarely wake up in the morning without having to scratch, as the fleas, lice, and cockroaches seem to flourish here. As with our trip from St Helena, we ensured we brought plenty of camphor to treat insect bites. We have decided to have the four boys sleep in one family bunk at the lower level, with myself and Kas on an adjacent bunk to assist in supervising the boys. Isabella, Bessie, Rose, and Margaret will occupy bunk beds directly above the boys and me. There is just sufficient head room to enable us to sit up on the bed, but the ceiling height of steerage is barely six foot and Onesiphorus has to duck his head when moving around the area.

Anthony and Onesiphorus sleep at one end, just in front of the partition to the family area. John Burt has his own cabin on the upper deck, as does Catherine Monk and her daughter. Traversing the length of the steerage deck is a long, wooden bench securely bolted to the deck, with fixed seating also bolted to the deck in a very similar style to *Justina* when we travelled from St Helena. On that occasion I was the joyful one, looking forward to reuniting with my family, and Anthony was grieving the loss of his heritage. How our positions are reversed now. Anthony's optimism since making the decision to travel to Australia has continued unabated.

All meals are taken here, and once cleared away, the space is used as an education space, or for mending and sorting clothing. We ensure the hatches are open when we are expecting good weather, as they have to be firmly closed, even in relatively calm seas, to avoid flooding the area. Despite this precaution, everything has a damp feel to it. It is very dark, as we are limited with the times that oil lamps can be used because of the danger of fire. To access the top deck requires ascending or descending a ladder via a companion way or hatch, with one hand in contact with the rails at all times. The younger children have become quite adept at this, but our clothing can get trapped underfoot if we do not take great care.

Married couples' accommodation in steerage accommodation: an emigrants dinner[204]

The toilet facilities at one end consist of a very basic enclosed water closet. We try to ensure it is cleaned several times a day, as the ventilation is very poor. It is reserved for women and children. Flushing of waste is achieved by scooping sea water from a nearby bucket. The rags or cloth or clouts are washed in a vinegar solution. We try to change them as often as possible. Very basic washing has to be accomplished using cold seawater. Any rainwater collected on deck is used for drinking. At times, it is hard to maintain a pleasant demeanour, although I try to reassure the children as much and as frequently as possible that this is all part of an exciting adventure. It is certainly better for all to encourage a spirit of cooperation. The men risk their lives, particularly in stormy weather, as they are required to conduct their ablutions near the bow of the ship on the leeward side. At times, the stench below deck is unbearable, particularly if the ventilation has been shut for a while. The first mate attempts to purify the air using a red-hot iron that he dips into a pail of tar and causes smoke and steam to rise up and deaden some of the worst odours. The most dangerous and dreaded illnesses aboard ship include cholera, typhoid fever, measles, chicken pox, and dysentery.[205]

We are permitted to go on deck, but there is little room to move. There is livestock and fodder, boats, ropes, and hatch covers, and sailors' hammocks. Food is brought down to us from the galley, and at times it is almost impossible to do this if the weather is rough. Once we run out of fresh food, our basic diet consists of salted pork and beef, bread, pease, and oatmeal. The water is 'fresh' but unpalatable. Even the younger boys are drinking ale, except on the rare occasions that fresh rainwater is available. Buckets and canvas are lain over the deck when it rains to try and capture as much as possible, and then the precious liquid is transferred to barrels. Occasionally, a sheepskin is hung out and the water squeezed from it. The liquid has a faint taste of wool, but is not displeasing.[206] Our rations abroad *Cecelia* are tightly allocated and supplemented as required from our own food supply. Sailors occasionally catch fish that is shared between passengers and crew.[207]

Our final English Christmas was overshadowed by the death of my brother Charles on 9 December at Guildford. His funeral was held on 15 December, 1838, at St Luke's church in Chelsea, a building largely funded by local parishioners. He was only 53. His widow, Elizabeth, and children Charles, 13, Georgina, 12, and Margaret, 3, will continue to live at Hans Place, the western part of Hans Town, which is approximately nine miles from Blackheath.[208] It is thought that Charles may have developed an illness as a result of the voyage he made on *Justina* that sailed on 1 December, 1837, to Bengal, and only returned to England shortly before his death. James's ownership of the ship caused him to believe he inadvertently played a part in the death of our brother.

We also had concerns about James' health. His wife, Elizabeth, confessed that he has been unwell, possibly something to do with his heart, as he has been getting increasingly breathless. It is fortunate that their son James Halliburton Young is a great support to them. He and Onesiphorus enjoyed celebrating their first cousin relationship, and both young men were of great assistance to Anthony in constructing the pre-fabricated house that we have brought with us, basing its design on the original Longwood House. Regrettably, during our time in England, we did not see Isabella, who has never really recovered from the death of her daughter Catherine.

The hardest goodbye was to my sister Elizabeth. It awakened feelings, long dormant, of our previous parting, in 1813. Sadly, this time, there is no hope of a future reunion. We held each other wordlessly on that final day. Through the open window, a faint peel of church bells could be heard from the bellringer's practice night at St Margaret's. It may have one of the last times the bells ring before a planned rebuilding of the church commences.[209] I reflected how bells have marked such important occasions in my life to date.

The ship is expected to arrive at George Town in Van Dieman's Land in the second week of July. Once we have procured suitable lodgings, Anthony and Onesiphorus will travel to Melbourne, which is part of the colony of New South Wales. They hope to purchase land in Newtown and erect the house before returning to collect the rest of the family. During the voyage, we have developed a close friendship with John Burt Esq, late of the East India Company Service, where he was employed as a master mariner. He has left his house in Westminster, London, to explore business opportunities in the new colonies. He seems to be particularly fond of Kas, who is some twenty years younger than he.

Anthony's mood has fluctuated over the course of the voyage. He is greatly concerned about how we will manage our finances in our straightened circumstances. We are so grateful for our beautiful children, who have not once on the long voyage expressed regret or concern about our future, but are approaching it with anticipation and a sense of adventure. Meanwhile, Anthony has occupied himself making a series of sketches on how the house will look once it is erected, and his plans to establish a garden to enable us to grow enough food for our needs and sell any surplus. He wants to enclose an area for horses and storage of their hay, and some pens so that we can purchase a pig, some chickens and geese, and goats. I have begged him to ensure that priority is given to construction of an earth closet with suitable privacy.

Disembarking from our most recent home[210]

In Captain Waddell's cabin, Onesiphorus tells me there are two pictures of barques. One with bare rigging may be *Cecelia* or a very similar ship. A smaller one beneath pictures a barque under sail. It has three masts with fore and aft sails on the mizzen mast and square sails on all other masts.

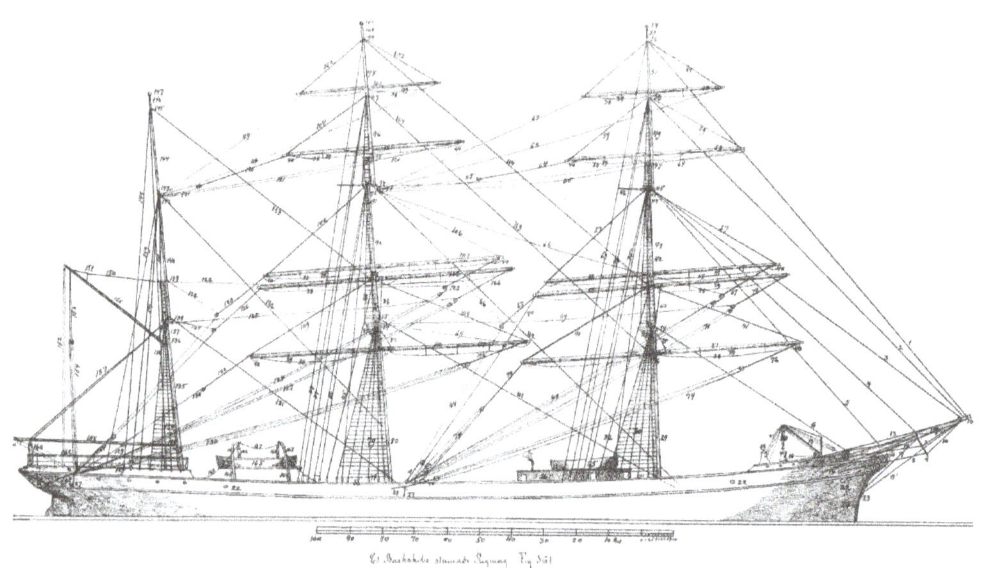

Barque rigging[211]

Barque under sail[212]

Chapter 38

Journal extracts
31 August, 1839

Our hearts are breaking. We arrived in Launceston on Monday 29 July, farewelling some of our new friends we met aboard *Cecelia*, including Catherine Monk, who appeared to develop a fondness for Onesiphorus, and Captain Waddell. The Captain had promised to come and visit us before *Cecelia* departed for Sydney on 14 August, prior to returning to England.

We had been in Van Diemen's land barely sixteen days when our beloved Onesiphorus disappeared without trace. We think it is possible that he went to farewell Captain Waddell, as unfortunately the Captain had been unable to visit us for as long as we had anticipated. We wondered whether Onesiphorus slipped and fell into the River Tamar, which is extremely cold at this time of the year. None of our children can swim, and his clothes would have been heavy. We have a close relationship with all our children, and it is unthinkable that Onesiphorus would not have returned home unless something dreadful has occurred. Despite our very best efforts, we have been unable to discover where he might be. The children are distraught. We are so grateful for John Burt and his support at this time. He assisted Anthony in placing the following advertisement that appeared in the paper today:

> *The Cornwall Chronical Launceston Tasmania Saturday
> 31 August, 1839*
>
> FIFTY GUINEAS REWARD.
>
> Whereas about 10 o'clock on Wednesday night, the 14th last, a Young Gentleman named Onesiphorus James Beale, late a passenger by the *Cecelia*, left his father's house for the purpose, it is supposed, of going on board that vessel, but has never since been heard of, having it is feared fallen from an insecure plank into the River.
>
> This is to give notice, that the above Reward will be paid to any person who will give such authentic information to his afflicted relations, as shall be the means of recovering his body, and upon their obtaining possession of the same.
>
> Or should he be alive, a like reward will be paid to any person who will give me immediate intelligence where he may be found. ANTHONY BEALE
>
> His dress when last seen, was a White Hat; blue pilot cloth Coat, brown blue striped trowsers, coloured Stockings and Shoes. Age 24 years, height about 5 feet 9 inches.
>
> August 16, 1839[213]

Advertisement re: Onesiphorus 31 August, 1839

Anthony has reluctantly decided he must depart in the morning, and he will take Adam, 10 years old, with him and Edwards, whom we have employed to assist us in the move. The house, a water cart, and various sundry items including livestock, have been put into the hold. It is Anthony's intention to finalise the sale of three acres of land in Newtown and erect the house. To provide for our immediate needs, he will take the water cart that he purchased in Launceston, with the plan to get water from the Yarra River and sell it door to door. Edwards will be responsible for this. After erecting a house, he will employ a fencer to enclose the property and to start clearing the land in order to commence work on the garden.

He has spent much of the voyage to Australia creating possible designs based on our discussions with John Lindsay, and drawing sketches, some humorous, in his journal.

In the meantime, we are staying in lodgings in Launceston, where we have basic cooking facilities and spending some of the time taking walks alongside the River Tamar, always hoping that one day we might find some evidence of what occurred to Onesiphorus.

29 September, 1839

The body of our beloved oldest son was discovered by a fisherman on Friday 20 September on the left bank of the North Esk river, a tributary of the River Tamar, a very short distance from our lodgings. I was unable to bring myself to go to the inquest. Katherine attended in the company of her now betrothed, John Burt, and described his state of dress. John Burt organised for me to receive a copy of the inquest's findings. Catherine Monk, whom we got to know well from *Cecelia*, was called upon to give evidence as an independent witness.

We plan to hold a memorial service for Onesiphorus when Anthony and Adam return, before our planned departure on *Perseverance* in November. My faith in the goodness of God had been tested on many occasions, but never more so than in the months following our departure from England.

'Sleep, my babe, hear not the rippling wave,

Nor feel the breeze that round thee lingering stray,

To drink thy balmy breath,

And sigh one long farewell.

Soon shall it mourn above thy wat'ry bed,

And whisper to me, on the wave-beat shore,

   Deep murm'ring in reproach,

   Thy sad untimely fate …

O sleep, my babe, nor heed how mourns the gale

To part with thy soft locks and fragrant breath,

   As when it deeply sighs

   O'er autumn's latest bloom.'[214]

The Cornwall Chronicle Saturday 21st September, 1839

INQUESTS. * Catherine Beale = Katherine Anne Sibella (married the following year)

* An inquest was held on Saturday last, the 14th instant at the Ferry House, at the Bridge before PA Mulgrave, Esq, Coroner, on the body of Mr Onesiphorus James Beale, a young gentleman who came out in *Cecilia*, and has been missing for the last month, and for whom a reward of 50 guineas has been offered by his disconsolate father who has just left the colony for Port Philip.

Witness Catherine Monk – I came from England in the barque *Cecilia* with Mr Beale's family; we landed at Launceston on the 29th July. The deceased Onesiphorous James Beale was 24 years of age, always in good spirits, and on the best terms with his family; I never heard him express any intention of leaving them. He was quite well and in his usual good spirits on Wednesday the 14th.

Captain Waddell, of *Cecilia* spent a part of that evening at his father's house, he left about 10 o'clock; I saw the deceased about 9 o'clock that evening; he wore the same clothes that are now on the body, as viewed by the inquest; I can speak positively as to the coat and trowsers; and I know, by the marks on the arms, viz., an anchor on the right arm, and two hearts and a dart on the left, that they are the remains of OJB. I know he left his father's house about a quarter of an hour after Captain Waddell that evening, I supposed he had gone into the garden; some time afterwards search was made for him, and it was discovered he was absent; we supposed that he has followed Captain Waddell, to whom he was much attached, and who he knew purposed leaving the post next morning.

Captain Bateman – I am the Harbour Master at Launceston. The barque *Cecilia* was lying alongside the wharf on Wednesday, the 14th; the stage from the wharf to *Cecilia* had been taken to pieces prepartory to her sailing the next morning, and there was only a plank on the evening of that day from the wharf to the vessell; it was a very narrow plank, and required great caution in passing over it; I came onshore on it after dark that evening. *Cecilia* was bout a fathom and a half from the wharf; I t was low water between 10 & 11 o'clock that night; There was only 3 feet and half water between *Cecilia* and the wharf, the mud was very soft and deep. Captain Waddell left Launceston about 3 weeks ago, and before he went the deceased was missing, and he (Captn Waddell) told me that he passed part of the evening with the deceased at his father's house and that he (the deceased) said he should call and see him on board that night, it was a dark night.

Miss Catherine Beale – I am the sister to the deceased OJB; the last time I saw him was on Wed evening, the 14th in my father's house; he was in very good spirits that evening; Captain Waddell spent part of the evening with us; the deceased wished to accompany him on board; Captain Waddell advised him not to do so; about 10 minutes after Captain Waddell left the deceased wished us all good night; we supposed he had gone to bed; a few minutes afterwards I heard him go out the back door, and shortly after, as he did not return, he was sought for, and it was then discovered he had left the house, and had taken his hat with him from his bed room. He had the mark of an anchor on one arm, and 2 hearts and a dart on the other; he had not had any difference with any person that evening, and was not labouring under any depression of spirits.

Dr Pugh – I examined the body of the deceased OJB. There is not any mark of violence upon it, and I have no doubt his death was caused by suffocation from drowning; the body appeared to have been lying in the water for a month or upwards.

John Snailhurst – I am a fisherman; I found the body which has been viewed by the Inquest about 10 minutes before 7 o'clock yesterday morning, on the left bank of the north Esk river abt … bank; the other part of the body was in the water; except the upper part of the back; it was in the same state as it is now. Verdict – found drowned.

The inquest into the disappearance of Onesiphorus 14 September, 1839

Chapter 39

**Journal extracts
1 December, 1839**

We departed Launceston on 4 November on the schooner *Perseverance*, 45 tons, that carried a general cargo. Captain George Dryden was taciturn, but he assured us he had made the voyage across the Bass Strait on many occasions and was familiar with the possible hazards we may encounter. We were told the journey could take up to two weeks, but if the weather was fine and the sea calm it would likely be considerably shorter. Rather worryingly, Captain Dryden told us that the Bass Strait is one of the most treacherous bodies of water in the world, with strong currents and powerful waves as well as semi- submerged rocks and reefs. There are more than fifty islands between Van Diemen's Land and the mainland.[215]

Our fellow passengers included Mrs Catherine Monk and her child, with whom we travelled from England. She shared a cabin with her friend Mrs Downie and her three children. Both ladies were to join their husbands, who came out from England earlier in the year. Compared to *Cecelia,* we travelled in luxury, with our family accommodated in a very generous-sized cabin. Two brothers, William and Alexander Rogers, and their friend Michael Roberts were in a third cabin. The ship's manifest was published in The Cornwall Chronicle (below).

November 4— Perseverance, (schooner,)
45 tons, Dryden, master, for Port Philip —
6,000 feet timber, 44,000 shingles, 800 paling,
2 cases apparel, 9 trunks ditto, 16 cases of slops
(Ready-made clothing possibly for naval ratings or more generally
for people)
1 cask vinegar, 1 cask ironmongery, 2 casks
beer, 4 chests drawers, 7 cases slops, 2 bed
steads, 6 kegs 1 jar provisions, 1 book-case, 1
hamper, 1 crow-bar, 1 anvil,' 1 vice, 1 bundle
rakes, 1 bundle spades, 1 filterer 1 cask wine,
1 bag coffee— Beale;

6 bags Sour, 1 butter
churn— M'Lean; 20 bags flour- Button &
Waddell; 2 sofas, E packages chairs— Dryden }
1,251 feet limber— Cowell j 8 cawi tiont—
Edilic & Co. ; S gigs. 1 package harness, 1 cast
riops—Crey; 2 bundle kangaroo skins, 1 ditto
leather— Lukin.

Shipping News for the Perseverance (1839) published in The Cornwall Chronicle[216]

MARRIED.—By special license, by the Revd. Dr. Browne, at St. John's Church, Launceston, John Burt, Esq., late of the East India Company's Service, to Katherine, Ann, Sibella, eldest daughter of Anthony Beale, Esq., late Paymaster to the East India Company's Establishment at St. Helena.

The Cornwall Chronicle (Launceston, Tas.: 1835–1880) Sat 18 Jan, 1840, Page 2[217]

Katherine remained in Van Diemen's Land and continued to live in the lodgings we recently vacated, caring for the elderly lady who owns the property. The latter is a parishioner of St John's Church of England in Launceston, where Katherine and John Burt plan to marry in January. John Burt has separate accommodation in Launceston. As Katherine is underage, it has been necessary to acquire a special license which was unable to be facilitated before we had to leave for Port Phillip. We visited St John's whilst we were living in Launceston, and had several conversations with the Rev Dr Browne, who agreed to conduct the marriage. The marriage announcement was printed in the Cornwall Chronicle of 18 January, 1840.

We hit a rough part of the Bass Strait with a violent storm and lightning, that for a worrying few hours made us wonder whether we would capsize. Fortunately, the captain and the crew are experienced, and the ship appeared sturdily built. We arrived in Port Philip on 13 November 1839, after nine days at sea and without any loss of our animals. Anthony had arranged for two bullock carts to be at the wharf when we arrived – the first to carry us to our new home, and the second, under the supervision of our hired man, Edwards, to carry our belongings. The livestock, principally fowls, had been stored in the hold and were unloaded later. Our plan was to sell the surplus eggs to generate some income. Anthony intended to return with a bullock cart and, with Edwards to assist him, to collect the remaining items from the wharf.

Anthony's sketch illustrating how our belongings will be transported to our new home

As the bullock cart reached the site, we were greeted by our new neighbours, the King family, whom Anthony and Adam had met previously. Anthony recorded the momentous occasion and the first days of our arrival in his journal:

'On a hot day, we landed on the beach and in crossing the punt was in danger of being backed upon by a team of restive bullocks – got across safe and with difficulty & great fatigue from the heat of the day reached home where we found an empty & very leaky house. I went to town to get bedding which was to have been brought to the wharf by the {ships' crew}. After waiting there until 8 o'clock I left & lost my way in the bush & did not get home until 10 o'clock.

'King had been dispatched to get 2 gallons of shrub which finding upon my arrival we all felt rejoiced to enjoy and happy with our lot – viz – once more at home – ever so homely – ever so wet – umbrellas in requisition during the night sleep or awake – after having been provided by Mrs. King with bedding to the best of her ability. My wife having very comfortably stowed herself away in one of my coloured shirts in lieu of a nightgown, the cart arrived with our bedding, boxes and poultry, all safe, a very great load for which I paid 5/-.

'My joy was great at beholding the fowls all safe after the trouble I had had with them in the furious gales which accompanied us on our journey from Launceston – 9 days.'[218]

Anthony erected our new home on an acre, but hopes to acquire further land, increasing to up to five acres so that we have plenty of room to farm our stock and grow necessary vegetables and herbs. The cost of the land in total will be £252. He plans to buy several cows before Christmas so that we can sell the surplus milk to retailers in town.

In the seventeen days since our arrival, we have had no time to mourn Onesiphorus. The first priority was to plug the holes in the roof. Anthony has been shown how to use a technique employing mud mixed carefully with straw or grass as a temporary solution, and we have draped canvas over our bed areas and purchased more buckets. We are grateful to have arrived in late spring, which gives us sufficient time to make the house habitable before the autumn. The weather has been very warm, but less humid than in St Helena and a pleasant change from the cold of England.

We have purchased goats that we stake in the areas of our land we wish to prioritise clearing, as they seem to have insatiable appetites for anything that grows. All the family contributes to the physical work, with even the youngest boys charged with the responsibility of collecting eggs. We have farmed rabbits for fresh meat. Edwards travels around the local streets carting fresh water he obtains from the Yarra River for use by other settlers. He is quite adept at driving the bullocks, which are yoked together as a pair.

Anthony has pegged out areas of our land where he intends to put plants, and he and Edwards have started digging holes for fencing, as securing our stock is a priority. He is planning to plant melons and cucumbers. We have had to spend more money than planned on purchasing tallow candles, but Mrs King has promised to show us how to make candles from mutton fat, and said she will purchase a mould for our use. I will try to record our new life as far as is possible in my journal, but already most of the daylight hours are fully employed in looking after the children, mending clothing, preparing meals, feeding the fowls, and keeping a wary eye out for snakes, which we have been told start to make their appearance in the hot weather.

The practicalities of getting food and wine to the table have been recorded in Anthony's diary in a series of sketches:

Breakfast on the hoof![219]

Teaching the boys[220]

Decanting a ten-gallon cask into bottles[221]

Bottling is a family affair[222]

Christmas, 1840

It is remarkable that twelve months have passed since our first dramatic Christmas. It rained for three days and nights, and the Yarra flooded to the extent that large parts of Melbourne were underwater. Brickmakers lost their kilns and huts, and the only reliable transport was by boat. A wharf, only recently erected, was totally engulfed by the water and floated out to sea.

We received a rare letter from Edward some weeks ago to advise us that he has received another promotion. Effective 24 February this year he is a lieutenant.

On 15 June, we completed 25 years in the marriage state. Anthony made four beds for flowers before the door. We had a party consisting of friends Mr and Mrs Williams, Messrs Grey, James, and Lee, who dined with us in the evening. The latter three guests stayed the night, and Anthony went into town for lunch with them the next day. The following Sunday, Mr Brooke, whom we knew on St Helena, took Issy and Rose to the English church. Mr Brooke is becoming a fine teacher for the boys.

Anthony took me and Bessy to Mr Waterfield's chapel. Margaret and the little boys remained at home under the supervision of Edwards. The Independent Chapel is the first permanent place of worship completed and opened in Melbourne; it has a facial plainness which consorts well with the neat conveniences of the interior. It is built in Collins Street, and neighbours the Scots' Kirk. The sittings are capable of accommodating about six hundred, which nearly approaches the total muster of its congregation. Our amiable pastor, Rev Waterfield, arrived in Australia the year before us.[223]

Collins Street East from Mr Waterfield's Chapel[224]

We have had a year of great excitement interspersed with times of great concern, mainly due to drought. The arduous toil on our land has been balanced by a social whirl of visits, picnics, and balls. Fortunately, whilst in England, my sister Elizabeth found she still retained a number of silk bolts in varied colours, that had been protected against insects. We were able to pack them carefully alongside our bedding for the voyage on *Cecelia*. The older girls begged me to make them a silk gown just in case they had the opportunity to wear one. It reminded me of making my yellow silk gown prior to departing for St Helena. Each of our daughters chose a different colour: Katherine has reddish hair and chose a shade of green that brings out her colouring; Bessie selected light blue; Issy always loved my gown and chose yellow for her dress; and Rose, a deep pink that suits her name. I also made a special dress for Margaret using a light pink shade that flatters her colouring. With silk remnants, each of the boys was provided with a pair of breeches.

Our dear son Anthony was nominated by Captain Stanley Clarke and recommended by my brother James for Assistant Surgeon in Bengal, India and, following his exams on 22 January, the post took effect on 8 February. He is enjoying sketching local Indian scenes in his rare spare time. Barely days later, although the news took two months to arrive, we heard from our nephew James that my brother James died on 24 February at Lee, possibly still heartbroken that he may have inadvertently caused the death of our brother Charles.

Katherine and John are very happy following their marriage in January. Sadly, we did not see them before they decided to make their home in England. The early weeks in Van Diemen's Land and having to speak at the inquest into Onesiphorus's death took their toll. Kas was very close to her oldest brother. She has recently spent some time with Edward, who is in England for a brief period of leave. He is a very poor correspondent. He is apparently doing well in India and continues with the rank of 2nd Lieutenant. We will always be grateful for the generous bond of £200 from John Lindsay and his brother George. The latter is a merchant and continues to live in the family home at Lawrence Poultney Lane. The sureties extended to Edward on 6 March, 1834, enabled him to complete his Cadetship at the Greenwich and Military Seminary.

Like Katherine, Bessy has also married well. George James is 10 years her senior. He was born in London at Mile End. He is a merchant dealing with wines and spirits. Bessy and Issy both met their future husbands at a society ball in Melbourne soon after our arrival. George lives in Richmond but has property in Collins Street and fourteen acres on the hill at Northcote, well situated for building sites. I can easily picture their wedding day that was recorded in detail in Anthony's journal:

'On Saturday 15 August, Messrs James and Nodin came in the latter's gig at half past ten, followed by Mr Welshe's carriage-and-pair driven by Mr James's servant John, dressed like a gentleman. Anthony walked to the church. I travelled in the carriage, following George and Francis's gig, with Issy and Bessy in her wedding finery. Rose started behind us in the gig driven by John: she went at a rapid pace and got to the church too early, so they drove away again as the clergyman, Mr Grange, had not arrived. Anthony had invited the minister to dine with us following the wedding, but he had declined on account of the darkness of the winter night and the distance to reach his home in the bush. The witnesses to Bessy's wedding were Anthony and Francis Nodin. Their marriage notice appeared in the *Port Phillip Herald* of 22 August, 1840, and the *Port Phillip Gazette* of 26 August.

'For the return journey, I was in the lead carriage, with the bride and bridegroom and Anthony riding upon the box. Issy travelled with Mr Nodin in his gig – Rose as before – and upon their return home had a very good cake that I had spent hours making. We served wine, but not from the bottles that Anthony had drawn the previous Saturday which amounted to 60 bottles or 10 gallons of wine. After the celebration, the bride and bridegroom took the family gig and, with Mr Nodin and Issy in the other gig, went out to Pascoeville[225] for a drive. Issy very nearly got capsized in a hole but got home in good time and the rest of the day we spent very agreeably with friends.'

Issy married on 12 December this year. Her husband, Francis, was born in England in October, 1803. He travelled on *Persian* from London, arriving in Hobart on 1 August, 1835, establishing a business selling linen, drapery, silk, haberdashery, hosiery, and sundry items. At some point, he was living in Launceston, having become insolvent in April, 1836. He subsequently went to Sydney but sailed from there on 16 October on the schooner *Paul Pry,* arriving in Melbourne on 7 November, 1838. As Francis explained to Anthony and me, a year earlier, in November, 1837, he purchased for £34: 'allotment 16 of town section 21 – a block with a frontage of a chain to Great Lonsdale Street, extending south to Bourke Lane.'

He manages a large store to the west of the marketplace in Melbourne on behalf of Mr J.F. Strachan of Geelong, who works as a squatter's provider. Since March, 1838, he has been Secretary and Treasurer for Melbourne Race Club.[226] The first race meeting in Melbourne was held on 6 and 7 March, 1838.[227]

Our house seems roomier now, with Margaret and Rose sharing a small room. The four boys occupy a larger nursery that doubles up for a school room where I give the younger children lessons in reading, writing, arithmetic, bible studies, and Latin each morning before chores are undertaken in the afternoon. None of the children, nor Anthony and I, have any difficulties falling to sleep quickly each night, exhausted from the full day of activities. We keep Sundays free, for church in the morning and socialising in the afternoon.

Wood for the animal pound[228]

22 June 1840 Anthony completes the calf and cow pound[229]

A census was conducted earlier this year. We are always interested in following information about people who have chosen to settle in Australia.

Christmas, 1841[230]

This entry will be the final entry in my journal until, God willing, I feel the need to record further information. My hands have become increasingly arthritic, and I find holding a quill and writing painful even on good days. We were blessed with our final child, Alexander Beale, who was born at our new property, St Helena Park, near Greensborough. He appears to be thriving despite my milk supply not as abundant as with past babies. I am now 47 and Anthony was 51 on 3 November. He will continue to record important observations in his journal and significant family dates in the family bible. We believe our observations in the journals we have kept to be a valuable record of such momentous times, as well as our individual lives lived across three continents.

I have been sincerely blessed with aunts, uncles, sisters, brothers, their spouses, my nephews and nieces, and not least by seventeen children. We mourn the loss of our children that pre-deceased us, and make a point of lighting a candle and reflecting on their individual lives on their birthdays: 3 January (Robert, b. 1819); 3 January (Adam, b. 1825); 20 February (Robert, b. 1820); 8 March (Charles, b. 1834); 22 March (Onesiphorus, b. 1815).

350 births as against 198 deaths.

A census taken (2nd March, 1841) showed the total population of the Province as 16,671, or 11,254 males and 5417 females. The inhabitants of Melbourne numbered 4479, or 2676 males to 1803 females, of which total 152 were children under two years, and only two persons over 60. Geelong had 454 residents, or 304 males and 150 females, including 10 under two years, none over 60, and only one individual between 45 and 60. In all the rest of Port Phillip, outside Melbourne and Geelong, there were only six sexagenarians, and 305 persons under two years. The social condition of this human aggregation was:—Males married, 2581; males unmarried, 8673. Females married, 2485; females unmarried, 2932.

In the town of Melbourne there were 809 married, and 1867 unmarried, males; whilst the married females were 783, and the unmarried 1020.

2nd March 1841 census of Port Phillip[231]

During the year, we received word from young Anthony. He has been promoted to Assistant Surgeon in Calcutta. Along with two other surgeons, he was directed to proceed to Cawnpore and to do duty under orders of superintending surgeon at that station.[232] From December, he is to proceed to Bandah, approximately 82 miles south of Cawnpore.

Chapter 40

Revisiting my journal
June, 1854

In clearing out some drawers, I 'rediscovered' my journal, long put away for more than a dozen years. It was one Anthony gave to me to replace my original calf skin journal that no longer had an inch of space. There are a number of blank pages. My hands are sufficiently recovered to write, so I plan to put these pages to good use to copy out and reflect on poems and hymns and the autumn of our lives. The cover is looking old, as unfortunately it has been difficult to protect it from damp. The lower right border is flaking from too-frequent handling.

Inside the back pages, I found some loose clippings from newspapers relating to Anthony's insolvency that caused us such concern. Why the date is incorrect by thirty years on the final clipping will forever be a mystery.[233] [234] [235] [236] We will forever be grateful that, with legal reforms, the need for severe consequences diminished and Anthony escaped going to prison.[237] The increased judicial regulation of insolvency avoided a particularly harsh feature of bankruptcy and insolvency law, namely imprisonment for debt.

WILLIAM H. KERR,
(2960) *Chief Commissioner of Insolvent Estates.*

In the Insolvent Estate of ANTHONY BEALE, Settler, near the River Plenty.

WHEREAS the Estate of the above-named Insolvent was placed under Sequestration in my hands, by order of His Honor Mr. Justice Willis, dated the 20th day of September, 1842, this is to give notice that a Meeting of the Creditors of the said Estate will be holden before me at my Office, Melbourne, on Wednesday, the 12th day of October instant, at 1 o'clock, for the proof of Debts, and that another Meeting will be holden at the same place, for the like purpose, and for electing Trustee or Trustees, on Monday, the 17th instant, at 1 o'clock.—Dated at Melbourne, this 3rd day of October, 1842.

WILLIAM VERNER,
(2970) *Chief Commissioner of Insolvent Estates.*

In the Insolvent Estate of A......

Notice of meeting of creditors re Anthony Beale's insolvency 3 October, 1842

335

In the Insolvent Estate of ANTHONY BEALL.

ARCHIBALD CUNNINGHAME having been confirmed provisional Trustee in the above Estate, this is to give notice, that all Debts due to the same are to be paid to him; and that a third Meeting of the Creditors will be holden before me, at my Office, at Melbourne, on Monday, the 12th December next, for the proof of Debts, receiving the report of the Trustee, and directing him in the future management of the said Estate.—Melbourne, 18th October, 1842.

WILLIAM VERNER,
Chief Commissioner.

(3062)

Notice re third meeting of creditors 18 October, 1842

In the Insolvent Estate of Anthony Beale, of Port Phillip.

NOTICE TO CREDITORS.

ON Friday, the 22nd day of September next, ensuing, I, the above-named Insolvent, intend to apply to the Honorable the Supreme Court for the district of Port Phillip, for the allowance of my certificate, in pursuance of the provisions of the Act of the Governor and Council of New South Wales, passed in the fifth year of the Reign of Her Majesty Queen Victoria, No. 17.—Melbourne, 29th July, 1843.

2758

ANTHONY BEALE.

Notice re application to the Supreme Court 29 July, 1843

*In the matter of the Insolvency of Anthony
Beale, of the River Plenty, in the District of
Port Phillip, and Colony of New South
Wales, Settler.*

NOTICE is hereby given, that I, Anthony
Beale, the above-named Insolvent, do
intend, on Wednesday, the twentieth day of
November next, at the hour of one o'clock in
the afternoon, to apply to William Verner,
Esquire, Chief Commissioner of Insolvent
Estates for the District of Port Phillip, that a
certificate be granted to me, in pursuance of the
provisions of a certain Act of the Governor and
Legislative Council of New South Wales, made
and passed in the seventh year of the reign of her
present Majesty Queen Victoria, No. 19,
intituled " An Act to amend an Act, intituled
'An Act for giving relief to insolvent persons,
and providing for the administration of insolvent
estates,' and to abolish imprisonment for debt.''

Dated this twenty-sixth day of September,
A.D., 1844.

ANTHONY BEALE.

Notice re relief of insolvent persons 26 September, 1844 (not 1814)

INSOLVENT COURT.

NEW INSOLVENT.

No. 279. George Wilmott, of Melbourne,
Plumber. Debts, £155. Assets, £16. Balance
deficiency, £139.

20th November, 1844.
The following insolvents came up before the
Chief Commissioner for allowance of their certifi-
cates:—
Hugh Lang—Granted.
Thomas Aekerly Robins—Adjourned for four
weeks at insolvent's request.
Alfred Woolley—Granted.
Daniel Stodhart Campbell—Granted
Norman Roderick M'Leod—Granted.
Anthony Beale—Granted.
James Clerk Wallace—Granted.
John Hunter (of Watson and Hunter,) no ap-
pearance.
John Seller—Granted.
John Maude Woolley*—Granted.
These certificates will be presented to-morrow
morning, at ten o'clock, for confirmation of allow-
ance, to his Honor the Resident Judge.

* In this case a caveat had been lodged, but
the opposing creditor having failed to appear was
saddled with the costs.

Insolvent Court 20 November, 1844 Certificate granted to Anthony Beale[238]

Another clipping was census figures from 1851: a huge increase in population in ten years:

The census returns for 1851 supply the following particulars :—

SOCIAL CONDITION.

	Males.	Females.		Males.	Females.
Married ...	12,529 ...	12,498	Single... ...	33,673 ...	18,045

CIVIL CONDITION.

	Males.	Females.		Males.	Females.
Born in the Colony or arrived free	43,006 ...	30,784	Holding tickets of leave ...	62 ...	3
			In Government employ ...	79 ...	0
Other free persons ...	3,053 ...	356	In private assignment ...	2 ...	0

RELIGION.

Church of England	37,433	Roman Catholics	18,014
Church of Scotland	11,608	Jews	364
Wesleyan Methodists	4,988	Mahommedans and Pagans	201
Other Protestants	4,313	Other Persuasions	424

HOUSES.

Stone or Brick	4,864	Finished	10,237
Wood	6,128	Unfinished	698
Shingled	9,912	Inhabited	10,866
Slated	132	Uninhabited	69

Melbourne Census, 1851[239]

Last year, our friend Lieutenant - Governor La Trobe provided 10 acres of land in Yarra Park to the Melbourne Cricket Club. The 15-year-old Club was forced to move from its former site that has now become part of the route for our first steam train. This 2.5-mile track goes from Flinders Street Station, which was opened this year by the Melbourne and Hobson's Bay Company, to Sandridge. The first university buildings have opened at Parkville following the passing of an Act of Parliament on 21 January last year. A museum has been started in the Government Assay Office in LaTrobe Street. The Melbourne we first saw has changed beyond belief.

15 June, 1854

'A day to remember. On this day, now forty years, I became a wife, may that here call to mind, all the way the Lord our God has led us through this wonderful world and how gently, how mercifully in his dealings with us. Corrections we have had, but blessed be God I can say "It has been good for us to be afflicted." Yes, it has brought us near to our God in the loss of our dear children I trust are in Paradise and we still have twelve of these as far as we can know.

'On this day, I do remember my firstborn and weep bitter tears. His death awfully sudden in the midst of robust health, full of youth and joyous feelings until in a moment swept away. A tragedy not of our making. It is the Lord's doing and therefore must be right. May God grant me grace to live to his glory. I am but a poor, frail creation, may my soul grow in grace. And may my dear husband and myself strive to walk in the way of righteousness and be ready when our own time comes.'[240]

> 'While I am a pilgrim here,
>
> Let Thy love my spirit cheer;
>
> As my Guide, my Guard, my Friend,
>
> Lead me to my journey's end;
>
> Lead me to my journey's end.'[241]

Since our first Christmas, when we experienced the effects of three days of relentless rain on the Yarra River, it flooded on three further occasions. Not long after we had moved to St Helena Park, the river rose to such an extent that the centre of Melbourne was reduced to a string of islands. There were further huge floods in 1844 and 1849. In the former, the water at Dights Falls rose by 37 feet. We had a picnic there when we first moved to Newtown as it was but a mile distant from our home.

6 July, 1854 – a poem

There are still three blank pages in my journal, and I feel well enough to copy out a poem from a favourite book *The Casket – a Christmas and New Year's Present for Children and Young Persons,* published in 1829.[242]

The poem is 'To a dying infant'. When I read it, I remember the four infants we lost on St Helena. The last verse reads:

'And when the hour arrives,

    From flesh that sets me free,

Thy spirit may await

The first at heaven's gate,

    To meet and welcome me.'[243]

4 August, 1854

This day has been set apart by our Bishop for prayer and humiliation on account of the war in Crimea. Our little circle of four only, met together in Spring Street. I am sure that our Heavenly Father may lend an ear to the prayers of his believing people and give succour to those who have gone forth against the aggressors. My heart aches for the thousands lost and the struggle of those poor persons left behind. I have had intelligence of a beloved child been again brought through the pain of childbirth. Another dear child had a narrow escape from being killed by his horse falling and how often had this been repeated. I praise the Lord for all his manifold mercies and deliverances.[244]

3 November, 1854

My dear husband has been spared another year, how gracious is our Heavenly Father. We have heard of our child being safely through her confinement and that she may up again in health and her dear babe be spared to be a blessing to her. Isabella Mary Anne Nodin is Isabella's seventh child. We also heard from Bessy and George. Their eighth child, Elizabeth Maria James, was born in Southgate, England on 27 May, 1854, my 60th birthday. We pray that the safe arrival of their beautiful daughter will in some way bring the happiness that was so missing following the unexpected death of their infant son, Edward James, so soon after they arrived in England.

For a treat we have started subscribing to a new daily paper entitled *The Age*. The first edition was published on October 17, and it is printed on a steam-driven press at the Melbourne Exhibition Building, known locally as the 'Crystal Palace,' situated on the corner of William and LaTrobe Streets. Items include shipping news, land for sale and public notices. We are informed that the population of Melbourne has grown to almost 80,000.[245] Other changes seen in Melbourne this year include the opening of the new public library on Swanston Street and the opening of Railway Pier on 12th September.

4 April, 1855

How long since I wrote in this book. I can scarcely believe it how time flies away. Another year has begun and already one quarter is gone. Our lives like the seasons are hastening and I cannot tell which of our dear circle may be taken away before the beginning of another year. My loved companion in youth has been restored … He is my all in all.

11 October, 1855

Yesterday was the anniversary of Alexander's birth, and while looking at our cheerful little family of dear ones in the morning, I could not but remember that, at the same house 14 years before, I was lying senseless, to all appearances in a dying state. The Lord has generously spared me at this time and enabled me to raise him. My dear boy, who in infancy was sickly, I pray you guide him to the truth of You and that he may eventually bear abundant fruit.

Chapter 41

5 August, 1856

Katherine awakes with a start. Her daughter Margaret is sitting beside her.

'How are you, Mama?' Margaret asks. 'I did not mean to startle you.'

'I have had such a strange dream.'

'Would you like to tell me about it? I can get you a cup of tea if you like?'

'Thank you, but I am not thirsty. In my dream, all my children, the ones still living and the ones no longer here, were sitting in a circle. Each was as I remembered them at a particular point in their lives. It did not seem to matter that the ages were wrong. We were sitting under the spreading branches of the Cedar of Lebanon at Terrace Knoll on St Helena. The sky was blue, and we could see the sea sparkling in the distance, reminding me of when Anthony took the children out on a boat to show them our home from the sea. One by one, with the babies carried by an older sibling, they approached me and placed a kiss on my forehead.'

'That is a beautiful dream, Mama. I know that the loss of so many of your children has been felt as a great sadness to you, especially Rose so few weeks ago,' said Margaret.

'But I have also been looking at the pictures on my wall. I don't know whether I ever told you that the picture of Christ as a shepherd was a gift from my sister Margaret, when I left for St Helena all those years ago. As you can see, it is a scene of gentleness and innate goodness. I have been reflecting that shepherds watch for enemies who might attack the sheep, defending them when necessary. They tend to sick or wounded sheep and search for, or rescue lost or trapped ones. They are kind, loving, patient, strong, and self-sacrificing. St Margaret has been depicted as a shepherdess.'

'I am honoured to have been named for her,' Margaret said with a smile. 'I have the family bible here. Would you like me to read to you?'

Katherine looks at Margaret as though seeing her for the first time.

'Please, I would love you to read the verses from John about the Good Shepherd. I love the sound of the old words.'

As Margaret reads, tears come into Katherine's eyes.

'Mama, you are crying,' says Margaret. 'Here, use this handkerchief.'

Katherine starts to sob before she wearily apologises to Margaret, who is holding her gently.

'How could I have been so blind, so oblivious and indifferent to you, a beloved daughter? How I have ignored your goodness over the years, more focused on my other girls, the grandchildren and the children that predeceased me? I am so sorry Margaret,' says Katherine. She experiences a sudden feeling of warmth that starts in her chest, radiating outwards before slowly encompassing her whole body. Her breathing is easier. She feels lighter. She grasps Margaret's hand, not wanting her to leave.

'You know I love you Mama,' says Margaret, her eyes filling with tears. It is as though all the confused feelings she had concerning their kinship have melted away in an instant. Her heartfelt prayers, spanning so many years, have been answered. Katherine takes a deep breath, exhales with a small sigh, and is quiet. Margaret continues to hold her hand. Outside the window a pair of honeyeaters or bell miners are taking nectar from one of the native shrubs. Their song is like delicate bells. The sun is setting as the evening star rises.

Margaret wipes her eyes, gently kisses her mother, closes the shades at the window, shuts the bedroom door, and leaves the house to find her father.

Chapter 42

Two private letters
5 August, 1857

My dearest Rose,

I am looking at your picture on the first anniversary of your death and reading the poem you left for me. It is an unseasonal winter's day, with sunshine and high winds. This morning, I walked over to the River Plenty and remembered all the picnics we took in the grasslands. There was a mob of about one hundred grey kangaroos running up from the riverbank. I could barely see them for the early morning mist. Sometimes I lie in bed and think of you whilst watching the gum trees sway and the leaves and branches move in a complicated dance. Life goes on all around me, but my heart is heavy.

Our beloved daughter Isabella, who had been grieving the untimely loss of Francis, remarried in July. Charles Maplestone proposed to her earlier this year. The wedding was held at St Helena at Sunny Side on a cold, frosty morning. Like you, I am very fond of Charles. This is his sketch of the house in April this year. He is hoping to purchase a property, Ivanhoe Lodge, that will comfortably accommodate their large family. It is closer than Richmond, so I hope I will be able to see him and Isabella regularly.

The house in which I was married (second time) 15 July, 1857' Sketched 13 April, 1857

John Lindsay married Emma Bennet in 1856, not long after you passed. Charles gave them this picture of their home as a wedding present.

Lindsay Beale House drawn by Charles Maplestone 1857

I know that you wished there had been a church closer than Heidelberg. After looking with longing eyes at the spot it was to be built on, but waiting patiently until the Lord decided the time was right, work has begun on the building of a chapel in commemoration of your life. Charles will assist me with the final design, and it will be built using local materials and labour from the Estate as far as possible. I will call it the Rose Chapel, as a memorial to you (your mother's special name for you) but also to acknowledge our beloved daughter Rose, who died so tragically just fifteen months ago. After Herbert Foley left, I find I spend most mornings in the cottage where he and Rose lived, as it helps me to feel close to her. It is quite near the spot where you and Rose are buried.

I have employed an old man, Hill, to make about thirty thousand bricks on the farm, close to the spring, which will be handy as a supply of water for the brick making. The man agreed to make them for 50 shillings per thousand if I supplied the firewood. Once again, Margaret's cart and oxen are being used to facilitate this, as well as carting bricks over to the site for the church, which takes considerable time.

We have also had to source stone for the foundations, loam for the mortar and lime, timber, and slates that have to be brought from Melbourne.

I have designed an engraving on a neat stone to be placed over the door of the small church:

'Dedicated to the honour and glory of God,

In commemoration of the happy life

And beautiful death of Katherine Rose Beale

A faithful follower of the

Lord Jesus Christ

Who died 5th

August 1856

Aged 61 years

Blessed are the dead who die in the Lord.'

My body is heavy although I am losing weight. There are days when I find it very difficult to get out of bed at all. I have lost interest in most things and spend much of the day in prayer and contemplation. Margaret continues to cook meals in the large cast iron pot over the fire, otherwise I don't think I could be bothered to eat. You had the lion's share of courage in our family. I was in awe of you: how you always put on a bright face, even in the most trying times; how you managed to find time to record your life in your precious journal; how you kept in touch with your sister Elizabeth and somehow still managed to find moments to read your beloved English novelists.

I remember the first time I saw you in your pretty, yellow silk dress for the Christmas party at Plantation House in 1813, hosted by Colonel Mark Wilks. You told me it had been made from a bolt of silk left over from your mother's work in the trade. Mark's daughter Laura was a vivacious character with great beauty, but I only had eyes for you, your dark hair and deep blue eyes suggesting an intelligence and maturity beyond your 19 years. I cannot imagine the courage it must have taken to leave your life in London, to say farewell to your family and take such a potentially dangerous journey out to St Helena. I know it was only meant to be for 12 months but our marriage in June 1814 changed all that.

We were blessed with so many children and sadly we have had to mourn the untimely loss of several of them. I long to join you again and perhaps eventually we will all be together in one place. My plans for the chapel near our home include a family graveyard, designed to be large enough to accommodate all our descendants in perpetuity if that is their wish.

Most of my days are taken up with making bricks. I have saved money, and will eventually pay for the construction myself. Haliburton has agreed to help me when he can, and Alexander has also pledged to spend a day a week assisting me. Today I am visiting a monumental mason to make a lasting memorial to you. There will be space left on it for my name so that we will always be linked together. It is my fervent hope that, in generations to come, people will come and worship at the church and perhaps wonder about the family remembered here.

I am reading Edward Young's *Night Thoughts*.

I have copied out this verse in memory of the verses you liked to write in our journal:[246]

'I tremble at the blessings once so dear;

And every pleasure pains me to the heart.

Yet why complain? or why complain for one?

Hangs out the sun his lustre but for me,

The single man?'

Edward Young

Chapter 43

Postscript
5 August, 1865 – St Helena Park

My dearest Rose,

It has been nine long years since we parted. I feel that I am close to the end of my life. There are days when I feel very muddled. The little chapel I built with handmade bricks is called the Rose Chapel. It is a single room with a fireplace. Praying there has given me much comfort and time for reflection on our marriage. When it gets dark, I use the old lamp we brought from St Helena. I wrote My Prayer to you when you were dying and thought it lost, but found it only yesterday when reading through the bible you gave to me so many years ago.

'My Prayer.'[247]

Pray for thee? ah! have I not always prayed
With quivering lips, and eyes oft blind with tears? –
With heart and hands alike to Heaven raised,
So have I prayed thro' all the long sad years.

I cried to Him who rules all earth and sky

To give thee joy – he only sent thee pain.

And when I prayed, Heaven's sunlight on thy way

Its rays were lost 'mid clouds and mists of rain.

With drooping hands, and low on bended knee,

I prayed that love – that crown of earthly bliss –

Might cast its charmed circle round thy head –

Alas! And Heaven refused me even this.

And now I kneel beside thee once again,

And know this is 'farewell' for evermore,

Just lay thy hands in mine love, while I pray

As I have never prayed for thee before.

And ere' ere the light fades from yon crimson sky,

Or sleep has come to calm thy wearied breath,

An answer to my prayer shall swiftly fly –

Ah! Be to her more kind than Life – oh! Death!

We built a tank to the south side of the church. Old Hill, the bricklayer, was a good choice; as was Wiggins, who was responsible for the carpentering work. The church was finished in 1861.

I moved into the cottage near the chapel that replaced the one Rose and Herbert lived in. Our granddaughter Kate kept house for me, but she is now twenty-three, and married Charles Symons Wingrove on 16 July, 1862, with the wedding at our property. Her stepfather, Charles Maplestone, formally adopted the Nodin children after he married Isabella. Luckily, Ivanhoe Lodge in Heidelberg was sufficiently large to accommodate all the children who have grown up together. Margaret now lives at Sunny Side, since Isabella vacated the house, although at various times Isabella's children stay with Margaret as they are close to their aunt.

The ship's bell remains in the fork of the lemon gum tree and is rung each Sunday. I will leave the choice of wording on our gravestone to John Lindsay, in consultation with our other children. Two prayers over time have brought me solace. I wish both to be part of my funeral.

Firstly, the prayer by Cardinal John Newman:

'May He support us all the day long,

till the shades lengthen, and the evening comes

and the busy world is hushed, and the fever of life is over

and our work is done!

Then in His mercy may He give us a safe lodging,

and a holy rest, and peace at the last.'

John Newman, Wisdom and Innocence, 19/2/1843[248]

The service to conclude with the Song of Simeon:

'Lord, now lettest thou thy servant depart in peace according to thy word.

For mine eyes have seen thy salvation,

Which thou hast prepared before the face of all people;

To be a light to lighten the Gentiles and to be the glory of thy people Israel.'

Nunc Dimittis, from the 1662 Book of Common Prayer

Chapter 44

Death of Anthony Beale

THERE IS A ROSE.

'There is a rose, a fragrant rose,

Which oft perfumes the Eastern gale;

That in its changes can disclose

The varied scenes of life's short tale.

For when the dawn springs forth in light,

Like childhood's first and earliest days,

The rose's blossom then is white,—

And early innocent displays.

At noon, like man, the changing flower

Shows all his heat, and blood, and strife,

And flaming red in every bower,—

Portrays the ripening age of life.

But like the darkening clouds at e'en,

When sultry suns have scorched the morn,

The rose in purple garb is seen,—

Life's evening, when young Hope is flown.

How often are our youthful hours,

Our Spring, our noon's of life o'ercast,

While darkness o'er our ev'ning lowers

In gloom of night, or winter's blast!'—[249]

Anthony Beale died on 4 September, 1865. He and Katherine are buried beside each other.

'They were lovely and pleasant in their lives and in death they are not divided.'

They were lovely and pleasant in their lives and in death they are not divided.

"Rose Chapel"

Afterword

Napoleon: 'It must be recognized that the real truths of history are hard to discover.'[250]

Why write about an ordinary person who lived more than two hundred years ago?

I first heard of Katherine Rose Beale in 2016 when I became a member of St Katherine's Church in St Helena,[251] following a move to nearby North Eltham, a green wedge suburb twenty kilometres north-east of Melbourne. I usually sat behind a delightful old lady, Isla Heddle, a great granddaughter of Katherine Rose and Anthony Beale. The church was originally the Rose Chapel, built as a tribute to his wife by a grieving Anthony, following her death in 1856. Half of the cemetery is set aside for the Beale family and their descendants. There are many memorials within the church, including stained glass windows commemorating the lives of Katherine and Anthony, and a large, grey, stone plaque honouring their first-born son, Onesiphorus. I thought it might be interesting to try and bring Katherine's story to light as she and her family were the original pioneers of the area. She had been born in England, but at some point in her life had travelled to St Helena, a tiny, remote tropical volcanic island in the South Atlantic. She had given birth to seventeen children. These experiences seemed extraordinary for a woman born in the latter years of the 18th century.

My professional and volunteer background

I grew up just north of London and emigrated to Australia in 1981 as a qualified nurse and midwife. In early 1983, I commenced a Bachelor of Arts, studying in the evening whilst working fulltime as a nurse unit manager. The final year of university was devoted to the study of Australian literature. A book that made a particular impression on me was a slim volume of short stories: *Bush Studies* by Barbara Baynton, written from the perspective of women in early Colonial Australia. The powerful and haunting stories of the suffering these women endured, eking out a living with few resources, a world away from friends and family, were inspired by Baynton's earlier life in the bush. Katherine's life as a pioneer in Australia, after a relatively privileged life on St Helena, was likely equally challenging.

During my career, I gained further professional qualifications including two master's degrees – in health services management, and in advanced nursing practice – and was a Fellow of the Royal College of Nursing, Australia. I was privileged to walk alongside literally hundreds of vulnerable people in their health journeys. My practice and professional interests included maternal and child health nursing; infection control and immunisation; oncology; palliative and aged care. I continue to volunteer in residential aged care in my retirement.

Midwifery is an ancient craft. I have chosen to use practice examples, or personal accounts of women having babies, particularly without pain relief, to reflect Katherine's likely experience of giving birth to her many children. I am most appreciative of those women who were prepared to share their private recollections. The birth of the premature baby aboard *Sir William Pulteney* is based on a delivery I witnessed as a young midwife. Recognition is given to the role of complementary or non-pharmaceutical interventions, particularly originating in other cultures, that could feasibly have enhanced the welfare of mothers during Katherine's lifetime. It was dangerous to give birth in the days before the reason for handwashing was understood, or effective pain relief, or safe anaesthesia, or antibiotics, were available. Katherine's grief at losing her 30-year-old daughter Rose, when she gave birth to a stillborn infant, was profound. Rose Foley and her baby are buried at St Katherine's Church, their deaths only a few months before Katherine's. At various times in my own professional career, I encountered people that had great faith in the power of complementary or alternative therapies. Many of these approaches, as integrative medicine, are now part of mainstream health care.

I have a lifelong interest in music and perform in community orchestras and ensemble groups. I love the sound of church bells and enjoy visiting centuries-old churches, particularly in England. Church bells are used as an ongoing motif throughout the book to mark important stages in Katherine's life, as are butterflies and trees.[252] The present-day remnant Anthony Beale reserve, where the Beales lived and the Rose Chapel was built, has become an important conservation area for flora and fauna.[253]

The Cedar of Lebanon tree was chosen for its symbolism and reminded me of my childhood, where I was fortunate to live on what had once been a grand estate with hundreds of specimen trees including two beautiful Cedars of Lebanon. Benjamin Grant in his descriptive guide to St Helena mentions different types of cedar trees throughout the Island.[254] An excellent book about lost and old gardens of St Helena has recently been published.[255]

The research process and choice of appropriate genre.

In preference to the structured format of research required of a higher degree (as I no longer had free access to university resources), my starting point was to examine a carrier bag of information about St Katherine's, added to over the years by the late Isla Heddle. Contents include various WikiTrees; extracts of diaries written by Anthony Beale and his son, John Lindsay Beale; copies of articles published in the popular media; and a few handwritten observations. I began to question some of the assumptions about the Beales that were put forward as 'real truths.' That included the understanding that Katherine had travelled to St Helena to visit her uncle, the Governor, and even her place and date of birth.

I had planned to employ the genre of creative non-fiction for this book, where characters, events and quotations are informed by research and verifiable by credible sources. I had anticipated finding useful information in the four volumes of journals attributed to Katherine, held by the State Library of Victoria. Unfortunately, extended lockdowns were imposed on Melburnians because of the Covid-19 pandemic and public buildings were closed. Confined to a five-kilometre radius of our home, I embarked on a virtual journey, travelling in time and a spatial sense. I had barely heard of St Helena and was unfamiliar with the part of London where Katherine spent her childhood. I mentally travelled back two centuries, using information available on the internet, including academic resources and non-academic, or informal writing, such as blogs. I sourced online documents from world-wide libraries and museums, read contemporaneous books and journals, downloaded very long historical documents available via Google books, and read academic papers. I initiated correspondence with local history societies, libraries, and the profile manager of the family WikiTrees, to try and resolve some discrepancies. I sought and received permission from direct descendants of the Beale family to ensure they and their families were agreeable to me writing about their ancestors, possibly in fictional format. I also wanted to check whether anyone else was currently working on a history of the family, as I did not wish to duplicate their work. Isla Heddle told me that there had been several people over the years proposing to write about the Beales, but as far as she knew that was no longer the case. I accessed old newspapers via Trove. The various people who helped me bring the book to fruition are listed under acknowledgements.

Part of my research entailed a detailed study of contemporaneously printed local maps, covering London and England more broadly;[256] St Helena;[257] Tasmania and mainland Australia, and looking at places via Google Earth and other media. The maps of St Helena were particularly important to inform Katherine's various journeys around the Island. I wanted to avoid having her walk or ride impossible routes, in the manner that Betsy Balcombe describes in the story.

I used maps to better understand stagecoach routes in 19th century London and to identify localities.[258] The departure point from the Bolt in Ton, in London,[259] the route taken to Portsmouth, the types of horses used, the Inn Katherine stays in at Guildford, the description of the Guildhall, and the layout of Portsmouth in 1813, are historically accurate. I learned more about the Green Chain Walk, a series of linked parks in South London developed in 2023 that partially follow ancient pilgrimage routes to Canterbury and along part of which Anthony walks whilst contemplating his future.[260] Katherine's birth family had largely settled in Blackheath and Lee, just south of Greenwich, living in a number of grand homes, by 1836. I am grateful to my nephew who lives in Wapping, close to where Katherine grew up in St George-in-the-East. He confirmed that the Thames is tidal where Katherine purchases her fish. He took photos of the stone staircase alongside the Prospect of Whitby, that coincidentally is his local pub, complete with a hangman's noose on the wall that marks the site of Execution Dock. He said that mudlarking has increased in popularity over the centuries, with approximately 5,000 registered mudlarks today.

The information from the John Lindsay about pollarding trees, the different properties of wood, the composition of traditional British hedges and the wildlife the Anthony observes during his meanderings, is factual. On a recent visit to East Devon in England, my brother invited me to a field he owns, demonstrating how he pollards trees for fuel and experiments with crops. He has constructed a simple but effective pump, to harness water from a local stream running through the property. Presumably Anthony Beale, during his three-year furlough in England, used his time productively to gather information about care of stock and farming practices. It is unlikely he had much practical experience in land management, as he had been a civilian employee of the Honourable East India Company. Domestic and gardening work on St Helena in his time would have been undertaken by servants or slaves.

Many of the males in Katherine's family were master mariners, employed by the Honourable East India Company, or were connected in some way to the Company. Interactive online maps are available to trace the routes taken by the East Indiaman ships to India, Canton, Java, and back to England.[261] The descriptions of the localities visited by these ships during their trade is fascinating, as are the details of the exotic goods that were loaded onto the ships in precise quantities. I learned about the important influences of tides, winds, currents, and navigating by the stars, to the expansive British trade empire. For example, it was important to avoid the 'doldrums', a belt around the Earth near the equator that has little to no horizontal wind. Ships could become becalmed, stranded for days or weeks, and run out of food and fresh water to drink. In the context of our own pandemic caused by an infectious agent, it was interesting to research the prevalent infectious diseases of the time and better understand the multiple hazards for mariners.

I had no idea that Nelson's body was preserved in a vat of brandy,[262] but logically Katherine's brother-in-law James Halliburton, who died at sea but was interred at St Helena some weeks later, had a similar fate. Most passengers or crew who were unfortunate enough to die during a voyage would be consigned to the sea, as happens with the fictional baby William. This was also the fate of Betsy Balcombe's older sister, Jane, when the family came out to Australia from England, with her father taking up the position of Colonial Treasurer for the Colony of New South Wales in Sydney in 1824. Betsy's youngest brother, Alexander, eventually made his home at The Briars on the Mornington Peninsula, Victoria in 1846.[263]

In later life, Katherine was a signatory to an 1842 petition to Governor La Trobe, her ex-neighbour in Newtown, from the 'Resident Ladies of Plenty' who were terrified that they would be attacked by bushrangers that hid in the forests of Montmorency.[264] The paintings Katherine hangs on her wall or refers to in other parts of her story, are real. Her son Anthony was a notable water colour artist, her daughter Margaret sketched scenes from their domestic life, and her future son-in-law Charles Maplestone drew sketches of various family homes. The houses her siblings and daughters occupied in England, and their extended family members, are identified through census reports within the Descendant Report.[265]

State Library of Victoria January 2022

Prior arrangements were made with the Heritage Room at the State Library of Victoria to have the two boxes consisting of four diaries attributed to Katherine Beale retrieved from the archives and ready for me to read.[266] In one box are a series of notebooks written by Anthony following the death of his beloved Katherine Rose. They are in stark contrast to his earlier writings where observations are reasonably objective, if not austere in their lack of emotion or regard for the sensitivities of his wife or children. The maudlin tones of the later writing with frequent invocations to higher powers and God, combined with the overly sentimental references to Katherine and others, induces in the reader a degree of unease. These later diaries are perhaps much more revealing of Anthony's character than his objective observations, or even the amusing sketches of their early life in Australia.

It should be noted that a transcript of all the Beale family diaries held by the State Library Victoria is currently a work in progress by Mr Tim Gatehouse, a local historian who has authored articles about the Beales,[267] so my access to the most valuable 1833 diary was limited. A pattern of silver links traces the edge of the cover with diagonal chains from the four corners joined to a rectangular inner border. Within the centre are the faint remnants of the embossed crest of the East India Company: a partial Cross of St George, surrounded by a shield shape. Sadly, the overall condition is poor, with fading writing and damaged pages. Pictures of the Company coat of arms can be found here.[268]

The front cover of Anthony Beale's 1833 journal held by the State Library of Victoria

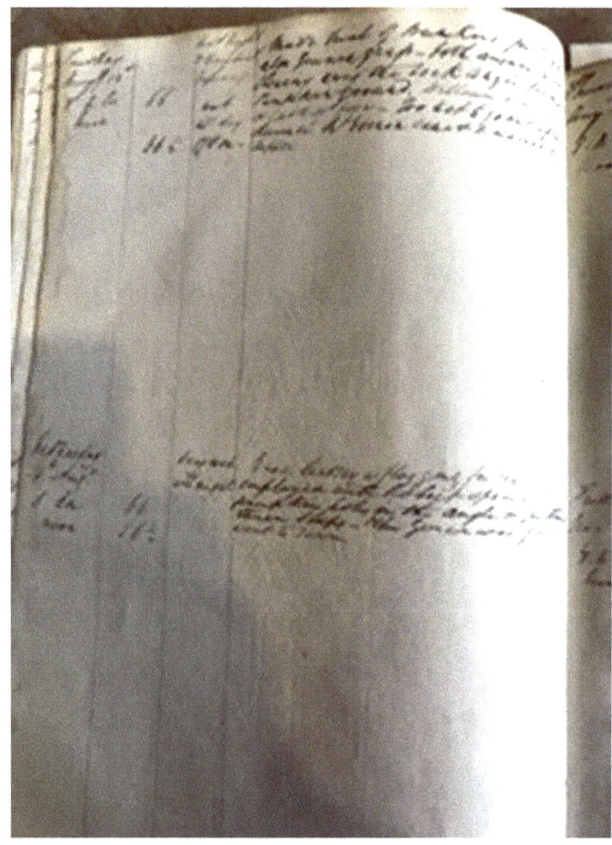

A typical page from Anthony Beale's 1833 journal is laid out with four columns

Katherine's Christian faith

The 19th century was one of the richest periods in the history of Christianity[269] that saw the rise of Biblical criticism, new knowledge of religious diversity in other continents, and above all the growth of science.[270] The fictional Katherine, Anthony, and Laura allude to this in their discussion of the geological origin of St Helena and the other islands that form a volcanic chain from the South Atlantic to Iceland. It was disappointing that entries in the journals held by the State Library of Victoria written by Katherine, are largely confined to copies of hymns or poems and what I have termed stylised writing, that takes a non-naturalistic, conventional form. Her reflections and invocations to God are not dissimilar in form to Anthony's later diaries. In part, this may be that Katherine, observing the customs of her time, was reluctant to commit her truer feelings to paper, never knowing who may read what she recorded. The texts are personal but not private. Sense-making of historical journals and letters is explored by Steven Stowe.[271] Nevertheless, it was quite fun to chase down the possible sources of the passages Katherine chose to copy, as presumably these books were available to early pioneers and important to her. Some texts appear to have been sourced from William Carus Wilson's *A Book of General Psalmody*, a weighty tome containing 'portions for the whole of the Psalms and above a thousand hymns.' The original was published in 1838, with a third edition published in 1853 so no doubt it was a popular book.[272] Other quotations in Katherine's hand are taken from poems or hymns written by Anna L Barbauld (1772). Written in full, on 6 July, 1854, is a poem 'On the death of an infant' by Caroline (Bowles) Southey (1787–1854).[273]

Below this poem, in Anthony Beale's hand, is written:

'Thou art gone to the grave' ...[274]

I visited my elderly mother who was seriously ill in England in late 2024. I spent part of the day reading poetry to her and discovered a book of poems written by her paternal grandmother. I chose to use examples of Evelyn Fairman's poems at various points in the narrative as they are very much in the style of Katherine's writing, despite being written about fifty years later. Katherine Beale's trust in the divine appears to have sustained her through the grief of losing several of her children. The various churches she patronised over her lifetime included: St George-in-the East in the East End of London, where she and several siblings were baptised, her mother buried, and her sisters married (evidence from census reports and other evidence-based reports collated in the comprehensive Descendant Report); and St James and the Country Church — now St Paul's Cathedral — on St Helena and close to Plantation House where Katherine possibly lived when first in St Helena.[275] Evidence to support her church attendance on St Helena includes her marriage certificate and other records relating to the baptism and funerals of her infants, copies of which were sourced from St Helena archives, and the choice of burial site for her brothers-in-law, Adam Baildon and James Halliburton. Katherine quite likely attended St Margaret's in Blackheath – located a close walking distance to the family properties in Blackheath and Lee – and St Luke's in nearby Charlton where several members of her family are buried. In Australia, she worshipped at Mr Waterfield's Chapel; St James Church that later became St James' Old Cathedral in Melbourne; and possibly a church in Heidelberg; as well as partaking in home-based church services with a visiting priest.[276] Evidence for this is recorded in Anthony Beale's journal.

Writer's block followed by a breakthrough

The lack of any personal information about Katherine presented a dilemma. I was unsure how to progress. I was having difficulty imagining her character. It was eighteen months before I had a breakthrough and felt I could resume writing about her. In the interim, I worked as a volunteer biographer with three elderly ladies, two of them in their nineties, to enable them to tell their unique stories. Working with each individual was a way of both honouring and affirming the rich life they had lived and allowing their voice to be heard. Through our shared journey I learned that story telling is not linear, as that is not how the brain works. Sometimes the recollections were delivered in a stream of consciousness, but more usually the anecdotes covered different decades and generations, sometimes jumping from one to another in a single sentence; the characters in them overlapped and were sometimes muddled; thoughts prompted other thoughts that sparked reminiscences; but ultimately the story became a coherent narrative. A relationship of trust was built over several weeks or months, where information was shared in a safe, private space. Through active listening and validation of what the person had to say, the process was as valuable as the end product. What was left out was sometimes more important to the storyteller than what was eventually included in the finished biography. The process allowed us to travel back to a different world, capturing the essence of 'ordinary' or 'domestic' lives of these women in important narratives, about a world that is gone forever. Above all, it was fun. It helped me to explore how best to write a story about someone's life and reaffirmed my commitment to telling Katherine's story.

I revisited the information in the original WikiTrees and realised there was a second profile manager whom I had overlooked. Unknown to me, she happened to be a direct descendant of Anthony and Katherine through her mother. In January 2024 Deborah Green, Katherine's great, great granddaughter, forwarded to me a very detailed, forty-page 'Descendants' Report' that was the culmination of years of expensive research about the family. The document added much needed verisimilitude to support Katherine's story. I tried to adhere as closely as possible to the report detail, in imagining and bringing Katherine's very large, immediate, and extended family to life. As a consequence, I rewrote several of the earlier chapters and it gave me confidence that this book truthfully portrays historical figures and facts as closely as is possible more than two centuries later.

Katherine's early life in Regency England

Katherine Rose Beale, nee Young, was most likely born in May 1794, not 1795 as recorded on her gravestone, in today's East End of London. She was the youngest of eight children. Many of her male relatives, including her brothers and brothers-in-law, were employed under the auspices of the Honourable East India Company, as commanders or captains of East Indiamen ships. Reciprocal trade, strictly regulated, was conducted with present-day Indonesia, China and India. Tea was one of the more important cargoes, alongside spices, silks, ivory, and other exotic goods. Further information about the Honourable East India Society 'club' and the lives of its senior commanders has been collated into a readable document.[277]

The new London Docks were being developed at Wapping, to accommodate the myriad ships and their imports. The River Thames was the key to Britain's hugely successful worldwide trade and maritime supremacy. A safe anchorage for the ships was located in a sheltered area known as The Downs, between the Thames Estuary that flows east into the North Sea and the Straits of Dover. The Thames also hosted rotting hulks of prison ships. England had recently lost the American Colonies, so sending unwanted felons to that country was no longer an option. In an ironic nod to the past, the *Bibby Stockholm*, a barge moored at Portland, Dorset, is controversially used to house asylum seekers in 2024 and likened to a prison.[278]

Many local industries in that part of London were intrinsically linked to the shipping trade. Examples include making ropes and sails. To rig Admiral Lord Nelson's flagship *Victory*, launched in 1765, required four acres of sail, 26 miles of rope and 768 pulley blocks. She was built at Chatham Boatyard, which has recently been repurposed to include demonstrations on traditional ropemaking.[279] *Victory* was badly damaged in the Battle of Trafalgar in 1805, one of many conflicts resulting from the Napoleonic Wars (1803–1815) that were the culmination of decades of antagonism between Britain and France, who both resented the other's attempts to expand their empire. The hulls of war ships and the East Indiamen were designed with a pronounced tumblehome, wider at the waterline than the upper deck, to provide the necessary stability to carry heavy cannon. A twist of fate meant Katherine was living on St Helena when Napoleon was exiled there in October, 1815.

The stagecoach routes and departure points, the design and payloads of East Indiaman ships and barques travelled on by Katherine, the influence of winds, currents and navigational instruments during the age of sail, the topography of volcanic islands, the multiple church and bell ringing histories, the minor characters and major events occurring on St Helena, are factual. The lives and professions of the prominent characters in the book: the Young, Beale, Wilks, and their extended families, are also based on fact. Information about secondary persons or places is informed by historical accounts. For example, the hanged men the fictional Katherine observes in London, and the murders of the Marr family, were true events. The Prospect of Whitby was – and still is – a real pub. The rivalry between the two resident chaplains on St Helena, Rev Jones and Rev Boys – and their uncompromising positions on morality – was well known throughout the Island and documented in various books.

The East Indiaman trading voyages could last up to eighteen months and had many inherent dangers, including disease, fire, enemy engagement, and shipwreck. Death and desertion rates were high, with new crew, including Lascars, taken on at various ports. Katherine's father was lost at sea, most likely dying a few weeks or months after his wife Katherine, nee Raitt.

'Crossing the second bar' was a significant point in the journey when returning from the Far East, as well as being a metaphor for death. It is usually recorded in the voyage details. This sense of distance and imperilment is captured in the poem *Crossing the Bar*, by Alfred, Lord Tennyson:[280]

'Twilight and evening bell,

And after that the dark!

And may there be no sadness of farewell,

When I embark;

For though from out our bourne of Time and Place

The flood may bear me far,

I hope to see my Pilot face to face

When I have crossed the bar.'

The River Thames below the Prospect of Whitby inn where Katherine buys fish (2024 copyright Oscar Pearson)

Stone steps adjacent to the Prospect of Whitby (2024 copyright Oscar Pearson)

St Helena and the Honourable East India Company

St Helena, a remote tropical island in the south Atlantic Ocean, is geologically part of a volcanic chain that extends northwards to Tenerife and Iceland. The prevailing theory on how such islands were created was attributed to Neputism: that islands had thrust themselves out of an Earth covered by ocean. This fitted well with the Creation story and Noah's flood as espoused by Christians of Katherine's time. Emerging theories established the foundation for modern geology and debunked the notion that supernatural intervention was necessary in forming the Earth's landscape: rather that rocks were birthed by processes driven by heat contained in the Earth's interior.[281] St Helena itself is thought to be the product of two separate volcanic eruptions.[282] Photographs of the Island, perhaps not so different from two hundred years ago, are captured in an excellent series by Pauline and John Grimshaw.[283]

St Helena was a vitally important strategic outpost, particularly for ships returning from India and the Far East. It was owned by the Honourable East India Company. The Company maintained two regiments on the Island: the St Helena Foot Regiment and the St Helena Artillery, and employed many of its civilians.[284] Ships had to approach from the northwest, usually on their return journey from the Far East. It could be challenging to navigate and occasionally ships missed the island altogether, which likely had dire consequences if the crews were running short of essential food and water. Marine chronometers were only just starting to be used on ships, were expensive, and were not uniformly fitted. Other navigational instruments included sextants, marine compasses, and telescopes. A detailed knowledge of the night sky, that assisted in navigation, was essential.

It is generally accepted that Katherine went to St Helena see her 'uncle, the Governor,' presumably Colonel Mark Wilks. It is likely this assumption was erroneous and referred to Dr Adam Baildon, her brother-in-law, a shore-based surgeon with the Honourable East India Company, who was eighteen years older than Katherine. He was married to her older sister Isabella, and they had moved to St Helena around 1807. Extensive research has been unable to establish a kinship link between the Young,

Raitt, and Wilks families. Wilks, as incoming Governor, took up his post on St Helena in June, 1813, travelling on *Sir William Pulteney*, an East Indiaman 'country ship.' Charles Hardy's fascinating Register of Ships including the supplement, and the updated edition by his son Horatio, contains detailed information about East Indiaman ships, their crews, the dates and destinations of voyages, and is referred to throughout this book.[285] [286]

Slavery and Chinese labourers

St Helena was to play a significant role in the abolition of slavery. However, during Katherine's residence, most of the domestic work and hard labour were undertaken by slaves, ex-slaves, or Chinese indentured workers. An interesting document from 1827 names the slaves and Chinese who are 'owned' by the dominant white elite population.[287] Punishment for even minor infringements by slaves was severe. During the excavations for the future airport on St Helena, archaeologists uncovered the graves of thousands of slaves. Many of these remains are being DNA tested to try and discover their origin.[288]

The arrival of Napoleon 1815

The population of St Helena almost doubled, virtually overnight, in October, 1815. Napoleon Bonaparte was defeated at the Battle of Waterloo, on 18 June, 1815. The battle marked the end of the Napoleonic wars, and Napoleon was exiled to St Helena. He arrived on *HMS Northumberland* (not to be confused with the East Indiaman ship *Northumberland* that operated from 1805–1819) with a flotilla of ships carrying members of his family and political allies, as well as military men employed to guard him. The senior officer was Admiral Cockburn, who was responsible for Napoleon's care and custody for his first seven months on St Helena. In an act of great discourtesy, the incumbent Governor Colonel Mark Wilks had little notice from the British of Napoleon's impending arrival. There was no suitable housing, so the deposed Emperor was temporarily accommodated in the Briars Pavilion owned by the Balcombe family.

During the period of Napoleon's captivity that ended with his death in 1821, governance of the Island was invested in the British, taking effect in early 1816 with the arrival of General Sir Hudson Lowe, who was of senior rank to Colonel Wilks. Wilks was highly regarded by Napoleon, unlike his successor. The near-derelict Longwood House was eventually chosen by Admiral Cockburn and Wilks to house Napoleon and his retinue. Soldiers were deployed to make it habitable. Longwood is situated about six kilometres from Jamestown on an elevated plain that was easy to secure. Napoleon was transferred there in December, 1815. Wilks, along with his wife, Dorothy, and daughter, Laura, returned to the Isle of Man in 1816.

The St Helena Act 1833

The St Helena Act of 1833 resulted in ownership of the Island reverting to the British, when the Honourable East India Company sold its rights to the Island and its employees. St Helena was no longer the jewel in the crown, as the nature of trade was changing, and ships were becoming faster. The full effects of the legislation, effective 2 April, 1834, were not felt until 24 Feb, 1836. The Honourable East India Company employees regarded it as a great betrayal. Many men, who had reasonably expected to be employed for life and ultimately receive a generous pension, found they no longer had a job or income. Living standards for residents choosing to remain on St Helena deteriorated significantly. Many islanders moved to South Africa or returned to England. St Helena, along with Ascension Island and Tristan da Cunha, are today British territories with equal status.

It is likely that the decline in status for the commanders and captains of the East Indiamen ships was set in train much earlier in the 19th century. By 1803 the Honourable East India Company (HEIC), had lost its monopoly on trade with India and depended on the tea trade from China – Canton in particular. Over the next couple of decades, competitors established tea plantations in India and elsewhere. Trading conditions became more difficult, and this was reflected in a steady loss of income for commanders over time. In a petition dated 'Canton, 12 November, 1827', a committee of four commanders, elected by their fellow officers, petitioned the Company about the loss of actual income that they had suffered over the past 25 years. They compared the income of the captain of *Glatton* in 1806 with *Farquarson* and *Lowther Castle* in 1826, arguing that a captain would be financially disadvantaged in the trading circumstances which then prevailed. The petition, which was subsequently printed for a more general distribution and presumably for public consumption, was signed by Captains William Hay, John Charettie, Robert Locke, and John C Whiteman. [289] And who was the lucky captain of *Glatton* in 1806? None other than James Halliburton![290]

Anthony Beale, Katherine, and ten of their twelve surviving children, most likely lived in England between 1836 and 1839, probably dependent on the largesse of Katherine's extended family, several of whom had bought large properties in Blackheath and Lee, just south of Greenwich. They travelled in a ship from St Helena captained by Katherine's brother Charles Cobb Young (recorded in the diaries of John Lindsay Beale held in the State Library of Victoria). It was possibly *Justina* (information from Descendant's report). *Justina* was owned by Katherine's older brother James Young. She weighed 410 tons and was built at Deptford in London in 1825. There is a record of her voyage to Bengal in 1837, captained by Charles Young. A search of the *Asiatic Journals* for the time period covering 1834–1839 did not identify a record of the Beales travelling to England, despite detailed information about other families who departed St Helena. A possible explanation is that the arrangement was private rather than a more formal voyage on an East Indiaman. It would have made sense for their ship to have docked on the south side of the Thames, possibly at Rotherhithe, which is less than four miles from Blackheath, although I have not been able to find evidence to support this. John Lindsay Beale notes: 'on arrival in England the family were farmed out to various relatives and I boarded with Uncle John Lindsay.'[291] In the absence of information to the contrary, it seems more likely that the Beales would have left St Helena in 1836 once the full effects of the British Government changes were felt, so this earlier date has been used in this book.

Departure for Van Diemen's Land, Australia, March, 1839

Based on his service with the Honourable East India Company, Beale received a pension of around £500 per annum. It is thought that he sold his pension rights in order to fund his family to make a fresh start as free settlers in Australia. They departed from England on 14 March, 1839 with ten of their children, travelling on the barque *Cecelia* that arrived in Launceston, Van Diemen's Land, on 29 July, 1839. Their second and third sons, Edward and Anthony, remained in England to pursue careers in the military and medicine respectively, sponsored by their uncle James Young. The Beales moved to mainland Australia and lived in Newtown, renamed Fitzroy, from November, 1839, where they were friends with the La Trobe family, who were neighbours. They moved again in 1841, when Beale took up a pastoral lease that became known as St Helena Park, River Plenty, and later the district of St Helena. Katherine gave birth to one further son, Alexander, on 10 October, 1841, when she was 47 years old. On at least one occasion, Anthony Beale was declared insolvent, with Katherine's brother-in-law John Lindsay, the wealthy widower of her sister Margaret, and his son-in-law George James, married to Bessie, apparently his financial saviours.

Katherine's death

Katherine died on 5 August, 1856. Her devastated husband, Anthony, built the Rose Chapel in her memory, with the assistance of Charles Maplestone, a widower and church architect who later married their widowed daughter Isabella. Approximately half the cemetery where Katherine and Anthony are buried is kept for their descendants. The remainder of plots have been secured for public burial. The Rose chapel was eventually sold to the Church of England and renamed St Katherine's Church, becoming part of the parish of Diamond Creek. Descendants of Anthony and Katherine continued to worship there until a pandemic achieved what a terrible fire could not. The church was closed for regular services in 2021.

The legacy of the Rose Chapel, AKA St Katherine's

St Katherine's was rebuilt following the 1957 bushfire, using detailed plans and funded by public donations. In an example of life coming full circle, a donation was received from the Bishop of St Helena. The Cathedral Church of St Paul was the old Country Church where Katherine's two brothers-in-law and possibly her four infant sons are buried. Through much of the 20th century, St Katherine's Church was a tourist destination, as well as a place of worship. This affection continued into the 21st century, with significant celebrations marking the 150th anniversary of its founding, in May 2008. Tours of the church by school and community groups are still facilitated in 2024 and it remains open for weddings and funerals.

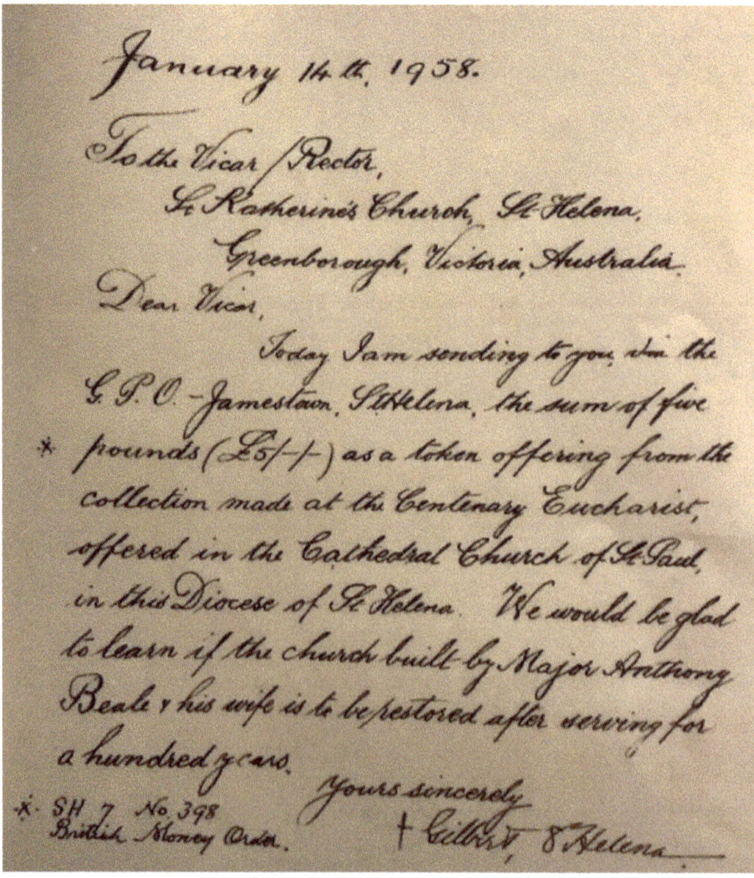

Letter from Bishop Gilbert, St Helena 1958

The coronavirus (COVID) pandemic of 2019 prompted a re-evaluation of how and where church services were delivered. In an ironic nod to the past – as Katherine's daughter Isabella laid the foundation stone of St John's Diamond Creek on 11 November, 1867 – the Church Council of St John's announced on 25 May, 2021, that St Katherine's and St Michael's in Yarrambat would be closed for regular Sunday worship.

Understanding Katherine's life and developing her story

One way Katherine's life might be understood is in the narrative archetype of a hero's journey or monomyth, as it fits well into the arch plot structure.[292] Her life may also be understood in the context of a quotation from Evelyn Underhill, a Christian mystic writer:

> 'Three deep cravings of the self, three great expressions of man's restlessness, which only mystic truth can fully satisfy.
> The first is the craving which makes him a pilgrim and a wanderer. It is the longing to go out from his normal world in search of a lost home, a "better country."
> The next is the craving of heart for heart, of the soul for its perfect mate, which makes him a lover.
> The third is the craving for inward purity and perfection, which makes him an ascetic, and in the last resort a saint.'[293]

Last words

In writing her story, the fictional Katherine became a very real person for me, allowing me to experience her world, sharing her thoughts and feelings, almost as though I was an invisible companion walking beside her across the trajectory of her life. I wanted her to become something more than Anthony Beale's 'Mrs B.' I sensed she was the vital partner in her marriage. Her strength of character, her loyalty to her husband who variously presents as impractical and sentimental, her love and acceptance of her children who went on to forge significant careers, is perhaps more important than the legacy of a church named for her. Her life was a lesson in resilience, resourcefulness, practicality and courage, whilst marked by significant grief, but in the few diary extracts in her hand, she does not indulge in self-pity.

As John Dunne, the great metaphysical poet, wrote:[294]

> No man is an island,
>
> Entire of itself.
>
> Each is a piece of the continent,
>
> A part of the main …
>
> Each man's death diminishes me,
>
> For I am involved in mankind.
>
> Therefore, send not to know
>
> For whom the bell tolls,
>
> It tolls for thee.

The church bell at St Katherine's was believed to have been brought to Australia from St Helena by Anthony Beale. For many years it was hung in a gum tree. I like to think that Katherine was able to look at it from her bed, as she was dying.

Stephen Hawes' (written ~ 1474) 'An Epitaph' seems fitting here:[295]

> After the day there cometh the dark night
>
> For though the day be never so long
>
> At last the bells ringeth to evensong.

The bell in in the fork of the gum tree – possibly dated 1957 around the time of the bushfire

References/Bibliography

1   Academy of American Poets. 2024. *Ulysses: Alfred, Lord Tennyson 1809–1892*. Accessed 25 August, 2024. <https://poets.org/poem/ulysses>

Character Profiles

2   The East India Company London. 2023. *St Helena and EIC*. Accessed 17 August, 2024. <https://www.theeastindiacompany.com/blogs/stories/st-helena-and-eic#:~:text=The%20Company%20was%20 granted%20a,undisturbed%20life%20in%20 the%20tropics.>

3   St Helena Government Gazette Extraordinary. 2021. *The Elections Ordinance, 2009. The Registration of Electors Regulations, 2009, Register of Electors*. Accessed 14 August, 2024. <https://www.sainthelena.gov.sh/ wp-content/uploads/2021/06/EX-GAZ-No-59-Register-of-Electors-June-2021.pdf>

4   Mason, Chris, & Whannel, Kate. 2024. *We can't change our history on slave trade – PM* Commonwealth Heads of Government Meeting, Samoa, 25 October 2024. Accessed 25 October 2024. <https://www.bbc.com/news/articles/c238lje181ko>

5   May, Leonard Morgan. 1908. *Charlton Near Woolwich Monumental Inscriptions of St Luke's Church*. Aspects of Kentish Local History. Accessed 23 August, 2024. <https://tedconnell.org.uk/LFH/GRS/CHW/01.htm>

6   i Museum. 2024. *Colonel Mark Wilks*. Accessed 23 August, 2024. <https://www.imuseum.im/search/collections/people/mnh-agent-29366.html>

7   St Helena Island. 2024. *Origins of Island surnames*. Accessed 23 August, 2024. <https://sainthelenaisland.info/surnames.htm>

8   Wikipedia contributors. 2024. *Devonshire (1804 EIC ship)*. Wikipedia, The Free Encyclopedia. Accessed 22 August, 2024. <https://en.wikipedia.org/w/index.php?title=Devonshire_(1804_EIC_ship)&oldid=1166301391>

9   Legislation.gov.uk. 2024. *Cinque Ports Act 1821*. Chapter 76. Accessed 23 August, 2024. <https://www.legislation.gov.uk/ukpga/Geo4/1-2/76/enacted?view=plain>

Prologue

10   Victorian Heritage Database. 2005. *St Helena Cemetery St Helena Road, GREENSBOROUGH VIC 3088 - Property No B6810*. Accessed 24 October 2024. <https://vhd-dr.heritage.vic.gov.au/places/64365>

11   Thorvaldson, Elke Haege. 2023. *Plants (flowers) favoured by native stingless bees*. Accessed 26 July, 2024. <https://www.elkeh.com.au/native-stingless-bees-sydney/>

12   Nillumbik Historical Society. 2022. *Joseph Stevenson and his Bullock Named Diamond*. Accessed 23 August, 2024. <https://www.nillumbikhistory.org.au/joseph-stevenson-and-his-bullock-named-diamond/>

13   Ferguson and Urie. 2013. *1869: St Katherine's Church, St Helena, Victoria. Ferguson and Urie Colonial Victoria's Historic Stained Glass Craftsmen 1853–1899*. Accessed 17 August, 2024. <https://fergusonandurie.com/2013/06/03/1869-st-katherines-church-st-helena-victoria/>

14   Croll, RH. 1928. *The Open Road in Victoria Being The Ways of Many Walkers: One Day Walks: St Helena*. A Project Gutenberg of Australia eBook 2014. Accessed 23 July, 2021. <http://www.gutenberg.net.au/ ebooks14/1402821h.html>

15   Montrose. 1930. 'A link with Napoleon.' *The Australian Women's Mirror*. Accessed 28 June, 2024. <https://nla.gov.au/nla.obj-407211414/view?sectionId=nla.obj-418804037&partId=nla.obj-407320041#page/n30/mode/1up/search/montrose>

16   Burns, A. A. 1946. 'In Memory of the Pioneers.' *Walkabout*. Accessed 28 June, 2024. <https://catalogue.nla.gov.au/catalog/2592481>

17   Wallis, Barbara. 1957. 'St Katherine's – old lamp still lights church rebuilt from bushfire ruin.' *The Australian Women's Weekly* (Vic Edition). Accessed 28 June, 2024. <https://ferguson andurie.com/wp-content/uploads/2013/06/australian-womens-weekly-6th-nov-1957-page-12-13.pdf>

18   Gwyther-Jones, Roy. 2017. *Light on the Hill*. A History of the Anglican Parish of Diamond Creek, 1867–2017. Greenhill Publishing.

19   Banyule City Council. 2024. *Anthony Beale Reserve*. Accessed 28 June, 2024. <https://www.banyule.vic.gov.au/Events-activities/Parks-and-reserves/Anthony-Beale-Reserve>

Chapter 1

20   Fairman, E. M. 1890-1934. *'A Mother's Wish'* in 'Poems'. A collection of poems written by the author's maternal great grandmother.

21   Carswell, Barbara. 2022. *Beacons of hope: Victorian lighthouses*. State Library Victoria. Accessed 23 August, 2024. <https://blogs.slv.vic.gov.au/our-stories/ask-a-librarian/victorian-history/beacons-of-hope-victorian-lighthouses/>

22   Morris, Rohan. 2024. *Rohan the Bullocky. Bullock teams facts and history*. Accessed 31 July, 2024. <https://www.glenedenfarm.com.au/>

23   Matthews, Sarah. 2018. *The ancient art of bellringing*. State Library Victoria. Accessed 28 July, 2024. <https://blogs.slv.vic.gov.au/such-was-life/the-ancient-art-of-bellringing/>

24   Edwards, Dianne H. 1979. *The Diamond Valley Story*. Chapter 7: Life in the Balance (1840s and 1850s). pp. 95. Copyright The Shire of Diamond Valley.

25   Superintendent, Port Phillip District (VA473). 1842. *Petition from the Resident Ladies of Plenty*. Public Record Office Victoria. Accessed 31 July, 2024. <https://prov.vic.gov.au/archive/EC9589D6-BD36-11ED-8BFF-D1F-085FE0A30>

26   State Library Victoria. 2024. *Beale, K. R., Beale, A., & Stadler, Y. (1828). Diaries, poems, 1828-[not after 1994].[manuscript]*. (Can be ordered and read in the SLV Heritage Room).

27   State Library Victoria. 2024. *Beale, K. R., Beale, A., & Stadler, Y. (1828). Diaries, poems, 1828-[not after 1994]. [manuscript]*. (Can be ordered and read in the SLV Heritage Room).

28   Fairman, E.M 1890-1934 *'My Rose'* in 'Poems'. A collection of poems written by the author's maternal great grandmother.

29   Oxford University Museum of Natural History. 2024. *William Burchell*. Accessed 23 August, 2024. <https://www.oum.ox.ac.uk/learning/htmls/burchell.htm>

30   Sandoval-Velasco, M., Jagadeesan, A., Ramos-Madrigal, J., Ávila-Arcos, M. C., Fortes-Lima, C. A., Watson, J., Johannesdóttir, E., Cruz-Dávalos, D. I., Gopalakrishnan, S., Moreno-Mayar, J. V., Niemann, J., Renaud, G., Robson Brown, K. A., Bennett, H., Pearson, A., Helgason, A., Gilbert, M. T. P., & Schroeder, H. 2023. *The ancestry and geographical origins of St Helena's liberated Africans. American Journal of Human Genetics*, 110(9). pp. 1590-1599. <https://doi.org/10.1016/j.ajhg.2023.08.001>

31   Fairman, E.M 1890-1934 *'Not long'* in 'Poems'. A collection of poems written by the author's maternal great grandmother.

32   Woods, Robert. 2023. *A Prayer Confirming that All Things Will be Well*, by Julian of Norwich. Accessed 20 July, 2024. <https://www.theccsn.com/a-prayer-confirming-that-all-things-will-be-well-by-julian-of-norwich/>

Chapter 2

33   Miller, Laura. 2023. *The powerful secrets of posies and how to make a medieval nosegay*. Accessed 11 February, 2024. <https://www.gardeningknowhow.com/garden-how-to/info/medievalnosegay.htm>

34   Read, Sara L. 2008. 'Thy righteousness is but a menstrual clout: sanitary practices and prejudice in early modern England.' *Early Modern Women: An Interdisciplinary Journal*, 3(1), pp. 1-25. <https://doi.org/10.1086/EMW23541514>

35   Hadden, R. H. 1880. *An East-end Chronicle: St George'-in-the-East Parish and Parish Church compiled from various sources.* Accessed 25 January, 2024. <http://www.stgitehistory.org.uk/media /eastendchronicle 1880. html>

36   Staveley-Wadham, Rose. 2021. *Horror and Hysteria – The 1811 Ratcliff Highway Murders.* The British Newspaper Archive. Accessed 22 June, 2024. <https://blog.britishnewspaperarchive.co.uk/2021/04/22/the-1811-ratcliff-highway-murders/>

37   Clarke, Richard. 2024. *Hanged at Execution Dock 1735–1830.* Accessed 28 July, 2024. <http://www.capitalpunishmentuk. org/edock.html>

38   Simon, Rebecca. 2014. *Pirate Executions in Early Modern London.* English Legal History. Accessed 22 June, 2024. <https://englishlegalhistory.wordpress.com/tag/marshals-dance/>

39   Wikipedia. 2024. *Execution Dock.* Accessed 23 June, 2024. <https://en.wikipedia.org/wiki/Execution_Dock>

40   Gingell, James. 2022. *A riverside walk to a famous old London pub: the Prospect of Whitby.* The Guardian. Accessed 22 June, 2024. <https://www.theguardian.com/travel/2022/may/27/a-great-riverside-walk-to-a-great-london-pub-the-prospect-of-whitby>

41   St George-in-the-East Church. 2024. *Cable Street.* Accessed 18 March, 2024. <http://www.stgitehistory.org. uk/media/cablestreet.html>

42   Grant, James. 1842. *Lights and Shadows of London Life.* Chapter 3: Rag Fair, The Dictionary of Victorian London. Accessed 18 March, 2024. <https://www.victorianlondon.org/publications8/lightshadows-00.htm>

43   White, J. G. 1901. *The churches and chapels of Old London. A short account of those who have ministered in them.* Forgotten Books, 2016. Accessed 18 March, 2024. <www.forgottenbooks.com>

44   Fox, Colin. 2011. *Table of slaves and their owners on St Helena 1827–1834.* Accessed 18 March, 2024. <https://sainthelenaisland.info/slavesalphabeticallybyname182734.pdf>

45   St Helena National Trust. 2024. *History of St Helena's Liberated African Burial Grounds.* Accessed 23 June, 2024. <https://www.trust.org.sh/shnt-conservation-programmes/cultural-heritage/st-helena-trans-atlantic-slave-memorial/>

46   Carroll, John M. 2020. *Canton days – British life and death in China.* Published by Roman and Littlefield. Accessed 10 February, 2024. <https://www.google.com.au/books/edition/Canton_Days/DDHNDwAAQBAJ?hl=en&gbpv=1&dq=typhus+in+Whampoa+1815&pg=PA101&printsec=frontcover>

47   Cotton, Evan. 1949. *East Indiamen: the East India Company's maritime service.* Wellcome Library. Accessed 18 March, 2024. <https://archive.org/details/b29828776/page/4/mode/2up>

48   McIntosh, Matthew A. 2020. *The New London Docks 1800–1830.* Accessed 29 December, 2023. <https://brewminate.com/the-new-london-docks-1800-1830/>

49   British History Online. 1994. *The East India Docks: Historical development.* Survey of London: Volumes 43 and 44, Poplar, Blackwall and Isle of Dogs, ed. Hermione Hobhouse (London, 1994). pp. 575–582. British History Online. Accessed 29 December, 2023. <http://www.british-history.ac.uk/survey-london/vols43-4/pp575-582>

50   Moriarty, Tom. 2024. *The History of Father Christmas: Festive folklore, winter traditions and very merry myths, the making of a festive icon.* <https://www.english-heritage.org.uk/christmas/the-history-of-father-christmas/>

51   Bowen, John. 1955. *The East India Company's Education of Its Own Servants. Journal of the Royal Asiatic Society of Great Britain and Ireland*, 87, pp. 105–23. JSTOR, Accessed 11 February, 2024. <http://www.jstor.org/stable/25222749>

52   Wikipedia contributors. 2024. *Sir William Pulteney 1802 Ship.* Wikipedia, The Free Encyclopedia. Accessed 22 June, 2024. <https://en.wikipedia.org/wiki/Sir WilliamPulteney_(1802_ship)>

53   Roberts, G. 2016. *Principle Departures for London Coaches (1819).* Accessed 23 July, 2021. <http://www.wickedwilliam. com/principal-departure-coaching-inns-1819/>

54   Sencicle, Lorraine. 2015. *Packet Service 1 to 1854.* The Dover Historian. Accessed 24 June, 2024. <https://doverhistorian.com/2015/03/21/packet-service-to-1854/>

55   Wikipedia contributors. 2024. *The Bali Strait Incident.* Wikipedia, The Free Encyclopedia. Accessed 22 June, 2024. <https://en.wikipedia.org/wiki/Bali_Strait_Incident>

Chapter 3

56   The Freemen of Deal. 2005. *The Downs.* Accessed 23 June, 2024. <http://home.freeuk.net/eastkent/deal/downs/downs.htm>

57   Whitten, Timothy. 2021. *Sea chest history and construction plans.* Marlin Spike Chandlery. Accessed 23 June, 2024. <http://www.marlinespike.com/index.html>

58   Chidell, Avril. 2021. Sea chest and the Bolt in Tun. Watercolours.

59   BBC Home. 2014. *Transport heritage: Portsmouth to London Road.* Accessed 30 December, 2023. <http://www.bbc.co.uk/hampshire/content/articles/2008/12/09/london_road_feature.shtml>

60   Harper, Charles G. 1895. *The Portsmouth Road and its Tributaries.* Accessed 23 June, 2024. <https://www.gutenberg.org/files/39234/39234-h/39234-h.htm>

61   Rowlandson, Thomas. 1780–1825. *Chelsea Stage Coach – caricature.* Courtesy Boston Public Library. Accessed 23 June, 2024. <https://jenikirbyhistory.getarchive.net/media/chelsea-stage-coach-89f0a9>

62   Smith of Derby. 2024. *Guilford, Guildhall, historic clock.* Accessed 23 June, 2024. <https://www.smithofderby.com/sod-assets/uploads/2019/02/Guildford-Guildhall-Clock.pdf>

63   The British Museum. 2024. *Morris Tobias and Co.* Accessed 23 June, 2024. <https://www.britishmuseum.org/collection/term/BIOG80160>

64   Makepeace, Margaret. 2021. *Sobriety and decorum – passengers on East India Company ships.* British Library Untold Lives blog. Accessed 18 March, 2024. <https://blogs.bl.uk/untoldlives/2021/06/sobriety-and-decorum-passengers-on-east-india-company-ships.html>

65   iMuseum. 2024. *Colonel Mark Wilks.* Manx National Heritage. Accessed 6 July, 2024. <https://imuseum.im/search/collections/people/mnh-agent-29366.html>

Chapter 4

66   Williams, M. R. F. 2022. 'Experiencing Time in the Early English East India Company.' *The Historical Journal.* 65(5), pp. 1175-1196. Accessed 24 June, 2024. <https://doi.org/10.1017/S0018246X2100087X>

67   Clarke, John. 2023. *Shipping wonders of the world: Life in the East Indiaman.* Accessed 24 June, 2024. <https://www.shippingwondersoftheworld.com/east_indiamen.html>

68   Chatterton, E. Keble. 2017. *The Old East Indiamen.* The Project Gutenberg eBook of The Old East Indiamen. Accessed 24 June, 2024. <https://www.gutenberg.org/cache/epub/54561/pg54561-images.html>

69   Thomas, B. C. 1990. *Portsmouth in Jane Austen's Time.* Jane Austen Society of North America. Accessed 24 June, 2024. <https://jasna.org/persuasions/printed/number12/thomas.htm?>

70   English Heritage. 2024. *History of Porchester Castle.* Accessed 24 June, 2024. <https://www.english-heritage.org.uk/visit/places/portchester-castle/history-and-stories/history/>

71   Thomas, James H. 2013. 'Country, Commerce and Contacts: Hampshire and the East India Company in the 18th century.' *Proceedings of the Hampshire Field Club and Archaeological Society.* 68, pp. 169-177. Accessed 31 July, 2024. <https://www.hantsfieldclub.org.uk/publications/hampshirestudies/digital/2010s/Vol_68/Thomas.pdf>

72   Butterfly Conservation. 2024. *Butterflies.* Accessed 24 June, 2024. <https://butterfly-conservation.org/butterflies>

73   Heard, Stawell. 2022. *A closer look at the Thames lightermen and watermen.* Royal Museums Greenwich. Accessed 24 June, 2024. <https://www.rmg.co.uk/stories/blog/library-archive/closer-look-thames-lightermen-watermen>

74   The Art of the Age of Sail. 2024. *Ship Types and Rates in the Age of Sail.* Accessed 24 June, 2024. <http://www.ageofsail.net/aoshipty.asp>

Chapter 5

75   Manx National Heritage. 2024. *Captain Crow and Colonel Wilks.* Accessed 12 February, 2024. <https://artsandculture.google.com/story/captain-crow-and-colonel-wilks/GwXhvHpEOjzu6w>

76   Kumar, A, Pandey, A. K, & Rao, R. K. 2017. 'Yoga and Pranayama during pregnancy.' *Indian Journal of Agriculture and Allied Sciences,* 3(2), pp. 47-52. Accessed 24 June, 2024. <https://www.researchgate.net/publication/>

77   Nori, W., Kassim, M. A. K., Helmi, Z. R., Pantazi, A. C., Brezeanu, D., Brezeanu, A. M., Penciu, R. C., & Serbanescu, L. 2023. 'Non-Pharmacological Pain Management in Labor: A Systematic Review.' *Journal of Clinical Medicine*, 12(23), pp. 7203. Accessed 24 June, 2024. <https://doi.org/10.3390/jcm12237203>

78   BBC News. 2013. *Manx: bringing a language back from the dead.* Accessed 12 February, 2024. <https://www.bbc.com/news/magazine-21242667>

79   Merriman, Samuel. 1814. *A synopsis of the various kinds of difficult parturition, with practical remarks on the management of labours.* 2nd edition. Accessed 24 June, 2024. <https://wellcomecollection.org/works/h957v24c/items>

80   PLSG. 2015. *Ian McBrayne talking about Three Colt Street, Limehouse.* The Port of London Study Group. Accessed 24 June, 2024. <https://portoflondonstudy.wordpress.com/introduction/>

81   British History Online. 2019. *Industries: Silk-weaving.* A History of the County of Middlesex: Volume 2, ed. William Page (London, 1911), pp 132–137. British History Online. Accessed 29 December, 2023. <http://www.british-history.ac.uk/vch/middx/vol2/pp132-137>

82   Sargent, Edward. 2015. *A history of ropemaking.* Docklands History Group. Accessed 24 June, 2024. <https://www.docklandshistorygroup.org.uk/ES%20%20Rope-making%20Talk.pdf>

83   McLeod, Lesley-Anne. 2011. *Education the key to riches: the East India Company College.* Accessed 12 February, 2024. <https://lesleyannemcleod.blogspot.com/2011/07/education-key-to-riches-east-india.html>

84   Burridge, Tom. 2013. *Scraping by on barnacles in Spain.* BBC News 23rd November. Accessed 24 June, 2024. <https://www.bbc.com/news/world-europe-24896788>

85   Barker, Joanna. 2024. *Letters from Elizabeth Montagu to Charles Robinson and Sarah Robinson Hougham.* Accessed 7 August, 2024. <https://emco.swansea.ac.uk/emco/correspondents/charles-sarah-robinson>

86   Govindappa, M. 2016. 'Mysore Residency and its Forms of Administration.' *International Journal of Innovative Research and Advanced Studies.* 3(10). Accessed 25 January, 2024. <https://www.ijiras.com/2016/Vol_3-Issue_10/paper_52.pdf>

Chapter 6

87   Tumlin Wallace, A. 2024. *The Liturgical Home: Laetare Sunday.* Anglican Compass. Accessed 24 June, 2024. <https://anglicancompass.com/the-liturgical-home-laetare-sunday/>

88   Wikipedia contributors. 2024. *Sextant.* Wikipedia, The Free Encyclopedia. Accessed 24 June, 2024. <https://en.wikipedia.org /w/index.php?title=Sextant&oldid=1228388526>

89   Marks, Tasha. 2018. *The 18th-century chocolate champions.* British Museum. Accessed 7 August, 2024. <https://www.britishmuseum.org/blog/18th-century-chocolate-champions>

90   Tyson, Peter. 1998. *Secrets of Ancient Navigators.* PBS online. Accessed 25 June, 2024. <https://www.pbs. org/wgbh/nova/article/secrets-of-ancient-navigators/>

Chapter 7

Chapter 8

91   Hall, Danielle. 2020. *Currents, waves and tides.* Smithsonian National Museum of Natural History. Accessed 6 July, 2024. <https://ocean.si.edu/planet-ocean/tides-currents/currents-waves-and-tides>

Chapter 9

92   History Trust of South Australia. 2021. *Whaling.* Accessed 27 August, 2021. <https://boundforsouthaustralia.history.sa.gov.au/journey-content/whaling.html>

Chapter 10

93   Zipes, Jack. 2015. 'How the Grimm Brothers Saved the Fairy Tale.' *National Endowment for the Humanities.* 36(2). Accessed 24 August, 2024. <https://www.neh.gov/humanities/2015/marchapril/feature/how-the-grimm-brothers-saved-the-fairy-tale>

94   Wikipedia contributors. *Arniston (East Indiaman).* Wikipedia, The Free Encyclopedia. Accessed 6 July, 2024. <https://en.wikipedia.org/w/index.php?title=Arniston_(East_Indiaman)&oldid=1223296709>

95   Beatson, Alexander. 1816. *Tracts relative to the Island of St Helena written during a residence of five years.* Biodiversity Heritage Library. Accessed 24 June, 2024. <https://www.biodiversitylibrary.org/bibliography/28652>

96   St Helena Island. 2024. *Education.* Accessed 7 August, 2024. <https://sainthelenaisland.info/education.htm>

Chapter 11

97   University College London. 2024. *A Brahmin and a Mohammedan in Earnest Converse for their Country's Good.* Monument to Major-General Sir Barry Close, Bart, 1815. Accessed 24 August, 2024. <https://www.ucl.ac.uk/culture/ucl-art-museum/monument-major-general-sir-barry-close>

98   Beatson, Alexander. 1812. *Report to the Honourable the Court of Directors for the Affairs of the United East India Company.* Biodiversity Heritage Library. Accessed 24 June, 2024. <https://www.biodiversitylibrary.org/bibliography/28652>

99   St Helena Island Information. 2024. *Brief overview.* Accessed 24 June, 2024. <https://sthelenaisland.info/brief-overview/>

100   St Helena Island. 2024. *Slavery on St Helena.* Accessed 25 June, 2024. <https://sainthelenaisland.info/slavery.htm>

101   Tyrell, John. 2017. *St. Helena 1813: Two Governors, One Execution and the Mistreatment of Slaves.* Accessed 25 June, 2024. <https://johntyrrell.blogspot.com/2017/03/st-helena-1813-two-governors-one.html>

102   Duncan, Francis. 1805. *A description of the Island of St Helena containing observations on its singular structure and formation and an account of its climate, natural history and inhabitants.* Accessed 23 July, 2024. <https://sainthelenaisland.info/duncanhistory1805.pdf>

103   Brooke, T. H. 1824. *History of the Island of St Helena from its discovery by the Portuguese to the year 1823.* Second edition. Published by Kingsbury, Parbury & Allen, London. Google Books. Accessed 24 June, 2024. <https://www.google.com.au/books/edition/History_of_the_Island_of_St_Helena_from/_EtpAAAAcAAJ?hl=en>

104   Chaplin, Arnold. 1919. *A St Helena Who's Who or A directory of the island during the captivity of Napoleon.* Accessed 24 June, 2024. <https://wellcomecollection.org/works/syay9ae9/items?canvas=33&query=Beale>

Chapter 12

105   Phoenix Forge. 2021. *How to forge an unwelded eye.* Blacksmiths Essential Skills. Accessed 24 July, 2024. <https://www.youtube.com/watch?v=yAKx6XaxDYE>

106   Dilhac, J. M. 2024. *The telegraph of Claude Chappe – an optical telecommunication network for the XVIIIth century.* College of the Holy Cross. Accessed 24 July, 2024. <https://mathcs.holycross.edu/~csci356/Dilhac.pdf>

107   St Helena. 2024. *Islands all around us.* Accessed 8 August, 2024. <https://sainthelenaisland.info/islands.htm>

108   Lambdon, Phil. 2024. *St Helena.* Royal Botanic Gardens, Kew. Accessed 8 August, 2024. <https://brahmsonline.kew.org/helena#:~:text=The%20community%20contains%20a%20moderately,dominated%20by%20the%20endemic%20St>

Chapter 13

109   St Helena. 2024. *Seabirds, Fairy Terns and many others.* Accessed 8 August, 2024. <https://sainthelenaisland.info/seabirds.htm>

Chapter 14

110   Barton, Matt. 2022. *Re-collections: William John Burchell.* Museum of Natural History, University of Oxford. Accessed 25 June, 2024. <https://morethanadodo.com/2022/07/26/re-collections-william-john-burchell/>

111   Harding, Graham. 2022. *The Food and Drink of the Nineteenth-Century British Picnic.* Food and Movement, Dublin Gastronomy Symposium. Accessed 26 July, 2024. <https://arrow.tudublin.ie/cgi/viewcontent.cgi?article=1253&context=dgs>

112   Dickson, Vivienne. 1973. *St. Helena Place-Names, Names.* 21:4, 205-219,DOI: 10.1179/nam.1973.21.4.205. Accessed 25 June, 2024. <https://sainthelenaisland.info/placenames1973_viviennedickson.pdf>

113   Lofy, Emily. 2024. *Prayer for a good husband.* Prayer and Spirituality Catholic Match. Accessed 25 June, 2024. <https://plus.catholicmatch.com/articles/prayer-for-future-husband>

Chapter 15

114   Kitching, GC. 1947. *A handbook and gazetteer of the Island of St Helena including a short history of the Island under the Crown 1834-1902.* Accessed 21 August, 2023. <https://www.friendsofsthelena.com/upload/files/A_Handbook_and_Gazetteer_of_the_Island_of_St_Helena.pdf>

Chapter 16

115   St Helena Island. 2024. *St James' Church: the oldest Anglican Church in the Southern Hemisphere.* Accessed 25 June, 2024. <https://sainthelenaisland.info/stjames.htm>

116   DeGreve, Daniel P. 2010. 'Retro Tablum: The Origins and Role of the Altarpiece in the Liturgy.' *The Institute for Sacred Architecture,* 17. Accessed 24 August, 2024. <https://www.sacredarchitecture.org/issues/volume_17>

117   Billingsley-Evans, Janet. 2024. *The Buchan School established 1875.* Accessed 25 June, 2024. <https://kwc.im/wp-content/uploads/2021/04/Buchan-Prospectus-web-version.pdf>

Chapter 17

Chapter 18

118   St Helena Island. 2024. *Important people: 3 Saul Solomon: 1776–1852.* Accessed 25 June, 2024. <https://sainthelenaisland.info/importantpeople.htm>

119   St Helena Island. 2024. *Shopping on St Helena: An unusual experience.* Accessed 8 August, 2024. <https://sainthelenaisland.info/shopping.htm>

Chapter 19

120   Gosse, P. 1938. *St Helena, 1502-1938.* Accessed 21 August, 2023. <http://sainthelenaisland.info/gossesthelena15021938.pdf>

121   Tyrell, John. 2008. *St. Helena Residents During the Captivity.* Reflections on a journey to St Helena. Blog. Accessed 28 July, 2024. <https://johntyrrell.blogspot.com/2008/12/st-helena-residents-during-captivity.html>

122   Abdul Amin, S. K. 2019. *Dr William Roxburgh, Pioneer of Indian Botany.* Peepul Tree Stories. Accessed 25 August, 2024. <https://www.peepultree.world/livehistoryindia/story/people/dr-william-roxburgh-pioneer-of-indian-botany?srsltid=AfmBOopnYzsZ-nmZdID3j1ed-KXWak7hHidEjMli__gN836K2tnlFQOf>

123   Cronk, Q. C. B. 1987. 'The history of endemic flora of St Helena: a relictual series.' *New Phytologist,* 105, pp. 509-520. Accessed 25 June, 2024. <https://doi.org/10.1111/j.1469-8137.1987.tb00888.x>

124   Grimshaw, Pauline & John. 2010. *St. Helena, Halley's Mount, Observatory Site.* Accessed 8 August, 2024. <https://www.flickr.com/photos/30593522@N05/5248277103>

Chapter 20

125   Janisch, H. R. 1885. *From the St Helena Records.* p 237. Accessed 31 July, 2024. <https://archive.org/stream/extracts-fromsth00janigoog/extractsfromsth00janigoog_djvu.txt>

126   Franks, I. 2024. *Sterling silver bells: Regency sterling silver bell.* Accessed 25 June, 2024. <https://www.ifranks.com/silver-ware/17033-silver-bells>

127   Chase, L., & Holloway Scott, S. 2011. *Milk below! (or maybe not …).* Two nerdy history girls. Accessed 25 June, 2024. <https://twonerdyhistorygirls.blogspot.com/2011/03/milk-below-or-maybe-not.html>

Chapter 21

128   Wikipedia contributors. *Atlantic raid of June 1796.* Wikipedia, The Free Encyclopedia. Accessed 25 June, 2024. <https://en.wikipedia.org/w/index.php?title=Atlantic_raid_of_June_1796&oldid=1056461032>

129   McGarry, Stephen. 2016. 'Close enough to toss a ship's biscuit ashore'—the French fleet at Bantry Bay, 1796.' *History Ireland.* 6(24). Accessed 25 June, 2024. <https://www.historyireland.com/close-enough-toss-ships-biscuit-ashore-french-fleet-bantry-bay-1796/>

130   Drummond, Charles. 1782-1786. *Glatton: Journal, Charles Drummond, Captain.* Qatar Digital Library. Accessed 25 June, 2024. <https://www.qdl.qa/en/archive/81055/vdc_100000001441.0x0000fe?utm_source=testpdfdownload&utm_%20medium%20=pdf&utm_campaign>

131   Hardy, Horatio Charles. 1820. *A Register of Ships Employed in the service of the Honorable the United East India Company 1760-1819 with an Appendix.* By the late Charles Hardy, revised with considerable additions by his son. Third edition, pp 160–163. Accessed 8 August, 2024. <https://www.google.com.au/books/edition/A_Register_of_Ships_Employed_in_the_Serv/f9hoAAAAcAAJ?hl=en&gbpv=1>

132   Pinkerton, John. 1812. *The World On Mercator's Projection.* David Rumsey Map Collection. Accessed 25 June, 2024. <https://www.davidrumsey.com/maps4695.html>

133   RootsChat.com. 2022. *East India Ships: Crossing the 'Second Bar'.* Accessed 25 June, 2024. <https://www.rootschat.com/forum/index.php?topic=867868.0>

134   Jackson, Norman. 2024. *Life and Death on the High Seas.* Accessed 25 June, 2024. <http://www.jacksontree.co.uk/Blunderfield_Thomas_B0714.htm>

135   Perdue, Peter C. 2009. *Visualising Whampoa Anchorage. Rise and Fall of the Canton Trade System – 11.* Massachusetts Institute of Technology. Accessed 25 June, 2024. <https://visualizingcultures.mit.edu/rise_fall_canton_02/cw_essay05.html>

136   Chester Beatty Library. 2024. *Traditional Chinese Clothing and Accessories.* Accessed 25 June, 2024. <https://artsandculture.google.com/story/traditional-chinese-clothing-accessories-chester-beatty-library/fQUByRYSK_TPLg?hl=en>

137   George, B. B, & Caesar, L. 2012. *St Helena and the abolition of the trans-Atlantic Slave Trade.* Copyright Museum of St Helena. Accessed 26 August, 2024 <https://www.museumofsainthelena.org/wp-content/uploads/2017/11/Fact-sheet-Slavery.pdf>

138   The Metropolitan Museum of Art. 2024. *Bed cover (Palampore) 18th century.* Accessed 25 June, 2024. <https://www.metmuseum.org/art/collection/search/453160>

139   Kapo, Remi. 2018. *Samuel Ally.* Accessed 25 June, 2024. <https://remikapo.org/samuel-ally/>

140   North American Anglican. 2020. *Feast of faith: High Church Eucharistic teaching and piety in the Church of England, 1800-1833.* Accessed 26 August, 2024. < https://northamanglican.com/feast-of-faith-high-church-eucharistic-teaching-and-piety-in-the-church-of-england-1800-1833/>

141   St Helena. 2024. *Unrest and Rebellion.* Accessed 8 August, 2024. <https://sainthelenaisland.info/unrest.htm#spirits-rebellion1811>

142   Adams, Christine. 2016. *List of Families and Cattle upon the Island St. Helena taken 30th Sept. 1814.* Accessed 17 August, 2024. <https://web.archive.org/web/20160426140837/http://www.archeion.talktalk. net:80/sthelena/1814census.htm>

Chapter 22

Chapter 23

143   King James Bible online. 2024. *Song of Solomon 5:15*. Accessed 25 June, 2024. <https://www.kingjamesbibleonline.org/Song-of-Solomon-5-15/>

144   King James Bible online. 2024. *Song of Solomon 2: 3–4*. Accessed 25 June, 2024. <https://www.kingjamesbibleonline.org/Song-of-Solomon-Chapter-2/#3>

Chapter 24

145   Naval Historical Society of Australia. 2024. *The Preservation of Horatio, Lord Nelson's Body*. Accessed 25 June, 2024. <https://navyhistory.au/the-preservation-of-horatio-lord-nelsons-body/>

146   Find a grave. 2024. *James Halliburton*. Accessed 26 June, 2024. <https://www.findagrave.com/memorial/215610563/james-halliburton> <https://graves-at-eggsa.org/main.php?g2_itemid=43>

Chapter 25

147   Reed, Susan. 2025. *Waterloo's Prussian Hero: Blücher and the British*. Accessed 24 July, 2024. <https://blogs.bl.uk/european/2015/06/waterloos-prussian-hero.html>

148   Hackett, I. 2006. *Balcombe Family and "The Briars" Park, Mt Martha, Victoria* East Melbourne Historical Society Accessed 26 October 2024 <https://emhs.org.au/system/files/catalogue/pdf_files/emdf0090_01.pdf>

Chapter 26

149   Abell, Lucia Elizabeth Balcombe. 1844. *Recollections of the Emperor Napoleon, during the first three years of his captivity on the island of St. Helena: including the time of his residence at her father's house, 'The Briars'*. p 141. Accessed 26 June, 2024. <https://archive.org/details/recollectionsofe00abeliala/page/n9/mode/2up?q=wilks>

150   Abbott, John S. C. 1855. *Napoleon at St. Helena; or, interesting anecdotes and remarkable conversations with the emperor during the five and a half years of his captivity*. Collected from the memorials of Las Casas, O'Meara, Moutholon, Antommarchi, and others. pp. 12–13; 67–77; 150–151. Accessed 21 August, 2023. <https://archive.org/details/napoleonatsthele00abbo/page/66/mode/2up>

151   Hicks, Peter. 2022. 'Catherine and Emily Younghusband's unpublished account of the Chinese indentured labourers on St Helena in 1816.' *Napoleonica®*, 1(1), p 147–160. Accessed 6 July, 2024. <https://www.cairn-int.info/journal-napoleonica-the-journal-2022-1-page-147.htm>

152   Moore, A. 1901. *Laura, Lady Buchan, nee Wilks (b. 1797, d. 1888)*. (1. F. Coakley, Ed.) Chapter 9 Manx Worthies. Accessed 31 July, 2021. <http://www.isle-of-man.com/manxnotebook/fulltext/worthies/p202a.htm>

153   Abell, Lucia Elizabeth Balcombe. 1844. *Recollections of the Emperor Napoleon, during the first three years of his captivity on the island of St. Helena: including the time of his residence at her father's house, 'The Briars'*. p 164. Accessed 26 June, 2024. <https://archive.org/details/recollectionsofe00abeliala/page/n9/mode/2up?q=wilks>

154   Heijtz, Stefan. 2024. *St Helena Postal History 1677–1903*. PDF document Nova Stamps. Accessed 10 August, 2024. <https://www.novastamps.com/StHelena.pdf>

Chapter 27

155   Kitching, G. C. 1938. *The English in St. Helena, Notes and Queries*. 175(14), pp. 236–243. Accessed 29 July, 2024. <https://doi.org/10.1093/nq/175.14.236>

156   Bourne, John Michael. 1977. *The Civil and Military Patronage of the East India Company, 1784–1858*. University of Leicester. Thesis. Accessed 29 July, 2024. <https://hdl.handle.net/2381/8425>

157   Chaplin, Arnold. 1914. *A St Helena Who's Who or a directory of the Island during the captivity of Napoleon.* Published by the author at 3 York Gate London, 1914. Accessed 24 July, 2024. <https://wellcomecollection.org/works/qucezja7>

158   iMuseum. 2024. *Colour prints of portraits of family of Col Mark Wilks.* Memorial tablet to Harriet Wilks and John Barry Wilks in Grosvenor Chapel. Manx National Heritage. Accessed 6 July, 2024. <https://imuseum.im/search/archive_record/view?id=mnh-museum-376868>

Chapter 28

Chapter 29

159   Lowell, Amy. 1821. *The Hammers V - St. Helena, May, 1821.* Excerpt. Accessed 30 August, 2024. <https://www.poemhunter.com/poem/the-hammers>

160   UK-St Helena Heritage Trust. 2024. *Valley of the Tomb.* Accessed 26 June, 2024. <https://www.uk-sthelenaheritagetrust.org/valley-of-the-tomb>

161   Mosborough History Meeting Group. 2024. *Napoleon Bonaparte – died at St Helena 5th May 1821.* Saunders's News-Letter – Thursday 12 July 1821. British Newspaper Archives. Accessed 6 July, 2024. <http://www.mosboroughhistory.co.uk/2020/04/18/napoleon-bonaparte-died-at-st-helena-5th-may-1821/>

162   Fenwick, Bishop R. 2014. *The Cathedral Church of St Paul, Island of St Helena.* Brochure. Accessed 24 July, 2024. <https://sainthelenaisland.info/stpaulsleaflet.pdf>

Chapter 30

163   Pipe, Simon. 2013. *Flowers for a St Helena slave.* Accessed 25 January, 2024. <https://sthelenaonline.wordpress.com/2013/01/18/flowers-for-a-st-helena-slave/>

164   Mason, A. W, Owen, Geo., & Brown, G. H. of the Secretary's Office, East-India House, London. 1825. *The East-India Register and Directory for 1825.* 2nd edition, p 352. [India]. Accessed 26 June, 2024. <https://archive.org/details/eastindiaregister-1825-2e/page/351/mode/2up?q=Beale>

165   Threedecks.org. 2024. *British Merchant east Indiaman 'General Harris' (1812).* Accessed 26 June, 2024. <https://threedecks.org/index.php?display_type=show_ship&id=29765>

Chapter 31

166   Jackson, E. L. 1905. *St Helena the historic island from its discovery to the present date.* p 249. Accessed 26 June, 2024. <https://archive.org/details/sthelenahistoric00jackrich>

167   St Helena Island. 2024. *Rollers.* Accessed 10 August, 2024. <https://sainthelenaisland.info/rollers.htm>

168   Jaffer, Aaron. 2024. *Who were the 'lascars' and why are they important?.* Accessed 4 January, 2024. <https://www.thewellingtontrust.org/wp-content/uploads/2021/06/Salt-fish-and-Shaitan-Lascars-lives-at-sea-1750-1850.pdf>

169   Willoz-Egnor, Jeanne. 2020. *It's a Disaster! The Rollers of 1846.* The Mariners' Museum and Park. Accessed 26 June, 2024. <https://www.marinersmuseum.org/2020/11/its-a-disaster-the-rollers-of-1846/>

170   Kipling, Rudyard. 1910. *A Saint Helena Lullaby.* Verse 8. Accessed 16 August, 2024. <https://public-domain-poetry.com/rudyard-kipling/st-helena-lullaby-3509>

Chapter 32

171   May, LM. 1908. *Charlton near Woolwich monumental inscriptions.* Aspects of Kentish Local History. Accessed 28 June, 2024. <https://tedconnell.org.uk/LFH/GRS/CHW/01.htm>

172   Engelhardt, E. 2017. 'Apoplexy, cerebrovascular disease, and stroke: Historical evolution of terms and definitions.' *Dementia & Neuropsychologia*, 11(4), pp. 449-453. <https://doi.org/10.1590/1980-57642016dn11-040016>

173   Duncan, Edward, & Huggins, William John. 1832. *The Honourable East India Company Ship Inglis (1812) leaving St Helena in 1830 in Company with H.M. Frigate Ariadne (1816) and the H.C.Ships Windsor (1818), Waterloo (1816), Scaleby Castle (1807), General Kidd, Farquharson (1820) & Lowther Castle.* Text from: "National Maritime Museum, Greenwich, London". Picture in public domain. Accessed 27 June, 2024. <https://picryl.com/media/the-honourable-east-india-companys-ship-inglis-leaving-st-helena-in-july-1830-e3442a>

Chapter 33

174   Asiatic Intelligence. 1834. 'St Helena Taxes.' *The Asiatic Journal and Monthly Register for British & Foreign India, China & Australasia*, XIV. Accessed 28 July, 2024. <https://www.google. com.au/books/edition/Asiatic_Journal_and_ Monthly_Register_for/CBAoAAAAYAAJ?hl=en&gbpv=1>

175   Gosse, P. 1938. *St Helena, 1502–1938*. Chapters 8–10. Accessed 21 August, 2023. <http://sainthelenaisland.info/gossesthelena15021938.pdf>

176   Green, Deborah. 2024. *Descendant report.* Includes details over three generations of the family.

177   Wallis, Patrick, Webb, Cliff, & Minns, Chris. 2009. *Leaving Home and Entering Service: The Age of Apprenticeship in Early Modern London*. Working Papers No. 125/09. Accessed 10 July, 2024. <https://www.lse.ac.uk/Economic-History/Assets/Documents/WorkingPapers/Economic-History/2009/WP125.pdf>

178   The Raitt Stuff. 2024. *Captain Charles Raitt's Court of Enquiry.* Accessed 10 July, 2024. <https://www.raitt.org/captain-charles-raitt-coe.html>

179   Caroline Bowles Southey. 1824. 'On the death of an infant.' *The Sydney Gazette and New South Wales Advertiser* (NSW: 1803–1842), p. 4. <https://trove.nla.gov.au/newspaper/article/2182533?browse=ndp%3Abrowse%2Ftitle%2FS%2Ftitle%2F3%2F1824%2F01%2F08%2Fpage%2F494772%2Farticle%2F2182533#>

180   Chatterton, E. K. 2017. *The Old East Indiamen.* Project Gutenberg, p 341. Accessed 28 June, 2024. <https://www.gutenberg.org/files/54561/54561-h/54561-h.htm>

181   iMuseum. 2024. *Colonel Mark Wilks.* Accessed 10 July, 2024. <https://imuseum.im/search/collections/people/mnh-agent-29366.html>

182   Find a grave. 2024. *Colonel Mark Wilks.* Accessed 28 June, 2024. <https://www.findagrave.com/memorial/148073125/mark_wilks>

183   Asiatic Intelligence. 1834. 'St Helena True Mean Time.' *The Asiatic Journal and Monthly Register for British & Foreign India, China & Australasia*, XIV. Accessed 28 July, 2024. <https://www.google.com.au/books/edition/Asiatic_Journal_and_Monthly_Register_for/CBAoAAAAYAAJ?hl=en&gbpv=1>

184   Cape Paper. 1836. 'St Helena: East India Company's establishment is dissolved.' Private letter. *The Asiatic Journal and Monthly Register for British & Foreign India, China & Australasia*, XX, p. 234. Accessed 28 July, 2024. <https://www.google.com.au/books/edition/Asiatic _Journal_and_Monthly_Register_for/-BEoAAAAYAAJ?hl=en&gbpv=1>

185   Carnac, J. R. (Chairman). 1836. 'Civil and Military Servants at St Helena.' Debate at East India House, 28 September. *The Asiatic Journal and Monthly Register for British & Foreign India, China & Australasia*, XXI. Accessed 28 July, 2024. <https://www.google.com.au/books/edition/Asiatic_Journal_and_Monthly_Register_for/gi4oAAAAYAAJ?hl =en&gbpv=1>

Chapter 34

186   Longfellow, Henry 1807-1808 "The Tide Rises and the Tide Falls" from *Ultima Thule* (1880) <https://www.poetryfoundation.org/poems/44651/the-tide-rises-the-tide-falls>

187   Chatham Historic Dockyard Trust. 2024. *Holy Stone.* Accessed 28 June, 2024. <https://collection.thedockyard.co.uk/objects/8897/holy-stone>

Chapter 35

188   Cooper, James. 2024. *UK Christmas History*. Accessed 24 July, 2024. <https://www.whychristmas.com/customs/uk-christmas-history>

189   Thomas, David, Tuckey, Ruth, & Yates, Youla. 1986. *London and Greenwich Rail Trail*. Greater London Industrial Archaeological Society. Accessed 28 June, 2024. <http://www.glias.org.uk/walks/15_train-trail.html #:~:text=The%20London%20and%20Greenwich%20Railway,journey%20takes%20only%20seven%20minutes>

190   Register – Bombay. 1837. 'Military Appointments, Promotions, Etc.' *The Asiatic Journal and Monthly Register for British & Foreign India, China & Australasia*, XXII. Accessed 28 July, 2024. <https://www.google.com.au/books/edition/Asiatic_Journal_and_Monthly_Register_for/dhIoAAAAYAAJ?hl=en&gbpv=1>

191   English Heritage. 2024. *A short history of Christmas Greenery*. Accessed 24 July, 2024. <https://www.english-heritage.org.uk/learn/histories/christmas-greenery-history/#:~:text=Christmas%20Trees,%2C%20Windsor%2C%20in%20December%201800>

192   Day, Ivan. 2013. *Some Christmas nightcaps*. Food History Jottings. Accessed 28 June, 2024. <https://foodhistorjottings.blogspot.com/2013/12/some-christmas-nightcaps.html>

193   Fox, Thomas. 2023. *Lewes avalanche disaster that left eight dead and families 'buried alive'*. Sussex Live. Accessed 28 June, 2024. <https://www.sussexlive.co.uk/news/history/lewes-avalanche-disaster-left-eight-7974736>

194   Dolan, Graham. 2024. *The old churchyard, St Margaret's Lee: the burial place of Halley, Bliss and Pond – the second, fourth and sixth Astronomers Royal*. The Royal Observatory, Greenwich. Accessed 18 March, 2024. <http://www.royalobservatorygreenwich.org/articles.php?article=1258>

195   Lewisham History. 2015. *Death by Falling from the Clouds in Lee*. Accessed 28 June, 2024. <https://runner500.wordpress.com/tag/robert-cocking/>

196   Catling, Chris. 2021. *Who will deliver me from this turbulent priest? How two Henrys failed to erase the memory of Thomas Becket*. The Past Current Archaeology. Accessed 24 July, 2024. <https://the-past.com/feature/who-will-deliver-me-from-this-turbulent-priest-how-two-henrys-failed-to-erase-the-memory-of-thomas-becket/>

197   All Saints Church Maidstone. 2024. *The Beale Memorial*. Accessed 28 June, 2024. <https://www.maidstoneallsaints.co.uk/beale.htm>

198   Ramblers. 2023. Green chain walk. *Ramblers with Transport for London*. Accessed 18 March, 2024. <https://innerlondonramblers.org.uk/ideasforwalks/green-chain-walk-guides.html>

199   National Trust. 2024. *What is coppicing?* Accessed 28 June, 2024. <https://www.nationaltrust.org.uk/discover/nature/trees-plants/what-is-coppicing>

200   Collins, Fergus, 2024. *How to identify common hedgerow species*. BBC Countryfile. Accessed 28 June, 2024. <https://www.countryfile.com/wildlife/trees-plants/hedgerow-plants-flowers-guide>

Chapter 36

Chapter 37

201   Longfellow, Henry Wadsworth. 1880. The Tides. Public Domain. Poetry. Accessed 30 August, 2024. <http://www.public-domain-poetry.com/henry-wadsworth-longfellow/tides-24299>

202   Beale, John Lindsay. Undated. *Extracts from diary*. Loose sheets in St Katherine's folder of information.

203   Klein, M. 2019. *Master Blockhead Goes to Sea: A Glimpse into the Experiences of Midshipman Frederick Marryat*. CORIOLIS, Volume 9, Number 2, 2019. National Maritime Digital Library.

204   Unknown artist. 1844. 'Married couples accommodation in steerage: emigrants at dinner.' *The Illustrated London News*, p 229. Accessed 31 July, 2024. <https://babel.hathitrust.org/cgi/pt?id=mdp.39015006972890&seq=237&q1=married+couples+accommodation+in+steerage>

205   Norway Heritage. 2007. 'Sanitary conditions on board – health and sickness on emigrant ships.' *The Transatlantic Crossing*. Accessed 28 June, 2024. <http://www.norwayheritage.com/health.htm>

206   State Library NSW. 2023. *Shipboard: the 19th century emigrant experience*. Accessed 23 December, 2023. <https://www.sl.nsw.gov.au/stories/shipboard-19th-century-emigrant-experience>

207   Copeland, Ann. 2012. *Salt beef, tinned carrots and haggis – the 19th century ships diet*. State Library Victoria Family Matters collection. Accessed 24 April, 2024. <https://blogs.slv.vic.gov.au/family-matters/collections/salt-beef-tinned-carrots-and-haggis-the-19th-century-ships-diet/>

208   British History online. 2024. *Settlement and building: From 1680 to 1865, Hans Town. A History of the County of Middlesex: Volume 12, Chelsea*, (London, 2004), pp. 47–51. British History Online, University of London. Accessed 28 June, 2024. <https://www.british-history.ac.uk/vch/middx/vol12/pp47-51.>

209   The Church Bells of Kent. 2023. *Lee, St Margaret*. Accessed 28 June, 2024. <http://kent.lovesguide.com/tower.php?id=296>

210   State Library Victoria. 2024. *Beale, K. R., Beale, A., & Stadler, Y. (1828). Diaries, poems, 1828-[not after 1994]. [manuscript]*. (Can be ordered and read in the SLV Heritage Room).

211   Wikipedia contributors. *Barque*. Wikipedia, The Free Encyclopedia. Public domain. Accessed 19 July, 2024. <https://en.wikipedia.org/w/index.php?title=Barque&oldid=1229103422>

212   Wilton, S F.. *File:Barque Under Sail.jpg*. Wikimedia Commons. Accessed 19 July, 2024. <https://commons.wikimedia.org/w/index.php?title=File:Barque_Under_Sail.jpg&oldid=817349033>

Chapter 38

213   Trove. 1839. *Fifty Guineas Reward*. Accessed 28 June, 2024. <https://trove.nla.gov.au/newspaper/article/65953770>

214   Coleridge, Sarah. 1837. 'Chapter XVI: O Sleep, My Babe.' *Phantasmion. A Fairy Tale (1837)*. Accessed 17 July, 2024. <https://www.bartleby.com/lit-hub/women-poets-of-the-nineteenth-century/sarah-coleridge-18021850-5/>

Chapter 39

215   Lynn, D. & M. 2024. *Bass Strait Islands, Tasmania*. Accessed 27 August, 2024. <https://justalittlefurther.com/bass-strait-islands>

216   The Cornwall Chronicle. 1839. *Ship news*, p. 2. Accessed 26 July, 2024. <https://trove.nla.gov.au/newspaper/article/65952205/6514905>

217   The Cornwall Chronicle. 1840. *Married*. Accessed 26 July, 2024. <https://trove.nla.gov.au/newspaper/article/66019858?browse=ndp%3Abrowse%2Ftitle%2FC%2Ftitle%2F170%2F1840%2F01%2F18%2F-page%2F6253345%2Farticle%2F66019858>

218   State Library Victoria. 2024. *Beale, K. R., Beale, A., & Stadler, Y. (1828). Diaries, poems, 1828-[not after 1994]. [manuscript]*. (Can be ordered and read in the SLV Heritage Room).

219   Ibid

220   Ibid

221   Ibid

222   Ibid

223   Rizzetti, Janine. 2017. *This Month in Port Phillip in 1842: April 1842 (Part 1)*. The Resident Judge of Port Philip blog. Accessed 20 July, 2024.

224   Jones, Henry Gilbert. 1804–1888. *Collins Street East from the Independent Chapel*. Accessed 20 July, 2024. <https://viewer.slv.vic.gov.au/?entity=IE1294148&mode=browse>

225   Broome, Richard. 2008. *Pascoe Vale*. Accessed 26 July, 2024. <https://www.emelbourne.net.au/biogs/EM01121b.htm>

226   Janson, Elizabeth. 2009. *Victoria before 1848*. Diary of Victoria Part IV, 1838 Geocities. Accessed 26 July, 2024. <https://www.oocities.org/vic1840/diary/vic4.html?202426>

227   State Library Victoria. 2024. *Melbourne 1838 - The first race meeting was held on 6th & 7th March at Batman's Hill*. Harold Freedman, 1989. Filename wp009915. Accessed 26 July, 2024. <https://viewer.slv.vic.gov.au/?entity=IE1344090&mode=browse>

228   State Library Victoria. 2024. *Beale, K.R., Beale, A., & Stadler, Y. (1828). Diaries, poems, 1828-[not after 1994].[manuscript]*. (Can be ordered and read in the SLV Heritage Room).

229   Ibid

230   Wilson, Bruce. 2009. *Christmas symbols and traditions - understanding our Australian Christmas*. Accessed 26 July, 2024. <https://www.wilsons.id.au/wp-content/uploads/Australian_Christmas.pdf>

231   Finn, Edmund. 2020. *The Chronicles of Early Melbourne 1835-1852, historical, anecdotal and personal, by 'Garryowen'*. La Trobe, p. 493. Accessed 31 July, 2024. <https://doi.org/10.26181/5f865718a3c7b>

232   Allen, H. 1840. *Asiatic Journal And Monthly Register For British And Foreign India, China, And Australasia*. Accessed 28 July, 2024. <https://archive.org/details/in.ernet.dli.2015.70750>

Chapter 40

233   Victorian Government Gazette. 1842. *In the insolvent state of Anthony Beale, Settler, near the River Plenty*, 84, p. 1574. Accessed 28 July, 2024. <https://gazette.slv.vic.gov.au/view.cgi?year=1842&class=general&page_num=1574&state=N&classNum=G84&searchCode=8056694>

234   Victorian Government Gazette. 1842. *In the insolvent estate of Anthony Beale*, 87, p. 1639. Accessed 28 July, 2024. <https://gazette.slv.vic.gov.au/view.cgi?year=1842&class=general&page_num=1639&state=N&classNum=G87&searchCode=5944927>

235   Victorian Government Gazette. 1843. *In the insolvent state of Anthony Beale of Port Philip*. Notice to creditors, 66, p. 1015. Accessed 28 July, 2024. <https://gazette.slv.vic.gov.au/view.cgi?year=1843&class=general&page_num=1015&state=N&classNum=G66&searchCode=8056694>

236   Victorian Government Gazette. 1844. *In the matter of the Insolvency of Anthony Beale of the River Plenty, in the District of Port Phillip, and Colony of New South Wales, Settler*. 40, p 164. Accessed 28 July, 2024. <https://gazette.slv.vic.gov.au/view.cgi?year=1844&class=general&page_num=154&state=P&classNum=G40&id=>

237   Edelman, J, Meehan, H, & Cheung, G. 2019. 'The evolution of bankruptcy and insolvency laws and the case of the deed of company arrangement.' *Lloyd's Maritime and Commercial Law Quarterly*, pp. 571–602. Accessed 28 July, 2024. <https://www.hcourt.gov.au/assets/publications/speeches/current-justices/edelmanj/EdelmanJ14Jan2019.pdf>

238   Insolvent Court. 1844. 'Certificate of Relief 20 November 1844.' *The Melbourne Weekly Courier*, Saturday 23 November, 1844. p. 2. Accessed 31 July, 2024. < https://trove.nla.gov.au/newspaper/article/228063461?browse=ndp%3Abrowse%2Ftitle%2FM%2Ftitle%2F1023%2F1844%2F11%2F23%2Fpage%2F22332239%2Farticle%2F228063461>

239   Finn, 1819–1898, Edmund. 2020. *The Chronicles of Early Melbourne 1835-1852, historical, anecdotal and personal, by 'Garryowen'*. La Trobe. Book. p 496. Accessed 31 July, 2024. <https://opal.latrobe.edu.au/articles/book/The_Chronicles_of_Early_Melbourne_1835_1852_historical_anecdotal_and_personal_by_Garryowen_/13087793>

240   Beale, Katherine Rose 1828- *Passages written in her handwriting* State Library Victoria. 2024. Beale, K. R., Beale, A., & Stadler, Y. (1828). Diaries, poems, 1828-[not after 1994]. [manuscript]

241   Newton, John. 1779. *Come my soul, my suit to wear*. v 4-5. Public Domain. Accessed 14 July, 2024. <https://hymnary.org/text/come_my_soul_thy_suit_prepare>

242   Bowles and Dearborn. 1829. *The Casket: A Christmas and New Year's Present for Children and Young Persons*. Accessed 14 July, 2024. <https://www.google.com.au/books/edition/_/P98sAAAAYAAJ?hl=en&sa=X&ved=2ahUKEwiU3r-j9lKWHAxVEzTgGHRhzBaoQre8FegQICxAF>

243   Moir, David Macbeth 1798-1851 'To a dying infant.' Accessed 10 October 2024 <https://allpoetry.com/David-Macbeth-Moir#t_main>

244   Hardwick, Joseph. 2017. *Special days of worship and national religion in the Australian Colonies, 1790-c1914*. Journal of Imperial and Commonwealth History 45 (3): pp 365–390. Accessed 14 July, 2024. <https://nrl.northumbria.ac.uk/id/eprint/31132/1/JICH%20article_Hardwick%20-%20complete.pdf>

245   Wright, Tony 2024 *The year that shaped a city* The Age Celebrating 170 years. October 17, 2024 p. 2

Chapter 41

Chapter 42

246   Young, Edward. 1742–45. *Night thoughts*. Project Gutenberg. E book. Accessed 28 June, 2024. <https://www.gutenberg.org/files/33156/33156-h/33156-h.htm>

Chapter 43

247   Fairman, E.M 1890-1934 *My Prayer* in 'Poems'. A collection of poems written by the author's maternal great grandmother

248   Mary Foundation. 2024. *Various Prayers by Saint John Henry Newman (1801-1890)*. Accessed 28 June, 2024. <https://www.catholicity.com/prayer/prayers-and-hymns-by-john-henry-cardinal-newman.html>

Chapter 44

249   The Australian. 1831. *Useful recipes: there is a rose*. Friday 17 June, 1831. p 4. Accessed 4 January, 2024. <https://trove.nla.gov.au/newspaper/article/36865810?searchTerm=NOT%20public TAG%3A%20recipe#>

Afterword

250   Bertault, Jules. 1916. *Napoleon in his own words*. Chapter V: Concerning the Fine Arts, p. 69. Translated by Herbert Edward Law and Charles Lincoln Rhodes. Accessed 11 July, 2024. <https://bootcampmilitaryfitness institute.com/wp-content/uploads/2015/09/napoleon-in-his-own-words-napoleon-1916.pdf>

251   Vic Screen. 2024. *St Katherine's Anglican Church and Cemetery*. Series of photos prepared for Banyule Council. Accessed 17 August, 2024. <https://vicscreen.vic.gov.au/choose-victoria/locations/st-katherines#0>

252   Association of Ringing Teachers. 2024. *The sound of bells ringing is deeply rooted in British culture*. Accessed 26 July, 2024. <https://bellringing.org/discover-bellringing/history-of-bellringing/>

253   Fetherston, Rachel. 2019. *The biodiversity secrets of Anthony Beale Reserve*. Remember the wild. Accessed 4 August, 2024. <https://www.rememberthewild.org.au/the-biodiversity-secrets-of-anthony-beale-reserve/>

254   Grant, Benjamin., Oliver, John Ryder. *A Few Notes on St. Helena: And Descriptive Guide*. Laos: B. Grant, printer, 1883. Accessed 27 October 2024 <https://www.google.com.au/books/edition/A_Few_Notes_on_St_Helena/QRYe-jEd3TYEC?hl=en>

255   McCracken, Donal P. 2022 *Napoleon's Garden Island: Lost and old gardens of St Helena, South Atlantic Ocean*. Kew Publishing Royal Botanic Gardens, Kew p 125

256   Baker, TFT (editor). 1998. *Stepney: Early Stepney*. A History of the County of Middlesex: Volume 11, Stepney, Bethnal Green. British History Online. Accessed August 7, 2024. <https://www.british-history.ac.uk/vch/middx/vol11/pp1-7>

257   St Helena Island. 2024. *Maps of St Helena*. Accessed 7 August, 2024. <https://sainthelenaisland.info/maps.htm>

258   Rosevear, A; Bogart, D; Shaw-Taylor, Leigh. 2019. *The spatial patterns of coaching in England and Wales from 1681 to 1836: a GIS approach*. Accessed 12 August, 2024. <https://sites.socsci.uci.edu/~dbogart/The%20Spatial%20patterns%20of%20coaching%2030%20july%202019%20final%20web.pdf>

259   Roberts, Greg. 2016. *Principal Departures for London Coaches (1819)*. Accessed 12 August, 2024. <https://www.wickedwilliam.com/principal-departure-coaching-inns-1819/>

260   Inner London Ramblers. 2023. Green chain walk. Accessed 18 March, 2024. <https://www.innerlondonramblers.org.uk/ideasforwalks/green-chain-walk-guides.html>

261   Brohan, Philip. 2015. *Mapping the shipping routes of the English East-India Company*. The Washington Post. Accessed 17 August, 2024. <https://www.washingtonpost.com/video/world/mapping-the-shipping-routes-of-the-english-east-india-company/2015/09/04/563c4dd4-532a-11e5-b225-90edbd49f362_video.html>

262   Stott, Romie. 2016. *The Scandalous Decision to Pickle Admiral Horatio Nelson in Brandy.* Accessed 18 August, 2024. <https://www.atlasobscura.com/articles/the-scandalous-decision-to-pickle-admiral-horatio-nelson-in-brandy>

263   Mornington Peninsula Shire. 2024. *The Briars Homestead and Gardens.* Accessed 18 August, 2024. <https://www.mornpen.vic.gov.au/Environment/The-Briars/The-Briars-Homestead-and-Gardens>

264   Greensborough Historical Society. 2021. *The 1842 Petition by the Resident Ladies on the Plenty River. Early Days: Greensborough and St Helena.* Part 3, p. 76. Busybird Publishing.

265   Green, Deborah. 2024. *Descendant Report.* Personal communication.

266   Beale, Katherine Rose. 1795–1856. *Diaries, Poems, 1828.* Accessed 12 August, 2024. <http://search.slv. vic.gov.au/permalink/f/1cl35st/SLV_VOYAGER1640396>

267   Gatehouse, Tim. 2015. *The Beale Diaries: A Precious Record of Early Colonial Garden Making.* Australian Garden History 26, no. 3 (2015): pp 4–6. Accessed 23 August, 2024. <https://www.jstor.org/stable/24918997>

268   Wikipedia contributors. 2024. *East India Company.* Wikipedia, The Free Encyclopedia. Accessed 17 August, 2024. <https://en.wikipedia.org/w/index.php?title=East_India_Company&oldid=1240696172>

269   Carrigan, Henry L. 2011. *Nineteenth Century Christianity. The Encyclopedia of Christian Civilization.* Abstract. Accessed 23 August 2024. <https://onlinelibrary.wiley.com/authored-by/Carrigan/Henry+L./Jr.>

270   Harris, Mark. 2024. *Biblical Criticism and Modern Science. St Andrews Encyclopaedia of Theology,* edited by Brendan N. Wolfe et al. University of St Andrews, 2022. Article published March 14, 2024. Accessed 28 August, 2024. <https://www.saet.ac.uk/Christianity/BiblicalCriticismandModernScience>

271   Stowe, Stephen. 2024. *Making sense of diaries and letters.* From the Making Sense of Evidence series on History Matters: The U.S. Survey on the Web. Accessed 17 July, 2024. <https://historymatters.gmu.edu/mse/ letters/letters.pdf>

272   Wilson, William Carus. 1853. *A book of General Psalmody: containing portions for the whole of the Psalms and above A thousand hymns.* Third edition. Compiled by William Carus Wilson, M.A. Rector of Whittington, and perpetual curate of Casterton. Digitalised by Google 29 March, 2023. Accessed 17 July, 2024. <https://www.google.com.au/books/edition/A_Book_of_General_Psalmody_Containing_Po/paaF7g_8qcwC?hl=en>

273   Caroline Bowles Southey. 1824. *On the death of an infant.* The Sydney Gazette and New South Wales Advertiser (NSW: 1803–1842) 8 Jan, 1824, p 4. Poetry. <https://trove.nla.gov.au/newspaper/article/2182533?browse=nd-p%3Abrowse%2Ftitle%2FS%2Ftitle%2F3%2F1824%2F01%2F08%2Fpage%2F494772%2Farticle%2F2182533#>

274   Heber, Reginald. 1818. *Farewell to a friend departed.* Accessed 28 June, 2024. Public Domain. <https://hymnary.org/text/thou_art_gone_to_the_grave_but_we_will_n>

275   Cannan, Edward. 1985. *A history of the diocese of St Helena and its precursors 1502–1984.* Printed at the Government Printing Office, The Castle, St Helena A.A. BIZAARE, Government Printer. PDF accessed 26 July, 2024. <https://sainthelenaisland.info/historyofthediocese1985_cannan.pdf>

276   Nunn, HW. 1947. *A Short History of the Church of England in Victoria 1847–1947.* Chapter 1, Early Years: 1803-1847. Project Canterbury. Accessed 4 August, 2024. <https://anglicanhistory.org/aus/hwnunn_victoria 1947/01.html>

277   Fuller, Tony. 2002. *Society of East India Commanders.* Mariners. The website of the Mariners Mailing List. Accessed 8 August, 2024. <http://www.mariners-l.co.uk/EICSocietyIntro.htm>

278   Andrews, Charlotte. 2024. *Bibby Stockholm migrant barge to be closed.* BBC. Accessed 12 August, 2024. <https://www.bbc.com/news/articles/cg640n3372qo>

279   Maisner, Stuart. 2024. *Chatham Dockyard: Reinvention of site 40 years after closure.* BBC. Accessed 12 August, 2024. <https://www.bbc.com/news/uk-england-kent-67873335>

280   Public Domain Poetry. 2005–2024. *Alfred, Lord Tennyson: crossing the bar.* Accessed 22 June, 2024. <http://www.public-domain-poetry.com/alfred-lord-tennyson/crossing-the-bar-475>

281   Taylor, Alexander H. 2024. *The foundation of modern geology.* University of Illinois Board of Trustees. Accessed 2 August, 2024. <https://publish.illinois.edu/foundationofmoderngeology/homepage/>

282   Cresswell, James. 2016. *The geology of Saint Helena, Ascension Island and Tristan da Cunha. Deposits Magazine.* Issue 45, p 21. Accessed 2 August, 2024. <https://www.geoworldtravel.com/resources/Mid_Atlantic/Geology%20TristanStHelAscen.pdf>

283 Grimshaw, Pauline and John pre. 2010. *St Helena History*. Accessed 8 August, 2024. <https://www.flickr.com/photos/30593522@N05/albums/72157624879923581/>

284 Chaplin, Arnold. 1914. *The Regiments in St Helena. A St. Helena who's who; or, a directory of the island during the captivity of Napoleon*. pp 33–34. Accessed 2 August, 2024. <https://iiif.wellcomecollection.org/pdf/b2803448x>

285 Hardy, Charles. 1811. *Supplement to a register of ships, employed in the service of the Hon. The United East India Company from the year 1760 to the conclusion of the commercial charter with an appendix containing a variety of particulars and useful information, interesting to those who were concerned with the East India Service*. Accessed 31 July, 2024. <https://archive .org/details/aregistershipse00hardgoog>

286 Hardy, Horatio Charles. 1820. *A Register of Ships Employed in the service of the Honorable the United East India Company 1760–1819 with an Appendix*. By the late Charles Hardy, revised with considerable additions by his son. Third edition. pp 160–163. Accessed 28 August, 2024. <https://www.google.com.au/books/edition/A_Register_of_Ships_Employed_in_the_Serv/f9hoAAAAcAAJ?hl=en>

287 Fox, Colin. 2011. *Table of slaves and their owners on St Helena 1827–1834*. Accessed 18 March, 2024. <https://sainthelenaisland.info/slavesalphabeticallybyname182734.pdf>

288 University of Bristol. 2012 *Archaeologists unearth slave burial ground on the island of St. Helena*. ScienceDaily. <www.sciencedaily.com/releases/2012/03/120308101621.htm> Accessed October 20, 2024 <www.sciencedaily.com/releases/2012/03/120308101621.htm>

289 Fuller, Tony. 2002. *Society of East India Commanders*. Mariners. The website of the Mariners Mailing List. Accessed 8 August, 2024. <http://www.mariners-l.co.uk/EICSocietyIntro.htm>

290 Green, D. 2024. *Descendants of James Young*. Descendant Report (personal communication).

291 Beale, John Lindsay. Undated. Extracts from diary. Loose sheets in St Katherine's folder of information.

292 Sundberg, Ingrid. 2013. *Traditional mountain structure handout*. Accessed 17 August, 2024. <https://ingridsnotes.wordpress.com/wp-content/uploads/2013/05/final-revision_traditional-mountain-structure-handout_8-5x14.jpg>

293 Underhill, Evelyn. 1911. *Mysticism: A Study in Nature and Development of Spiritual Consciousness*. Christian Classics Ethereal Library. Accessed 22 June, 2024. <https://www.ccel.org/ccel/u/underhill/mysticism/ cache/ mysticism.pdf>

294 Donne, John. 1624. *No man is an island. Devotions upon Emergent Occasions*. Meditation XVII. Accessed 30 August, 2024. <https://www.commonlit.org/en/texts/no-man-is-an-island#:~:text=%22No%20Man%20Is%20An%20Island%22%20by%20John%20Donne%20(1624,is%20in%20the%20public%20domain.>

295 Hawes, Stephen. 1424–1523. *An Epitaph*. Accessed 30 August, 2024. <https://www.poemhunter.com/stephen-hawes/biography/>